WHERE EVIL STALKS

I returned to my room to bathe before dinner. Ebulliently happy, I liberally sprinkled the bath powder. To my delight, suds rose above the rim like Alpine peaks. Cael the cat settled himself on the sink to observe. I immersed myself and was distracted by lost soap when suddenly the lamp was extinguished. Before I could rise, two hands grabbed my head and pushed me under the water. I flailed and splashed, but my assailant's grip was so well-judged that I was unable to right myself and was on the verge of passing out when I was released. Sputtering and gasping for air, I climbed from the tub to the sounds of a demented, blood-stained Cael. The cat had saved my life. The game had gone too far, I decided. I would leave Gay-wyck in the morning.

VINCENT VIRGA

AVON
PUBLISHERS OF BARD, CAMELOT AND DISCUS BOOKS

For J and V

GAYWYCK is an original publication of Avon Books.
This work has never before appeared in book form.

AVON BOOKS
A division of
The Hearst Corporation
959 Eighth Avenue
New York, New York 10019

First Avon Printing, November, 1980

AVON TRADEMARK REG. U.S. PAT. OFF. AND IN
OTHER COUNTRIES, MARCA REGISTRADA, HECHO EN
U.S.A.

Printed in the U.S.A.

Love is as hard and unbending as hell.
                    —St. Theresa of Avila

                Oh, sir, to willful men
The injuries that they themselves procure
Must be their schoolmasters.
                            —Shakespeare

Prologue

28 June 1969
Gramercy Park

I HAVE JUST RETURNED FROM A VISIT TO Gaywyck. Memories at eventide sustain me. The wonder of my life and the passion of our love triumph over Time's constraint.

Sweet, silent Donough, I command my heart:

Make me a willow cabin at your gate,
And call upon my soul within the house;
Write loyal cantons of contemned love,
And sing them loud even in the dead of night. . . .

Book One

One

I RESEMBLE MY MOTHER PHYSICALLY. When I summon her into time present, I become young as well. Both of us are small and ash-blond fair, with large green eyes and pellucid skin; but, while her face is oval, her features soft and delicate, mine—due to my father's Scottish influence—is squarer, my features angular and hard. Yet, the most striking aspects of my visage are unquestionably the ones I inherited from her—in particular, my eyes. It startles me that we look so much alike. And she was also an only child.

I consider our physical likeness an extension of our temperamental affinities. Neither of us liked people, and most people were wary of us. When not with each other, we were alone; since she held no fear of solitude, I was not taught to dread it. I don't know if as a very young child I enjoyed being so isolated, or if I acclimated. I do know that it felt comfortable and I soon consciously contrived to remain as much to myself as possible. Living in a small, rural community helped.

If forced into social intercourse by a neighbor's surprise visit or a birthday party for a peer, I was not a success, never having developed the art of feigning enjoyment. However, I discovered that most people, when rejected, moved from confusion to hurt to resentment to indifference with stunning rapidity. The few children I gravitated toward as friends were the weak or the halt or the lame. Such attractions my father discouraged, as I knew he would.

I was also a sickly child, asthmatic; the frequent lingering colds and fevers exactly suited my disposition, or perhaps formed it. Lacking the desire to be well—the rewards for robust health not being appealing—I managed to be ill constantly, and thus acceptably secluded from others, safe and secure in my house, in my room, in my bed. After my mother taught me to read at the age of four,

I felt no need for anyone—not even her. I knew I would never be lonely again.

Staying in bed for the day, no matter the season or the weather, was a delight almost beyond bearing. Mother baked special treats and brewed herbal teas. My parents argued endlessly about my indisposition; but since I was medically certified as ill, there was nothing my father could do without appearing irrational or unkind, and as the principal of our local school, he was anxious to avoid seeming either. (Until I was of school age, he contented himself with dark scowls and guttural, rambling presentiments of doom that never failed to send me into a frenzied panic: "Just wait until I get my hands on him . . . *then* this nonsense will stop.")

Unlike my mother and me, my father is large. Like us, the hair on the crown of his head is the color of sand, but it shades into dark brown at the sides and back, in his beard, and on the rest of his body. His eyes are small and blue, his body virile and muscular. He never tired of recounting growing up on a farm and laboring as a tram conductor in Boston at night to supplement his hard-won scholarship to Harvard College. Whenever he removed his shirt to chop lumber for firewood, I gazed from my window awed and frightened by the power of his arms and back. One hot summer day, I watched him bathe in the Allegheny River, then ran across fields and climbed a tree to hide myself in the foliage until I felt able to continue my meager and precarious existence.

I remember no one from my school days: not a face can I draw up from the well of memory to fill the seats in the classrooms. I thought I had no need of them; they, having each other, truly had no need of me. And the fact that my father hovered over us each day helped my cause. Rebuffed by my indifference, none ever pursued me for fear of being labeled a seeker of the faculty's favors. They never taunted me either; not even the bravest chanced igniting my father's rage.

Despite his threats, my attendance at school was poor. I moved from year to year with fewer and fewer days actually spent in the classroom; but with him as my private tutor, I had no fear of falling behind. On the contrary, without the other children retarding my growth, I was able to progress with such alacrity that it eventually became impractical for me to attend the class meetings.

Father's pleasure in my intellectual achievements soon displaced his impatience with my frailty. He began to see my confinement as a positive thing. He began to make plans for my future. To be a teacher (no matter how fine) in a small village in upstate New York was for him a disgrace; an accident of fortune. I was to become a lawyer. I was to have the most successful of public careers. I listened and knew otherwise. (I *know* he would have reconciled himself to what occurred. But that is neither here nor there.)

Our house, on reflection, was perfect for the three of us. It had the requisite number of rooms and a "spare" bedroom reserved for my expected sibling, but later converted into my mother's sewing room when I was six. The "finished" attic was my father's study. It was reached by steep ladderlike stairs that took up most of the narrow central hallway. The basement was used for storage. There always seemed so much space in that house. I was astonished on my last visit to see how small, in reality, it is. One often reads of this phenomenon, but it is strange and disconcerting to experience. One wonders if only spatial relationships are distorted by memory. Does anything survive the past intact?

To facilitate my studies, he built an oak desk the length of one wall in my room. He stained it to match the desks in his school. The surface accommodated my lessons and our evening tutorials. By my tenth year, to my relief, I was completely free of the classroom. I was no longer forced to expend energy overcoming my inadequacies on the playing field or at the convivial luncheon table or in any other group activity.

At five o'clock each evening, the family convened at the dinner table. Most often we ate in silence. My father and I read. My mother sat entertaining fantasies. After final grace, my father and I retired to our desk, where we worked until nine at a combination of subjects from Greek to differential calculus according to a strict program. Shakespeare was the one constant. Saturdays we worked from eight in the morning to noon; after lunch, he would real aloud one Shakespearean play: tragedies, histories, comedies, in ordered rotation by date of completion. My mother was allowed to listen; she darned or crocheted during my father's excellent performances. Each evening of the following week we discussed that play line by line.

Some assignments I was expected to complete after he retreated to his study for the evening. I would place that work on the steps outside my door for him to approve or reject. Other assignments I finished the next morning or afternoon, in preparation for our evening.

From my tenth to my sixteenth year my days were my own to structure. I held myself accountable for every waking moment. I imposed an order so compelling that it carried me beyond self-discipline into a realm of self-mastery that I cannot now imagine. Yet, I remember. And my journals corroborate it all.

For a long time, I would go to bed late. I never had trouble falling asleep. I would read until I felt tired; with my light extinguished, sleep would soon come. Often, over my head, I heard my father pacing in his study. My mother always retired early. No sooner had my father left me to my work, his step quietly ascending to the top of his private stairs, than my mother would appear with cookies and milk to kiss me good night. Her kiss was the harbinger of my most precious hours. Invasion no longer possible, I would descend to secret depths beyond the sound of my own voice, achieving exquisite solitude. Father's footsteps overhead merged with the wind-and-rain sounds of foliage rustling, and with the creakings of the ever-settling house to follow (or to lead me) into my dreams.

The mornings were of a different order. From my earliest years I was haunted by bad dreams. Their stray, elusive slivers pricked my nascent consciousness, inflaming it with fear and crippling anxiety. Knowing I could either surrender to the seizure or struggle against it, I kept distracting novels from father's library by my bed. They helped restore the equilibrium lost after sleep. (Years later, at the height of duplicity at Gaywyck, when nightmares returned, I again relied on novels to disperse the terrors that lingered upon awakening.) Since my father never realized how easily my studies came to me, I often continued reading for most of the day.

Father discouraged my appetite for novels, convinced that it encouraged daydreaming and passivity. It was mother who supplied me once father's meager supply was exhausted. She managed it with the help of Father Howard, the parish priest, who was in every other way a good friend to my father, his organist. The prelate administered the sacraments to me if I missed Mass several Sundays in a row. (Although raised a Quaker, Mother practiced no religion because there was no Quaker community in our area. Father Howard came to understand that Mother was not a candidate for conversion. They each acknowledged the other's right to a personal God of one's own definition. Mother said she doubted his sincerity on this count.) One morning she discussed my need with him. He offered to approach Miss Grimmond, a wealthy pillar of his church. She lived with a female companion in a Greek-revival manse at the center of the village, and with the assistance of Mr. Cullam's Bookstore, Gramercy Park, New York City, she too read novels voraciously.

I liked Miss Grimmond. We knew each other by sight from Sunday Mass, but had, of course, never spoken. She was small, like I was, and about twice my mother's age. She was the only person I ever observed who seemed as shy as I; she was rich enough to be affectionately termed "eccentric." Not only did Miss Grimmond read novels, but also every major weekly and monthly magazine published in the country. (Her father made his fortune in local crude oil. She attended private schools and had a European grand tour, but for personal reasons preferred living in that great parental house.)

The afternoon my mother spoke with Father Howard, a package was delivered by Miss Grimmond's friend Annie. It contained *Ivanhoe* (which I'd read), *Wuthering Heights*, *Mansfield Park*, and *The House of the Seven Gables* (read as well); also, old and new copies of *Century*, *Lippincott's Magazine* (where I was soon to discover Dorian Gray), and all the *Harper's* issues containing the *Trilby* serial. A note, written in clear, precise script, requested details of books read, preferences, and encouraged me to master French because I would soon be old enough, she said, to appreciate the current glorious Golden Age in that culture.

Whenever a package passed between us, there was always a letter—sometimes pages long—full of gossip about our favorite authors and books ordered from Mr. Cullam. She inquired which new ones I wanted (and why), and expressed mutual concern for our health. We devoured the journals, skipping the trash written for and by women who existed on impossibly high moral planes, or written for women by men with absurd worshipful notions. Miss

Grimmond and I pretended the heroines were friends whose behavior embarrassed us personally. We both preferred the "serious writers." (All this stood me well at Gaywyck.)

Our favorite modern novelist "in the great tradition" was Mr. Dickens. My letter to her after I finished *David Copperfield* for the first time (in my thirteenth year) brought her only visit. On that early autumn afternoon, we sat in the front parlor discussing novels in general and Mr. Dickens in particular, while my mother served tea. Miss Grimmond spoke to her spoon throughout the visit; I spoke to the sugar bowl. When she rose to leave, she handed me the packet she'd been holding on her lap all the while. It contained our copy of *David Copperfield* in which she had written: "To my special friend, Robert Whyte. Remember me! Angela Grimmond. 1895." When I left home for Gaywyck nearly five years later, it was the only book—aside from my journals—that accompanied me.

Referring to that time, I have called myself "shy." "Shy" is not a forceful enough word. "Shy" is an evasion of the truth. "Easily frightened," yes. "Morbidly sensitive," yes. "Timid and cautious," yes. But also much more than that. Much, much more. I was menaced by every other human being. I saw everyone's capacity to inflict pain and expected every intimacy to bring disaster, shattering my inner balance irrevocably. I knew myself capable of such horrors. Terrified of myself, I became terrified of others. How the change occurred from reclusive child to wretched adolescent, I cannot say. Sufficient unto the day. . . .

I prayed. I devoted myself to the Blessed Virgin Mary. Still no solace came. More in anger and disappointment than from intellectual curiosity, I began reading the philosophers who positioned themselves against the Church: Kant, Schopenhauer, Nietzsche. By middle adolescence I had repudiated superstition. I was pleased to know that God was dead. Not even to Him and His did I owe allegiance. I had myself. I had my books. I had my journal. And, of course, I had my mother. My father observed my progress, even encouraged it, never explaining his own attachments to the Church.

If I were well enough to leave my bed, Mother would call me to breakfast at seven immediately after Father left for school. If I were not, she would appear with a tray, kiss me good morning, and sit by my side making

pleasant conversation. We never spoke of our feelings or
of her past. We never spoke of my father beyond her
platitudinous praise of him as a good husband and a good
provider. We usually spoke about day-to-day things, like
her garden or my studies. All that changed when Annie
began delivering packages. Then we talked about the
stories we were reading. We studied the Penfield posters
in *Harper's*, and the Maxfield Parrish ones in *Century*, and
the Sartain mezzoprints in *Graham's Magazine*. It always
annoyed us that we couldn't decorate the house with them,
but they would have given away our secret. We satisfied
ourselves by staring at them and pointing out our favorites
to one another.

Miss Grimmond sent Mother *Godey's Lady's Book*. We
admired the elaborate wood-engraved covers, and pondered the imaginative costumes recommended for women
of fashion. The only time I ever saw her "silly" was when
we paged through the new *Godey's;* she excitedly turned
to the back to discover how a particular effect was achieved
"just in case" she was ever in need of it. (Once she laughed
so at an elaborately layered cape suggested for the opera
that she had to stretch across my bed and take deep breaths
to regain control over her convulsive giggles. That was an
exceptional experience! I have my journal open to the
morning's entry. It is scattered with exhilarating exclama-
tion marks.)

Sometimes, in the morning, I enjoyed helping her with
the lighter household chores. While she always complained
that they bored and fatigued her, I found them relaxing.
She particularly loathed dusting. We had very few *objets
d'art* in our house; inanimate things that had nothing to do
but collect dust, and people who had nothing to do but
remove that dust, she found equally absurd. "Spare, simple living," she said with pride, "is what God made us
for. No fancy whatnots in the Garden of Eden." Small,
beautiful things, she said, belonged in museums or in
magazines. Her notions of good living were not the stuff
of Gaywyck.

Afternoons, I was alone. She was occupied with her
chores or in her sitting room with the door closed. I read,
wrote in my journal, and prepared lessons for Father. My
journals for this period contain conversations with my
parents, records of dreams, plans for a healthful regimen
that would transform me into someone large and tall,

hirsute and muscular, and long rambling essays on life's meaning, as well as catalogs of my failings, lists of my favorite things, notes on books, and even "receipts" neatly printed among the desperate, confused notions that the time of which I wrote was my eternity. Thousands of pages: to read them today is to cradle myself in my own arms. Whispering assurances, I calm the sobbing child.

In the journal for my fourteenth year, there appear my first references to sex. Veiled and very carefully phrased, though detectable nonetheless, they are concerned with finding ideal beauty in a combination of my parents' best qualities. But while my mind was just beginning to explore the possibilities, an incident occurred that shocked me senseless—although search as I may, I can find no reference to it, beyond a report of the event. Suffice it to say that from that day forward I expelled all thoughts of my sexuality from my waking hours.

I remember the event so clearly that only the most cursory glance at the pages of my journal is required, and then just to make certain of the peripheral details. I was helping my mother dust the books in my father's study. I had just finished relating a long, detailed account of Jane Eyre's adventures. It was snowing heavily and the silence of the house combined with the silence of the world outside to make me feel in the warm center of a timeless universe. Mother seemed distracted and strangely withdrawn. Standing by my side, she began talking about Father Howard, who had visited that morning. A chance reference was made to a neighbor pregnant with her ninth child. My mother remarked—not without humor—on the perils of being a good Catholic wife. Then, free of hesitation, she looked at me and asked, "Do you know where babies come from?"

I blushed, mortified. I could not look at her. I muttered that Father had explained. I continued dusting.

"You're like me, Robbie, in the important ways. God is good not to torment us with any concern for . . . I feared you would take after your father in that regard, but God is good."

I prayed she was finished so we could continue our morning as if nothing had happened. There was more to come. Afterward I knew nothing would ever be the same again.

"When I was carrying you . . ." she began, then paused.

My heart pounded. I stared straight ahead at the wall of books, seeing nothing.

"While I was carrying you, I prayed for a daughter. When you were born, I was disappointed. But not now. You are so much like a girl, I feel God has answered my prayers."

She put down her dustcloth and kissed me. Those words chill my soul. Not the coldness of my schoolfellows nor the anger of my father at my incompetence and disinterest in masculine pursuits devastated me as did that affectionate kiss.

There are entries in a much later journal that point to my constant consideration of the masculine/feminine soul, but they are inconclusive as argument and unimportant beyond acknowledging the differences in male and female role functions inherent in the social order. But for a few lines, they are of no value, merely evidence that the subject was frequently on my mind. They are to be seen as the fulcrum on which future events will balance. I quote the lines of consequence:

I see plainly that I have the body and thus the soul of a man. It follows, then, that all of my actions are the actions of a man. Therefore, whatever these actions may be—according to the incontrovertible laws of nature—they are masculine.

Between my mother's loving words and the "death" of her spirit, three long years intervened. Slowly, imperceptibly she grew more silent; toward the end, it was like living with a mute. Developing monstrous headaches in the last year, she requested my father hang thick black drapes in her room to block the light. Wearing only her nightgown, she remained in seclusion for days, eventually weeks. Father and I shared our fears as she gradually ceased to function. The doctor said it was "woman's trouble." He assured us it would pass. We began to take long walks over the frozen fields on winter evenings after our makeshift dinners. We commenced becoming friends.

My journal for the early part of 1899, my seventeenth and last year at home, is full of grieving. It is concerned with the loss of my mother, who died to us one wet spring day when she withdrew into a wordless, unreachable world. Tears fell from her sightless eyes like rain running down empty windows.

I found her weeping at the kitchen table. It was morning. When I offered breakfast, she made no acknowledgment of my presence. I hastily prepared my own and, frightened, retreated to my bedroom. I wanted to talk but was afraid of provoking more intimate revelations on the order of those shared in my father's study; although, I confess, I was more afraid of what I sensed to be the truth of her condition. Ostensibly, I stayed closeted to read that entire day. In reality, I was paralyzed with guilt and terror, waiting for my father to come home.

Arriving nine hours later, he discovered her as I'd left her. I heard him speak softly and gently at first; then his voice began to rise in anger, until he was shouting frantically in panic and fear. He burst into my room where I sat holding *Nana*. I told him all I knew. He bellowed that I should have run for the doctor. (Had I gone, would anything have been different?) He tore the novel from my hands, cursing it and me. Dragging me into the kitchen to watch my soundlessly weeping mother, he rushed for Dr. Martin.

The doctor came. He pronounced that profound melancholia had deranged her nervous system. We put her to bed. Three days later, after silently lamenting for three sleepless nights, she was taken by Dr. Martin and my father to the state mental hospital in Rochester for examination. My father returned alone.

Rather than drawing the two of us together, the tragedy of my mother's madness ended the rapport that had recently developed. Rarely was there overt hostility, but no longer was there tolerance for my preferred way of life. I wrote in my journal that I felt he accused me of stealing her love. Whatever love she had for him had remained untouched by me. The love he craved, that he assumed I'd usurped, had never been but in his fantasy.

When he announced his plans for me to sit the Harvard's entrance exam, I knew the time had come for me to disabuse him of his ideas for my life. I refused although I knew it offered no threat. I was in no emotional condition, I said. He informed me that I had no choice, and contrary to my own fancies, I would not be able to spend the rest of my life in my bedroom. I said I had no desire to enter *any* university, least of all one as competitive and demanding as Harvard. Again he informed me that I had no choice: I was no longer welcome in his house. It was my fault, he shouted. Her worry and disappointment over me was the cause of it all.

I went to see Father Howard. He had frequently told me I could call on him if the need arose.

In four days, he had found a solution to my problem.

Two days later, on 28 September 1899, I left for Gaywyck.

My fate galloped to meet me.

Two

IT OCCURS TO ME THAT AT CRUCIAL moments alternate routes seem to exist. Life provokes illusion. By rejecting Harvard and all it represented, I thought to remain unplumbed. By embracing the hermetic world of Gaywyck, I hoped to stow away my heart uncharted and unknown. Seemingly to avoid self-revelation, I pursued life as though mirror-reflected: mistaking left for right and back for front. Fleeing from my demons, I arrived in their midst. Forced to do battle, I achieved victory over the dark in the depths of the cave of the heart.

I remember little of the journey from Rochester to Hoboken. I know I was strained and overtired. I had not slept the night before: my excitement and fears kept me pacing my room. When the sun rose, I walked through the woods that surround our house. The peace of the late-September dawn calmed me; I felt a momentary contentment recalling Father Howard's description of my destination. *Gaywyck*: a great, secluded mansion "in the classical style" on the southern shore of Long Island, surrounded by dense woods on three sides, the fourth exposed to the sea. Never having seen the ocean, I was exhilarated by the idea of living within hailing distance, of being summoned by its pounding surf as familiarly as I was now by this day's dawn. When I cleared the trees, I glimpsed my father's pale face in his study window. He appeared to be crying. Ashamed, I glanced away. I looked again. He was gone; the windowpane seemed wet in the sun's reflected light. I sighed, relieved. I felt too fragile to face another confrontation. I hurried to my room to finish packing and to dress in my best gray broadcloth suit.

According to my journal, the train left Rochester at 10:00 A.M., arriving in Hoboken at 3:00 P.M. The weather upstate was cool and bright-clear. Father Howard drove me to the station in Miss Grimmond's carriage. My father and I parted at the door without any show of affection or grief. Instead of the bustling world of Harvard and the law as he had planned, I was heading for a deserted estate on Long Island and the position of librarian to one Donough Gaylord. I respected his disappointment. I wished he could have respected my right to choose my own life. I waved good-bye.

Once on the train, as the tints of autumn slid by, I was stunned by a sadness too deep to sustain without tears. It was as if the seat had collapsed, dropping me through my life with not a soul to break the fall. I saw my scowling father standing rigid in the doorway, his hands by his side. I saw my absent mother's ghost, a weeping Madonna, framed in the window. I heard Father Howard officiously repeating instructions as if he were intoning some arcane litany of exorcism.

Opening the box lunch packed by Miss Grimmond, searching for a napkin to wipe my face, I found a note wound around a five-dollar bill:

> Dear Robert,
>   Such an important day! Be brave and strong, Robert, you who are so dear to me.
>   Do great things for me.
>
> All my love,
> Angela Grimmond

The comfort in those simple, perfect words! I looked through my own reflection and smiled with my complicitous self.

It grew warmer as we chugged south, and the conductor suggested we open the windows. I spent the journey reading *David Copperfield*, eating (Miss Grimmond had packed food for three), gazing at the scenery, and picking grit out of my eyes. By the time we reached Hoboken and I stepped off the train, the force of the heat slapped me giddy.

I was to be met at the depot by a Mr. Martin Head. I walked a few feet down the platform, then stopped in panic when a porter overtook me. I had no idea where he came from but the trunk he juggled was mine. He extended his free hand to take my gladstone. I surrendered it, convinced I'd never see either again. (I studied his face; a description might be required at a later time.) Bravely I resumed walking. Reaching the end of the platform. I positioned myself directly outside the gate and waited, heart pounding, for Mr. Head. The terminal was vast, every inch of it crammed with scurrying people. The porter disappeared into the crowd. Before I could shout after him, a very tall, very thin redheaded man approached me. He was short of breath and perspiring heavily. He introduced himself as Mr. Martin Head. He put himself at my service. Totally bewildered by the heat and the crush, relieved beyond speech by his having discovered me in the throng, I nodded meekly, muttering, "Yes, yes, yes, thank you," and fell into step beside him.

"My trunk and gladstone?"

"Been collected. Ferry over here."

"Is it always this hot in September?"

"Stinkin' Indian summer. Don't know why it's blamed on them."

We walked across the station, through a long wall of doors, down a gargantuan ramp where Mr. Head gave a uniformed man some coins, and across a cool dock to the waiting, churning ferry.

"I've never been on a boat before, Mr. Head!"

"She ain't much of one."

That doesn't matter, I thought. He conscientiously maneuvered us into a position that guaranteed a view of the skyline. Enormous birds flapped and squawked overhead. I wanted to ask their names but my guide was perspiring heavily and seemed submerged in some personal misery. I kept as still as I could.

The changing look of Manhattan Island was familiar to me from the dramatic pictures I'd studied in the pages of *Harper's Weekly*, but as it loomed into view, my jaw dropped. I never knew I had a passion for the gigantic until that skyline awakened it. I wanted to know, *now*, all about the great lives that sustained the mythic place, and especially about the greatest of saviors, Donough Gaylord, who held dominion over *my* life. I saw his city bright with imperial glitter, his streets walled, man-made canyons. Sailing across the calm river toward his seemingly silent fortress, awash in gleaming daylight, I felt storybook wonder: Atlantis and Ninevah! With a surge of joy I felt all my lost illusions restored. He would make everything well. He would grant my one wish: peaceful, never-ending solitude. Had I known . . . *had I but known.* . . .

At Pier 43 Mr. Head delivered me to the short, elegantly

dressed, elderly Mr. Edmund Goodwin, who wore gray spats with pearl buttons. Before I could thank Mr. Head properly, my second courier spun on his heel, exclaimed, "We're late!" and moved in the direction of the street. Alarmed, I followed, waving to a pale Mr. Head, who smiled and said something I did not hear for the noise. I think he wished me well. I could not have used anything more.

The pier and its surrounding area was so unpleasant, so foul-smelling, so god-awful *hot,* so crowded, so rotten to the eye and nose with garbage strewn underfoot, with crates stacked precariously everywhere, with vendors hawking fruits, vegetables, umbrellas, clothes, newspapers, animals. At the curb, a clutch of filthy, tattered urchins screamed and danced in front of a stately ebony brougham drawn by a pair of the most perfect black stallions I had ever seen. Buffeted, I was embraced and engulfed by the tremendous activity around me. I was lost. I felt sick. Where was Mr. Goodwin? I noticed again the splendor of the equipage and for the first time the ornately scrolled letter G embossed in gold on the door above my reflected, panic-distorted face. The door opened. My image slid off its shiny surface like a glazed bun off a tilted plate. Mr. Goodwin beckoned me with a wiggling index finger from inside the carriage.

"I slipped around the other side," he said.

I stepped up and found myself enveloped in a cocoon of the most gorgeous gray velvet. Gently closing the door, he rapped twice on the wall behind him, setting the jewel box of a coach in motion.

He never lifted the shades! My first impressions of the streets of New York were based solely on sound and smell and a few yards of sidewalk in front of Pier 43. Outside, the din lessened slightly as we pulled away from the pier, but what I assumed to be the ordinary sounds of the city were most disconcerting: I felt hounded by the thunder of construction, threatened by what seemed an irate mob, and pursued by enraged horses neighing and stomping on all sides. But the most appalling noise was the howl and clangor of the municipal transit system's cable cars. The enchanted labyrinth was inhabited by monsters!

Mr. Goodwin spoke twice. The first time, he identified the horrifying roar passing overhead as the Sixth Avenue elevated train. (From *Harper's* I was able to fit an image to the pandemonium. I nodded knowingly while smiling gratefully.) The second time, he announced we were at our destination. How he knew is beyond me. The carriage had stopped so many times, only to start moving again with a gut-wrenching jolt.

He descended, offering much-needed assistance. I was as shaken and wobbly as if I had been to sea in a rickety tub rather than riding for thirty minutes in high style through the streets of the world's greatest metropolis. For the first few moments I swayed on the sidewalk in the glaring heat. Hordes of strangers bustled by, smiling at me and gaping enviously at "my" carriage and pair.

As I cataloged my impressions, I gathered this piece of the island was far removed from Pier 43. It was relatively quiet, immaculately clean, there were no street vendors, and the people looked as if they'd leaped from the pages of *Godey's.* I took a deep breath and glanced at what rose before me: Saint Patrick's Cathedral on Fifth Avenue between Fiftieth and Fifty-first streets in the midafternoon sunlight. I was unprepared for the immediate impression it made on my dazzled senses; the gleaming white Victorian-Gothic structure looked like a huge cake!

An elderly, portly cleric interrupted my thoughts (such as they were) by introducing himself as Father William Collins of Saint Paul's on something-or-other street, "just off Fifth." He repeated his name. I stared blankly. Leaning toward me, he whispered gently, "Yes, it does overwhelm one with its majesty. Greater than Chartres, much greater! So fine! Take your time, my son; collect yourself. I do understand. So fine!"

I looked into his large blue eyes. Such a dear man, I thought. I also remembered who he was, which was more to the point; Father Howard had said his name at least twenty times in as many minutes.

He most courteously dismissed Mr. Goodwin ("You've succeeded beautifully, so beautifully!"), who returned to the carriage at the curb. The priest and I stood silent for several minutes among the parade passing on the sidewalk. He seemed lost in meditation. (I studied the New Yorkers, noticing the trim cut of the men's suits, and felt as if I were wearing a flour sack.) Then, turning to me, Father Collins informed me that he thought me calm enough to enter the cathedral, "to confront its magnificence."

"Live the experience, my son, as I know you will. Father Howard wrote me of your sensitive, gentle soul. Being pensive myself, I do understand."

He winked conspiratorially. Taking my arm, he slowly led me up the steps, guiding me into the cool gaping mouth of the edifice.

Devoured by a cake, I thought. Curiouser and curiouser. . . .

Father William Collins obviously loved Saint Patrick's Cathedral, and what *I* was doing there was a mystery soon solved. He told me in a mellow whisper as we moved down the central aisle that he had convinced Mr. Gaylord of the necessity of my seeing this great monument to Christ and to Saint Patrick during my brief sojourn, in the hopes it would inspire a rebirth of faith, "rekindle the divine light." The matter was of course just between me, Father Howard, himself, and God, since Gaylord had not been told of my "waning fervor."

"Not his concern, my son! Though he is concerned about *everything* in your sad history. So sad! Your mother is in my prayers, rest assured."

The mention of her made my heart race. I looked away. When he asked if I didn't see "an iridescent quality in the window tracery," I smiled politely, not having the heart to contradict the sweet old man.

What relief when I trudged out into the open air and stood on the cathedral's steps again! The balm of the bright hot sunshine! Father Collins checked his watch and announced the time approaching 4:12. My interview with my employer was scheduled for half-past six. Father suggested dinner before the ride down to the Gaylord town house at number 15 Gramercy Park on the corner of Irving Place. He gestured toward an empty black victoria at the curb. As we neared it, I spotted the same scrolled gold letter G that had adorned the previous carriage. Like that other vehicle, it was of rare finish and proportion, appointed in the same gray velvet upholstery. Black stallions, twins to the other pair, clopped the pavement, anxious to carry me farther toward my destination.

"Mr. Donough thought an open carriage would be acceptable from here to Number 15," Father Collins explained as we climbed aboard, "with a stop for dinner at Childs on Forty-second Street, which was *my* suggestion!"

The ride down Fifth Avenue was tremendously exhilarating. Such a variety of traffic! Such hustle and bustle! So many beautiful people! All the pictures in the world can't capture the fervor of it. The city pulsates! And all the while, my companion chatted delightfully about the glories of the town, pointing out those buildings he could identify by owner or occupant, most of whom were members of the Four Hundred or attended his church.

At the corner of Forty-second Street and Fifth Avenue, the carriage stopped without our signaling. We descended. While Father spoke with the driver, I looked about me. People of all shapes, sizes, and colors, yet with touching similarities, overheated and fatigued, thronged the streets. They wore the most astonishing varieties of costume; some looked dressed for the stage and others looked as if they'd only just arrived from foreign lands. They all seemed absorbed in private thoughts and impervious to everything, and all in a frantic hurry.

"What's the big rush?"

"They're hungry! Been working all day. Probably *all* going to Childs!"

Across the street, on the southwest corner, an immense excavation yawned. It was the widest, deepest man-made hole I'd ever seen. A large sign identified it as the proposed Forty-second Street branch of the New York Public Library.

Like me, I thought, a vacant space soon to be occupied by a splendid building and books.

We walked to Childs along Forty-second Street amidst thousands of souls speeding in various directions. The restaurant was a sparkling clean establishment, all tile and marble, with an endless number of tables. Between the tables, ten-foot standing fans churned the air above our heads. The waitresses wore white blouses, pert black bow ties, and full white aprons. It was a noisy place but (to me) inviting and exciting.

We sat at one of the round tables, joining four other gentlemen. Never having been in a restaurant before, I was relieved when he recommended the "regular dinner." ("Such a bargain at fifteen cents, Robert!") My veal was delicious, and Kathleen, our waitress, after promising to visit Saint Paul's that coming Sunday, gave me a second order of fried potatoes "on the house." I ate heartily, though silently, feeling comfortable with my companions, who soon were engaged in congenial conversation. I was thinking of the ride down Fifth Avenue, and imagining Donough Gaylord.

After dinner, we found the hansom waiting outside. Forty-five minutes remained before my appointment. The driver was instructed to go slowly down Fifth Avenue, then across Twenty-third Street so we might see Madison Square Park, then down Fourth Avenue to Twentieth Street. In the carriage, I found a thin gray blanket of the softest cashmere for our laps. When we spread the blanket to avoid the evening damp, a woven scrolled black letter G embraced my knees like some great spider.

We rode for several blocks until I summoned the courage to ask:

"Have you known the Gaylord family for a very long time?"

His mood changed completely. All traces of joviality disappeared.

"I have been the family's spiritual adviser for decades. I baptized Mr. Donough and, to my eternal sorrow, I buried his mother, his father, and his twin brother, Cormack. They are a remarkable family, remarkable!"

He began relating his version of the Gaylord family history. I sat enthralled, oblivious to all else.

Three

"AT THE AGE OF THIRTY, DONOUGH Gaylord is New York's most eligible bachelor. Keeping such tabs is of paramount importance in my line of work." Father William Collins chuckled. "He is the most generous, the kindest, and the most compassionate person in New York, perhaps in the entire world." Three years before, Gaylord had given Saint Paul's a new rectory. Three days before, upon hearing from Father Collins of my plight, he had sent an offer of employment, although he knew nothing of me.

"Most men admire him the way they admire the moon."

Before Donough Gaylord's mother, Mary Rose, took ill, the family spent every Christmas season in town at Gramercy Park. Father Collins, their pastor, her friend, had been a frequent visitor and companion. When the family retired permanently to Long Island, he and Mrs. Gaylord maintained a lively correspondence and during the summer months he visited them for week-long vacations. He had also been familiar with Donough Gaylord's grandparents. Grandfather Donough, like his son and grandson, though generous to Holy Mother Church, was not amenable to the religious influence; neither had the Southern-born grandmother furthered God's cause as Boston-bred Mary Rose had done.

Jennilee Turner had been one of the most sought-after belles in the Atlanta of her day. Although she was not classically beautiful (her brown eyes were too prominent), men seldom noticed when tangled in her charms as Grandfather Gaylord had become one lilac-scented afternoon in 1834 during lunch in the scuppernong arbor. The forty-four-year-old bachelor, visiting Georgia on business of another sort, asked for her hand after dinner that same day. His fortune, made in shipping, doubled in railroads, then quadrupled in Manhattan real estate, satisfied her ambitions; his impetuous passion convinced old man

Turner that his exasperating daughter had met her match. Theirs was the biggest wedding Atlanta had ever seen.

The house in Gramercy Park was purchased and work was begun on a summer retreat. Gaywyck was erected as a monument to her beauty and as a testament to their love. Set on a rise, it was built of the finest oak and teak to designs by James Dakin in his most lavish Southern style: three stories of porticoes and pillars with half-acre corridors and rooms upon rooms opening into more sun-filled rooms overhanging the sea. Willow groves and oak stands were laid out; an avenue of limes, an herb garden, shrubbery mazes, a Chinese teahouse, and of course a scuppernong arbor. Both homes were furnished and maintained in an extravagant style that made them justly famous. Until the outbreak of the Civil War, Jennilee and Donough Gaylord were the reigning couple of New York society, envied by everyone who knew how truly happy they were.

Their only child, Cormack Donough Gaylord, was born in 1835. He was educated by private tutors, and everything money could buy was bestowed upon him. He was endowed with astonishing beauty and a multitude of talents. At the age of five, he spoke five languages, not counting classical Greek and Latin. At eight, Franz Liszt advised his parents he had the makings of a concert pianist, "if he wishes to lead such a horrid life." At fourteen, he published an article in the *New York Times* evaluating Mr. Edwin Booth's New York debut as Cassio to the father's famous Iago. But at seventeen he touched upon his true genius. With money received as gifts and allowance, he made himself independently wealthy with "a killing" in peanut butter; he was the first to package and sell it as a grocery item. Then, during the Civil War, he shrewdly invested capital on both sides of the Mason-Dixon line, making certain his investments existed independently one from the other, so that whatever parts might be lost, the whole could not be destroyed. When the war ended, his money had increased two-hundred-fold and not even the depreciation of American currency disrupted his rise.

The Gaylord wealth, like a few other private fortunes, flourished as no others had done before. Economists explained the phenomenon as one due to bizarre coincidences and inexplicable fates, "like the collision of the sun and moon," one wag jibed.

There occurred other collisions less propitious.

As the war progressed, Jennilee Turner Gaylord worried herself into illness over her parents. Removed to Gaywyck to escape the chaos of the city, she built for them a brick cottage on the grounds, but they refused to leave home, never believing the war would reach Atlanta. Impetuously, without her husband's knowledge, she sped south to coerce them.

Traveling at night via the Gaylord steam yacht, she was guided by a renegade Confederate, Captain Scott, who had made millions jumping the blockade for her husband. She arrived the same day as General Sherman. In the midst of the carnage, while the Athens of the South blazed, they boldly confiscated an open buckboard. Collecting her parents, who insisted on carting the family silver, the portraits, the pets, and four devoted "nigras," they made for the outskirts of the city in the direction of the camouflaged boat. Close to the sea, a convoy of looting Yankee soldiers stopped them for the wagon, and senselessly shot them dead. Only Captain Scott survived.

Grandfather Gaylord did not accept his wife's death complacently. He became obsessed; violence surfaced at the slightest provocation. He abdicated in his son's favor, leaving the boy to manage the family's holdings while he devoted his life to avenging his wife. With the help of friends in Washington, he won General Sherman's approval to track down the men responsible ("War is not licensed barbarity!"). He set a huge reward on their heads, hired bounty hunters, circulated posters proclaiming Jennilee's martyrdom, and offered the tottering Confederacy vast sums (in gold) as well as hefty promises of material aid (steel, wood, cloth, seeds) for reconstruction. Before the war's end, each man in that marauding convoy was slain. He personally assassinated Captain Scott. At the helm of the renovated steam yacht, he sailed into retirement at Gaywyck. In 1867, aged seventy-seven, after being thrown from a wasp-stung horse while examining his potato crop for parasites, he died.

During the frenzied postwar boom, Cormack Gaylord was the most eligible bachelor, the most sought-after dinner guest in fashionable New York society. Like his future son, he was reputed to have only two passions: money and opera. The latter he discovered at the opening of the Astor Place Opera House, which his father helped build; that performance of Verdi's *Ernani* awoke in him at age twelve an interest that continually provided his richest pleasures. (He spoke of the American premiere of Donizetti's *Roberto Devereaux* two years later as the happiest night of his adolescence.) Throughout his youth and early manhood he attended regularly; in maturity he arranged business trips abroad to coincide with performances he wished to hear; and by the age of thirty-three, he was a prime mover in the project to rebuild the Academy of Music after the disastrous fire which he watched from the roof of his Gramercy Park home.

With the Academy reopened, joined by Pike's Opera House (later the Grand Opera House) and the famed Metropolitan, opera was for a brief time the center of attention in certain circles, for reasons far removed from musical appreciation. Ambitious young ladies, encouraged by scheming mothers, became staunch devotees, vying to learn the latest arias in hopes of enchanting Gaylord during the suppers arranged for after whatever piece all were attending that night. (Gaylord's valet made a tidy sum informing the anxious of the week's arrangements. Years later, when the current Gaylord was "about town," a similar interest in opera flowered, but with much less success.)

In March of 1868, on a visit from Boston, eighteen-year-old Mary Rose Reagen attended the opera with her aunt; coincidentally, it was by Verdi. She wept throughout the performance of *La Traviata*, observed clandestinely from the neighboring box by Cormack Gaylord. The performance was a mediocre one, and the very young Irish beauty in her gown of white mull with pale beige lace was of far greater interest to the middle-aged bachelor. Unlike her peers, she did not spend the overture chatting with friends, the first act waving to acquaintances in various parts of the house, the second on the grand staircase discussing the fashions of the day or the latest liaisons, and the third asleep or preparing to exit during the fourth in order to attend some gathering at which Gaylord was the headlined attraction. From the moment the performance began, she sat transfixed.

Initially, he was amused by her intensity. Her spontaneous responses touched him. Then the tilt of her head, the

impatient gesture she employed to quiet a companion who
attempted conversation during the *"Sempre Libera,"* the
audible sigh she made when the curtain fell on Act One,
and her quivering response to the rising gas light, conspired to draw him to her.

Mrs. Lacey, the chaperoning aunt, was an annoying,
fatuous busybody; but he was willing to concede that three
marriageable daughters were a heavy burden. She was
doing the best job she could within the confines of the
appalling "mating dance" devised, he believed, to give
women something to do. He had learned to forgive the
hounding.

Entering her box at the first interval, he was introduced
to the niece who smiled warmly. As polite conversation
was resumed, he noticed that she refrained from joining
in the general discussion, preferring to sit musing by herself. Until his comments on the performance caught her
attention, she did not address him directly. Then, dis-
pleased with his lack of enthusiasm, she declared *she* had
thought it a splendid performance and although it was
only her first *Traviata* she knew *she* would *never* tire of it
however poorly sung or gestured, and had *she* been at the
first American performance in 1856 *and* heard La Grange
she hoped nothing *nothing* would ever diminish its magic
for *her.* . . .

While everyone present stood or sat stunned by her
declaration, Cormack Gaylord smiled. He apologized for
his insensitivity and his unforgivable ennui. She blushed,
apologized for her impertinence, and informed him that
it was the most beautiful and important night in her life,
and even if he spoke the truth—something she refused to
consider—he must not insist she agree with him. He assured her he could never be tyrannical with one so en-
chantingly lovely. She laughed, blushing again, and held
his eyes with her own.

He returned to his box for Act Two. Amused, he
watched the aunt scold her penitently bent head until the
music started; then the bowed profile was lifted and its
attention turned toward the stage with such determination
that the chastisement was brought to an abrupt halt. Not
even a heated lecture on the Gaylord millions could distract her from *Traviata.*

During the second interval, he strolled. Miss Reagen of
the Boston Reagens was badly shaken by Violetta's plight.

He hoped she would have the stamina to endure Act Three. The evening had taken an exhilarating turn. His spirits were high. He impulsively accepted an invitation to visit a business associate's box, where the chilled champagne was delicious, until the resident twin daughters began straining for his attentions. Unamused, he quickly returned to his place. He was getting too old, he thought, for all the socializing required in the business world. He needed to make some changes. He needed something more acceptable as a private life, something that would make things easier.

The young girl visiting her aunt sat enrapt, oblivious to his presence. Bemused, he studied her. When she began to weep, he felt a rush of tenderness. Surrendering to her sorrow, she allowed her tears to flow unchecked; by the end she was crying uncontrollably. When the houselights went up, she continued to sob unashamedly in her aunt's arms, soothed by the other members of the disconcerted party. Cormack Donough Gaylord looked on. Already captivated by her beauty and what he perceived to be her integrity, he capitulated to her innocence and the absence of affectation. Such a one as this, he thought, needs to be protected.

He took no supper that night. Nor did he sleep. The next morning, and every morning thereafter, he sent her a cluster of camellias. The following week, to the day, he called. She and her aunt received him cordially. Thanking him for the flowers, she extended her hand, which he took. Leading him into the parlor, she began discussing music in general, opera in particular. She attended often in Boston, but her father had not considered *Traviata* suitable for a young woman, which she hoped explained why she was unfamiliar with it in performance. Her father, she added, found many things unsuitable for a young woman. She revealed above her aunt's protestations, that her ambition was the operatic stage.

"Past tense," she emphasized, sadly drawing his attention to her syntax. During the previous year, she had slowly come to realize that she lacked the physical stamina and fanatical discipline required; she had struggled to relinquish her ambitions without self-pity. Worried she would never "regain her senses," her widowed father had unwisely interfered. While not denying her abilities, he scoffed at her priorities.

"Women of your social class," he informed her, "do not have 'talent,' they have '*gifts*,' which are cultivated not for themselves but for their husbands' pleasure and their husbands' profit."

His meddling curdled her sadness into anger. She saw herself as chattel having no life (or "gifts") of her own. Dangerously depressed, she was given permission to visit her aunt, who suggested the opera to raise her spirits.

"And did it raise your spirits, Miss Reagen?"

"Oh, yes, Mr. Gaylord. I finally heard *Traviata*. It did make me feel much better."

He stayed for three hours. Before leaving, he asked her to sing something. Pleased, she sang "*Libiamo*" from *La Traviata* beautifully, accompanying herself on the parlor spinet. He accepted an invitation to dinner. At home, while dressing, he imagined her reactions to Gaywyck.

All of his visits were pleasant and encouraging. He found her intelligent, well-educated, thoughtful, kind, generous, and scrupulously truthful, a virtue he thought no longer extant in young women. She, for her part, found him constantly stimulating, patient, compassionate, gentle, and respectful of her ideas and feelings, which greatly pleased her. As each was beautiful, neither considered beauty extraordinary, accepting their mutual attraction as natural and preordained.

They were eager to know each other well. Visits occasionally began at breakfast; luncheon often extended to teatime. He arrived full of plans for the day: outings in one of his carriages, excursions on one of his boats, or tours in one of his private railroad carriages. Always considerate of her wishes, he was never annoyed if she preferred a walk through a museum, or a quiet day in the garden. The courtship extended for two months. On May 1, she returned to Boston. On May 3, he journeyed to Boston to ask for her hand. On June 6, they married.

At first sighting, she loved Gaywyck. She had the paintings from their honeymoon in Italy and England and France hung at Gaywyck. The expanse of the rooms, she said, suited them better, and the sound of the sea worked a perfect counterpoint. Masterworks were raised in various chambers, which were renamed and redecorated accordingly. The Rembrandt self-portrait was placed in the main library. The Botticelli Madonna she hung in her bedroom; the Crevelli she hung in his. The Vermeer she placed in her sitting room. The enormous Titian was hung in the main parlor, then removed to the third-floor library because she found it oppressive; in its place was put the mysterious Rossetti portrait of a woman who dramatically resembled her. The Della Francesca angel was set in the small downstairs study. The others were lovingly dispersed to rooms that were frequently used by relatives or friends; and after they were all settled on appropriate walls, Mary Rose Reagen Gaylord announced she never needed to visit New York or Boston again. The Empire furniture bought in France was shipped to Gaywyck.

But there was the opera. For that she endured "the endless journey" into New York via their steam yacht or private coach. For the music she tolerated separation from the sea, her pictures, and the serenity. Cormack, semi-retired, hired talented young men and trained them to oversee his business involvements, maintaining contact via his telegraph system and a courier service. An assistant ran his office at Gaywyck. More and more like his father, Cormack became the gentleman farmer. But together he and Mary Rose ventured into the city; for a week or two their house at Gramercy Park came alive with late suppers and musicales. Until she became pregnant. Then everything changed.

From the moment Mary Rose discovered herself with child, she withdrew into herself. After the initial shock and anger, her humor grew dark, her mood depressed. He had known of her loathing for children and her fear of childbirth; she felt betrayed. Her confessor, Father Collins, tried to foster her "duty" to the will of God, but she refused all guidance. Fleeing to Gaywyck in despair, she locked herself in her rooms. After five days she admitted her aunt and the priest; but not her husband. As the days became weeks, his anger and confusion became fear; although her two intimates assured Gaylord she was "coming around," he sent specialists of every kind to see her. When she refused them all admittance, he at least felt he was doing his best. Then, suddenly, she appeared in his study one evening, followed by a smiling priest and a nodding aunt.

"I have been very foolish," she whispered. "Forgive me."

There was no explanation for the change in her behavior. It was accredited to answered prayers.

She asked for new costumes, everything to be in white.

An apartment on the third floor was converted into quarters for three seamstresses and their designer-mistress, who arrived almost immediately. She asked for a doctor-in-residence; a family physician agreed to spend four days a week at Gaywyck. She asked for a full-time nurse; one was moved into her sitting room, which was destined to become the nursery. She asked to receive communion every morning; the local priest appeared to say Mass in the newly organized chapel in the third-floor library, with the large Titian supplying a proper sense of decorum and the magnificent jewel-encrusted chalice—a gift from Cormack to the local church—supplying the proper sense of occasion. (A special dispensation had to be arranged, allowing the priest to say Mass twice a day: once on his own altar for his parishioners and once at Gaywyck; owing to Cormack's friendship with Cardinal Fanning, the delay was of no consequence.)

She asked for music. A chamber orchestra was housed in the cottage built by Jennilee Turner Gaylord. Each day, at midmorning and after tea, they made music in the willow grove or in the main parlor or the music room, depending on her whim. Vocal soloists, stars of the various companies on her patron list, frequently visited to perform arias and entire scenes from her favorite operas. Boxes of music arrived daily for her perusal, and selections were rehearsed by the musicians in the mornings and afternoons. With performances and rehearsals, music was always in the air that summer, like the buzzing of the bees and the cries of the seagulls and the rumbling of the sea.

Mary Rose was amenable to suggestions from everyone. Except for this languid passivity, she seemed to have regained her senses. Father Collins, visiting in early July, attested to the healthy good spirits that pervaded Gaywyck.

"It was like a grand party at the height of the season. People you couldn't get a ticket to hear at the Met for love or money were warbling on the lawn! So exciting!"

The birth was expected at the end of November. Having grown larger than ordinary, and preparing for a "heavy" baby, the mother allowed herself little excess, spending most of her time reclining on divers chaises in and out of the house. Her day had a definite shape: Mass, breakfast, music, lunch, a nap, a walk, clothes fittings, tea, more music, another nap, dressing for dinner, reading, prayers, bed. She seemed to thrive on the order Gaylord

created for her, until the end of August. Increasingly
distressed by her figure, she announced herself "repulsive"
and retired once again to her quarters, venturing forth at
night with her aunt to walk along the beach, or in the
late afternoons on her second-floor balcony out of view
to hear Schubert, Beethoven, or Mozart. She remained in
seclusion, awaiting the birth of her son.

"It *will* be a son," she assured Father Collins, "for I
will never allow a child of mine to go through this torment. And if I know *anything*, I know God grants Cormack his wishes."

At midnight on the twenty-seventh of October 1869,
she became unduly anxious and profoundly agitated about
the impending birth. A fierce storm had risen outdoors.
The wind, encouraged by the turbulently hissing sea,
moaned brutishly, slammed against the house, and rattled
the windows through closed shutters. She awoke screaming.
The wind, she said, was sucking the baby from her womb.
The doctor was called, a sedative administered. Drugged,
she slipped past her dozing aunt and sleeping nurse.
Through the window of their office, Cormack and his
assistant saw her white form stagger over the rise and
descend to the sea. Bounding down the lawn to the rain-
swept slope, the husband jumped to the flooded beach
below and tore her, unconscious, from the roaring, battling
sea.

Within an hour, after an excruciating breech delivery, a
five-pound boy was born. He was named Cormack
Donough Gaylord. Ten minutes later, the doctor's
shout "There's another one coming!" electrified the household. A second boy, three pounds five ounces, was born.
He was named Donough Cormack Gaylord.

Mary Rose regained consciousness immediately. When
told she delivered twins, she laughed crazedly and shouted
for her husband.

"I hope you're pleased," she said to him. "Two for your
pleasure."

He remained silent. Thanking the doctor, he withdrew
from the room. She demanded the boys be placed at her
side. The smaller, Donough, caused concern, but the
doctor assured her he was perfectly healthy, neither pre-
mature nor sickly in spite of his tinier frame. Often with
twins, he explained, one draws more nourishment in the
womb; often one is larger; often one is heavier.

Nevertheless, she fretted. She demanded a specialist from New York. She raged that the infant Cormack should have "bullied" his brother even before birth. She raved hysterically until a stronger sedative induced sleep and allowed the doctor to attend her ripped and bruised body. To his astonishment, within two hours she awoke, screaming for her sons, who had to be nursed before she would rest quietly. Then she slept for twenty-one hours. When she awoke, Father Collins was at her side. She seemed calm. Relieved, the household prepared to celebrate the birth of the twin boys.

From their first to their fifth year, the boys were confined to the grounds of the country estate and were always in their mother's presence. The house in Gramercy Park was dark except for the rooms occupied by Cormack Gaylord Sr. when in town for business, an arrangement that occurred more and more frequently and for more extended periods. He began appearing at the opera without her, accompanied by Father Collins or whatever young protégé he happened to be training at the time. Everyone commented on what a faithful and understanding husband he was for one so handsome and still so young. He gave Mary Rose everything she required, never balking on grounds of expense or practicality.

One of the most eminent pediatricians, a specialist in twins, stayed at Gaywyck for the first precarious year, when children are most perishable. Cormack offered him an annuity equal to the value of his thriving practice, a laboratory and library in the now-deserted cottage, and a private railroad carriage to carry the more tenacious parents who insisted on keeping appointments with him. The Vermeer room, adjacent to Mary Rose's bedroom, was converted into a perfectly appointed nursery, and the rooms opposite into quarters for the nurses, the nanny, and the nursery maids (one for each baby). Detailed records were kept to make certain the growth rates, feeding schedules, and behavioral patterns were in order. Nevertheless, Mary Rose feared for their safety. Only when the wall between herself and the twins was removed did she feel at peace.

Whenever they cried, she tended to their needs herself, forcing the staff to stand about idly. *She* fed them, changed them, played with them, and sang them to sleep. She preferred them in her own bed, rather than in their ornate cribs. She walked with them when they howled, often through the night as one woke the other, so that both would have to be held and soothed. She dressed them for guests and undressed them for bed. She even took over the preparation of their food when she was forced to concede she was not producing enough milk; a wet nurse was forbidden. She would sit for hours watching them sleep, humming endlessly, softly, as if pausing would snap the thread of their dreams.

Regularly during dinner with her husband when he was at Gaywyck, if the sound of crying reached her ears, she would rise from the table, frequently not returning. One evening, when she seemed particularly overwrought and distracted, Cormack suggested she return to town with him and Father Collins for the new production of *Norma* at the Metropolitan Opera House, precipitating a scene of such violence that he feared for his person. In her rage, she accused him of every conceivable sin. Many he acknowledged. Many he repudiated. Many he had assumed concealed. Forced to call the doctor, he never again interfered with her obsessive concern for their twin sons. He returned to Gramercy Park hoping the current "phase" of her maternity would end.

Growth, as always, changed things; only Mary Rose's all-pervasive involvement with her children remained the same. The boys grew: Cormack first, Donough following. Cormack remained the larger for the first year, then Donough equaled him in height and weight; but the older retained the lead in all things. He began to crawl first, observed by Donough, who soon followed, copying his brother's movements. The same pattern was established with standing, walking, and talking. Since they were never alone, all of it was carefully noted. By the middle of their second year, they had a personal language of expressions, gestures, and sounds so impenetrable that a tutor was hired to help straighten the phrases and untangle the syntax.

Julian Denvers, a quiet, gentle man, religious and infinitely patient, was of medium height and slight frame, with thin, long brown hair, brown eyes, and a waxen complexion. He had studied most of his life to become a Jesuit, but, realizing before his final vows that "it was not God's will," he was recommended to the concerned Mary Rose by Father Collins. At their first meeting, the young

man and the anxious parent got on very well. She was
favorably impressed with the quality of his education, and
felt his disciplined presence would be a good influence on
her sons.

He was touched by her devotion to her children. When
she offered him the position, he accepted. From that day,
he never left the Gaylord employ. Spending most of his
time with the children, he also saw a good deal of the
mother, developing a rapport that gave him a mastery
over her temper and inexplicable mood shifts. This made
him invaluable to Cormack Sr.

The twins' second birthday marked a turning point. She
allowed the nanny more responsibility in the day-to-day
caring for the boys. She invited people to the house;
Gaywyck was again vibrant with social activity. It was as
if by living for two years, they convinced her of their
ability to survive. Also, she had detected during their
infancy what she considered a talisman, though the doctor
assured her it was not uncommon in twins. One child was
a "mirror image" of the other.

She discovered a birthmark under Cormack's left arm
in line with his left nipple; Donough had an identical one
on his right side. Cormack's left eye was slightly larger
than his right; Donough's right eye was the larger. The
hair whorl at the top of each child's head was exact, except
Cormack's grew counterclockwise. And, at a very early
age, Donough preferred his right hand, while Cormack
favored his left. Thrilled, Mary Rose took comfort in
displaying this "sign from God"; greatness lay dormant in
her sons. She celebrated their second birthday as a personal victory.

"God wants such perfect creatures as angels in heaven.
I forbade it. Now they're two, and each has two for himself and for the other. Jesus loves them."

Mary Rose requested her friends to visit, ostensibly to
renew aquaintance, but in truth to display her prodigies.
Eager mothers arrived, carrying their children. They seldom returned. Cormack was a rough little boy who instigated games that inevitably led to scraped knees and
bloody noses. "Boys will be boys," Father Collins offered
in supplication, but the mothers were not soothed. Soon
most of the visitors were single women or married women
without children, who often stayed a month at a time. The
house was filled with laughter. The musicians were re-

instated. Cormack Sr. returned for extended periods, pleased that matters were under control.

From their earliest days, when they slept together on their mother's breasts, and the nights when they slept side by side, each sucking the other's thumb, they were inseparable. When asked how she could tell one from the other, Mary Rose smiled sagely and answered, "A mother knows such things." Mr. Denvers, however, lacking a mother's powers, admitted difficulty. He was instructing them in four languages (the major "opera tongues"), and often became convinced the same boy was doing the responding or asking the questions. No matter how intensely he concentrated, they succeeded in confounding him. ("How severe can one be with a three-year-old tot?" he asked himself, answering: "Not very!") Since the lessons were given outdoors, they moved about or simply answered to the other's name at a strategic moment, always sensing those moments of doubt. Also, he discovered they were ambidextrous, a fact he never disclosed to their mother.

His idea for the gold rings expressed just how well he understood his mistress's mind. Knowing she would reject anything that disrupted her plans to make them reflections, one of the other, he acted accordingly. As he expected, she did not object; she was, in fact, delighted. Cormack was given a gold ring for his left pinky finger; Donough was given one for his right. For their mother, the duplication was complete. For the tutor, the exasperation was no more.

At about this time, the first of a series of young men was hired by Cormack Gaylord to oversee his sons' physical development and to guard them when they frolicked in the sea. A jetty was constructed of huge rocks; it extended into the ocean for fifty yards, creating a play surface, a picnic area, a tide breaker, a diving platform, and on the far side, a private place where the men swam, free from the prying, observing eyes of wives, mothers, nurses, nannies, and female visitors. Cormack Gaylord greatly enjoyed this privilege, romping for hours with his sons and their guard, occasionally joined by a male houseguest, or by Mr. Denvers, who shyly wore a bathing costume, or by the easily chilled Everard Keyes, the new music teacher.

"Don't you think it's a tad *early* to start them on piano and theory, my dear?"

"Early? It's *never* early!"

Everard Keyes, an amateur scientist and concert pianist of moderate reputation, with a temper remarkably easy and indolent, had retired from the stage, unable to bear the strain of a professional career. Essentially a private person, he could not maintain his equilibrium in the public arena. Meeting Gaylord at the opera, introduced by a mutual friend, he mentioned his awakening interest in teaching. "But not just piano, sir; music theory and composition as well." Several tempting offers had already been received from universities and musical academies; fearing academia would stifle him or not leave enough time for composition, he was hesitating, he explained, before commitment. The next morning an offer was delivered by messenger; the situation offered his own cottage on the estate, a valet, a cook, and as much money and free time as he desired. He returned a positive reply. In that way, he joined the others at Gaywyck.

Though Mr. Denvers's opposite in every physical characteristic (being corpulent and fair with a ruddy complexion), and in every spiritual one (being a confirmed atheist), Keyes and the resident tutor liked each other immediately, uncovering similar opinions and interests, including their theories of education and their shared passion for guidebooks as "manuals of sensibility." (Both treasured copies of Murray's *Handbook to Spain*, 1845, by Richard Ford, as "the masterpiece of the genre," and they laughed uproariously over Horrebow's *Iceland* and his section "Concerning Owls in Iceland," which they quoted simultaneously in its entirety: "There are no owls of any kind on the whole island.")

Keyes decided he must take his meals at the main house, and soon moved into quarters there. He instigated the use of surnames between himself and the tutor, a European style quickly adopted by the entire household, except for a brief period when the boys referred to them as Tweedledum and Tweedledee.

In the beginning, the boys were pleased with their music teacher and much impressed by his mastery of the keyboard. They brought their enthusiasm to Denvers and attempted a different language each day during their sessions together. Then, for a time, Donough rebelled. Everyone agreed the root cause was Mary Rose's fascination with the musician: she never ceased remarking to the boys that Keyes was the best thing their father had ever bought.

Donough shouted his hatred for French, German, and Italian. He hated Keyes and Chopin and Schubert. During this period he was constantly disciplined for recalcitrant behavior, such as lopping the blossoms off his mother's beloved tulips, or breaking Denvers's glasses, or burning Keyes's music, or, most outrageously, urinating from the second-story balcony onto his teachers, gossiping below. He never attempted to hide himself; he was not a sneak. Nor did he refuse his punishment, though it made him angry. Secretly pleased to see the reserved Donough displaying some temperament, the adults were not unduly severe. As Father Collins predicted, the "storm" passed.

Their sixth birthday was celebrated at Gramercy Park, setting a precedent that was not broken until Mary Rose became too ill to journey from Gaywyck. They traveled wrapped in sable cloaks and gray beaver hats trimmed with tartan ribbons, in the specially equipped family coach pulled by four horses; stopping for one night at an inn, they arrived the day before their birthday. They stayed to celebrate Christmas and the New Year with parties and theatergoing, operas, and excursions to museums and galleries, returning to Long Island by rail after Little Christmas. In town, the twins were an immediate success. Before the end of their first visit, they were quite famous, causing a stir wherever they appeared. Mary Rose's extravagances in dressing them became legend. Their radiant, dark beauty, reflected by nature each in the other, dazzled. With every succeeding year, their intelligences sharpened, tightening their features, rendering them fiercely intent. One observer noted they had the eyes of young hawks.

By age fourteen, when they arrived at the opening of the new Metropolitan Opera House, their perfectly poised splendor was as great a topic of conversation—and of greater interest to many—than the expense of the new *Faust* production, or the much-touted Golden Horseshoe. For Father Collins, that night was unforgettable. He experienced the exhilarating sensation of being among the inheritors of the earth and the old traditions at their shining hour. Everything revolved around the two perfect children whose lives lay stretched before them like miles of priceless silken fabric to be cut in patterns of their own choosing. He often remembered that night when he talked of the strange and wondrous ways in which the Lord works His relentless will.

The following year, Mary Rose grew ill with a weakness in her lungs that overwhelmed her completely. The family never appeared publicly again. When she died, Father Collins spoke her eulogy. A few years later, he spoke over the graves of her husband and elder son; in 1887, they perished in a fire. Young Cormack died trying to save his father.

Donough, distraught, went abroad. He traveled for three years incommunicado, finally settling in Paris until 1896, when he sailed to New York to take control of his vast estate. The grief-struck boy returned a formidable, intense private man. No one spoke an unkind word of him; no one called him friend. The aura of sadness that informed his extraordinary beauty seemed to excise him from the mundane concerns of life, isolating him in a shuttered reality. Father Collins reckoned him a unique, mysterious creature of God who followed the beat of a solitary heart.

I trembled in anticipation as our carriage pulled up to 15 Gramercy Park.

Four

I HAVE RELIED HEAVILY ON MY JOURNAL in recreating Father Collins's narrative, trying not to alter his version by adding information gathered subsequently or clarifying what he muddled. I have retained as much as possible the confusions he engendered as to what had in truth occurred behind the glittering facade. ("What is truth?" asked Pilate, washing his hands.) I have, however, made his narrative linear, eliminating the unrelated tangents that interrupted as we progressed down distracting Fifth Avenue.

The carriage followed its prescribed route, carrying us past the Stewart and Astor mansions ("such lovely people, who . . ."), the Buckingham Hotel ("not to be faulted, if . . ."), and under the arch honoring Admiral Dewey at Madison Square ("so elegantly aligned with the one farther down honoring Washington, where . . ."). So as not to be rude by cutting too sharply into his "tour" speeches, I spent much of the journey maneuvering him back to the desired topic. I managed quite gracefully in the beginning, but less so as the destination approached.

"How long did they wear the rings?" I blurted out finally.

"I don't know, but they worked, which is all that matters. So clever!"

Night had fallen when we turned into Twentieth Street and Gramercy Park appeared, enclosed within a black wrought-iron railing. Suddenly it became very quiet in this beautiful enclave; I could hear a fountain splashing from somewhere within the private park. I wondered why the sounds of the heavy traffic and public transport did not penetrate into the lovely square.

We folded the soft lap blanket and Father Collins descended to the street. I followed, slipping on the step. Then I stood speechless, staring at the five-story red-brick corner house. I told myself it was natural for me to be nervous. I told myself everything would be all right:

nothing happens by chance. Every step is counted, every step is measured.

"It's a very *large* house," I said.

"The largest in the square. So fine!"

I was terrified. I told myself it was natural for me to be terrified. Was not my life at stake? What if Donough Gaylord detested me? What would I, a foundling, do alone in New York with nothing but Miss Grimmond's five-dollar bill? I stood immobilized by this possibility, as a deer stands startled by a sudden light.

"Hurry along, Robert! We mustn't keep Mr. Donough waiting!"

The moment he rang the glistening brass instrument, the glass-enclosed lamp over the door grew in brightness, illuminating the building's lower facade and the area in which we stood. I could see our faces in the enormous black-lacquered door, which was suddenly opened by an elderly man formally dressed. He smiled.

"Good evening, Father."

"Good evening, Mr. Moore. This is Robert Whyte. Mr. Donough is expecting us."

"He asks that you wait in the front parlor for a wee while, Father. He won't keep you long."

Glancing over my shoulder as I crossed the threshold, I noticed the lamplighter at the corner. His beam expanded rapidly, like an instantaneous moonrise, merging with the light emanating from over my head. I noticed the carriage was gone. It had begun to rain.

"Thank you, Mr. Moore. Tell Mr. Donough we're here, please."

"No need, Father. He ain't deaf. And he's expecting no one else."

"Thank you, Mr. Moore."

"Thank you, Father. The main parlor, please. He'll be sending for you shortly, Mr. Whyte."

The deep-red entranceway was surprisingly spacious, nearly as wide and as long as a railway carriage. On the wall to my left, a large and ornately etched crystal globe covered the steady gas jet; it hung over and was reflected in a deeply polished walnut table that held a silver dish and a cut-glass vase containing a massive arrangement of fall flowers of every variety. These had been chosen with such an understanding of their color values and how each shape contributed to the whole, that I felt their presence as one would feel the presence of a very strong human personality.

The hallway divided at the far end into a stairway and a narrower, extended passage leading to a closed black door. Mr. Moore rolled open paneled doors to my right. The parquet floor began to shimmer around me, glinting with scattered luminosity, reflecting the bright lamplight in the parlor. Luxury enveloped me as I crossed into the room; the double doors shut silently behind. I thrilled to the beauty of it all.

The furnishings and the painting over the fireplace were too much for me to absorb. I had never experienced any of it in three dimensions, and meeting it gathered together made me laugh with excitement. Ornate Tiffany lamps hovered over elaborate art-nouveau *objets* like monarch butterflies. I crossed and recrossed the room, but kept scurrying back to gaze at the painting. At first, it made me think of the flowers in the hallway, flattened and crushed into the canvas. As I looked, a form emerged; a cathedral in blinding sunlight, like Saint Patrick's that very afternoon! Could the facade be *made* of sunlight?

"What an *astonishing* painting, Father! Whose is it?"

"Mr. Donough's! One of his French pictures. By some fellow named 'Money' I think. I know, dear boy, it *is* awful; but don't tell him that! How I miss the Turner watercolors and the comfy chairs."

These are the impressionists, I thought. How different they look in color. . . .

"If his mother were alive, she'd never tolerate it."

I looked to the other side of the room and found another painting so bizarre and thrilling, I gaped at it. It was different entirely from the Monet, but somehow similar. Not bright and hot, but pale and very cool to the eye; while the first seemed to be splashes of color, this seemed to be blocks or planes.

It's a landscape, I thought. It's more exciting than Monet.

I glanced around the room to see if I could locate any other paintings. As my eyes rushed by the now open sliding doors, I saw a Japanese man.

"Mr. Whyte?"

I nodded, anxiety rising again.

"Mr. Gaylord will see you now."

Father Collins moved to accompany me.

The servant spoke again, turning his attention to the cleric. "Mr. Donough wishes to see Mr. Whyte alone, Father. Would you like some sherry?"

"Oh? Yes! Thank you, Taio, I would. So kind! Does Mr. Donough want me to stay?"

"Yes, Father. He wishes to thank you personally for your kind help in this matter."

I looked at Father Collins, who smiled encouragingly. I smiled meekly. Taio bowed and invited me to follow. We walked back into the foyer, turned to the right, and I waited while Taio closed the parlor doors. Passing beyond the flowers, we began ascending the stairs. As we climbed, I noticed that the walls were covered with red silk, embossed with minuscule red velvet columbines. The foyer light dappled the stairwell, merging with a similar one shining out from a half-open door at the top of the stairs.

Taio announced our arrival by two light taps. A deep male voice answered affirmatively, authoritatively. Taio slowly pushed open the door and entered, saying my name softly.

Heart pounding in trepidation, I waited on the landing outside. I registered nothing at first but flickering light until I noticed on the blue wall inside yet another painting similar to the landscape downstairs. It shocked me; the jolt was not of bewilderment, but of delight. I had perceived it immediately as a landscape, not a palette or a puzzle, but a vision.

The more I see of these pictures, I thought, pleasantly distracted, the more I'll understand. It's learning to see. . . .

Taio passed me in the doorway. He bade me enter. I hesitated a few heartbeats before walking into Donough Gaylord's study.

Even now, aeons later, my senses quicken as the memory of that moment takes hold of me. My soul slumbered and was soon to awaken.

I want to eradicate all that has accrued around him. I want to regain in all its purity my first impression of our first brief encounter.

I am sitting in that same study now. It is approximately the same time of day at the same time of year. The Cézanne is still on the wall, and I glance at it whenever I look up from my writing. My journal for that day is open beside me, helping me reclaim states of mind long gone, helping unravel the skein of diverse feelings and uncover nuance buried by the decades. Happiness, once accepted, obliterates memories of fear and pain.

Last night I dreamed I climbed again that columbine-covered stairwell. In my dream, its walls were aflame. Undaunted, I moved upward, easily reaching the door. Encouraged, I take pen in hand. Walk with me into the maelstrom. Would it were as simple in waking life as it is in dreams to triumph over adversity. . . .

I hear his first words: a simple phrase, a thank-you to Taio for having brought me to him. Then, as Taio passes me in the doorway, *he* says my name, raising the last syllable to end in a question when I fail to appear. I take a deep breath and walk into his study.

He stood in front of the fireplace with his back to me. Something on the white marble mantel held his attention. He is just above six feet in height, but being broad-shouldered, he gives the impression of a much taller man. His hair is like a raven's plumage. He wore formal evening attire. When he finished inspecting the cluster of red needle-shaped crystals, he turned his attention to me.

His eyes are enormous—almond-shaped—and of the palest gray, a silver dusk on a summer's day. They sought my gaze and held it. In their depths I recognized genuine interest, not momentary curiosity. I blushed and looked away. Then I returned his gaze, drawn by those twilight eyes.

If he had an imperfect beauty—if his nose were hooked, his chin nonexistent, his ears fleshy, his skin marked by enlarged pores—then with these negative aspects a picture could easily be drawn. But when male features are regular yet impart astonishment to the beholder, one must resort to "a face on a Roman/Greek coin/statue" or "a primeval god" or even "a hero in a romantic novel," though most heroes are never too clearly described, so that the reader may be allowed to satisfy each and every personal inclination.

Truly, Donough Gaylord is this and more. He has a perfect dark Irish beauty. Centuries of breeding have refined the coarser West Country aspects, honed them, burnished them until his flawless profile was thrust upon us. His is the majesty of face that one confronts in the miniatures of Hillyard, such as one finds in the frescoes of Della Francesca. There is magic in a beauty such as his.

He gave me a small, qualified smile. Walking the several paces from the fireplace to the door, he then gave me his hand in greeting.

"Welcome, Mr. Whyte. I hope this weather hasn't distressed you too much. Your trip was pleasant?"

"No, sir. Yes, sir. I . . ."

I was about to say something simple, like: "I'm pleased to know you," when, looking away dartingly, I saw yet another French impressionist over his desk.

"They are the most *incredible* paintings, sir. I agree with Mr. Brownell of *Scribner's*. I think they are wonderful! They *are* light. I can't take hold of them in my mind yet. Are there any at Gaywyck?"

"Why?"

"To look at. To get to know. To understand even . . . perhaps . . . somehow . . ."

He stared at me as if I were a needle-shaped crystal. I lowered my eyes. He turned and walked back to the fireplace. I waited for him to speak, but when I glanced in his direction, I saw him gazing into the fire. In profile, he seemed slightly flushed and irritated. After an interminable pause, he spoke very softly.

"Did Father Collins tell you how fond I am of these paintings?"

"No, sir, only how unpleasant *he* found them. Why, sir?"

"I was curious. The answer to your question is no; there are none at Gaywyck. There are other wonderful paintings, but none of these. Keyes hates them—Everard Keyes, that is, my old music master. He hates them. Do you want one?"

I thought I'd misheard him. "Do I *want* one?"

"Yes. I have several in storage ready to be hung. You can take one with you tomorrow."

"Have you any more by him?" I asked, dazed, pointing to the landscape.

"Cézanne? Yes, I have several more of his. You can have that one. It's time I shifted them around; I'm beginning not to see them. By the way, I agree with you about Mr. Brownell."

"I read the Japanese do that, too. They claim seeing things in different settings keeps them fresh in the mind.

I can't imagine ever becoming accustomed to these pictures, though. But it always struck me as a fine idea, once I thought about it."

"Yes," he said gravely, staring at me again. "Taio gave me the idea originally."

I blushed. The extraordinary house, the radiant art, the beauty of the man, had exhilarated me and made me forward. I had risen from my shyness like a bird from a thicket, and suddenly, shocked by my boldness, unaccustomed to such freedom, I flew back to the safety of my defenses.

"Are you interested in the Japanese as well, Mr. Whyte?"

"Yes, sir. But I know very little. . . ."

I blushed a deeper scarlet. I felt humiliated by not being able to control the suffusion. I felt bewildered by my sudden collapse.

"I am as well," he said, approaching me.

Looking up, startled to see him in motion, I fought the impulse to flee, to hide. I stood still, locking my knees. As he neared, I read compassion in his eyes. I felt calmed, though my heart raced. Placing his right hand clemently around my forearm so that his fingertips barely touched me, he smiled, comforting me in my distress.

"There are several other impressionists in the library. Come, let me show them to you. We can continue our talk there. Would you like some sherry or port?"

I shook my head, still unable to speak. Then I bravely looked into his eyes. We both smiled. His cologne was dry and musky, redolent of autumnal flowers. It gave me courage.

"Thank you for being so kind, sir. And so patient with me."

Holding my gaze while releasing my arm, he flushed slightly. "Mr. Whyte, I am neither kind nor patient."

"Mr. Gaylord, sir, methinks you lie."

Laughing, relaxed, we walked to the door side by side.

On the way to the library, we paused to examine some Japanese prints hung along the corridor. He explained the ways in which they had influenced the French artists. Having the two forms alive before my eyes, I was able to grasp the concepts immediately. I heard names spoken aloud that I had only read in magazines; I was amazed at how much I had retained. He seemed delighted with our conversation, but mostly I listened, intoxicated by his splendor. When animated, he was even more fascinating. He surrendered totally to his enthusiasm, revealing a vulnerable and tender spontaneity that surprised me. And I was charmed by his obviously sincere concern for my enjoyment.

The collection in the library was very impressive. (The *library* was very impressive! I'd never seen so many books and periodicals gathered in one place.) Every major artist involved in the movement was represented. He told me of the great exhibit in Paris where he purchased several of his paintings. He described it with such fervor and with such an eye for details (the stupid jeering crowds, the space filled with these paintings, etc.), that in the following years it appeared in my dreams. I felt comfortable with him, secure in his gentleness.

This is a *farouche* man? I mused.

Only during the silences that occasionally intruded, did I sense his reticence: the way his eyes dropped from mine, the quick smile that flickered across his face to allay panic. Those signs I easily recognized, and they helped me understand the bond between us. Beneath his dazzling exterior, I knew the uncertainty he, too, lived with. I saw it as my own.

I think we introverted people, those of us who find it difficult to make contact with the outside world, know one another instantly. (It is all in the eyes.) Yet each of us fears to acknowledge the other, lest by some bizarre chance we have misread him, and in acting too hastily, expect a particular sensibility where none exists.

He showed me the catalog from the 1895 exhibit and was delighted with my facility in French. We exchanged a few short pleasantries in the language, and though I read French, Italian, and German fluently, I had never spoken them with anyone but my father. When he asked after my talented father, I spoke of him without restraint or difficulty. I cannot say the same of my reactions to his discreet questions about my mother. He neither prodded nor interrupted with exclamations of condolence once I had begun. He listened. He was the only person who had asked me how I felt when I lost her. He listened to my sorrow, and when he did speak, it was to ask the precise question that helped me over whatever was blocking the telling of the simple story. At its completion, I burst into tears.

I was so startled by my behavior that I became flustered, but before I could do anything foolish (like experience shame), he rose from his chair and put a hand on my shoulder, consoling me with the warmth of his presence and the absence of any tension in his silence. Then he told me that he understood because he had experienced the same grief. His revelation confounded me. Still collecting tears, my eyes met his. After a pause, he told me that his mother had suffered the same fate as mine.

"But Father Collins said—"

"Father Collins says what everyone believes. It was what my father wanted. It was the easiest way. Very few know the truth. . . ."

He smiled. With that sweet smile he let me know that I had been told the truth because I had given of the truth. It was an exchange open and free of compromise.

"When Father Collins told me about you, Robert, I hesitated before suggesting Gaywyck. Then we decided it would be the best thing, given the circumstances. For now. You don't have many alternatives."

"There is no place for me to go."

"Then it's settled. For now. If later you change your mind and decide on a career, I'll assist you in any way I can. Perhaps, after seeing New York today, you'd prefer to stay in town?"

"Good God *no*, sir! Please, sir, let me go to Gaywyck!"

"Gaywyck is a vast and lonely place. I am rarely there in the winter, and there will be nothing to amuse you."

"*Nothing?* A great library! Miles to walk! The sea! And what about Denvers and Keyes? Besides, sir, I have no interest in society. Books are my life."

"So I understand."

I sensed a brooding hesitancy in his manner.

"Of course, if you don't *want* me to go . . ."

"I *don't* want you to go, but I've convinced myself that everything will be manageable. I'm probably behaving foolishly, but I do think *for now* it's the best place for you. Denvers seemed pleased you were joining them; that's a good sign. He will be your friend. Keyes, on the other hand, is not well. He's living in the past and is regularly quite mad; but he's harmless."

Then we talked of my duties, which consisted of devising a system for locating specific volumes in the vast

collection of books. There were more than 75,000 titles in
the two libraries at opposite ends of the first and third
floors. I was not to alphabetize, because the time and
energy required to shift the books were prohibitive and
were to be spent on more productive things.

"Like what, sir?"

"Like reading, and walking miles, and bathing in the
sea! And enjoying the music room. Do you play an
instrument?"

"No."

"Fine! A new pupil might be just what Keyes needs."

"But what about the books, sir?"

"Do the best you can with them. Concoct the simplest,
cleanest plan. I don't care what, as long as it works! I'm
bored with setting two servants to find a book whenever
we receive a request. It's a great collection, and several
universities use it. There is a catalog, neatly and correctly
done, but it's useless when searching for the book itself.
Every time a scholar writes, the staff goes into hiding!"

A knock at the door interrupted us. Taio entered and
informed Mr. Donough that he must leave for the opera
if he did not wish to be late. He reminded the master of
Father Collins, asleep in the front parlor.

"Good Lord! Father Collins! I forgot all about the
man! Asleep? So much for my uncomfortable furniture!
I'll be down immediately, Taio; thank you. Robert, would
you care to join me at the opera tonight? It's an interesting cast in *Le Nozze di Figaro*, for a change."

My heart started to pound with fear.

"No, sir," I mumbled. "No, thank you, sir, no . . ."

"Next time with more notice," he said gently. "I'm
certain you must be exhausted after your journey. Taio
will show you to your room. We will talk again in the
morning at breakfast."

I nodded to him and watched him stride from the room.
His candid, warm manner had been transformed before
my eyes at the arrival of Taio. Still gracious, yes, but
suddenly cool and slightly distant. I was disarmed by the
way he avoided embarrassing me for my startling panic
at his invitation; I was not intimidated by the alteration
of his tone, I was intrigued. He was regrouping his forces
to do battle with the world. I envied his self-control.

Taio showed me to my room: spacious and beautiful,

on the fourth floor, overlooking the park, with pale green walls that reminded me of spring and brought trees into the room. A full bathroom opened off to the left, and a silk-vested young man, a few years younger than myself, stood drawing my bath. An arrangement of flowers, smaller than the one in the foyer but similar in selection, sat on the writing table in the corner. In its presence, I felt Donough Gaylord.

The room delighted me. Even now, sitting at the writing table, its elegance envelops me. The delicate colors and sweet symmetry satisfy an internal sense of order. With all the refurbishings and modernizations, it has been changed very little. Why meddle with perfection?

The walnut furniture is still here. The gold-and-china Dresden clock ticks on the desk beside ever-present flowers. The translucent drapes are white with a pale green stripe. The carpet, a complex weave of white, green, and golden threads, covers most of the dark wood floor. The long wall opposite the two windows is still blessed by the same five enchanting Utamaro women arranged around the fireplace, but today they do not glance over shoulders and from under large umbrellas at my gladstone bag and wooden trunk placed beside the lustrous brass bed like two intruders from another world.

How easily the tenses shift the weight of years. How long ago it was; how present it is. The more I write, the more the one becomes the other.

After an hour in the bath, using an orange-scented soap that floated on the water like a marigold blossom, a lime-smelling creamy-white shampoo, and a golden oil the young man had carefully measured under the running spout, I dried myself (feeling smooth all over) with a massive soft, thick white towel, G-monogrammed in green. It had amused me to lie in a huge tub that balanced on four gilded paws, and to follow the complex traceries made by the silvery pipes that twisted gracefully around corners and up the steamed walls, providing at a touch not only cold water but an inexhaustible supply of hot as well. I would have stayed soaking and dreaming through the night if the young man had not knocked to announce my supper.

Some cut sandwiches, cakes, and a pot of tea had been carried up, with G-engraved silver cutlery and china as white as the snow moon. The tray waited on the low table set in front of the fireplace. The sandwiches were the most delicious I had ever eaten: cold meats mixed with mysterious cheeses. The teapot was a delicate white porcelain; its tea, lemony fragrant and light brown, was perfect for that time of day.

This is Elysium, I thought as happiness rose; but an equal and opposite sadness immediately seized me when the association of my mother in *her* kingdom of the shades overtook me. I reflected on her for the first time with a modicum of detachment. Having verbalized my weighty sorrow to Donough Gaylord, having sounded the depths and not been lost, I began to extricate myself from its numbing, paralyzing guilt. I touched my sorrow and wept again, aware that much of the pity was for myself.

Whoever unpacked my nightshirt and robe placed *David Copperfield* on the bedside table, but had the discretion to leave my journal in the lining pocket of my gladstone. I carried it to the desk, and finding some black ink in the drawer (there was also some blue and some mauve, but I only use black), I unscrewed my pen from its cork and began to detail the day. When the young man arrived to prepare the room for my sleep and to remove the tray, I rose and stood watching while he drew the drapes and turned down the bed.

Since his hands were full with the tray, I opened the door for him. He thanked me and said, "Good night, sir." Sir? I thought. Me, *sir*? I laughed to myself and allowed, for the moment, happiness. Returning to my journal, I wrote for hours (7:45 P.M. to 10:35 P.M.), until my hand began to resemble a secret code and my head started nodding into the flowers. Then, after lowering the lamps, I scaled the vast bed, disturbing it as little as possible. Though it was firm and deliciously pliant, and its sheets of the coolest, softest linen, I could not sleep. The white coverlet, of a light, satiny material, rustled whenever I moved. I fingered its luxurious texture and began counting the silk summer clovers attached to its surface. The night's sounds of horses' hooves clopping on the cobbled street, of strolling people in conversation, of strange dogs barking, of footsteps and creakings within the house, were all ordinary urban noises to those initiated, but for exhausted me not conducive to sleep.

"I can't sleep!" I sighed to one of Utamaro's dimly visible women. "Shall I take another bath?"

Deciding against it (too noisy), I went down to the library for something to read. I wanted something light, something entertaining, something that would help me relax yet not keep me awake all night. Having read most of the periodicals, I perused a bookshelf near the door, hoping to avoid the temptation of those paintings (I was *tired*; I wanted to go to bed). Finding an old friend, *Emma* ("Familiar faces and all that sublime prose"), I turned to go, then surrendered with a sigh to the pull of the canvases.

Around the room I walked from one to the other. Third time around, while moving closer to examine a Cassatt, I spotted a group of gothic novels exquisitely bound in red leather. Eschewing *Emma* for the unknown chills of *Carmilla* and her famed coffin of blood, I removed it from its place, catching sight of a mysterious reflecting surface behind. Taking down the other volumes, I uncovered a small glass display case. It contained thirteen mounted headless bees. A legend attached to it read:

> *La Vendetta*
> *13 Queens Revenge*
> *1 Undeserved Sting*
> *King Cormack/18 May 1883*

I shuddered. At thirteen years of age, Cormack was a little old for such childish cruelty, or so it seemed to me. I returned everything to its proper place, including *Carmilla*, and then restored *Emma* to its niche as well. Cormack's perversity upset me. I needed something exotic to distract me. Seizing a French novel with an odd title that I vaguely remembered reading about, as well as a French dictionary, I returned to my room. It was 11:30. After making myself comfortable in the bed, I opened the book. Nearly two hours later, while laying it aside to check a word, I was startled by the sight of Donough Gaylord standing in my doorway.

"I'm sorry if I frightened you, Robert. I saw the light under the door and thought you'd fallen asleep without extinguishing it. Forgive me for disturbing you, but when you didn't respond to my knock . . ."

"You aren't disturbing me, sir. Please come in."

He walked into the room, pausing halfway to the bed. He carried a program.

"You're up rather late, Robert. I assumed you'd be exhausted and fast asleep long ago."

"I am exhausted . . . but I probably won't be able to sleep until I finish this amazing book!"

"What are you reading?"

"*Là Bas* by Huysmans."

"You probably won't be able to sleep *after* you finish it, either."

We laughed. There was a pause. He moved closer.

"I hope you don't mind, sir. I chose it because of its title. I couldn't sleep. I found it in the library."

"*Mind?* Why on earth should I mind? You may read whatever you wish. Huysmans, however, is not the path to pleasant dreams."

"I rarely have pleasant dreams, sir." After an unfilled pause, I added, "Do you, sir?"

"Do I what, Robert?"

"Have pleasant dreams, sir?"

"No. Rarely."

He began pacing, turning his slightly flushed face from me in embarrassment. When he ceased to pace, he rested his arms on the brass railings at the foot of the bed. A smile expanded into a grin on both our faces. I think of this quiet moment as the genesis of our friendship. Cautiously we drew toward each other. For an instant we dropped our guards. In our innocence we perceived nothing beyond an incidental amity. And the shock of communion.

A lull, imposed by mutual reserve, opened between us a deep ravine. We peered at each other across it, then glanced away, both still smiling dumbly. I heard myself speaking and felt as if I'd leaped into the air in an attempt to cross the divide. I could not believe the words I uttered: "Is what troubles you . . . your dreams, sir, your brother, Cormack?"

Donough Gaylord turned as white as an autumn mum. "My brother is long dead," he said coldly. "He died in a fire trying to save our father."

"I know," I said, flustered by his suddenly frigid manner. The decapitated bees buzzed in my brain. I wanted to explain, to apologize if I could, but he did not give me the opportunity.

"Good night," he stated abruptly. "I suggest you put out the light and get some sleep, lest tomorrow you be too tired to enjoy the rest of your journey."

Then he was gone.

Instantly I cursed myself. Jumping out of the bed and rushing about the room like a person demented, I burst into tears.

What in God's name made me say a thing like *that*?

I prowled, repeating the conversation over and over, unfastening the link that had pulled Cormack Gaylord into my stupid, vacant mind, only to hook it all together again in stunned disbelief. As I retrod the way of our discourse, I became more crazed. I felt anew those fleeting seconds of harmony which I'd shattered—perhaps irrevocably—by my insensitivity. With great effort I calmed myself. My first impressions of Donough Gaylord returned. My belief in his kindness, gentleness, and compassion sustained me.

Though I knew I could not sleep, I turned out the lamp and got into the bed. A dull, persistent ache tormented me. I wanted to believe he would forgive me. I *needed* to believe he would forgive me. Closing my eyes tightly, I fought against tears. I whispered soothingly that there was nothing to be gained by torturing myself. It was done, finished. Why was I in such a condition over innocently offending him?

In a few hours, it would be morning. I would be going down to breakfast. If he . . . *when* he appeared at table, his eyes would reveal all.

I relaxed. Dozing intermittently, I waited for the urban birds to herald the dawn.

Five

TAIO KNOCKED AT 7:30 TO ANNOUNCE breakfast in thirty minutes. I was washed and dressed and sitting at the writing table contemplating flowers, awaiting the summons. For twenty minutes I gave my attention to Utamaro's consummate art. When the clock read 7:50, I walked slowly down to the foyer, where Taio, hearing me descend, appeared to guide me to the breakfast room behind the front parlor.

The sunlit room was empty. My heart failed. Taio left me in the care of a young uniformed woman who offered her services. I thanked her and accepted a cup of tea before she left me alone.

He was not there. I was not forgiven. I could barely raise the cup to my lips, so great was my sorrow. And I could not accuse him. It had been *my* atrocity that had killed our nascent affinity.

Observations previously made of my own character were proven true again: I was incapable of friendship. Always rushing about like a terrified rabbit, trampling people's feelings like so many blades of grass, hearing nothing but my own thundering heartbeat, I violated privacy and breached every boundary of decorum. For an unlovable, unacceptable creature such as I, retiring to Gaywyck was the most responsible behavior.

Taio entered. Nodding in my direction, he poured a cup of tea at the place set opposite. Then Donough Gaylord, dressed in a gray morning suit a shade lighter than his eyes, hurried into the room.

"Good morning, Robert. You aren't hungry?"

"No, sir."

I was so relieved and so happy to see him that I reddened to magenta and laughed as though I'd misplaced my sanity. He stared at me. Revealing the whitest teeth, he smiled and recommended oatmeal.

"Taio, give Mr. Whyte some oatmeal and a croissant. *Two* croissants with plenty of jam and butter!"

He asked if I slept well. I lied and said I had. He said he had as well. He apologized for having been late to table, explaining he had personally supervised the packing of my Cézanne. I expressed gratitude. He expressed his pleasure. Taio was ordered to bring me ham and eggs and two more croissants. I was suddenly ravenously hungry. I ate everything Taio set before me.

We talked of the opera and the difficulty of assembling a first-rate ensemble for Mozart, of the Huysmans, which he wanted me to finish (Taio had packed it in my gladstone), of my journey, and of the possibility of his visiting soon. When breakfast was done, he walked me into the parlor to show me the Van Gogh he had hung over the fireplace. While we stood in front of the magnificent sunflowers, he told me I was to make myself at home in Gaywyck.

"You have my permission to make any changes you wish in your rooms. Denvers has already been informed. If you need anything, write to me. Now, about your salary . . ."

"My salary?"

"Of course. Did you think you'd be working for nothing?"

"I don't want any money. Room and board are enough."

"Nonsense."

"I'm serious."

"If you wish to work for me, you will accept a salary, Robert."

He was no longer smiling. His voice had acquired an edge that I took to be annoyance. I nodded, fear rising.

"Is one thousand a year, paid quarterly, satisfactory?"

"It's far too much!"

He lifted his right eyebrow. "It will be deposited in an account at my bank in your name. You'll be able to withdraw by post whatever amount you wish. The first payment will be settled today."

"A salary in advance?"

"It will balance at the end of a year."

"What if I don't stay a whole year?"

"Then you'll be in debt."

"You don't even know me."

"I'm a good judge of character."

He wished me a good journey before handing me over to Taio, who led me out of the house to the carriage waiting at the curb.

The day was clear and beautiful, cooled by the past evening's rain. As I stepped up into the carriage, I glanced back at the house. Donough Gaylord stood in the parlor window with the white curtains pushed aside. I waved. After a pause, he waved in return. Taio closed the carriage door. The vehicle, shades drawn, carried me from my new friend.

I was assailed by feelings and thoughts, by the experience of Donough Gaylord; nothing from the outside world penetrated. I saw his face and gray-suited form as clearly as if he were riding with me. I felt a collapse of internal barriers as I studied those perfect features, scrutinizing each in an attempt to comprehend the workings of the whole. His elegant attire at breakfast, displaying his superb figure, had appeared but a marker on my mind's periphery until I sat musing in the cab. So it was with many other things.

> Thy tongue, thy face, thy limbs, actions,
>   and spirit,
> Do give thee fivefold blazon. Not too fast.
>   Soft, soft!

Attitudes, gestures, inflections absorbed unconsciously were conscientiously examined. We spent not quite two hours in each other's company, but that made sufficient impression to endure a lifetime.

Why had he impressed me so? I wanted to *be* Donough Gaylord, and the reasons seemed clear to me: beauty, perfection of form, always fascinates. It is truth incarnate.

"For beauty, my Phaedrus, beauty alone is lovely and visible at once. For, mark you, it is the sole aspect of the spiritual which we can perceive through our senses, or bear so to perceive."

When the carriage arrived at its destination, Taio, much to my amazement, opened the door. I had not gotten much beyond the obsessive concept of beauty; I was startled from the closed circle of my thoughts by the sight of water and a ferry at the end of a dock.

I scurried after Taio and another man who was carrying my baggage as if it were weightless, balancing the trunk on his shoulder. No sooner had we boarded than the boat started to move. Again I remembered Manhattan is an island; to depart in any direction, one must cross water.

When the ferry docked, Taio hurried me into another carriage pulled by a large dray. Taio was so agitated, I hesitated to ask for an explanation. The great horse dragged us at a stupefying speed through the streets, and I gathered we were late for a very important appointment.

The train of four cars stood at the extreme end of a long platform; three cars were blue, one was gray with matching gray shades. A uniformed guard stood on the landing of the gray car. He nodded at Taio and stepped aside to allow us entry. I assumed this was the Gaylord private carriage Father Collins had mentioned. If I had not been prepared for something extraordinary, I know I would have disgraced myself, for it was not a railroad car I entered but a thickly carpeted, superbly furnished room with paintings, glass-fronted library shelves, armchairs, a divan, and chessmen set up for play.

Rather than block the doorway as I gaped at the interior, I unhesitatingly strode to the nearest chair and sat. It faced a desk and another chair on the opposite side. It looked as if a second interview was pending, the first having gone too well. Around me, various shades of blues and grays were carefully coordinated. The walls and ceiling were covered with a white wood I had never seen before. Nothing hung from any part of the carriage; there would be no rattling or swinging while we were in motion. But the wonder to me was the way the colors and the artfully arranged furniture conspired to force the visitor's perspective from oblong to square! Palladio would have been pleased.

Taio was describing to the guard, Mr. Tibbs, an elaborate accident on the ferry in which the wheel of our carriage had lost several spokes. (I gathered the train had been delayed because of it.) While he talked, he moved about lifting shades and fluffing pillows. Kneeling beside my gladstone, he undid it; removing *Là Bas*, he placed it on the desk in front of me. The train began to roll.

"I'll serve luncheon at one, sir. If you should require anything before then, press the button near the door."

I thanked him and asked what time we would be arriving at our destination.

The guard answered, "Usually at three-thirty. Today, Sterling Harbor at four. Unless some other unforseen delay occurs. . . ."

Taio sighed. I thanked them both; both departed. I went to the gladstone immediately to retrieve my journal. The journey had primed me. Was isolation so easily ended? What excuse had I but innocence in matters of the heart? Donough Gaylord had not found me strange, an aberration; he had empathized, and seemed to know my unhappiness.

> It is too rash, too unadvised, too sudden,
> Too like the lightening, which doth cease to be
> Ere one can say, "It lightens."

In my journal I wrote: "We are the same person, Donough Gaylord and I."

I wrote of my joy in having a new friend. I wrote of platonic love. I wrote about my mother. I could not doubt she loved me in her way, nor I her in mine. She was *the* exception. My affection for her proved that before its Dark Ages, my heart had known a kind of loving. Yet, as I studied its history, I abandoned all hope of a Renaissance. I saw fear and self-loathing conspiring to keep it a cold, bare, ruined vault. I saw myself devoid of grace. The truth was inexorable: spiritual beauty was only his.

The idea that Donough Gaylord could be my friend was absurd. Donough Gaylord, the man I wanted to be, the man I had briefly allowed myself to become. I blushed for my arrogance. I shook off my romantic illusions and reclaimed my reason.

Mortified, I closed the book and stared unseeing out the window.

Taio interrupted my brooding with preparations for my luncheon. The preliminaries were much more diverting than the flat scrub-pine woodland through which we were passing (though the foliage had begun to color, the maples most ostentatiously). A large table was unfolded from the wood paneling and a ceiling lamp descended on a rod to brighten the newly created dining area. A white damask cloth, china, crystal, and silver were brought in by a steward.

I was seated and served.

I asked Taio if he had cooked the meal.

"Oh, no, sir. *I* am not a cook. I am a gentleman's valet, Mr. Gaylord's personal servant. Mr. Willows travels with the kitchen."

I resolved to chart the household hegemony. I sent my compliments to Mr. Willows and resumed writing in my journal. At 3:15 Taio reappeared with the steward to prepare the room for tea. I was pleased to see them and the spice cake, still hot from the oven. Its smell filled the place with a sense of civilized well-being. I rose and followed it to the table.

After my first taste, I sent a message via Taio to Mr. Willows informing him that his cake was a highlight of my journey.

The train arrived at Sterling Harbor without any complications. I spent the final minutes with Huysmans. The excitement of seeing Gaywyck, meeting Denvers and Keyes, making a new home, convinced me I would not be able to concentrate on the book; I had opened it anyway —as a prop if for no other reason—and was soon so engrossed, I did not feel the train's lessening speed. Taio and the steward helped me step down into the cool, clear air.

"This is the end of the line, sir."

"Or the beginning," I countered giddily.

Taio nodded several times. "Or the beginning? Yes, sir. Thank you, sir. I had not thought of that. . . ."

A young man with blazing red hair rushed toward us. He was dressed in overalls and a thin green sweater. He had a slight limp; the trouble was with his left leg.

"Here's Brian," Taio whispered, waving. "He'll take you up to the house. A word about Brian, sir, in case Mr. Donough forgot to mention it. I wouldn't waste words asking him what cannot be answered with a nod or shake of his pretty head. He is a mute."

I thanked Taio for everything. Before I could elaborate, Brian was upon us, smiling. We were introduced and shook hands. (He *is* pretty; "pretty" is the perfect word, with his small, frail features, his golden freckles, and his cornflower-blue eyes. I thought of Tom Sawyer full-grown.) I bid Taio good-bye again and began walking down the platform with Brian, who made happy guttural clucking noises while bobbing and waving to different railroad personnel of his acquaintance, all of whom seemed delighted to see him again.

Someone called my name. Turning, I spied Mr. Willows rushing toward us, carrying a blue tin.

"Your spice cake, sir," he panted.

I caught up with Brian, who had not waited during my brief exchange with Mr. Willows. He was grunting angrily. I asked him if anything was wrong. He spat, shrugged, and quickened his pace to move ahead of me.

Good Lord! I thought. What *have* I done?

The Sterling Harbor station was then a one-room wooden structure, white with green trim; marigolds grew in its windowboxes. Built at the end of a narrow stone platform, it resembled a Victorian child's dollhouse. Where the platform ended, the tracks ended as well, at a wall of trees. I glimpsed a road parallel to the tracks. In the center of the road, an open carriage waited with a gargantuan black-and-white Belgian in harness.

A thin man in the uniform of the railroad was tying my baggage to a rack in the rear (the painting had been placed on the seat). Brian gave him a coin and motioned for me to take my place beside the Cézanne. The man winked at me while Brian climbed to the driver's place.

"Ever seen such a gorgeous thing?" he asked, twitching his head toward the horse.

"Only in magazines."

"Makes the carriage look like a toy."

"I didn't know they were used to pull such small loads."

"They're not, usually, but our Brian gets a kick riding with Frenchie."

Brian snorted, cutting our laughter short. The man tipped his hat and left hurriedly as the train whistle blew. The horse snorted. I moved to claim my seat, but stopped when I noticed Brian descending from his. Frowning, he came toward me with his arms extended. I looked from his hands to his scowling face for a few moments before I realized he was staring at the cake tin. I handed it over and sat down. He stood there sniffing at the open box. I knew he knew its contents, so I said nothing. Did he want a piece? Without an explanation, he turned and gracefully sprang back up to his place.

From his higher perch, he glanced back at me and laughed happily. He kept my cake.

I guess we're friends again, I thought, perplexed.

The carriage was lifted from the ground by Frenchie's initial enthusiastic strides, but settled into an even roll as we moved down the road.

Curiouser and curiouser. . . .

We drove at quite a clip into the falling sun along the deserted tree-lined road. For a short while the familiar country sounds were blissful after the noise of Manhattan and the rumbling train, but then the howling locomotive sped by, to our left, shaking the trees to their roots. How fragile is peace! We rode for a long time toward that very slowly sinking orange ball before I noticed in the foliage to the right a stone wall covered with honeysuckle and ivy. I had no idea where it had begun. Could it have been there all along?

Another mile brought us to a sudden halt. I heard a lock turn. Leaning from the carriage, I watched an elderly man pull back a tall black gate with an ornately scrolled G circled in the central latticework. On the top, winged dragons perched.

Not as exciting as a barbican, I thought, but not bad.

We took a sharp right into the grounds, passed the gatehouse and the gardener's cottage, then rolled onto a narrow graveled way. Branches formed a leafy umbrella overhead. A light breeze rustled the greenery. Suddenly I sensed the sea. It flavored the air cooler and brisker, and played a counterpoint to the softer rippling of the leaves. The sun darted hide-and-seek among the trees to my left and splashed me with golden light. White birches appeared, first singly, then clustered, mingling with pine trees and fir, with maple, oak, and elm.

"It perches on a ledge overlooking the sea," Father Collins had said. As we rode, drawing nearer, the waves began to echo thunder. I was breathlessly eager to reach my new home. Set away from the road, behind a great stone wall opening to a seemingly endless wood, it made me think of Prince Florimund, trapped, thicketed, searching for the legendary Sleeping Beauty. But where stalks Carabosse?

Who can forget his first sight of Gaywyck? For a fleeting orchestrated instant, glimpsed from a landscaped rise, its countless symmetrical windows and enormous white columns flash. Immediately it disappears behind a screen of junipers. We quicken our pace in search of apparitions. The sea sounds louder and the park grows

more dense. We ride the curving, rising, dipping road
through the eventide's descending light. As we burst into a
clearing to the roar of the surf, the sun spills inversely,
willingly, into the dark. In the gray-mauve dusk is
Gaywyck.

I stepped down and stood between two circular groupings of red salvias that resembled pools of blood. Before
me was the most massive antebellum mansion imaginable.
Veiled in sea mists, it has neither beginning nor end.
Perfectly proportioned, its lucent white elegance and grace
beckoned me to climb its wide stone steps. Flowers pro-
liferate and rows of rhododendron lead the eye to the distant right wing imprisoned by tendrils of ivy. Gaywyck
is without time or place. But the sea is near! I surrendered
to its sound and to its smell. The lofty columns embraced
me. Soft gold light streaming from the stained-glass fan-
light enveloped me. I felt calm and secure. The porch held
solid beneath my feet.

Ambrose, lamp in hand, opened the door. Tall, very
straight, and slight, he seems the Ancient of Days with
tufts of white hair growing in every direction from the
top of his well-shaped head. He reminded me of a ragged
lily! Quick dark eyes offered a discreet greeting as he
formally nodded me entry. Enter I did; but after barely
three steps I stopped to wonder at the sight across the
dusk-filled foyer.

At the head of a grand staircase is an oval window
through which I saw the rising, brightening moon. My
mortality floated in the oval onyx, reflected like the evening star on the silvered surface of the sea. The stairway,
dividing under the window, climbs up, around both sides
of the vast foyer, like two outstretched arms joining hands
over my head to form a choir. The heady scent of flowers
and a piano's sepulchral pianissimo added the final
touches.

Enraptured, I missed the three descending steps. Ambrose caught me and prevented my fracturing a hip or a
head. For such an old man, his strength and reflexes surprised me. His officious manners disappeared in a blush of
pride when I told him so; he confided in accented English
that he was ninety-one and spry as a guppy. Still gripping
my elbow, he led me to the right. Our footsteps echoed off
pale marble, drowning the piano's melody.

A figure taller than I stood at the center of the room. As we passed, the lamp revealed a dancing bronze faun. I moved closer. The creature played a flute while gripping in its left hand a fistful of priapic abundance. I blushed, shocked by the detail, but thrilled by the miraculous vitality. Ambrose whispered, "Shockin', ain't it? First thing the guests always sees! I'll *never* get used to it, I won't! Benvenuto Cellini was no gent, I can tell you!"

I agreed, half-hearing, until the name registered.

"Cellini? *The* Cellini?"

"Are there two?"

"I don't think so."

"Then 'e's the one! Them Eye-talians is all the same. If this one gets to you, wait till you see 'is mate in the sunroom."

"There's another one?"

"You'da thought one woulda done it for 'im. Obscene, I calls 'em. Always 'ave. Lotta good it does . . ."

I walked around the statue. I half-expected it to leap at me. Even in the dim light, the nipples on the breast and the fine hairs that covered the body, could be clearly discerned. In the background, the piano had grown louder, fiercer, as if accompanying the faun's sybaritic display and presciently encouraging me to take part. I spotted something in my peripheral vision move down the right staircase. A white, long-haired feline walked to the center of the landing to bathe in the moonlight.

"What a gorgeous cat!"

"Cael. Named after an angel, 'e is. Came all the way from Persia."

"Cael," I whispered. "And rightly so; an angel, indeed!"

I stared at him. His fur glistened. Our eyes met and held until he glanced away as if to listen to the music undisturbed. Leaning forward, he folded his front paws under his breast; his long, silken hair formed a radiant cape. Motionless, he seemed lost in meditation.

"Come along, now, Mr. Whyte. Denvers awaits you."

I followed Ambrose to enormous blond-wood double doors with brass fixtures. Silently they slid apart. We crossed the large room to another set of doors and stepped into a deep hallway. The small stairway at the end was illuminated by a gas lamp. Firelight flickered over the shiny parquet floor, slanting in from a room on the left near the end of the corridor. As Ambrose closed the doors, he emitted an uncouth expletive; Cael shot through a second before they slammed together.

"That bloody puss! Someday 'e's gonna part with that fluffy tail of 'is!"

"How old is he?"

"Donough got 'im when 'e returned from Paris, Europe. Like everything else around 'ere—exceptin' me, 'a course —'e's worth the bloody earth!"

We laughed. Walking toward the flickering light, I watched the cat bound to the end of the hall and fly up the stairs; stopping suddenly, tail flicking, he turned and crouched, staring at me. I wanted to play with him, but turned instead into the study. There, in front of the fireplace, Denvers stood facing me, his arms behind his back.

"Good evening, Mr. Whyte. Thank you, Ambrose."

His voice, though light in timbre, was firm and commanding. He nodded to a chair near the fire. I sat, oblivious of everything but his formidable presence focused in his searching, intense eyes. But for a white shirt, he was garbed entirely in black. He looked severe. His iron-gray hair, combed back from his high forehead, abetted the impression. His mouth, set in a tight smile, could have been taken for a grimace, had I not been predisposed to like him. Visions of Miss Murdstone skidded across my mind.

"I trust you had a pleasant journey."

I nodded, thanking him. His mouth stretched a bit wider, but his eyes remained cold, uncommitted. I was thoroughly intimidated, and could not utter a syllable. Then the Gaylord treasures came to my rescue once more. Glancing above his head, I discovered an enormous oval mirror in a gold rococo frame with *putti* holding flowers (and each other) or busily arranging draperies. Behind his shoulder several hosts of angels hovered. I moved my eyes from the cherubs to his face and declared impulsively, "Mr. Gaylord said you would be my friend."

Astounded, he jumped as if the flames at his rear had singed his trousers.

"*What* did he say?"

"He said you would be my friend, as you've always been his."

Nodding his head slowly, he studied my face. He had paled and was obviously disconcerted. There was nothing more for me to say. I waited anxiously. Slowly he brought his arms from behind his back. He extended the right one to me. Shocked, I saw he was missing fingers. I gaped. Coughing to cover my rudeness, I rose to accept his gesture.

"If Donough told you that, it must be. Welcome to Gaywyck, Robert Whyte. It should not be difficult being your friend. You seem as direct as you are beautiful. It will do us good to have youthful virtue under our roof once more."

Then he pulled me toward him and kissed me on my right cheek. I began to draw away, but catching myself, held still and received the kiss. I was flustered by this bold expression of affection. In my family, no one touched; we rarely kissed. And he called me beautiful. I was more than flattered; I was proud to have my mother's and my own perceptions seconded. I worried everyone thought himself beautiful.

When he released me from the embrace, we took facing seats. The fire blazed between us. His face was flushed, his eyes soft, his voice a gentle baritone. Excitement rushed his words.

"I will do my best, Robert, to disappoint neither you nor Donough. But you, for your part, must be patient. There was no friendship here. We spend our days in hiding. All must change now. *You* must change everything."

"I?"

"Yes! You, *puer*! There is much sickness here, much pain in this dark backward, this abysm in time. Things will quicken now. Donough was right to send you here."

He asked what else my benefactor promised of Gaywyck. I spoke of Keyes.

"At *times* quite mad?" he exclaimed, interrupting. "Better to say at times nearly sane!"

"He plays the piano beautifully," I said, flustered by his outburst. "At least, I assume it was his playing I heard as I came in."

"Yes. He plays ravishingly well. At least Beethoven does. One must give him that."

"I don't understand."

"Didn't Donough mention Beethoven?"

I shook my head and tried not to appear worried.

"Well, my dear boy, for the past three years . . . *no*, it

must be closer to four, because it was a year after Donough returned and near the time Cael joined us that Keyes announced the 'Moonlight Sonata' understood him so well, he must have composed it. Before that, he was content with triolets and madrigals, but after young Cormack's death it was touch and go with the old fool and suddenly he was gone before we could catch him. It all defies augury. Sometimes he is Beethoven and sometimes not. One must be quite careful. I've no idea what influences his decision, but if one has, say, Mahler songs before or after tea, one may assume with some certainty that Keyes will descend for dinner. If one has silence, Ludwig will be dining alone, having just completed the C-Sharp Minor Sonata, Opus 27, Number 2 for performance at dusk, as we heard tonight, or perhaps the Sonata Number 9 for violin and piano in A, Opus 47, another favorite. He sings a rapturous violin."

I filled the pause with "Good Lord!"

"You must not be alarmed! At worst, it's an inconvenience, though I confess the sudden deafness infuriates me. It would be simpler were he Mozart. Easier for us and painless for him once we convinced him he was alive and awake each morning."

We laughed conspiratorially.

"It could be worse," I added bravely, to his delight. "He could be Schubert. . . ."

At that moment Cael arrived. His round owl eyes gleamed in the firelight, and his silky coat was streaked with auburn near the long, feathery tail. Under his pale pink nose was a bow-shaped pink mouth. Long whiskers made his heart-shaped head look kittenish. He balanced on the arm, wrapping his tail around his legs. As I moved my hand to the top of his head, he stretched to meet it, grunting, then gingerly stepping to the center of my lap, he curled his body and commenced purring.

"Well, Robert! It seems you've captured two hearts tonight. In all my years with that animal, I've never seen him go to anyone but Donough. Not even Goodbody can charm him!"

"I don't usually like cats."

"There aren't many like Cael. He hates Keyes, but he loves Beethoven. I'm certain he understands.

"For the first year Donough kept him in town, but he

was forever hunting in Gramercy Park. The outraged caretaker complained; Donough exiled him here."

"*He* killed?" I asked, pointing to the fluffy ball lounging in my willing lap.

"A dissimulation of birds! He has an ongoing feud with a raccoon in the tomato patch. Before the week is out, he'll raid several rabbit warrens to bring tokens to you. That enchanter is a predator of the first rank. There are two sides to everybody. Men are rarely what they seem."

We spoke of life at Gaywyck. Breakfast was laid at eight on the patio; luncheon at noon in the small dining room, where supper was served informally at 6:30, unless Donough Gaylord was in residence, then supper was a formal occasion and served in the main dining room at 7:45. Tea happened at four in the Rossetti parlor or on the rear patio. Weather dictated.

"Mr. O'Shay requires promptness at table, and Brian is positively maniacal if his croissants are not eaten hot and his spice cake devoured the second it appears at tea. He attends no man, and once threw a perfect *genoise* into the pleached hawthorns because the *crème au beurre* had gone pudgy in the sun. We were most fortunate it was not heaved at us!"

"He bakes spice cake?"

"Excepting Monsieur Henri's, the best in the world. Are you partial to spice cake?"

I related my experience. Denvers was giddily amused.

"He *hates* Willows. When Donough took Brian into town to apprentice with Henri, the boy set his heart on that train. He adores trains almost as much as he adores Donough; that mobile kitchen was the answer to his prayers."

"What happened?"

"Donough said no. He wanted him here, safe from mishap. That was over two years ago, but the boy still broods as though it were this afternoon. I'm certain he fed Willows's cake to Frenchie!"

"Was he born mute?"

"No."

There was a long pause. Just when I assumed I must seek an elaboration elsewhere, he continued.

"He suffered an accident many years ago which left him a gimp and mute. It eclipsed his mind as well. As well it might! There are frequently unpleasant scenes, which, to my great sorrow, you will witness soon enough. We—"

Ambrose announced dinner. Denvers became distressed: I had no time to wash and change and inspect my apartment before sitting down to my first meal at Gaywyck. I assured him I was not disturbed. He rose and walked to the door.

"There will be plenty of time for talking, Robert. Winters are dismal in this kingdom by the sea. '*We two alone will sing like birds i' a cage.*' "

" '*When thou dost ask me blessing, I'll kneel down and ask of thee forgiveness. . . .*' "

Denvers smiled. The tutor surfaced with pleasure at my matching quotation from *Lear*. I pushed forward in the chair, shifting my legs to arouse Cael, who grunted and stood hunching his back in a stretch. He extended his paw to descend, but a second before jumping, froze, staring up at the mirror.

I cried out in disbelief. There, in the mirror, was my mother's face! Not the face I had recently been parted from, but the ravaged, aged face that would arrive with time and suffering. It floated like an image reflected in a deep pool. I fell back in the chair with a gasp. My heart pounded. A cold sweat broke out on my brow. I called her name and collapsed in a faint.

I have no idea how long I remained unconscious. When I revived, Denvers stood over me, repeating my name. Ambrose held a glass to my lips. A strange voice spoke.

"Poor boy! The journey was too much for him. . . ."

Denvers smiled at me, gently caressing my face. He answered the unfamiliar voice:

"Yes, Mr. O'Shay, you are right as always. Come, Robert, we'll help you to bed."

I said nothing. Helped by Denvers and Ambrose, I shakily stood. I glanced at the mirror. My white face and trembling body, held by the two men, appeared in its center. The rest was a dark void. None of the area beyond the circle of firelight was reflected. On the hearth, Cael sat washing his face. He paused to stare at me for a moment before continuing his ablutions.

I left the circle of light. Led by strong arms, I ventured into the void.

Six

WHEN I AWOKE, A SUNBEAM PROBED between the drapes beyond the foot of the bed. I could hear waves breaking on the shore and smell the keen, piquant air. Cael slept against my right hip. Brian sat reading beside the bed, his right hand covering mine. I felt rested and calm. I remembered much tossing and turning and a profound agitation in trying to escape from a clutch of nightmares. My mother's face, like a water lily, floated on the surface of memory, superimposed over every other image.

I had awakened several times not knowing where I was. Gentle hands had comforted me, bathing my forehead, feeding me, returning the blankets when I threw them off; of these ministrations I was dimly aware. When the tumultuous chaos lifted, peaceful sleep descended for the first time in seven days.

"What are you reading, Brian?"

Looking up at me, he laughed and showed me the spine of the book.

"*Wuthering Heights*. I love that book. Poor Catherine and Heathcliff!"

He shook his head vehemently, anger in his eyes.

"No? Why not?"

He opened the book to the frontispiece, depicting them embracing on the heath. Grimacing, he pointed to Heathcliff. Placing the book on the bed facedown, he raised his hands to form horns on his forehead.

"But don't you think he suffers enough for that?"

He shook his head furiously. He would have none of it. I began to argue for Love. He put his fingers in his ears. When I closed my mouth, he placed his hand over it. I lay still. He smiled. I frowned. He nodded happily.

"Your fever is gone."

Denvers stood in the doorway. Brian made laughing, guttural sounds and trotted from the room. Cael woke, stretched, made his own guttural sounds resembling a rumbling birdcall, and jumped from the bed to follow my nurse.

"Never moralize with Brian on Romantic Obsession, my dear boy. You and I may agree with Dr. Johnson that 'He who makes a beast of himself gets rid of the pain of being a man,' but Brian, for all his pain, would consider that a poor bargain. He's taken better care of you than of his precious bumblebees."

I asked how long I'd been ill and was amazed at the reply: three days! He explained that I fell into a fever the first night and the doctor had confirmed the fact that I was overstrained and suffering from nervous exhaustion. He had left detailed instructions and medicaments to be administered. While helping me to my bed, Brian had heard me call for Donough Gaylord and had refused to leave my side. He commandeered the sickroom, following the doctor's orders precisely, ignoring all else, and demanding the household behave accordingly.

"He's lived here with you. It seems you've made *three* friends! He's the most valuable of us all, trust me! Our kitchen is a commissary; we've eaten nothing that isn't journeying toward or *fait accompli* soup! You've no idea how pleased we are to see you well!"

While he spoke, he marched around the room, opening the drapes and the French windows, fluffing my pillows, and wagging his index finger at me like an angry tutor.

"Don't scold him, Denvers, not even in jest!"

Donough Gaylord leaned on the doorframe, a crooked smile on his empyreal face. He wore dark blue trousers and a maroon striped shirt, its collar unattached, open at the neck. Windblown hair fell over his brow.

"If this is the result of his first meeting with you, I see you've lost none of your powers!"

"Once a Jesuit, my boy, always a Jesuit."

"Though maybe I flatter you. I wonder if this wasn't a ruse to gain your sympathy and win Cael's and Brian's affections."

"Whatever . . . he's succeeded brilliantly. Not completely, however. He hasn't taken Keyes away from Beethoven."

"But they haven't yet met."

There was a warmth and shared camaraderie in our laughter. I felt my heart expand. Brian returned with a bowl of steaming chicken soup, which he carefully placed on the bed table. Cael sprang onto the bed, his yellow eyes as round as asters. He paused, studying my face to ascertain a welcome, then carefully made his way to my hand, which he cleaned before settling beside me. His nose was wet and shockingly cold. Brian walked around the bed to the other hand to take my pulse. He entered some figures in a small green notebook after consulting the clock on the mantel.

"Thank you, Brian," I said, grasping his hand. "I hear you've saved me."

He shook his head. Donough Gaylord crossed from the doorway to his side. Putting an arm around the boy's shoulder, he squeezed him affectionately.

"Brian is the best, Robert; the finest. Do everything he tells you and you'll never have to worry."

Brian sounded a long, extended "Ah!" and rested his head on Donough Gaylord's shoulder.

"How many more days in bed for me, Brian?"

The boy held up three fingers. I moaned and asked if I could bathe before then. A brief conference ensued. Yes, if I did not dally in the water *and* if I finished my soup. Brian left to run a bath; I drank the broth; Denvers and Donough Gaylord, in conversation, walked out to the railing of the porch.

I looked around me. The bed had an ash head and base, the same color as the walls and ceiling. The comforter and drapes were chocolate brown. An ornate radiator with a G crest rested like a piece of sculpture opposite the fireplace. Atop a Queen Anne bureau sat my *lares* and *penates*: *David Copperfield*, a stone paperweight, a small wooden box with cuttings of my parents' hair, and an old brass ruler that had become a good-luck charm. My journals were neatly piled on a small table in the corner. To the right of the bed, a most exquisite Madonna hung on the wall.

"Good Lord! A Crevelli!"

"We know," called Donough Gaylord. "Don't you like her?"

"Yes. Of course I like her. She startled me, is all."

"Then we'll leave it," he said to Denvers as they walked through the billowing drapes.

"I can certainly think of more startling things to find in one's bedroom."

"What's in your bedroom, Denvers?" I asked.

"Only a Rubens, alas."

Donough Gaylord laughed. "My parents were very fortunate when it came to buying pictures."

"They were very *rich*, which is far more important, Donough; and they took no chances. They lacked a sense of adventure, which you've more than compensated for, my boy. The *thing* in the other room is actually quite nice, by the way; much more to my taste than the others done by those hyperactive bohemians."

"I've hung the Cézanne in your sitting room, Robert. He hates to admit it, but he likes it."

"I *don't* hate to admit it. I admit it! I like it! But one is divinely vulgar, two would be impertinent."

"There's a Vermeer in my bedroom, Robert, and the Della Francesca in the small study is very special. Did you notice it on the wall opposite the mirror?"

"Yes, he did. He saw it reflected in the mirror. It gave him quite a fright."

I stared at Denvers, then glanced away. It wasn't the Della Francesca image that had frightened me. Donough Gaylord's voice broke in on my thoughts.

"If the Crevelli excites you, we must administer a sedative before allowing you downstairs."

Trying to be cheerful, I told them I was eager to see Cellini's obscene satyr in the sunroom.

Denvers snorted. "That twit Ambrose will never learn. Those luscious fellows remind us that all good things come in pairs."

"Denvers! You always forbade us to generalize. Surely, not *all* good things. There must be an exception."

"And who, didymous, knows that better than I?"

The tutor raised his mutilated limb to emphasize his point. The weight of the gesture was lost on me but not on Donough Gaylord. Having one moment been so carefree and jocular, he suddenly stood pale and drawn.

Brian pulled back my blankets. When I tried to stand, I discovered the debilitating effects of my illness. I rested on the edge of the bed. The two men had moved back to the portico. Denvers was speaking animatedly to Donough Gaylord, obviously distressed, head bowed. He looked very young beside the gray-haired man, nearly as young as I. Brian caught his attention. He carried me to the tiled bathroom, where a frothy white tub awaited.

"Brian loves bathing powders," he said softly.

I removed my nightshirt and with their assistance stepped into the bath. After standing for a few moments to prepare myself for the water, I knelt slowly into the herbal-scented foam. Viewed over my shoulder, Donough Gaylord stood frowning, lost in thought; Denvers studied him intensely. Their eyes met and locked for an instant, until the flustered younger man excused himself and walked from the room.

I was allowed to soak for three minutes. Brian washed me, using a coarse cloth that was surprisingly invigorating. Normally I would have been self-conscious and ill-at-ease being seen naked and being assisted, but it happened so quickly and matter-of-factly that I had no time to reflect on anything but the pleasures of the bath. Stepping from the tub, I was wrapped in a thick brown towel and rubbed dry, then helped into an emerald-green flannel nightgown that Denvers said had once belonged to the twins.

When they were ten years old, no doubt, I thought, looking at my small, taut face reflected in the steamy mirror.

I noticed a brown leather case on the sinkstand beside my old brush.

"What's that?"

"It's for you. Brushes and some toilet things."

I opened it. The light danced on silver and gold manicure pieces and china-backed combs and brushes and tiny crystal bottles filled with colored liquids. The first one I unstopped contained the scent I recognized instantly as Donough Gaylord's. I felt him standing close again.

Thank you for being so kind, sir. And so patient with me.

Mr. Whyte, I am neither kind nor patient.

"Enjoy them, Robert. Use them well."

"Thank you, Denvers. Whose were they?"

"No one's. Mrs. Gaylord loved Fabergé pieces. We were the New York branch of his business!"

Back in the bed, wrapped in clean linen, I was served hot chocolate and fruit. It was time for my nap, a fact Brian made clear by closing the windows, drawing the drapes, removing the extra pillows, and tucking the blankets over my head. Seizing the moment when Brian went to fill my water jug, Denvers sat by my side and spoke very softly.

"I don't know how much you remember . . ."

"All of it. I remember all of it. I saw my mother in the mirror."

"Robert, you were greatly fatigued from the journey and from your experiences with her illness. What you saw was the Della Francesca lit by Ambrose's lamp."

"But—"

"Do you recall his entering the room?"

I thought back and realized his simple explanation was most likely the correct one.

He observed the relief on my face. Rising to leave, he said, "I'm pleased we've settled that. Now, go to sleep."

"Yes," I said. "Yes, yes, I will."

There's no other explanation, I thought. Unless I've gone mad. Please, God, don't let me be mad. . . .

Alone with the cat, I arranged my body around his in the wonderfully comfortable bed.

"Was ever there a pair as fortunate as we?" I whispered to Cael. He opened his eyes a slit, yawned, stretched his back legs, and began purring. Enveloped in a sense of well-being, I slept soundly. Cael's purr became the loveliest of lullabies.

Brian woke me. He opened the drapes and propped me up with pillows before ceremoniously presenting an overloaded tea tray. I recognized the smell of spice cake, but there was none in front of me. Scanning the room, I spotted a linen-wrapped mound on top of my journals. After silently devouring a large portion of fluffy softscrambled eggs, I smiled at him and awaited the inevitable.

He removed the empty dishes, then fetched and unveiled the cake, which he placed on the tray. Tense and anxious, he paced the room.

I poured a cup of tea, sweetening it with honey. "Is this from your hives?"

He nodded.

"It's wonderful."

He nodded.

I cut the cake. He gazed out the window, suddenly interested in clouds. Fortunately, his spice cake was ambrosia. Delighted, I told him truthfully that it was the best, the most nectareous dessert. He turned and studied me, flushed with unalloyed pleasure.

"It's my secret recipe," he whispered.

Startled, I sat very still, the second morsel of cake bal-

anced on my fork halfway between plate and mouth.
Brian had spoken. He hadn't "spoken" in clearly formed
syllables, but rather in a modulated hum that I understood
perfectly. I wanted to shout and tell him how wonderful
it was that he was *not* a mute. Instead, I said calmly, "Who
gave you the recipe?"

"Monsieur Henri, but I've changed it almost completely."

"Has he tasted it?"

He nodded.

"Did he like it?"

"He asked for the recipe, but I wouldn't give it to him."

We laughed as though it were the most wonderful joke
in the world. We talked together while I finished my tea.
He asked me how I'd met Donough Gaylord. I told him
how I came to Gaywyck. And I told him about my
mother's face in the mirror. I also told him that I was
afraid of going mad as my mother had done. He assured
me I was no longer to worry, because if I did, Donough
would take good care of me.

"Thanks," I said. "There's some comfort in that. Not
much, but some. . . ."

"Some is better than none."

"Uh-huh."

Before he left, I took the last of the prescribed sedative. Unaccustomed to drugs, I was frightened by the
force with which sleep overtook me, and I could remember, during the previous three days, losing the sense of
demarcation between waking and sleeping reality. I complained that hurtling into sleep terrified me and probably
did to my brain what Alice's "Drink Me" potion had done
to her body; but I swallowed the medicine.

Instantly I was spun into a tumultuous dream. A searing warmth filled me, fusing images and causing a buzzing
sensation in my ears that woke me into a night room loud
with the carping of cicadas and the singing of whippoor-
wills. A sibilant whispering occurred. I had been dreaming
of the sea. The voice at first surfaced from its depths beneath the horizon; I grasped fragments of sentences as
though they rode the great distance on the crests of
waves like slivers of moonlight. Surrendering to the pull
of the drug, I tumbled backward into the self's darkest
reaches.

The voice persisted. I struggled against answering its

summons until, quivering with recognition, I imagined it
Donough Gaylord's. Totally numb, I opened my eyes.
Cold air chilled me. I shivered and groped for the receding waves. He laughed an echoing laugh. Sitting on my
bed, he took me in his arms. Tugging on my nightshirt,
he deftly pulled it over my head.

"You smell lovely," he whispered.

Kind and patient, I thought.

He pressed me back to the pillows. I lay curled in the
gelid hollow of a wave. He caught it; I tumbled upward,
opening. He hovered, naked, poised above until I pulled
him down. The heat of him and bright lights blinded. His
hair was wet and smelled of the sea. He grasped me
tightly, murmuring, "Ah, *yes*." I slept in his enveloping
arms beneath a heaving sea.

The wind rustled the drapes, moving them sufficiently
for me to see that the French windows were open. My
visitor fully clothed, stood to the left, staring out at the
night. Unsteadily I rose from the bed. My body ached
and I had great difficulty standing; my mouth tasted salty.
As I approached him, he turned, catching me before I fell.

"Go back to bed!"

"I want to be with you, Donough."

Angrily he pulled away. Stepping out, he vanished. "Go
back to bed, I said!" hung in the air.

I followed him, but he was nowhere to be seen. Staring
at the moonlit sea, I shivered drowsily, then looked around.
I was straining against a railing on a second-story balcony.
Automatically walking to the right, I reached a balustrade.
Leaning over, I discovered myself outside the oval window; I could see Cael sitting on the landing. Across the
egg-shaped window, the balcony continued, but the gap
made by the glass was too vast for me to leap across.
Glancing upward, I discerned that what I had construed
as roof was actually a similar balcony for the third floor.
Turning, I saw a stairway at the end connecting it with
mine. Perhaps a similar stairs descended to the ground
below?

Supporting myself on the railing, I moved in that direction. I was freezing cold and dizzy from the shock of it.
I spotted him walking the border of trees that edges the
lawn at the rise. Quickening his pace, he glanced over his
shoulder as though looking for me. I raised my arms. He
stopped. Our eyes met, telescoping the yards between,

eradicating distance. A strange smile broke upon his face, a smile filled with pain and bewilderment. Raising his right arm, he tapped it to his forehead in salute. Turning away, he hurriedly walked in the direction of the sea. I wanted to be with him. Descending the steps, I stumbled after.

He sat on the rise between two great yews, contemplating the sea. When he heard me aproach, he spun around. Stupefied, he muttered my name. Standing, he quickly removed his jacket to cover my nakedness.

"Good Lord! Robert!"

"I only wanted . . ."

Before I could explain, I collapsed. He carried me back to the house. Once in my room, he set me on the bed, and taking his jacket from me, replaced my nightshirt as gently as he had removed it. Why this sudden modesty? I began to shiver violently.

"Have you always walked in your sleep?" he asked. He piled blankets on me, then built a fire.

"You've probably caught your death. Brian told us you were sleeping soundly."

"I was, until you woke me."

He stared at me for an instant. Frowning, he turned away. "You were dreaming."

Bewildered, I felt compelled to contradict. I was certain I had not been dreaming. The face in the mirror may have been the product of an overwrought imagination, but his presence and his warmth most certainly were not!

"I was *not* dreaming! I was not!"

"Stay still, for God's sake," he shouted. "I'll get you something hot to drink."

He left me alone. Upset and gradually overtaken by fear and shame at having spoken to him in so bold a manner, I began to whimper and shiver uncontrollably. The door opened. Cael entered, followed by Brian. The cat jumped on my bed, sniffed my face, and gently, softly touched his cold nose to my cheek, bestowing a kiss, the first he'd ever given me.

"What happened?" Brian queried groggily.

I shrugged, fighting back tears, unable to answer him. Donough Gaylord crossed toward me. "Drink this!"

I obeyed the stern, low-voiced command without hesitation. The drink was very hot, and there was whiskey in it. It warmed me quickly.

"You must try to sleep, Robert. I'll send for the doctor immediately."

"I don't need any doctor."

He raised his right eyebrow.

"No more sedatives?" Brian interjected nervously, attempting a joke.

"Exactly! Now, go to sleep, Robert! Brian's bedded in your sitting room. He's been there all night with the connecting door open. If you need anything, call him."

The tone of his voice made it clear there was to be no more conversation. Suddenly I was terribly confused and uncontrollably tired. A chill shook me. The thought of his anger terrified me.

"Brian, please fetch Robert an aspirin powder before you go to bed."

My young friend left us. Donough Gaylord smiled at me as if in forgiveness. I forced myself to smile in return. He put his hand on my forehead and brushed back my hair. My eyes collected tears; my heart responded: gratitude pervaded me, submerging reason in the mysterious comfort I drew from him.

"Forgive me," I mumbled.

"There is nothing to forgive. I should have been more careful. I should have put Brian in the room here with you to protect you. In time you'll be fine."

"Oh . . . Mr. Donough . . ."

Brian brought the aspirin powder.

"Go to sleep, now, Robert. Brian, go to bed. You are exhausted, and we mustn't have *you* coming down with something."

I watched them walk to the door. Donough paused, while Brian continued out of the room. Turning to me, he smiled again, then quickly raised his right hand to his forehead in a salute similar to the one he had just given me from the garden. The gesture surprised me, but before I could comment, he was gone. Could I have imagined that? I could see him standing in the garden. But I could also see him standing at his Gramercy Park window with the curtains pushed aside. He was waving to me. Or was he saluting? No longer certain, I meekly acknowledged it was always the more ceremonial courtesy.

I *was* dreaming . . . must have been . . . from whence come such bewildering dreams as these?

Dimly awake, I felt Cael make his careful way to my pillow; curling himself, he pressed against the top of my head, purring heavily. I felt protected, guarded. Together we journeyed by coracle. He knew the constellations well. For a time we wore armor, but I, alone, jousted with Culwich-cum-Gaylord, who was also a shimmering sea. In a grove of golden ginkos, I held out my hands to catch the fanlike leaves that spiraled to the earth, but they burned me. We bathed in chilling waves. One by one, they donned helmets of steel. In a castle lived a cyclops with a clowder of cats.

The chill took its toll. I awoke with a heavy cold. Since I'd earned it, I made no complaints but stayed quietly abed eating and drinking all the food put in front of me. The cold did not linger. Two days elapsed without incident, but without a visit from Donough Gaylord. On the third day, I asked Denvers about my employer.

"He left for town yesterday on urgent business."

I was stunned. Why should I have expected otherwise?

"Will he be back soon?" I ventured.

"I shouldn't think so. In any case, not before Thanksgiving."

Though unable to completely conceal my disappointment, I managed to mask the extent of it, even from myself.

Denvers abruptly changed the subject to the book he held in his hand. "Have you read much Whitman?"

I shook my head, then added, "Only a few pieces in magazines."

Why didn't he say good-bye? I wondered, knowing full well he had more important things to do than visit with me, an employee.

"Read him now, dear boy, and learn something."

Denvers handed me the volume.

"It's the 1881 edition," he explained, sitting by my side. "I wanted the complete 1892 edition, but as usual, I couldn't find it. Nor could I locate the 1888 *November Boughs* with 'Sands of '70' and 'Good-bye, My Fancy.' It is so frustrating! One can never find a goddamn thing! And I was convinced I knew where they were, which makes it even more irritating. We *all* await your ordering our books."

"How did you find this edition?"

"It was on Donough's desk. That's what set me thinking about Whitman. I'll be very happy to see that 1860
edition; it's inscribed . . . one of my favorite volumes.
Things have a way of vanishing in this house."

"They turn up again, surely."

"Eventually, while one is searching for something else.
Years skitter by that way."

He asked if I had decided upon a strategy. I said I
hadn't given it much thought. He assured me I was not to
feel pressured. He suggested I rest a few more days, then
left me to Whitman. The book had been resting on my
lap. When I placed it on its spine, it opened to a marked
page. I read the poem in front of me.

When I Heard at the Close of Day

When I heard at the close of day how my name
        had been
    receiv'd with plaudits in the capitol, still it
        was not a happy
    night for me that follow'd,
And else when I carous'd, or when my plans were
        accomplish'd,
    still I was not happy,
But the day when I rose at dawn from the bed of
        perfect health
    refresh'd, singing, inhaling the ripe breath of
        autumn,
When I saw the full moon in the west grow pale and
        disappear in
    the morning light,
When I wander'd alone over the beach, and
        undressing bathed,
    laughing with the cold waters, and saw the
        sun rise,
And when I thought how my dear friend my lover
        was on his way
    coming, O then I was happy,
O then each breath tasted sweeter, and all that day
        my food
    nourish'd me more, and the beautiful day pass'd
        well,
And the next came with equal joy, and with the next
        at evening
    came my friend,

And that night while all was still I heard the waters
    roll slowly
  continually up the shores,
I heard the hissing rustle of the liquid and sands as
    directed to
  me whispering to congratulate me,
For the one I love most lay sleeping by me under the
    same cover
  in the cool night,
In the stillness in the autumn moonbeams his face
    was inclined
  toward me,
And his arm lay lightly around my breast—and that
    night I was happy.

My heart raced ahead of me. The poem's sentiments
agitated me. The words sang of love. I reread them, anticipating the rush of emotion. The phrases rooted in my
memory. I closed the book. Was the marker inserted for
my benefit? Dare I presume Donough Gaylord meant me
to see it? That he was speaking to me?

I felt joy rising. I fought against seizing it. It was beyond
my ken that I, with my tightly governed spirit buttressed
to preserve order, harmony, and uniformity of feeling,
could surrender so easily to the chaos, the anarchy, the
deranged regions of emotions. Nature must truly abhor
solitude.

To calm myself, I turned to the beginning of the *Calamus*
group. Every poem aroused me.

  . . . *By the love of comrades,*
  By the manly love of comrades. . . .
  . . . *The dear love of man for his comrade, the*
  attraction of friend for friend. . . .

Then I was gazing again upon the poem beneath the
marker. The exhilaratingly beautiful verse moved me to
tears. Surely we had all become comrades! Why else had
Denvers acted as messenger? Blissfully I charged into the
next poem. With nine lines, I was devastatingly routed.

Are You the New Person Drawn Toward Me?
Are you the new person drawn toward me?

> To begin with take warning, I am surely far different
>   from what you suppose;
> Do you suppose you will find me your ideal?
> Do you think it so easy to have me become your lover?
> Do you think the friendship of me would be unalloy'd
>   satisfaction?
> Do you think I am trusty and faithful?
> Do you see no further than this facade, this smooth
>   and tolerant manner of me?
> Do you suppose yourself advancing on real ground
>   toward a real heroic man?
> Have you no thought O dreamer that it may all be
>   maya, illusion?

The shock of truth was more than I could physically
bear; I could not catch my breath. Having lowered my
defenses, I now sat helpless and trembling at the cruel,
crushing onslaught. The message was not loving tidings
but one of admonition, a caution, a warning.

I caught my breath. It seared my breast. I was overwhelmed by the shame of having made this indirect means
of communication necessary. Obviously, I had evinced
signs of instability, and no other approach seemed feasible.
The succinct Whitman statement left no room for doubt.

Tears dropped on the page, punctuating the poem anew.
I cried myself to sleep. I slept suddenly. I slept soullessly.
I slept to overcome a death of the spirit, a death of the
heart.

When I awoke, Dr. Anders was standing beside my bed.
After his examination, he declared me "a fine specimen"
and suggested one more day convalescing, then "business
as usual."

Just what the doctor ordered, I thought, a return to the
old, sensible life of effort.

Denvers found me in good spirits.

"Did you manage any Whitman?"

"Yes! More than enough. He's a great poet. Thank you!"

"You're welcome. But I really did very little. It was
Donough who put the poems before me, and Whitman who
wrote them."

"But you were the emissary."

I thought of sacrificing the messenger who embodied
bad tidings in an attempt to controvert their ill effects. The

image of Denvers being flung from the balcony into the sea careened through my mind.

"Emissary? You are a strange young man, Robert. Emissary, indeed!"

I studied his face. He accepted my scrutiny.

"Yes, Robert, I suppose 'emissary' is an appropriate word . . . if one thinks about it."

I nodded. He smiled and left the room. Stroking Cael, I reopened the book and reread the poems.

Seven

NEXT EVENING, I SAT DOWN TO MY first official dinner at Gaywyck. Keyes did not appear. At dusk I heard the "Moonlight Sonata" while standing on the portico outside my room and watching the sun slip behind the horizon. Gaywyck rests on the edge of a small peninsula, and from my vantage point gives the impression of being surrounded by water, a ship adrift in the ocean. The music soothed me. My heart, newly extinguished, went out to the sun, and I knew the night and the sea and I were ruled by the dead white moon.

I felt calm. The days in bed had replenished my energies. I was no longer a stranger to myself. Sleep restored me the way the sun returns a flooded field to dry pasture land. The confusion was gone. Only a suspicion of *tristesse* remained. I drew a deep breath. As far as I could discern, all was battened down. I felt secure in the knowledge that soon everything would be forgotten, buried, hidden away.

Ambrose knocked to announce dinner in half an hour. Five minutes later, Denvers called to accompany me to the small dining room. He carried a large Wanamaker's catalog which he dropped on a chair. I instantly retrieved it.

"You'll be needing a few things. I've taken the liberty of checking articles I think you could use. Go through and mark colors and sizes. We'll send your measurements to Donough's tailor for evening clothes and other necessities."

"But you've marked every section!"

"Because, dear boy, you *need* something from every section, and usually *several* somethings, at that."

"Won't that be extravagant and expensive?" (I spoke the final word as though it were blasphemy.)

"There is no such thing as extravagance hereabouts. And the only thing ruder than talking about money is thinking about money."

The Cézanne had been hung in the sitting room. There were many splendid pieces, but Donough had set the painting in the perfect spot. I marveled at his sensitivity.

"Donough's rearranged everything. Many years ago, a guest once remarked that each room contained a 'headliner.' Reynolds is the gent at the top of the bill in this room, or *was* until the Cézanne replaced him. I wasn't *really* paying attention when they began shuffling them about. I *think* he replaced Rembrandt, who then shoved Rossetti out of the front parlor. Or has he done in Stubbs?"

"Where's the Rossetti portrait?" I asked suddenly.

"The Rossetti left with Donough. He's given it to the National Gallery on permanent loan; they've been after it for years. Why so disappointed? It was *not* one of his better efforts."

"I understood it resembled Mr. Donough's mother."

"Who told you that?"

"Father Collins."

"That silly celibate! It's a typical Rossetti portrait of a young, androgynous thing. It resembles *you* as much as Mary Rose."

"Me?"

"Yes, you. It's the eyes. When I mentioned it to Donough, he agreed, said he'd gaped at you rudely on first sight. It *is* remarkable, you know. I never thought anyone could have eyes as lovely as she. Just goes to show! Of course Keyes will be thrilled. He'll grasp you to his woolly breast as a fellow reincarnate. Mother of God! What a world you've entered, Robert Whyte."

"Mr. Donough warned me. He tried to change my mind, but I was adamant. I was destined to come to Gaywyck."

"I pray to God you don't live to regret it." He paused, staring at me intensely. His eyes brightened. "But you are going to change all that! You will; I believe you will. We must chance it. To give up hope is to die. Now, let's go down to dinner."

Chance and change. Seeing those two words together, I realize that the only difference between them is the letter c and the letter g. cg. CG: the initials of the enigma. Whatever made me think that *I* could escape the malediction of Cormack Gaylord? Perhaps I thought their combined efforts would spare me? Or more likely, Donough

Gaylord thought death destroyed his brother's evil by appeasing it? In either case, we were wrong. Evil is never obliterated. Even now, after all these years, his raging spirit haunts my dreams. Chance and change, key words of human existence. CG. Truly our destiny is written in the stars.

My rooms, I discovered, were at the end of the second-floor corridor, left wing. I was the only person inhabiting that wing. Denvers and Mr. Donough were on the second floor as well, but in the right wing on the other side of the oval-windowed foyer. Keyes was on the third floor, above Denvers. The others lived "below stairs," in quarters near the kitchen area. The "dailies" commuted from the village of Sterling Harbor.

Denvers and I sauntered down the wide corridor toward the central staircase. The windows at either end would fill the space with daylight, but the lamps made the pieces of sculpture and floral arrangements barely discernible. I wondered if the twins had ever roller-skated over its shiny wood floor.

"Most of the rooms are never used anymore. The ones next to yours are occupied by Donough's friends Goodbody and Mortimer whenever they visit, which, alas, is very infrequently. These are opened only to air them and for the annual spring clean."

"What a waste of all this beauty."

"Beauty is never wasted. And if you saw the guests who inhabited these rooms—bores of every feather—you wouldn't grieve over the now vacant beds."

Descending the stairs, I paused to look at the eternal sea through the vast window. Glancing upward, I noticed a milk-glass dome.

"Charming touch, that, don't you think? Originally, it was stained glass in the Daikin style. Our Donough said the colors shifting on the landing frightened him. That was his first change."

"Has he made many others?"

"Quite a few, yes. Outside, he's allowed the park to reclaim some of the ornamental grounds. The gardens have been simplified and in some cases replaced by lawns. The great knot garden has been reduced to its barest tracings. It was all too much to maintain. He's stocked several museums with Meissen and coins and early Roman heads, and pictures, too, making room for his own. This place will always be a baroque hodgepodge, but he's put his classical touch here and there."

We crossed the foyer, pausing to greet the Cellini satyr and to admire its musculature, then opened the pair of blond doors opposite the ones that I'd passed through on my first night. A beacon lamp burned on a white piano in a far corner. It shimmered in the satin Sheraton coverings, the buhl, porcelain, and wood surfaces, the Parian marble, biscuit china, and gilded mirrors.

"There's the Reynolds! That takes care of him. He replaced Gainsborough. I should have guessed; Whistler's too dark; Rembrandt's too small. You can look later. We'll be late to table."

When we reached the Louis XVI dining room, with its floor of quartered oak parquet and its wainscoted oak walls, Ambrose awaited. He showed me to my place at the round table. An arrangement of autumn zephyr lilies and showy autumn crocus was removed to the sideboard and placed beside Cael, who sat silent, attendant. The remaining candles were lit.

"I thought you'd prefer a hot salad as a first course. One *does* get tired of soup."

Never having seen one, I had no idea how to eat the green flower placed before me. I asked. He demonstrated. Removing one leaf ("scale"), he dipped it into the porcelain cup of drawn butter.

"Drawn butter?"

He explained. I dipped and nibbled the bulbous, succulent tips. All the while, he talked charmingly of the vegetable, delighting in my discovery of it.

". . . a native of Barbary . . . species of sunflower. . . . Donough adores them stuffed with shrimp . . . beware of the choke. . . ."

Ambrose removed the fuzzy mass with an experienced flick of a knife. I savored the bared heart of the artichoke and tried to draw some lessons from nature to parallel the defenses of the human heart, but found Denvers's erudite "nonsense" (as he called it) much more instructive.

A roasted capon followed, stuffed with chestnut-thyme dressing, covered with an orange sauce; then a pumpkin soufflé, and a broccoli with hollandaise (each a separate marvel to me); then, fresh, still-warm cheddar-cheese bread ("one of Brian's specialty acts"), which Brian himself delivered in one of his rare appearances at table. Den-

vers applauded with great gusto, joined by Ambrose and
Mr. O'Shay, who stuck his head in through the kitchen
door: "He's been working all afternoon on that concoction."

The baker cut his bread. We all "oohed" and "aahed."
The baker bowed. We applauded again. Ambrose muttered
under his breath that he for one hated cheese bread, preferring either cheddar or bread but not some "mucky
marriage" of the two. Denvers frowned, called him "a
cranky old fart," and ordered the rest of the meal to be
served. Indian squash and baked yams appeared.

"This is a feast!"

"Not quite, Robert, my boy. It's all wonderful stuff,
but common enough fare. The feasts will come later on,
and there will be plenty of them, I promise. We celebrate
everything here. We rifle *The Farmer's Almanac* to fill
the leaner periods."

He told me that the acreage cultivated to grow the
vegetables filling the table had been expanded during the
recession of 1893, and the excess food was sold to the
village at a token price; similar arrangements were made
for meats and dairy products. Though the recession had
long passed, the villagers still reaped benefits from
Gaywyck.

He toasted me and wished me happiness. I thanked him,
and toasted myself. The chilled, dry, fragrant wine
thrilled me. Delicious wines in crystal glasses dominated
the dinner parties in Constance Cady Harrison's glamorous
metropolitan novels, and I finally understood why. I loved
the wine. Wine for me had always been heavy, sweet, and
medicinal; this one was decidedly pleasurable, delicious,
and exhilarating.

"It's one of Donough's favorite wines."

I took the opportunity and plunged. "I'm sorry he had
to leave so quickly."

"Yes, so am I, but he's a busy man and we see little of
him here at Gaywyck. His latest project has absorbed him.
He's raising funds and organizing prodigious feats for two
old friends of his, Jane Addams and Ellen Starr. They've
actually managed to open their place!"

"Hull House?" I asked, stunned.

"Yes, exactly; thank you. Those buccaneer ladies are
only two of many."

"Who else is there?" I mumbled totally undone by this conversation.

"Well, his major involvements, besides the Chicago venture, are with that madwoman Lucy Stone and her suffragettes, and with the Garment Workers' Union. Both hopeless tasks, if you ask me, but fortunately, he rarely does. I *should* be delighted he took seriously all that manure about human rights I fed him. . . ."

"And aren't you pleased?" It was a rhetorical question. The tutor's pride in his pupil was evident.

"Of course I am! I'm also a little guilty. God knows, I didn't produce this Parsifal by myself. His mother was a splendid creature, a shining light of virtue and probity just like her son. She embodied *the* best qualities of the Bostonian Age. She worshiped Emerson, Thoreau, and Channing, and when the great Emerson died, she made us all don mourning. Now people confuse morals with manners and have reduced the Bostonian tradition to meaningless phrases. Materialism is all!"

We had arrived at one of his favorite topics. Fortunately I was well versed in the Bostonian Age. My father was devoted to Emerson and to Holmes; he taught me to revere that period in our history as golden. When I mentioned how vehemently against Louisa May Alcott and her myriad imitators my father was ("Purveyors of pernicious pabulum"), Denvers could not have agreed more heartily. My especial fondness for *Little Women* and *Eight Cousins* surfaced, perversely.

After dinner, he suggested I retire early to prepare for my first workday. I agreed. As we climbed the staircase, Keyes could be heard playing the piano and humming loudly, accompanying the instrument's clear, brilliant sound with his own warm, musical head tone.

"You were right, Denvers. He does sing a rapturous violin."

We parted at the top of the stairs. Cael ran ahead as if to show me the way. Everywhere I'd gone, the cat followed or appeared beside me to observe my every move. If at any time I approached him or expressed interest in his behavior, he ignored me or scurried away, bearing his tail like a white plume. Yet the instant I settled, he would bound for me, stand in my lap with his right front paw crooked, and gaze into my eyes until I welcomed him.

Then he gave his greeting: a guttural chirrup. The purring began when I spoke to him; by the time he stood close enough to be hugged, he was literally vibrating with pleasure.

"What a handsome friend you are! Yes! What a *tesoro*! What a gorgeous puss! What a darling spicy cake!" I'd chant, becoming more inane as he revolved excitedly, politely offering first his rear for me to investigate, then his head for me to pat. "Peach Pit, Biscuit Tin, Fond d'Artichay. . . ." He remained standing, accepting the homage. Suddenly flinging himself onto his side, with a grunt, he began a meticulous wash before napping. At night, when I extinguished the bed light, he would make his way to the pillow in the darkness and settle coiled for sleep above my head.

That night, I had no intentions of sleeping immediately. The wine excited me. I wanted adventure. Opening the French windows in my bedroom, I stepped out to view the still-full moon and the familiar constellations, all sharply evident in the cloudless October sky. Then I saw the sea. My wonder at the mild night was instantly replaced by a sense of astonishment that I had not yet visited the beckoning expanse of water before me.

I descended to the back lawn and crossed quickly to the edge of the rise. Great patches of silver-lavender leaves glimmered in the yew trees. I could smell spices planted in the area. I found a gravel path leading to a flight of wooden stairs near where Donough Gaylord had been sitting. The far side of the rise was a rock garden that sloped precipitously to the sandy shore below. While stepping down, I spotted blue lobelia and thought how surprised my mother would be to see it thriving in that wind-blown place.

Feeling the sand beneath me, I removed my shoes and socks. I left them on the bottom step. Looking up and down the deserted beach, I headed into the surf. The water was warm! Holding up my trouser legs, I splashed in, heading to my left toward the rocks. By the time I reached the jetty, I had made up my mind. A story read in some magazine had deterred me for a few paces, but the young hero had drowned on a full stomach because he disobeyed his sainted mother; *I* was not disobeying anyone. I wasn't planning to swim. I didn't know how.

I would wade. I would not go a depth beyond my collar-bone.

Standing on a wide ledge to the far side of the rock pile, I undressed and folded each garment carefully, stowing them in a flat niche to my right. The jetty reminded me of playing blocks my father had carved for me when I was a child. Agilely I lowered my naked self into the churning water; it reached only to my knees.

I waded. After a few cautious attempts, I sat. A small wave slapped playfully. I laughed. A larger one broke over me. The brackish water flooded my open mouth. With a jolt I remembered the dream: clasped in the tenderness of Donough Gaylord, I felt in the swirling water a scalding erotic current that forced a sudden intake of breath, and a goodly amount of the onrushing wave.

Choking, I staggered upward and sputtered about. The first sight my stinging eyes registered was Cael sitting on the beach looking distressed. His fur was standing on end and his eyes were round as my own taut nipples. The metaphor embarrassed me. Glancing down at myself, I turned and plowed my way into the water, submerging my decidedly overstimulated body up to its collarbone. The experience was extraordinarily pleasurable; the wet caressed and offered solace. Bobbing a bit, I distracted myself from my self by riding the swells and navigating toward the jetty.

My clothing was gone. In place of my garments lay a dead bobwhite. My initial response was disgust. The poor bird had had its throat slit; blood was still trickling from the wound into a carmine pool that partially covered its head. Then I caught the significance of the savage gesture and began searching for my clothing with a growing sense of urgency and fear.

There was not a thread on that pile of rocks. Growing angry, I looked around me. I wanted to tell the thief it was not a fair trade. I stood hands on hips wearing bright October moonlight for all the world to view. What world? Except for the light in my own bedroom, the house looked dark. The world consisted of me, Cael, and my ghoulish trickster.

Timidly I shouted a weak "Hello?" Cael answered. We stood studying one another from opposite ends of the jetty. He looked quite calm. I scrambled down the other side of the stone playground and splashed into the cold water. It reached above my chin. I hurled myself forward and swam to shore with an improvised flailing that kept me afloat.

My shoes and socks were gone. Shaken, I felt desperate for a warm bed. Unfamiliar with any of the paths winding through the dense woods, I made for the house without cover, Cael in tow. My bare legs brushed the leaves of the geraniums and azaleas that border the trees; a cluster of rosebushes did minor damage to my right thigh as I approached the flagstone patio that is screened from the sea breezes by a wall of pleached hawthorn trees.

Inside the library, Denvers sat reading. My rooms were directly above him. Hastily rounding the L-shaped, leafy barricade, I cautiously mounted the steps. Safely on the portico, I stood for a second surveying the grounds. Not a soul was visible. Whoever had taken my clothing not only indulged a bizarre taste for the macabre but also knew the area well enough to vanish. It was like something from a Wilkie Collins novel. Even such a simpleton as I could have found a leafy patch in which to hide after perpetrating the bloody prank.

Neatly folded on my bed, with my shoes to the side, was my clothing. Inside the left shoe was an enormous mottled red-and-white slipper orchid. I removed the exotic bloom and accepted it for what I assumed it to be: an apology for a game that had failed to amuse. I placed it in the water jug beside my bed.

Cael sat on a pillow cleaning the vestiges of our night's passage from his paws. I noticed a red streak under his chin. Leaning closer, I saw it was blood. I felt such relief! Grabbing the startled animal, I told him between hugs and kisses that his gift was appreciated even if it was poorly timed; I forgave him the poor bobwhite because his distress over his messily executed prey had been punishment enough. He howled, rightly annoyed.

I laughed at my foolishness. Did the mysterious prankster have the slightest notion why I had reacted so strangely? Perhaps he had seen Cael delivering my present and had laughed at my absurd conclusions and behavior. I dropped the cat. He set about washing himself, and I followed his example, sponging away the salt water. Once in bed, I immediately fell asleep.

Many dreams visited me. In the last, I was chasing butterflies. I said something to anger Cael, who began pummeling me with his front paws. I shouted and awoke to find him poking my cheek with his cold nose.

I opened my eyes to the room's dim predawn light and sighed. He jumped over me and hurried to the bedroom's closed door. I sat up. He danced by the door. Walking in circles on the tips of his paws, his back arched, his tail straight up and quivering, he squeaked softly, signaling me to make available the sitting room. He looked very annoyed. As I got out of bed, he sidestepped over to me and rubbed against my legs. There was such a stillness, I could hear his mild purr.

I opened the door to let him into the adjoining room. Before I could climb back into bed, he was again on my pillows.

"What *is* the matter now, my sweet?"

His eyes were narrowed. No longer purring, he glared at me steadily, while whining and revealing his tiny pink tongue and sharp white teeth. After a moment he jumped from the bed and disappeared into the sitting room. When I did not immediately follow, he stuck his head in the doorway, his eyes now wide in bewildered astonishment. I walked toward him. As I passed, he emitted a squeaklike sigh. The door between the sitting room and the hallway was also closed.

"All right! All right! I didn't do it on purpose. What can you expect from a novice?"

I crossed the room, expecting him to follow. When I reached for the doorknob, he remained on the other side of the room looking cagey.

I began to turn the knob.

"Don't trust me, eh? Think I need slapping?" I asked, as I pulled the door toward me.

The moment the hallway was revealed to him, he sprang to his feet, arching his back and hissing in a crazed frenzy. His claws dug into the carpet, pulling it toward him. With his fur on end, he looked twice his normal size.

"*Cael!*" I shouted, startled. "Cael, what's wrong?"

"He hates me. That's what's wrong."

I spun around, frightened witless by the unknown voice. A fat old man with shoulder-length white hair stood barefoot in the doorway. He wore a ruffled nightshirt. His glazed blue eyes were half his face; a receding chin was weakened by the absence of teeth.

"You *are* wise," he said, "for one so young and savory. Everyone needs to be slapped occasionally."

During the pause that followed, I nodded and grinned stupidly, still aghast at the sight of him. I mumbled a few hasty thank-yous so as not to offend. When in doubt, I thought, be polite.

"Who are you in this life?"

"I'm Robert Whyte, sir. I'm to be the librarian."

He laughed at me. "A likely story! Do you know who I am?"

"Yes, sir," I said crisply, hoping to project self-control.

"Did you enjoy the Kreutzer? I dedicate it to you!"

"Oh? Really? Thank you, sir!"

"I saw Donough leave your room. Does he *always* run away after? When you hung over the edge, I hoped you would fall into the oval window. Why must you take him from us?"

My mind spilled outward, unable to contain a thought. I could barely hear him. With no teeth, he slurred words. And Cael's hissing, though less frequent, was still distracting.

"Did you enjoy your swim?"

He laughed maniacally, miming with his hands the wringing of a neck.

"You won't take him away this time."

He stepped toward me. His eyes, seemingly benign, suddenly filled me with dread. I shrank from him. He took another step, entering the room. Cael darted from behind and clawed his bare foot. The old man shrieked, turned, and fled back into the darkness. Shaking, I stood leaning against the doorframe. Cael slunk into the hallway a few paces before rushing back into the room. I closed the door and locked it. The old man's words had battered me senseless. The cat pressed against me. Picking him up, I hugged him tightly, attempting to ease my anxiety and fear by nattering to him about his heroism. He sporadically hissed and growled.

"Cael! Cael!" The pads of his paws are wet with perspiration. "You weren't attacking that old warlock. You were defending us! You were as frightened of him as I was! You were sweating along with me! Yet *you* managed to clobber him."

Slowly I walked back to my bed and curled on top of the coverlet.

"The old man saw Donough and me. I wasn't dreaming. Why should anyone lie to me? I'm not worth lying to. I'm no one."

Cael was calming, and began to clean away the smell of fear. I opened the drapes. A soft breeze came through the partly open French windows.

"Cael! You could have gone out here!"

The cat yawned. Danger past, he curled for sleep. I looked at him, stupefied.

"When you awaken, my Persian angel, I must inform you that cats don't do such things. Whoever heard of a watch*cat*?"

The morning was brightening, but neither sun nor moon was in the silver sky. The hour of the wolf hung heavily. I dressed quickly. Going down again, I crossed the dew-soaked grass to the pebbled path and followed its curving way to the cliff's edge. At the bottom of the wooden steps, Cael waited.

The time was quiet, a sigh of muffled waves the only sound in the intense stillness. A deathlike tranquillity reigned.

Sitting on the edge of the rocks with Cael on my lap, I looked out into the vastness of the ocean. A primal awe moved me to tears. I strained for a sense of union; motionless, I plunged and dissolved. Then I turned back to Gaywyck. In the morning light, it wasn't quite as immense as I had first assumed. It wasn't *small* by anyone's standards, but neither was it Versailles. The light around me heightened and the off-center oval portal gleamed. Birds set up their alarm at the approach of day. Suddenly I saw the porticoes with their iron supports as bars, and the central glass as a massive glinting eye.

"The eye of Polyphemos," I said aloud, and shuddered. "The cyclops is watching! He whom Odysseus tricked, declaring, 'I am No One.' "

The dawn rippled in the glass, infusing life.

"The cyclops is waiting. And I too am No One! *I* am the clever no one."

I laughed at the connection; my spirits soared as the new golden day rose. I made my way over the rocks to take up my duties at Gaywyck.

I had conquered fear and doubt in an instant. As if by magic, the moment was all that concerned me.

near the end of the corridor. As Ambrose closed the

Book Two

Eight

THOSE INITIAL WORKWEEKS ARE RE-membered in a daze of mellow contentment. With a peace-ful, orderly existence came comfort and false security.

The Indian summer spun a web of perfect days. The tonic beauty of the Gaylord estate was further enhanced; hypnotic, it drew me from the house (and out of myself). Upstate New York, the land is mostly dense forest or ploughed field, hilly to mountainous; but on this piece of Long Island shore, the terrain is flat. A delicate, carefully tended park extends a mile in three directions, just twenty paces from three sides of Gaywyck.

As Denvers explained, "A brigade of gardeners and horticulturists toiled fiercely to civilize this double-dune wilderness. Grandfather Gaylord imagined a miniature Central Park; he nearly succeeded. Only the rock forma-tions are missing."

The first afternoon Denvers and I set out to explore my new home. He knew the names of virtually every animal, vegetable, and mineral that inhabited the area, and I date my interest in the language of the natural world from these walks along the paths that twisted and turned, crossing and recrossing one another like the unwound string of Theseus, always returning us adventurers to the point of embarkation. It was then as it is now. Behind the pavilion, a willow grove slopes to the beach; in front, a triangular acre of birches fans out from its steps. (The birch grove became a retreat; the tall, slender trees, with their ethereal grace, soothe the spirit.) My *favorite* spot was the wrought-iron bench in the midst of a six-hundred-year-old stand of white oaks (it afforded a separate peace from the birches, and was sought at particular times). The pavilion was the attraction closest to the house, and we would often sit under its round slate roof to talk or, if the mood was right, play a game of chess, using the port-able set Denvers always carried.

"For a time it was very lively here. I do recall one healthy spring there were fifty gardeners! For weeks they lived in colorful tents set up along the beach. Almost all the cultivation took place on this side of the house where the fresh water ponds are. I can still see those gardeners, all busily pruning and planting and weeding. '. . . *The noisome weeds which without profit suck/ The soils fertility from wholesome flowers.*' " Denvers seemed far away. " '*Had he done so to great and growing men,/ They might have lived to bear and he to taste/ Their fruits of duty. . . .*' Father Gaylord never understood," he said slowly. "I think he felt aversion from the time of Cormack's birth. The two were forever cursing each other, and Gaylord grew to fear Cormack's mad ferocity. Fear it was that curdled into hatred, *I* believe. One night after a particularly fierce argument, Gaylord lunged to slap his adolescent son. Cormack grabbed a poker.

" 'If you raise that, you'll be dead,' threatened his father.

" 'You can't stay awake forever, Da.'

"From that moment, the father's towering will submitted to the son's firmer one. The boy was accepted as an adult opponent."

"What happened?" I asked.

"Gaylord tamed him. They became devoted to each other. Hatred is but the undertow of love."

"Tamed him *how*?"

"Love. One can work miracles in the name of love."

I nodded, thinking I took his meaning. I nodded, swallowing his bait whole.

Another day, after tea, we walked straight to the columned gazebo. Its wrought-iron, stained-glass roof was designed in imitation of the pinnate leaves of the surrounding ash trees. To reach it, we walked down the cool cloistered avenue of towering lindens; then, turning right, we followed a trodden path that skirted the fruit trees and revealed the gazebo before sloping down to the beach and stone jetty.

When we arrived, Denvers sat in silence, watching twin ruby-throated hummingbirds hover over a Dubbonet Buddleia. "Cormack rode the wind in a rebellious battle for deliverance. Like Icarus, he flew too near the sun. . . ." Suddenly he excused himself and disappeared. I was not the only person haunted by past sorrows. The sound of ospreys drew me to the water to watch their spectacular feasting dives.

Walking up from the beach at sunrise my first morning, I listened to the migratory and resident birds sing. A bouquet of pheasants and several deer grazed on the back lawn while a dray of squirrels gorged themselves. Of course I'd seen wild animals, but never casually and calmly feeding, indifferent to my approach as if I were one of their species. They seemed entirely fearless. Instinct should at least have warned them.

When I sat down to breakfast, Denvers was in a radiant mood.

"I awoke this morning with a sense of renewal! God help me, but I've decided to resume work on my book."

"Fiction?"

"Lord, no! I'm not that brave . . . *yet*! We have a fine collection of Early American literature in this house, Robert. For years I've been making notes with an idea to someday assembling them into a book. The time, she is now!"

Immediately after breakfast, we traversed the house. We "did" the manse by way of its paintings, since they are what most interested me. The complete trip took several hours.

"Gaywyck was the first large summerhouse built at this distance from the city. It set the style, especially along the south fork. The three hundred acres were wrested from the Indians, complete with a prophecy: *No happiness until the blind shall see*. Imagine!

"There are forty rooms. The Dixie architect gave no thought to Long Island winters. He took a peek and scampered home, enchanted by the light. To be fair to Daikin, it was intended only as a summerhouse."

We roved from room to room, and time and again I was bowled over by the splendor of the place. That I was to live in the midst of such treasures filled me with unsettling excitement.

"By 1850, most of this stuff was here. Remember, fifty years ago, one could buy *anything*. That Hepplewhite cabinet cost more to crate and ship than to buy. And those Ming porcelain vases were so inexpensive, they bought a dozen!"

Denvers had to drag me from the rooms, from the furniture, the carpets, the china, silver, and glass, the wall hangings: tapestries, icons, carvings, paintings—especially the paintings. "Come," he repeated over and over, "come, Robert, they aren't going anywhere." I stood unable to move, the art inducing rosy flushes. In the small study, he left me to the Della Francesca while he went in search of the key to the art room.

"Ever since Beethoven lost the Rembrandt etchings in the knot garden, we've kept the room locked."

We did not enter Donough Gaylord's quarters, though Denvers did not think he would mind. I said I would rather wait for him to show me what he had selected for his own. When Keyes refused to answer our knock, we did not force the issue.

"I don't know when you'll meet him, Robert. If ever."

"We've already met."

"How did that happen?"

We stopped walking.

"He was outside my rooms the other night."

"What did he say?"

"That he saw me standing on the portico."

"Nothing else?" he queried apprehensively.

"He said something about my taking Donough away."

"A common euphemism for death. He thrives on unoriginal euphemism. *And* death. I'd be careful, if I were you, Robert. I think the old fool is dangerous."

"Oh?" I asked, feeling a chill.

"He's never forgiven his world for the absence of Cormack. The boy had an Olympian beauty the likes of which we shall never see again. It was intensely sad to see him smile."

"Like Donough?"

"No. There was something malevolent about Cormack. He was capable of anything. It gave him a certain majesty. He leaped for the stars; probably could have separated the Gemini."

When we passed the door to the art room, I did not think twice about his mumbled explanation that he had misplaced the key; we visited his own rooms instead. Seeing them gave me a delightful surprise. Puritanlike in his dress, the tutor possessed the heart of a squirrel. His sitting room was crammed, every inch of wall space covered. One wall was devoted to Michelangelo drawings of the male nude. We proceeded to the libraries. We visited the one on the third floor first. The Titian hung on the only open wall space.

"These are the most valuable books. That glassed-in area is the Caxtons and the folios and quartos from the late fifteenth, early sixteenth centuries: Shakespeare, Marlowe, that lot. The chest, third shelf from the bottom, is a Gutenberg Bible. That entire wall is English literature in no order, of course, except for that shelf there, which holds Johnson. *Most* of this stuff is firsts, and rarely used except for special reference. Some of the reprints are on that wall. There's the collection of Americana I mentioned, about a thousand pieces; some additional newspapers and periodicals are downstairs in the small study."

The downstairs library was a much more comfortable room. It was furnished with soft overstuffed chairs. A mahogany desk filled one corner; I immediately christened it "my office." A narrow tapestry hung between two windows opposite: hundreds of butterflies woven in silken brightness on a red background.

"It belonged to Anne of Brittany. It was a Christmas present to young Cormack; he adored the insects. Somewhere there exists a chart he made identifying each and every pair of those membranous wings."

"Did Donough share his interest?"

"No. He preferred semiprecious stones. They were just as beautiful but caused no pain to gather. For that Christmas he gave me a paperweight of Swedish tremolite."

"What was Donough's gift that year from his father?"

"The Christmas tree was in this room. That morning, a sheet covered the tapestry. Gaylord gave an unveiling speech, a very funny one about the travails of capturing and weaving so many butterflies into the woof and warp. Then he ceremoniously presented Donough with a dented milk container and instructed him to remove the lid and pour its contents into the center of the room. Donough slowly and very dramatically undid the top. We all waited breathlessly."

"What was it?"

"Two dozen uncut precious stones. As they bounced and rolled all over the floor, a large orange diamond scudded into my shoe. When I knelt to retrieve it, I could think of nothing but lust. We all gathered them, except for Gaylord, who stood like Jove delighting in the havoc. The boys scrambled under the furniture and I remember

Cormack bowling a black diamond the color of his most
secret self, and Donough tossing an unblemished white
one into the air. I fondled a purple amethyst the color
of my grief. . . ."

Suddenly he was weeping. He turned from me. I moved
to touch his arm, but with a murmured apology he
withdrew from the room. I was so startled, it took me
several minutes to grasp what had transpired; he had been
calm, and then, seemingly without transition, distraught.
There are perhaps wounds that never heal, I concluded
naively.

To distract myself, I roamed the room examining the
crowded shelves. A collection of illuminated manuscripts—
all books of hours—sprawled across one, above a collection of dime novels which someone had stacked according
to size. Emerson in gorgeous calf-bound volumes stood
beside sets of Braddon and Thackeray, Defoe and Scott,
Richardson and Marie Corelli. A first edition of *Emma*
rested on top of the twenty monthly installments of *Our
Mutual Friend* and several volumes by William James.
One shelf was a complete set of *Spectator*s jumbled with
various sized volumes of Pepys's diaries.

Yet, the Roman playwrights sat huddled together. And
Plato (at least thirty separate volumes in every size, shape,
and color) had not only been neatly segregated but alphabetized as well. Someone had imposed an order, but indolent hands had demolished it. I made a mental note to
search rooms for books left lying about.

Then I began familiarizing myself, quickly grasping the
general groupings in several of the cases. By the time
Ambrose called me for lunch, I had evolved my plan of
attack and was eager to discuss it with Denvers, but he
was absent from table. Having been taken ill with headache, he dined alone in his rooms. I ate my chop reading
Cicero's *On Friendship*:

> . . . to put friendship ahead of all human con-
> cerns, for there is nothing so suited to man's nature,
> nothing than can mean so much to him . . . all men
> are meant by nature to have some sort of com-
> panionship one with another . . . there arises a
> mutual feeling of affection—the sort of thing that
> occurs when we find someone with whose character

and nature we feel ourselves in sympathy, because
we think we see in him a bright and shining
light. . . .

". . . *a bright and shining light*," I sighed.

After luncheon, I went for a walk. Wandering, wanting
to read more of Cicero, I started for the music pavilion,
but at the boulder I went right, intending to sit by the
waterfall. The day was warm, nearly hot, and the running
stream that paralleled the path looked cool and inviting.
By the time I reached the pool, rippled by a graceful
waterfall, I wanted to swim. To my delight, I discovered a
waxed-string hammock among the sweet-smelling cedar
trees to the left. While I swam, I would be able to keep
my eyes on my clothing.

I stepped onto the ledge where the waterfall splashed
before it poured into the purling pool. Standing under the
cascade was deliciously refreshing. I closed my eyes and
turned around several times. When I opened them, I was
staring through the falling water into a cave. A cave! I'd
never been in one before. True, it was a speck compared
to Huckleberry Finn's along the Mississippi, but it was
taller by several feet than I, and deep enough for several
people to picnic or hide in, perhaps even live in.

As my eyes became accustomed to the dark, I noticed
the remains of a straw mat in the far corner; the walls
were covered with drawings or symbols. Gradually the
lines and forms became clear to me: two naked men
wrestling, one large and bearded, the other thin and small.
The refracted light glinted and shifted over the pictures.
I moved closer to examine them and realized the men were
not wrestling. In the first one they appeared to be locked
in a hold, but the other drawings clarified their activities.
I blushed from head to foot.

Mesmerized by these bold and obscene glyphs, I felt a
series of sharp, aching pulsations deep in my sapling
frame. I knelt, shaken by sudden expanding recognitions.
Memories of forgotten dreams and arrested images rose
to full height. Suddenly fearless, guiltless, at peace with
the kinetic figures, and animated by the realization that
their dance was mine, I experienced light pouring into my
heart's remotest corners.

The sounds of the waterfall covered the onrush of my

own moaning; all echoed together in the cool cave. While the figures watched over me, I wept for discovery, finding in myself the ability to love myself, to intimately know and to caress my own flesh, to commune with my own spirit.

Quickly I leaped through the falls and jumped down into the pool. I daydreamed as I swung drying in the hammock. Who could have drawn those pictures? Whom, if anyone, did they represent?

Denvers was awaiting me in the downstairs library. I told him about the swim, but withheld the news of the cave. I felt as if I had trespassed on someone's privacy, and I preferred keeping my transgression a secret. Or had my caution been awakened with my desires?

He ordered a pot of tea and we discussed my system for ordering the books. I would give each bookcase a letter from the alphabet, and each shelf a number; the cases would be lettered clockwise, the shelving numbered from ceiling to floor. The downstairs library would be known as I, the upstairs as II, the art room as AR, the music room as MR, etc. For each book a card would be made, coded, and alphabetized.

"There's a typewriting machine in Donough's study, Robert. Have you by any chance acquired the skill? No? Well, not to worry. If all those young women can do it, it can't be all that complicated! There's an instruction booklet. If you typewrite the card, it would be less wearing, and with a sheet of carbon paper you could make two at one time. Then each library, I and II, would have a set."

I wanted to see the machine immediately. Up we went to Donough's study. I had no compunctions about entering his rooms now that there was a legitimate reason. His study was beautiful; I felt comfortable in it immediately. A tremendous art-nouveau desk was set between the French windows. It was piled with papers and books and square manila folders. Brightly colored rock formations acted as paperweights. A bronze casket sat on one end.

"Open it, Robert."

Inside lay the precious stones he had told me about that morning. I let them fall through my fingers, lifting the black diamond and the amethyst to the light. When I closed the lid to the box, it slammed. I felt the sound reverberate in the stillness.

Donough Gaylord's delicate scent hung in the room. I glanced around me. A Renoir hung over the mantel. The third wall was covered with shelving, stuffed with books and glass artifacts; the fourth had a large leather-upholstered couch with Japanese prints arranged behind it. On the couch, a book lay open. I crossed around the chairs and table to look at it: the poems of Rimbaud. In a far corner, on a metal stand, the telegraph sat hooked to a cable that passed out through the wall. Between the French windows hung Manet's full-length portrait of my employer.

I crossed back to stare at the painting. He wears formal evening garb, a red-lined cape, a tall hat and cane. His face looks stern, his mouth tight. It was an expression I had never seen but would soon know well.

"How severe!" I observed.

" 'Staunch' is my word for it," Denvers responded. "It was done in a difficult period for him. He said he tried desperately to appear jaunty, but Edouard searched him out."

In his bedroom I discovered a portrait of the twins. It hung like an icon over the bed. While I stared at the two, the import of their double image entered my life. Insidiously, my fate was sealed.

We moved the typewriting machine to my study and set it on a suitable table. We were reading the instruction booklet and following the diagrams for correct finger placement when Brian interrupted to take my measurements for evening wear. Denvers left us. All went smoothly until Brian asked me whether I wore myself on my right side or my left. I was embarrassed because I did not understand. He explained by means of a few simple gestures. I was embarrassed because I did not know. He made me walk around the room. I consider those few paces one of my rites of initiation into manhood, as well as my leap into the world of fashion. I spent the remainder of the afternoon with the Wanamaker's catalog.

Dinner was especially pleasant and festive that night. Brian caught some lobsters for me, and Denvers ordered a bottle of a delectable Pouilly-Fouissé to celebrate my first experience with the ten-legged sea crustacean, as well as my first workday. Keyes did not descend. His mournful, poignant, and wonderful music had underscored the dying of the light. I walked in the garden wondering when we two would meet again. I had not long to wait.

The next morning, after learning how to correctly arrange my fingers on the typewriting machine's keys to achieve maximum efficiency and speed, I visited Library I to sort through the books in Case A. I found a silk-bound third volume of Mozart's letters. Obviously a refugee from MR. Should I make a pile? I looked around at the piles already made.

The music room is one of the loveliest rooms in Gaywyck. It is as large as the main parlor downstairs, but painted the palest gamboge. Empty of furniture, except for three enormous mirrors, two pianos, two harpsichords, and one dozen matched Chippendale straight-back chairs, it is dominated by the Botticelli Madonna who is reflected in the mirrors alone, like the morning star. One portion of a long wall is a bookcase stuffed with bound volumes and loose sheet music. I opened the heavy white drapes; the sunlight flooded in and reflected off mirrors and crystal chandelier. I began searching for Mozart I and II. My concentration was soon broken by three sharp sentences.

"So you're the culprit! *You* took the third volume! Who are you, anyway?"

I answered rather quickly, considering my fright at his silent and sudden approach. I was relieved to see him wearing teeth. In the sunlight, with birds singing and the drapes fluttering in the breeze, it was difficult to imagine anything menacing about the plainly dressed old man.

"I'm Robert Whyte, sir."

"And what's that when it's at home?"

"Robert Whyte, sir? It's . . . I'm the librarian."

"Yes? Well! Do your friends call you bob*white*? Sweet!"

"No, sir," I answered softly, trying not to grimace.

"Do you play the piano?"

"No, sir."

"Shall I teach you?"

"Oh, yes, sir, *please*!"

And so, my lessons with Keyes began. Every morning after practicing one hour on the typewriting machine, I reported to the music room with limbered fingers. The time spent with him was of indeterminate length, some mornings twenty minutes, some mornings three hours, depending on his whim. A piano appeared in my sitting room after my first lesson; I practiced my scales and the

Chopin ballad for an hour after lunch and an hour before dinner, unless Keyes was playing, in which case, with heightened awareness, I would sit on the portico or stroll in the garden below his windows. He played fewer and fewer evenings during this period, and regularly joined us for dinner, completing our threesome. With him present, some of the meals were actually boisterous! After a glass of wine, he developed a raucous laugh. At our first meal together, when Denvers teased him about his interest in me, he retorted, " 'Young men of intelligence and character are a source of delight to thoughtful and perceptive old men; age is much less burdensome to those who enjoy the affections of the young.' "

I wasn't surprised. He reminded me of Cicero. When I placed the quotation, he sighed happily and lectured me on the importance of an education. He reminded me of Polonius as well. He was a perfect foil for Denvers. I was pleased to be in their company.

The rhythm of my days continued unbroken until the end of the month, when Donough Gaylord appeared, announced in my sitting room by a large case that I found upon returning from a long walk after tea. The case contained a formal evening suit and a note from Ambrose asking that I be ready by 7:30 for him to assist me with my dressing. I bathed and waited excitedly. At precisely 7:30 he knocked. He brought with him a tiny, beautifully wrapped box which he said was a gift from Denvers.

"What is it?"

" 'Ow should I know? Open it, for Gawd's sake! My guess is scent. What else could it be in that tiny a box? Never use the stuff myself. See? What did I just say! Open the stopper and let's 'ave a whiff. Ummmm. Nice. If you ever get a package from Keyes, toss it out the nearest window."

After trimming my hair and shaving my neck, he insisted I remove my cotton undergarments to wear the silk monogrammed set from the case. He helped me into the starched white shirt, and attached the collar, using pearl studs also found inside the traveling case. He tied my tie, held my trousers so I could step into them without bending my shirtfront, and effortlessly changed my socks when he noticed I wasn't wearing the proper silk hose. Then he stood me in front of the mirror. After brushing my hair straight back from my forehead, he put a dab of scent on my neck and a touch on top of my head.

"You smell good enough without this, mind you, but it's the icin' on the cake, so to speak. It's like Mr. Donough's, only milder. Must be careful with it. Don't want to appear tarty. You're all set, my boy. They're collecting on the lawn before din, and I'm serving the befores. Big night tonight: the master's thirty-one!"

"Today's his birthday?"

"Fumes from that bit of scent gone to your brain? Didn't I just say today 'e's thirty-one?"

"Yes, yes, you did, Ambrose. I am sorry. It's all this excitement. No one's ever helped me get dressed before."

"All right, then. Go down to the back lawn, now. I expect they're all waiting to get a good look at you. And you're well worth the wait, if I do say so myself."

He left me to my image in the mirror. From the tips of my new black patent-leather pumps to the top of my slightly scented head, I looked immaculate, freshly minted, fine. In the weeks I'd been at Gaywyck, the black circles had vanished from under my eyes, and hours in the sun had lightened my hair while coloring my skin to a healthy sanguine tone. My face had grown fuller, and I thought I could detect a slight shadow on my upper lip. I was pleased with my appearance and honestly startled by how elegant and gentlemanly I looked.

If only Mama could see me tonight, I thought as I turned from my reflection.

Instead of going down to the lawn directly from my rooms, I went out to the front of the house.

That morning I had admired a late-flowering white rose-bush. Selecting the most perfect bud, I broke it off from the stem to give to Donough Gaylord. He stood talking to Denvers and Keyes; Cael sat at his right foot. When I appeared, rose in hand, they all stopped talking. I approached him and presented the flower. He thanked me and, after pinning it to his lapel with a pearl stickpin, he shook my hand.

"I didn't expect you from that direction, Robert. You looked like an apparition. You quite startled me."

The night was warm. A mist was rolling in off the sea. I found the heavy, smokelike vapor mysterious and exciting. It curled around us, linking us even after he released my hand. He seemed larger than I remembered.

"You look *vrai chic* . . . very presentable in that outfit, Robert."

I thanked him for my new clothes. His eyes were a paler gray than I remembered.

"I hope everything is well with you, Robert."

"Everything is perfect, Mr. Donough, perfect."

Denvers handed me a glass of cold champagne, addressing me as "*der Rosenkavalier.*"

"Happy birthday, Mr. Donough!" I toasted.

"I could not have done it better myself," Keyes applauded.

As we walked in to dinner, I noticed his hair was longer in the back and he was wearing sideburns.

"That's why you look different! You've grown your hair."

"You are observant, Robert. Do you like my sideburns?"

"When I was a gallant," interjected Keyes, "they were the fashion; then they were no longer the fashion. Have they returned *à la mode*, dear Donough?"

"I've no idea, Keyes. Perhaps I'll grow a beard again."

"I'd like to see you with a beard."

"Would you, Robert? I had one in Paris. When I came home, Denvers pleaded with me to take it off."

"Why?"

"Because he looked like a bear, that's why."

"My father always wore one."

"I remember, too, dear Donough. You looked like a wild man! It was thrilling, but very Cormack."

"Shut up, Keyes," Denvers snapped, "and have more champagne."

"That's actually the reason I removed it. It made me look like someone else."

"But, dear," Keyes jibed, "you were twins. He looked just like you."

"I never thought so."

"Neither did I," said Denvers. "Robert, you were born to wear that suit."

"I, for one, dear, could never tell you two apart. No one could, *really*, until he thought up the rings, and even then I had my doubts every once in a while."

"Robert, hearing you practice that ballad each morning does bring back memories! Wait until you hear him, Donough. Fingers, you still use the same teaching methods, I notice."

"I know you're changing the subject, Denvers, even

without your using that ridiculous cognomen, and I assure you it's agreeable to me. I'm as pleased as the rest of you that he's gone, but it's *his* birthday, too, tonight. He would have been thirty-one, as well, had he lived. . . . Forgive me, dear, but he must be in your mind tonight, or am I wrong and speaking out of turn *yet again*?"

"No. You're right. Of course he's on my mind."

"Wouldn't it be better to talk about these things?" I asked.

"Isn't he beautiful, gentlemen?" asked Keyes.

"Here's to beauty and truth!" toasted Denvers.

"Beauty and truth!" we shouted too lustily.

The main dining room was gorgeously arrayed. When I took my place, I was afraid I wouldn't know what to do with all the cutlery and china and crystal in front of me. Ambrose poured more champagne. My worries faded as dinner was served; the table was so large and everyone so distant from me that no one would be able to see what piece of silver I was using, if any. I wanted to continue the conversation about Cormack, but they had gone on to other subjects. I was disappointed, but I sensed we had moved a step closer to the heart of the matter. I sensed wrongly. It was becoming a habit.

Another tradition: we were served champagne throughout the meal. Donough Gaylord explained apologetically that it was the wrong wine for the meal but it always had been and they all agreed it probably always would be. From my first sip, I loved the taste of it and I drank more than I should have, but I came to that realization far too late. Suddenly everything was "glorious," and everything had to be toasted. At one point I spilled some wine on my new jacket, and I'm told (by Denvers) that I behaved as if I'd been stabbed: howling for assistance.

Then I became so riotously jolly that I declared it the best birthday I'd ever had, at which point a witty toast was made (by Keyes) that I found the funniest thing I'd ever heard and laughed tempestuously. My champagne glass was confiscated and I was ordered (by Mr. Donough) to clean my plate. I ate so much food he became concerned for me, until Denvers assured him I was still a growing boy ("that miracle of digestion occurs every night") and that the wine would do no harm.

To my great chagrin (and everyone else's amusement),

after the lavish cake was brought in and we all completed a round of "Happy Birthday to You," I fell asleep at the table! I remember thinking that I felt strangely tired, that the singing had mysteriously exhausted me, when Donough Gaylord was standing beside me, and I was the center of attention, instead of the cake.

"Wuzza matter?"

"Nothing's the matter. It's past your bedtime."

"Party over?"

"Yes, for now."

"I had a wonderful time. Thank you for inviting me."

"You're welcome. You must come again next year."

"Oh! Thank you! I'd like that!"

"So would I. Come, now; I'll help you upstairs."

"No! That is *not* necessary! I'm a little tired, but I'm fine."

I stood. I sat. "I think, maybe, I *could* use a little help. Thank you, sir."

He helped me to my feet. Standing, I tried to bow good night to my fellow guests, lost my balance, and nearly fell into the cake. Fortunately, he caught me.

"I don't know what's wrong with me," I mumbled, stalling on the landing under the oval window, unable to move my foot up to the next step.

"You're fine, Robert. You drank a little too much champagne tonight, that's all. Nothing to worry about."

"You mean I'm *drunk*?"

"Yes, you could say that."

"*This* is drunk?"

"Yup."

"I like it."

"I was afraid you were going to say that."

At that moment, the moon, full and enormous, came out from behind some clouds as if to bear witness to my happiness.

"Hi, there, moon!"

"Robert, turn around and lift your feet."

"Moon, I love you. Donough, Mr. Donough, have you ever seen such a beautiful moon?"

Then a miracle occurred: I began to fly! I levitated, turned, and slowly floated up the stairs.

"My God! I'm flying!"

"No you're not. I'm carrying you."

"I love you."

We stood still. Halfway up the staircase, looking into my eyes, smiling, Donough Gaylord paused.

"I love you, Mr. Donough."

"Me and the moon?"

"Yes. You and the moon. And Cael."

He continued smiling as he carried me up the stairs with my head resting on his shoulder and my right arm flung around his neck. Impulsively I kissed him on his warm right cheek.

"I love you more than the moon," I whispered, "and even more than Cael."

When I awoke, I was in my bed. My head felt furry, and my tongue swollen. I thought I'd slept for several days. It was night again. The Fabergé clock chimed 1:30. I sat up. I was wearing my nightshirt. I tried to remember how the party ended, but I couldn't, until suddenly, I did.

"Good Lord! I kissed Donough Gaylord!"

My heart, yet again, had run ahead of me. I did not want to know.

I walked out through the drapes onto the portico. I felt myself careening into shame, swooning into horror-filled agony.

I'm not up to any of it, I thought, taking deep breaths and counting to ten.

The stars seemed so close, I wanted to grab them the way I'd handled the precious stones in Donough Gaylord's study, and let them slip through my fingers into the sea. To distract myself from the feelings I still wanted to deny, I forced myself down to the lawn, then down to the yew trees on the rise. There was a battle raging within me, but I wanted no part of it.

As though sucked into a vacuum, thought ceased. I stood breathless, adrift outside time, staring at the sight below: Donough Gaylord, clothed in luminous moonlight, rose from the sea. The water opened, revealing him to me. He rose with a fiery brightness discharging light into the universe. When he tossed his head, a galaxy of stars exploded. Stepping toward me through the glistening foam, he lifted his firm legs high; bending his tightly muscled knees, he walked through dilating space.

Cael, running along the shore, distracted me. When I looked back, Donough Gaylord was chasing the cat. Both soon disappeared beyond the jetty.

Like an afterimage of the too-bright sun, he, rising, accompanied me across the lawn and up to my room. I felt recklessly alive. The battle raging inside me had been won. He had conquered me, bringing terror to my heart as all angels do. To deny any longer my love for him would have been an evil.

To say I dreamed of him is an understatement. That night, he came to dwell in my soul.

Nine

THE MORNING AFTER THE BIRTHDAY party, I was torn from restless sleep by wailing outside my windows. The voices, sharp and violent, merged with my dream of a funeral, where a field full of people mourned aloud, swaying like tall weeds in a fierce wind.

When I pulled the drapes open, a flock of enormous long-winged gray-and-white birds was revealed wheeling and diving and circling overhead. I had seen these birds from the ferry crossing to Manhattan Island. It was their keening that sounded in my ears.

I stepped out onto the portico to get a closer look; several, perching on the balustrade, calmly turned their mottled brown heads askew to examine me. In the garden below, Donough Gaylord was the still center of the birds' activity. Wrapped in a white robe, he stood feeding the squalling tribe, all the while chatting to them, his baritone voice rising and falling amidst their calls.

"Robert, good morning! Come help me feed them."

"What are they called?"

"Gulls. Seagulls. On a visit from the port."

"What are you feeding them?"

"Bread. They eat anything but lettuce, fruit, and onions."

"How do you know that?"

"I once had several for pets. Come join me."

I dressed quickly and went down to the garden. There were dozens of gulls. The bread we threw to them was still warm.

"Is this our breakfast bread?"

"Yup. I used up all the other."

I started feeding the bread to myself.

"How do you feel this gorgeous morning, Robert?"

"Hungry and tired and ashamed, all at once."

"Ashamed? Why on earth ashamed?"

"I disgraced myself last night."

"Nonsense! That's what birthdays are for."

"But it was *your* birthday!"

I hadn't planned to say anything. I thought I'd slip away from them before tea and nap; until then, I'd hoped to smile a lot and keep my mouth tightly closed. But, standing beside him in the morning sunlight, receiving his smiles and the bread from his outstretched hands, watching the wind ruffle his hair and billow the robe he wore, I was overcome with guilt for having violated his nocturnal solitude. My heart pressed inward from the chaotic euphoria. I fastened on the seemingly obvious cause for my uneasiness.

"I made a fool of myself, Mr. Donough."

"Nonsense! Anyone who doesn't get kite-high on his first encounter with champagne is the fool. Be grateful you have such a small capacity. Let's hear no more about it!"

I began to thank him and career into a lengthy speech about him always having to forgive me, when Denvers appeared, sparing us both. He had some white garments thrown over his arm.

"Stop feeding those goddamned birds, you two," he shouted. "They'll be coming around every day again screaming for food. They nearly killed us the last time, bouncing their whelks and mollusks off our heads and smashing them into our teacups."

"They're visiting Mr. Donough!"

"Yes! I can see their calling cards all over the lawn, and on the hem of his caftan. Tell them to go home now, Donough, please! It's time for *our* breakfast. What a dreadful day! Brian's in a state; his bread's disappeared. Oh, God! Donough! You haven't given those monogamous aviary horrors our bread? How could you? Is that the thanks I get for ferreting out these shirts of yours? Where's Cael?"

"Cael is busy hiding in the library pretending to be asleep."

"Cael! Come out here and eat these gulls. Here, Robert, these tunics are for you."

"If he wants them."

"Want them? Yes, please, I want them! They're wonderful."

He handed me the belted shirts: four, all white with extraordinary embroidery on the fronts—one design in blue, one maroon, and two white-on-white.

"Denvers thought they'd suit you, Robert. Thank you, Denvers. What would one do without you?"

"I'm sure I can't imagine!"

I asked to be excused, and ran to my room to put on one of the new shirts. They were of the softest fabric and featured only two buttons on the right shoulder. I chose the maroon embroidery with its intertwined wild flowers and butterflies.

"A perfect fit!" Denvers exclaimed as I took my place at table on the patio. "What good luck! I'm pleased something is going right this morning. You quite resemble a Russian aristocrat; a Georgian, I'd say. Wouldn't you, Donough?"

"What's Georgian?" asked Keyes as he appeared around the hawthorn hedge. "Certainly not our morning visitors! I'd know their young, healthy American voices anywhere; once heard, never forgotten! I thought I was in a Roman piazza! Why are you rudely gaping at me, dears? For Donough I'm always down to breakfast."

He took his seat and only then noticed my new shirt.

"Goodness! Where did you find that?"

Before anyone replied, Brian walked through the door carrying fresh rolls. He looked preoccupied until he saw my shirt; then he started as though pinched, dropped the silver plate, groaned, and dashed back into the house.

"What's wrong?" I pleaded, flabbergasted.

"It's Cormack's shirt," Keyes started to explain, when Donough, annoyed, interrupted.

"That's absurd! Nothing is Cormack's anymore! They are *my* shirts and I want Robbie to have them."

Startled, I looked at him. He had never called me Robbie before. My family always called me Robbie; how would he know that? A feeling of intimacy pierced me, as though he'd gently stroked my face or kissed me on the forehead.

"It's hunky-dory with me, dear," Keyes continued, unruffled. "But please explain that to Brian."

"He's probably hiding in the stillroom among the pickles and the fruitcake. Would you prefer me to go, Donough? The shirts *were* my idea."

"No, thank you, Denvers. I'll go and try to put an end to this nonsense once and for all."

"Well, hurry back, dear, before the eggs congeal."

Donough exited. We remaining three sat in silence. Denvers frequently glanced upward, nervously expecting something unpleasant to drop into our midst.

"Do you remember—?" he began, but Keyes, sighing, interrupted.

"Denvers, be a dear! Retrieve those rolls from the ground and pass me one before those feathered vertebrates convene a raiding party. Isn't there some Mediterranean adage connecting dropped breads with ill fortune?"

"More than likely, Keyes, more than likely. What a heinous morn!"

It was quite a while before Donough returned. When he did, he assured us quietly that all had been "sorted out." No one questioned him. No one seemed surprised or relieved. That he should take care of everything seemed the natural order of things. I blindly followed their lead.

After breakfast, he invited me to go horseback riding. The horses were stabled on the far side of the cottage; as we passed the deserted house, I told him how much it attracted me. He offered to take me through it after lunch, and then to take me boating on the pond.

We rode the horses westward along the beach while farm workers collected seaweed to fertilize the fields.

"It always saddens me to see that," he said. "It's proof that summer is over."

We rode in and out of the surf, passing the main house, the jetty, and beyond the white oaks, the boathouse where the steam yacht and sailboats were secured. He talked of summer outings to his neighbors', the Gardeners, who lived on an island in the bay, and even projected a trip for the following spring to his own island, Key Gaylord, off the coast of Florida. I was content riding beside him, listening to him happily planning our lives.

"Could we reach the New York ferry by riding along this shore?"

"Yes, with a little help from a bridge or two. If we were riding toward Sterling Harbor, now, we would reach the end of the island before lunch."

"Life is wonderful!" I said, musing aloud.

"When it is pure and whole, yes."

"And when is it not whole?"

"When it's shattered beyond repair."

"It's never beyond repair."

"You're very young."

So are you, I thought.

"Oh?" I said.

I glanced at his face. He was staring straight ahead. We rode in complete silence. I found great solace in his comradeship.

"I mean," he said, "you're very innocent."

"As you are," I whispered.

He snorted, cantering ahead. I caught up with him, then hurried by at a fast trot. I had never ridden for pleasure before; galloping along the sea's edge magnified the sense of exhilaration and freedom. When the breeze quickened, turning the capped waves one upon another, flinging the spray into our paths, we gamboled back toward the stable, pausing at the cove just behind the cottage to watch the osprey feed. He took as much delight in their skills as I; he called them by another name, fish hawk, and told me that, unlike the gulls, they could never be tamed.

"They won't trust, and always keep their distance. They're quite wary of humans."

As you are, I thought, and as I was. . . .

Eager to explore the cottage, I hurried us through lunch. There was something about the place that intrigued me— the romantic connotations of large, empty houses with a prevailing aura of sadness over lost opportunities. But since no lives had been shared there, it seemed aglow with possibilities of promises yet to be exchanged. When I attempted to explain to the others, they grew perplexed, and I fell silent until apples and cheddar were served for dessert.

"No pastry from Brian or Monsieur Henri!"

"Don't be disconsolate, dear! There *are* worse fates than apples and cheddar."

Donough laughed. Denvers consoled.

"M. Henri is sound asleep. He abhors the country and has difficulty sleeping at night; the quiet unnerves him. Mr. O'Shay does breakfast and lunch for us. Brian has vanished."

"Vanished?"

"Yes, but not to worry. It happens now and again."

I wished to pursue the subject, but I noticed a flush suffuse Donough's face. I suggested we pocket the apples and leave for the cottage.

"Don't get too dirty, boys," Denvers called after us. "That place hasn't been cleaned in years."

From the moment Donough unlocked the front door, I wanted to live there. I hadn't seen any of it, but I *knew*. The oak door was built to human scale, *my* human scale; and the lock sounded softly, echoing inward, announcing our arrival. This was a house that could easily become a home, I thought as I crossed the small foyer to look up the curving wooden staircase.

"Who was the last person to live here?"

"I was."

"You were? When did you live here?"

"Before I left for Paris."

"I thought you left for Paris immediately after . . ."

"No, not immediately. I lived here before the fire, too."

There is so much I must learn about you, I thought, frowning.

He moved into the room to the right of the foyer; I followed. White sheets covered everything.

"The library," he said, raising both arms. "This way to the dining room, please."

"Uh-oh!" I moaned. "Something tells me this is going to be very quick."

"Quick, but exemplary! The tiles in this foyer are from Liverpool. The chandelier is Waterford. Notice the wainscoting, please: oak."

He slid open the double doors to the left of the foyer, crossed the music room, and disappeared into the dining room. I did not follow. I stood gazing out the windows at the pond and the towering trees at its far end. The four swans looked carved from alabaster. Early-afternoon light warmed every corner of the room.

"We await your presence in the dining room, Master Whyte!"

I went toward him, but stopped in the doorway. The elm tree, ancient and massive, grew directly outside. It filled the window. I told him I would live in the house just to be near the tree.

"It's a wych elm, very special and rare in this part of the world. The Indians revered it. There are legends attached to that tree. No one knows how my grandfather convinced the Indians to leave their sacred elm. When I was a child, they camped during each solstice, praying to lift the curse."

" 'No happiness here until the blind shall see,' " I recited respectfully.

"We Gaylords are a doomed race. Our history bears it out."

"Perhaps you *were* but are no longer? Perhaps the prophecy's been played out?" I offered, thinking: If not, *I* will end it.

"Fate *is*. Mine's disastrous." He smiled.

"Love *is*," I said boldly. "Love works miracles."

"That kind of love exists only in novels."

"Art imitates life."

"Don't confuse the two. Let's go upstairs."

The room above took advantage of the tree's breadth. A narrow balcony thrust us into its center.

"If I lived here, Mr. Donough, this would be my bedroom. I'd wake in the morning to the sound of leaves, and in the fall watch them defoliate. You look shocked. Do I sound mad?"

"When I lived here, this room was my bedroom. Everyone thought *me* mad."

"Great minds, et cetera," I said.

Great hearts, ditto, I thought.

The third floor, he had used as his study.

"Did you keep servants with you?"

"No. I cooked and kept house for myself."

"And your brother?"

"He'd visit."

"This was your Walden."

"I often thought that."

I wanted to go into the attic above to view the tree from overhead, but he nervously cautioned it was unsafe.

"If you're with me, Mr. Donough, what danger is there?"

"I'm touched by your faith, Robbie, but it's structurally unsound."

"Someone may want to live in here someday." I paused, then added, "For instance *me*. We librarians *require* a certain solitude. You know, stealing from the farm, a Whitman could write poems here forever, undetected!"

What would have happened had we walked up those attic stairs then? Could it have been that simple?

While he was locking the door to deter vagabonds, I remembered the art room and asked for a key.

"Why?"

"I want to work with the art books."

"Don't worry about them."

"But I'd like to see the Turner watercolors, and the butterflies, and your stones!"

"We'll do that tomorrow. No one's been in there for years. I lock it to prevent the staff from damaging anything."

"Uh-huh," I mumbled, annoyed by his not having checked his story with Denvers. Why was he so protective toward Keyes?

He led me behind the cottage along a curving path to a toolshed concealed by overhanging foliage. Inside were gardening implements, and to the rear, folded yellow canvas tents, large striped umbrellas, wooden tables and chairs, cushions, pillows, inflatable toys, and several peculiarly shaped boats and floats.

"And what's *that* when it's at home?" I asked, mimicking Keyes.

"It's a raft."

"Yes, but what's it supposed to *be*?"

"A peanut-butter sandwich," he answered quietly, verging on discomfort. "It was meaningful at the time. My father dabbled heavily in whimsy."

I laughed, honestly delighted. "I think it's delicious!"

He moaned and relaxed, laughing along with me. He had so many sensitive areas; I hoped I would always find them so easily detectable. We dislodged a small round wooden craft that had to be emptied of pails, balls, shovels, sand molds, and various other children's toys.

"What a bizarre-looking boat! It looks like a walnut shell."

"That's exactly what it is. The other half is in here somewhere. Cormack and I each had half a shell. We grew up confusing the world with this boat. Whimsy can be a dangerous thing."

"It's a lovely little boat."

"I'd forgotten all about it."

We carried the boat effortlessly and eased it into the water. The swans swam over to investigate. Dragonflies darted and hung suspended. Yellow flag iris swayed; marsh marigolds bobbed; and the ripples disturbed the pickerel weeds and the myriad water lilies. He stepped in first, then helped me aboard. Under the "ribs" we located and detached the small paddles.

"I feel . . . *enchanted* floating in this thing. What's it made of?"

"Walnut."

"Why did I ask?"

"Okay, if this makes you feel enchanted, we must have a float in the halved watermelon."

I laughed loudly, and spontaneously clapped my hands together.

"There's a rowboat for the entire family decorated in the form of half a watermelon, with its alternate slices removed. The hull is bright green, and one sits on the remaining pink sections on oval black cushions that look like seeds. It was Nanny Welles's favorite 'silly.' It would make her laugh as nothing else could. I used to love to ride in it with her."

He fell silent and stopped rowing, lifting the dripping oars out of the water. We drifted near the still center of the tiny lake. A skein of geese in migratory formation flew overhead. To my left, I spotted Brian emerging from the trees at the far edge of the water. I waved to him. He did not respond. When Donough waved, calling a greeting, he stopped walking; after a long pause, reluctantly, he lifted his right arm before disappearing in the direction of the beach.

"He's going to the mud flats."

"What for?"

"After the tide leaves, it's great fun to flop and slide in the 'primordial ooze,' as Cormack called it. It's a good place to be alone. In the summer, there's a forest of sunflowers along one side. Some of them grow to over six feet in height; one can vanish safely and comfortably among them."

I looked after Brian. Cael sat on the bank watching us.

"Mr. Donough," I began cautiously, "was Cormack responsible for Brian's accident?"

He began rowing again. I trailed my hand in the water, touching the water lilies as we moved by them. I was sorry I hadn't waited to ask Denvers, but there was something about the mood in the boat, the rapport between the two of us, that told me the question was acceptable at that moment.

"What makes you think that?"

"The way he reacted to this shirt this morning. One need not be Holmes to deduce—"

"It was thoughtless of me to have allowed Denvers to give you that shirt." He stopped rowing. We drifted again, this time toward the shore. "It suddenly brought my brother's presence back into the house."

"Is that so terrible?"

"The night we met, you asked me if my dreams are disturbed by him. Yes they are. He's been dead thirteen years, and I'm not the only one still haunted by him. He was cursed with a violent temper which he never controlled. That's not fair. I shouldn't say that. He tried. He just didn't succeed very often. Everyone has suffered because of it. He was in a horrible boating accident with Brian; the boy hasn't spoken a clear word since. Denvers is cruelly maimed. Keyes is a broken man. Cormack left us empty creatures. It's as if we, too, are made of walnut. . . ."

The boat reached the shore. We disembarked.

As we approached the house, Taio ran to meet us. He handed Donough a message. I was remarking how pleased I was to see him again, when a gasp from our mutual employer interrupted the exchange.

"What is it?" I asked.

"An employee of mine has been brutally murdered! Taio, pack my bags; we'll be leaving tonight. Send Joshua to the stable; we'll need a carriage. I'll wire for the train immediately. We'll have to send Lonnie for Mr. O'Shay. Excuse me, Robert. I've a great deal to do before I can leave. Taio, tell Henri I'll take tea upstairs."

With that order, he walked quickly toward the house. Pausing to search his vest pockets, he turned and threw some keys to Taio. "For the cases," he called over his shoulder, disappearing through the open library windows. Seeing the keys change hands reminded me of the locked art room. When I ran after him, catching him in the foyer, he bade me follow.

In his room, from the center drawer of his desk, he produced a large ring of keys. He detached one and handed it to me.

"The watercolors are in the large cabinet behind the door. Take the entire Turner portfolio in the top tray. Take the Girtin portfolio, too, the *Panorama* series; they're worth studying. And take the Cotman, *and* the Veronese. And the Sandbys. I'd love to go through them with you, but I can't. Never mind; next time. Take whatever you want. They're *all* in the cabinet with the narrow drawers behind the door."

The telegraph machine on the desk began clicking, printing a message on a strip of paper that unwound from a roll somewhere within. I turned to leave. M. Henri nearly trampled me into the carpet. He was enraged that his special birthday tea was not being treated with the proper respect ("Business, *always* business; why not business afterward?"). Then Denvers appeared, pale and shaking ("Is it true about Jones?"), trailed by Keyes in tears ("So soon, dear, why so *soon*?").

Joshua ran in to report the horses ready. Lonnie, cape in hand, inquired whether Mr. O'Shay was required that evening. Ambrose stood in the doorway to announce the hour for tea arrived, and to ask whether or not Mr. Lewison and his son were to receive instructions for the roses or were they to spend the night in the sunroom leering and snickering over "that filthy faun."

Calmly Mr. Donough answered each question. Yes, he would go down to tea. Yes, Jones was dead. ("Murdered?" "Yes, strangled and dumped in the East River.") Yes, he was leaving too soon, but would return for Thanksgiving ("perhaps").

"Good, Joshua, thank you. Ten o'clock will be fine."

Yes, Mr. O'Shay would be needed that very evening. Denvers was asked to have Mr. Grouse take care of the Lewisons.

"Come, Robert, let's go down to tea."

My head was revolving. Who were all these people? Why had I never seen or heard of them before? When I met Mr. Harrington and his son in the stable that morning, I was not surprised, but then I'd assumed someone was caring for Frenchie and the other horses.

"They're the staff, Robert. Do you think Gaywyck runs itself?"

I shook my head. Of course not! I knew large houses had servants. I was forever reading articles in magazines about the shortage of good ones. I'd read shelves of novels where their importance was made quite clear. I simply had not *seen* them doing whatever it was they did.

"There are a dozen people below stairs every day. If you should happen across one working somewhere in the house, all you have to do is smile. They won't hurt you."

"I'm sure they won't! It's just strange I haven't seen one of them."

"Not really, Robert. You haven't seen them because they haven't wanted you to; they are trained to be invisible. If it weren't for them, and for Denvers's management, Gaywyck would be uninhabitable."

Tea was an elaborate affair. A field of flowers decorated the patio; a Lyonnaise lace tablecloth under the china and silver and crystal signaled the event. We drank a dry white wine (M. Henri did not approve of tea) and sang another round of "Happy Birthday." None of us was very talkative. Keyes sniffed discreetly. When Donough left, we three remained at table.

"Denvers," I asked, "who was Jones?"

"A business associate, Robert."

"Were they very close?"

"No."

"They were close enough, dear. Not as close as Abel and the late Cain, but close enough—"

"Shut up, Keyes, you are *worse* than an old fishwife!"

"Yet a widow before a wife!"

"If you don't keep still, I'll wedge a pie where your brains ought to be!"

We finished our tea in silence.

The lock on the art-room door stuck. I had to fidget with it before the lock sounded and the door opened. The air inside was heavy. Cobwebs clustered in corners. Against the wall, to my right, stood a great rolltop desk exactly like the one owned by my father. It, like his, must have been assembled in the room, because it could never have been maneuvered through the doorway or the narrow windows. I was amazed to see the desk. I had tremendous affection for the one in my father's study, and had always naively believed it one of a kind. Seeing its twin here in this room surprised me.

Behind the door was the file: a large wooden bureau with a dozen wide, shallow drawers. Each but the bottom drawer was neatly labeled. Each but the bottom drawer was unlocked. Why had someone locked it? What could be more important than the Rembrandt etchings stored in the unlocked drawer above it? As if by reflex, I crossed to the familiar rolltop desk. It rattled open, revealing an identical arrangement of little knobbed drawers that concealed, no doubt, secret places similar to the ones I'd uncovered one spring morning long ago.

I found the key to the file's bottom drawer. I knew immediately in which tiny niche it was secreted.

Instead of returning to the cabinet, I knelt in front of the desk and, out of curiosity, slid open the concealed panel in its right side. It contained two books, each bound in black calf, and wrapped once around with a leather thong. I undid the top knot. Bold black letters leaped from the page: "PRIVATE!"

The word was printed in a child's hand. I turned to the second page.

> BEING HIS *private*
> BOOK
> DONOUGH GAYLORD

I hesitated before turning to the third page.

> ON YOUR HONOR
> IT IS STILL NOT TOO LATE

I turned another page, my heart pounding as I read:

> CORMACK, IF YOU READ THIS,
> I WILL KILL YOU.

I closed the book. It *was* a child's hand. How old was he when he started his diary? I opened it to check the date on the first entry: 4 July 1877. He was seven years old! I read the first entry:

> C STILL SWITCHING RINGS. THEY ARE STUPID NOT
> TO SEE. I WOULD TELL BUT C WOULD KILL ME.
> I WILL TELL IT HERE AND I WILL FEEL BETTER
> LIKE LAST WEEK IN CONFESSION.

I closed the book. Picking up the second volume, I undid the thong and opened it at random. 9 November 1884:

> C VISITING D. AT LEAST HE'S LEAVING ME ALONE.
> I'M ASHAMED BECAUSE I'M JEALOUS AND I MISS
> HIM. JEALOUS OF WHOM? OF BOTH. I HATE THEM

BOTH. D CALLING C BY MY NAME. HE SAYS HE
WILL PUNISH D. IT SCARES ME. I DON'T KNOW
WHAT TO DO.

Two lines from a poem in Latin followed. Catullus. I
translated:

I HATE AND LOVE; ASK HOW? I CANNOT TELL,
BUT I FEEL IT AND I AM TORN IN TWO.

I flicked the pages forward. 18 July 1885:

I TRIED TO DROWN MYSELF LAST NIGHT, BUT
AFRAID, I SWAM ASHORE. I WILL DO IT YET, AND
SOON. I SHOULD HANG MYSELF FROM THE WYCH
ELM, BUT WHY DO SUCH A THING TO MY TREE?

"Fade far away, dissolve, and quite forget
What thou among the leaves hast never known,
The weariness, the fever, and the fret
Here, where men sit and hear each other groan. . . ."

I flicked backward. 3 November 1882:

LAST NIGHT C LET ME BE FATHER. I LIKED IT AS
MUCH AS BEING S. WE AGREED TO TAKE TURNS
BEING FATHER.

I flicked backward to 5 May:

C CUT A HOLE IN THE DRAPES. HE WAS TELLING
THE TRUTH!

I closed the second book and sat on the floor in front
of the desk. If I studied the diaries, I would learn everything I wanted to know about Donough Gaylord. I would
also learn the truth about Cormack. and what had transpired at Gaywyck. But I had no *right* to read his books.
Would I want anyone to read my journals? The mere
thought of anyone—*anyone*—reading my words, invading
my privacy to that extent, made me feel queasy and light-
headed.
Carefully I retied the two books and returned them
to their hiding place. I did the same with the key. I took

the watercolors he had suggested, and went to his rooms to return the art-room key. His door was locked; he did not answer my knock. I returned to my room.

It was a brisk evening; someone had lit a fire for me. I spread the watercolors on the carpet and immediately realized a book was needed if I were to fully understand what lay before me. Hastening back to the art room, pleased the key had not been returned, I found exactly what I wanted with no difficulty. I also found a loose-paged sketchbook entitled *Copies*. It was a record of all the paintings at Gaywyck; each in pen and ink with dabs of oil paint denoting the colors, and information detailing size, peculiar markings (signatures, stamps, damages), date of completion, date of purchase, etc. I took it with me.

Donough did not descend for dinner. He did appear for dessert, however; Henri had worked with Brian on an outrageous concoction, and had threatened hara-kiri if it were not "appreciated." He seemed in good humor though a bit restrained. Champagne was ordered. Henri and Brian were toasted. Again we sang "Happy Birthday." Some good cheer was generated and immediately dispersed when he said good-bye and left us, to wrap up "odds and ends."

"I feel all odds and ends, my dears."

"Have some more champagne."

"*Où sont les neiges d'antan*, my dears?"

"I couldn't agree more! Give me your glass."

I left them when they opened the third bottle. Luggage sat on the foyer landing, ready for the carriage. I wanted to head for the art room to see what was locked in the bottom drawer of the watercolor cabinet just behind the door; instead, I went to my room feeling virtuous and wrote in my journal.

The entries in Donough Gaylord's books had aroused my imagination. One line I logically followed to its bitter conclusion:

> HE SAYS HE WILL PUNISH D. IT SCARES ME. I
> DON'T KNOW WHAT TO DO.

". . . going to punish D . . . punish Denvers . . . punish . . ." No! He couldn't have! *Denvers is maimed*, he had said that just this afternoon. It simply wasn't possible! I refused to believe anything so ghastly.

I put my pen down and once again headed for the art room at a brisk trot. I was willing to violate the sanctity of those two volumes to prove myself wrong.

"Please, God," I whispered as I hurried up the side stairs, "please, God, don't let me be right!"

I did not need the key. The door was unlocked. I opened the secret panel on the side of the desk. The books were gone. I checked the hidden drawer, knowing the outcome; the key had been removed. The bottom drawer of the watercolor cabinet was unlocked and empty.

On my couch, in my room, I tried reading Boswell's *Johnson*, but could not concentrate. Headless bees buzzed in my brain. Taking a collection of Keats from Library I, I walked out into the garden, suddenly beckoned by the sea. Keyes grieved through the "Moonlight Sonata."

Once at the beach, I knew why I had come. On the edge of the jetty, my sea-soaked glistening angel of light, my Donough was poised at the moment of plummeting. In my heart, pandemonium reigned as he soared and fell to the moon-inflamed waves.

Back in my room, with Cael on my lap, I opened the book of Gaylord paintings. They were in alphabetical order. The Rossetti portrait induced a palpable sense that any moment the stars would fall and crush me to dust. It was the image of my mother! I hugged Cael.

"Love is my strength. Love is my only defense," I whispered blindly.

Love was my greatest enemy.

Ten

IMMEDIATELY FOLLOWING HIS DEPARTURE, I spent the days alone in meditation, attempting to manage the feelings that attended this access of love. My will to succeed kindled the desire to understand, and fastened a leash of longing that led to reliving shared moments, paring them to their essential truths.

I had pressed myself to seek and find a friend. A great cloud of unknowing had been lifted. I knew the more accustomed I grew to this mystical surrender of will, the more fully whole I would become. I was beginning to see the difference between self-interest and self-love: the former is the death of the soul, the latter the way to loving another. "I long for no other treasure but love, for it alone can make us pleasing to God," I read in Saint Thérèse of Lisieux's autobiography. I bade myself look forward and let past time be. But that was easier said than done.

About this time, nightmares again tormented me. I frequently collapsed into bed after dinner, barely able to remove my clothing, only to awaken in blackest night from horrifying images involving the loss of my vision. Blunt and sharp instruments gouged out my eyes. But always by accident: a tree branch snapped back by an unknown hand. "Oh, God, not again!" I would moan before being wrenched from sleep by my own screams. The toll was a heavy one. I would feel out of focus the entire next day, as though I'd overindulged in champagne the previous evening, and the absence of rest exacerbated minor tensions. I never connected the dreams with the liquid in my bedside water jug. I had no reason to. . . .

A letter arrived from my father. It was short and direct: he wanted me to write my mother, who was still lost in the abyss of her mysterious depression; he thought a letter from me might have some therapeutic effect. He enclosed her new address. She had been moved to another hospital.

I was ashamed for having forgotten her. Oh, she was
ever-present in my heart, but she was of another world;
the idea of writing a letter had never occurred to me,
fascinated as I was by the newly discovered science of love.
I sat down immediately after breakfast and began: "Dearest Mama," but could go no further than that. I had never
written to her before. What was I to say? I went out for
a walk.

Off the avenue of lindens, toward the sea, there is a
sunken garden. Down three stone steps is a small circular
clearing in the woods, a hollow, connected to the beach
by a narrow tunnel through the trees and tall underbrush.
At the center of the hollow is a druid's dolmen from Con-
nemara. I sat contemplating the autumnal tints; the wych
hazel was still a distance from the quince color it would
achieve.

Everything around me is changing, I thought. How
could I expect to remain the same?

I opened my writing pad and began:

Dearest Mama,
    I am having the greatest adventure of my life.
I am making a friend. I have wanted to write to you
often, but I could never decide where to begin.
Today, I'll begin at the beginning. . . .

I described the house and the gardens in detail. It was
an optimistic letter, with all the shadows excised; she had
enough of her own. I was quite pleased with it. I read and
reread it, delighted I was able to express succinctly much
of what I was feeling. I enclosed a white spider mum, one
of our favorite flowers.

At luncheon, I asked Denvers how to post the letter.
He explained that Ambrose was responsible for the mail
pouch, making certain it reached the gatehouse every
morning in time to be collected. I had missed that day's
run; he suggested I take advantage of the beautiful afternoon and deliver it to town myself. If I rode along the
main carriage path, turning left at the gatehouse, I could
ride through the park to the heart of town.

"How do I get out of the park?"

"There's a second gatehouse near the farm, operated
by Saunders. The post office is directly opposite the
bound tree."

"The bound tree?"

"An ancient oak that once marked the parish boundary. It's the only tree left on the wharf. Have you never heard of bound trees? No? And you a country boy, too! Good Lord! Soon there will be nothing left of our heritage."

I was delighted with the prospect of a long, solitary ride. I changed into the old boots I used for riding and walked to the stable, where I politely requested Anita. Mr. Harrington was pleased I would be exercising the mare; his son had twisted an ankle playing with Cael.

The puss does gad about, I thought as I trotted down the curved path toward the carriageway.

The letter weighed heavily in my pocket. Had I been too glib? Had I placed myself too securely at the center of Gaywyck, aggrandizing my position as librarian by painting myself companion to the lord of the manor? Good Lord! Taking it from my pocket, I tore it in half and threw it into the undergrowth. I felt rage coming. Reining in the horse, I turned her back to the stable, determined to compose a more sensible missive. It took minutes for me to regret my hasty actions. There were several perfectly acceptable paragraphs that would be more than adequate. I need not include everything the first time I wrote.

I went back to collect it. The letter was not to be found! Up and down that path I rode, at one point dismounting to cover the area by foot. My foolishly romantic letter had mysteriously disappeared.

When I got back to the stable, I assured Mr. Harrington that I hadn't ridden at a frenzied gallop but had stupidly lost the letter and planned to write another, which I promptly did. Retracing my way on docile Anita, eyes raking the underbrush, I nearly rode over the object of my search. The epistle lay in the middle of the path. There was no wind strong enough to have carried it. There was no way it could have rolled or slithered of its own volition. Yet, there it was, in the center of the trail. And, stranger still, it looked mended. The two portions were side by side, forming a perfect packet. I dismounted only long enough to retrieve my property. The mum I had enclosed was missing. I was flabbergasted at the idea of someone—*anyone*—perusing that ridiculous emotional disclosure. I saw myself reading Donough Gaylord's journal and cringed, causing Anita to quicken her pace. Who would remove the flower? Had it fallen from the torn letter when the kind soul who retrieved it had put it in the path of someone going toward the house?

I put it out of my mind. The day was brilliantly clear and cool. Indian summer seemed on the decline. I studied the trees. I listened to the birds. I sang. I talked to the mare, who flicked her ears to let me know she appreciated the attention.

In the distance, where the path veered leftward, I could see the gatehouse. Somewhere, a cow coughed. Overhead, somber clouds banked.

At the honeysuckle-covered (smaller) gatehouse, a hulking elderly man introduced himself. Saunders seemed to know all about me. We discussed the weather; then he called his wife to meet me. After we exchanged greetings, she asked if I had noticed anything "peculiar" or "out of the way" on my ride through the park.

"The missus means, Whyte, did you see any ghosts!"

I shook my head solemnly. I believe in ghosts. I also believe that if I'd passed a ghost, I'd know.

"The missus swears there's ghosts in the park. I tell her it's the poachers, but she don't believe me. Let her have ghosts, I say, if it makes her happy."

"Poachers don't steal pies, Gregory, and you know it."

"Poachers steal anything they have a mind to! And your pies are pretty special, missus. Everyone in the village knows it. Don't you got something to do in the house?"

"Good day, Mr. Whyte. Ride careful, and take good care of Anita."

There you are, I thought. Ghosts!

I was jesting, but was closer to the truth than I realized.

The port, according to Denvers, had originally been settled in 1641 by English Puritans who colonized Long Island because Massachusetts was becoming too populous and too licentious. They purchased the land from the agent of the Earl of Sterling, and in his honor called it Sterling Harbor. After bartering with the Indians (sixteen "coates" and sixty bushels of corn), they built their dugouts and planted crops of hay, oats, and corn in fields fertilized with fish, in the Indian manner.

In the beginning, all the men were farmers, fishermen, and soldiers at once, but as the years passed, Sterling Harbor became a whaling port of some reknown. To its future regret, others were allowed to acquire lucrative

import connections with the West Indies that would have
maintained Sterling Harbor's prosperity when the whaling
industry died as the whales departed for safer waters.

The village of one hundred and twenty souls was transformed into a poor fishing port long before the great
storm of 1845 destroyed its harbor structures, the boats,
and every piece of net in the area. Grandfather Gaylord
rebuilt and replaced everything. He lent the capital, charg-
ing a token interest so the proud villagers would not scorn
his offer as charity.

To show their collective gratitude, they renamed the
Meigs Tavern, Gaylord's Inn. Grandfather Gaylord was
very pleased and never informed them that their local
bank, which for years bought land and foreclosed on
scores of outstanding mortgages, was owned by himself.
Unknowingly, the village had placed Gaylord's name on
his own property. He offered his railroad to transport
their (his) fish, clams, oysters, lobsters, and scallops. By
means of judicious management, he kept the now prosper-
ous village a limited but profitable investment.

Donough's Lane, the main street, follows the plan of
the original Pond Road of 1645. Circling the pond, it
runs through the center of the village and stops just short
of the harbor. Several yards beyond the pond, the ancient
gnarled oak grows imperiously, encircled by carefully
tended flower beds in a tiny green of its own. To the right
is the post office. Next to it is the shop of Thomas Adams,
Esquire, Cordwainer. The sign intrigued me.

Mr. Adams, a shoe- and bootmaker, greeted me at the
door. I asked him about the sign. On the walls inside, old
lasts and awls were hung for decoration. He offered me a
seat opposite his worktable and discoursed on his an-
cestors, workers in cordovan leather, who had founded
the business in 1670. After generations, he refused to
change the sign, though the word "cordwainer" had passed
from the language.

"Everyone around here knows what I do," he explained,
"and Gaylord prefers it this way, too."

Before leaving, I introduced myself. He said he had an
order from Gaylord to cobble me a pair of riding boots.
He measured my feet and took impressions of both. He
showed me sketches of different boots. When I made my
selection, he remarked that I'd chosen a pair exactly like
a pair he'd made for Donough Gaylord.

"He must have been wearing them when we went riding."

"More than likely. Every time he comes into the village, he stops to tell me how pleased he is with them. I'm making another pair now. Your foot's very similar to his. You his kin?"

"No."

"Funny. I could've sworn you were related. You can learn a great deal from people's feet. You certain you're not?"

"Positive. Can I have these in brown leather?"

"I'll make them as Mr. Gaylord ordered: shagreen leather boots; only the finest shagreen. You'll be satisfied. If not, you come and tell me why, and I'll fix 'em."

I thanked him and went to post my letter. Afterward I rode down Donough Lane to the harbor. Turning right along Harbor Lane, I proceeded several hundred yards in order to have a complete view of the church. The narrow bell tower had caught my eye, but the white-shingled oblong structure beneath it did not captivate my imagination until I noticed the cemetery behind its black-iron fence. Dismounting, I climbed the small rise. Overhead, dull gray clouds, swollen with rain, darkened to black. At the gate, I paused to search for the Gaylord plot. A marble figure of the angel Gabriel beckoned from under an expansive chestnut tree. On his pedestal were inscribed the glad tidings that the Gaylords rested in his guarded domain.

"Gabriel presides over Paradise," my father's voice instructed. "He is the spirit of truth. It was he who dealt death and destruction to the sinful cities of the plain. It was he who brought man the gift of hope."

There were three small headstones carved with names and dates of father, mother, and son Cormack. I stood beside Cormack Gaylord's grave and introduced myself as I would have done to formal family portraits. Bending, I plucked some cinquefoil to be pressed into my journal. The wind had risen. The storm was racing closer.

"Gabriel!" I whispered. "May they rest in peace. Lead the blind to sight. Love your kindred spirit, Cormack, a dark antagonist as well."

Gulls screeched. I attended the rumblings of the heavens and scrambled back to Anita, who eagerly turned homeward.

I was about halfway through the park when it began to rain. The birds had ceased their singing. I urged Anita on, anxious to reach home before the storm broke. That talk of ghosts and poachers had made me edgy.

We galloped all the way to the stable, where I returned Anita to Mr. Harrington's charge. Crossing from the stalls to the main house, I heard the roar of thunder.

Terrified by the lightning, I detoured hastily, running at tremendous speed, and reached the far side of the cottage just as the deluge came. I pressed up against one of the library's French windows to protect my body as best I could, pleased I had not made for the wych elm on the other side. Lightning flashed nearby.

At first I thought I'd magically tumbled through the panes like Alice through her looking glass, but the rain soaking the rug around me was coming in through the open window. My weight had forced the lock. I stood up to close the window. I felt dazed. If the heavy carpet hadn't broken my fall, I might have done serious damage to my spine or my neck or my head or my . . . I stopped in mid-conjecture. I no longer felt anything. I no longer heard the storm. In front of the fireplace, scattered on the hearthstone, I saw a torn white spider mum.

Reader, I was dumbfounded. Could I be mistaken? Taking the damp envelope from my pocket, I searched through it again. No flower. Crossing to the hearth, I knelt. Heat emanated from the coals in the grate. Someone had been in the room not too long ago. I picked up a small mound of the mum's petals, stamen, sepal, and pistil. Someone standing in front of the fire had dismembered the mum and dropped it, piece by piece, to the hearthstone. While reading my letter?

Somewhere in the house, a door closed. Outside, thunder crashed. I thrust the flower's fragments into my pocket. I hesitated a moment before lighting the lamp on the mantel and carrying it out into the foyer. I cannot explain my foolhardy behavior beyond my feeling of comfort in that house! It could not be haunted by some dreadful poltergeist; I reasoned I would sense it. Someone, an amiable poacher, was living or resting there. I believed it was my duty to protect my employer's property. In the foyer I listened for a sound to guide me. There was only the rain.

Up the staircase I went to the second-floor landing.
The sitting room was empty. A bolt of lightning outlined
the wych elm in the windows. I walked down the corridor,
pausing at each closed door as if to divine by inner logic
the one hiding the object of my search. At the end of the
hallway I found stairs leading to the third floor.

I climbed and peered down the corridor. Another flash
illuminated the passage. Nothing to stimulate suspicion.
I turned and continued up the stairs to the unsound attic.
There is something about attics, I thought, and if the door
is locked I . . . The door swung open. Another flash
traced the top branches of the great tree outside the panes
to my left. Under those attic beams, the light revealed a
mattress, a table, and a square object leaning against the
wall below the window.

I turned up the lamp and held it above my head. The
square object below the window was a painting in an
ornate gilded frame. I moved closer. The picture was of
a woman in a blue robe. She had long white arms and stood
in an open door with sunlight streaming over her. Her face
was in darkness. I moved closer. The open door was stained
glass. This was the Rossetti portrait! Light exploded. I felt
the house move and leaped into the air with a terrified
shout. A demented bellow from a room below echoed
mine. I started to tremble violently. Glancing at the painting as I turned to flee, I saw the face was not in darkness.
There was no face. Someone had cut it from the canvas!
Turning, I fled. Sobbing from shock and fear, I knew the
lies would soon consume me like fire from heavan.

I rushed down the flights of steps and sped along the
corridors. Halfway down the main staircase, I realized
the library door was open. I had closed it. There was no
way out except the way I'd come in. I could go back up,
but what then? Looking over the banister, I noticed an
open doorway under the stairs. I could hear a distraught
person pacing in the library. I lowered my quaking self
over the banister and made my way with footsteps muffled
by the storm.

The basement turned out to be a room with a stone
floor, brick walls, and a wooden door. It was empty. Beyond that door was a storage area for wine; thousands
of bottles in bookcases set perpendicular to the walls. I
tiptoed down the narrow central aisle. There was not a

window to be seen. Another wooden door opened on
stone stairs. I descended, counting to fourteen.

At first glance there was nothing extraordinary about the
square room where I stood, so I sat on the bottom step. It
was a windowless dungeon. The perfect place to be buried,
I thought, nothing festive about it. Holding the lamp
high to make certain I was not overlooking anything, I
saw the wall, directly to my right, slightly ajar! Moving
toward the aperture, I extended my hand. Just like something from Mary Shelley, my touch set the wall in motion. Silently, it began to close. By the judicious interven-
tion of my foot, motion was halted before the way was
sealed. I stared. The door had been camouflaged to blend
in with the wall. In short, a secret passageway! I had
stumbled upon the entrance. "Or the exit," I mumbled.
Thrusting the lamp into the tunnel, I saw that the narrow
way was endless, like Hugo's Parisian sewer system.

Suddenly, above and behind me, I heard footsteps. I had
no choice. Stepping into the passage, I closed the wall.

The tunnel was tall enough for me to hold the lamp
aloft, and wide enough so when walking in the middle,
I could not touch the sides. I could see ten feet in front
of me. The square tunnel was red brick; the effect was
somewhat like walking up a moldy chimney. The air was
damp, but plentiful. I walked quickly, free of strain until
a blank wall loomed in front, giving rise to an attack of
panic and claustrophobia that nearly caused me to fold
at the knees, until my shaft of light took a sharp left,
forming an acute right angle. I stopped to reconnoiter. I
had fled the cottage near the rear, on the left side, behind
the wych elm. I had walked under the garden, beside the
pond, and was now turning toward the main house.

I walked for another ten minutes, when the passage
abruptly widened into a room and ended at a heavy
wooden door. The door was locked. The door was huge.
I faltered. Retracing my steps was no problem, but what
awaited at the other end decidedly was. Placing the lamp
on the floor beside me, I sat down to rest and to think.
I studied the door: a great, noble door of sturdy wood,
studded with immense square-headed tenons. But no knob.
Impossible to break down, burn down, shoot down,
and very difficult to chop down. It would probably hold
back a marauding army.

"Of course!" I said aloud, feeling brilliant. "If the South attacked the North, or if the North attacked the Southerners occupying this territory, what a wonderful place to hide."

And to make certain they weren't trapped, there was an escape route. To my right, at the base of the door-frame, I noticed a small ring attached to one of the red bricks. Slipping my forefinger into the brass circle, I pulled. Nothing happened. I pulled harder. Still, nothing happened.

"Surely *something* should be happening! Goddamn it! The brick should come loose, uncovering a key on a niche. I've read too much Braddon not to know that. Maybe nothing does happen and I go back to discover one crazed cow in the sitting room and . . ."

While muttering to myself, I changed position for better leverage. Knees apart, head resting on the door, I yanked with all my strength. The ring slid out of the wall on a chain six inches long. The door gave way, pushed by my skull as I toppled forward. I scraped my head, and a tiny trickle of blood ran down the side of my face.

"No simple key for these people . . . build one into the wall . . . never misplace it. . . ."

I brushed my trousers and patted my head with a hand-kerchief.

"I've finally drawn blood with my meddling! Thank Christ it's my own!"

I found myself in another dungeon. A circular staircase on my left led up to a door. A long corridor extended to my right. If I was correct in my calculations, I was standing under the ivy-covered right wing, but the high room encompassed the first floor as well, which included the area behind the small study with the reflecting Della Francesca. Somewhere keys jangled and footsteps sounded. Turning down my lamp seconds before light flashed out at the end of the long corridor, I slipped behind the door and peered through a space retained for that purpose. I wanted to see who approached and why. A slight ache marked the place on my head where the bleeding had stopped.

The corridor light, dim at first, then brighter and brighter, passed, balanced on a tray with covered dishes carried by Mr. O'Shay. When he moved out of my field of vision, I opened the door farther to see him maneuver up the circular stairs. At the top he paused, fumbled with keys, but the door opened by itself.

"Right on time, as always, dear," a woman's voice spoke.

"I made you something special for tea today, Ruby. Scones and rum butter. Are you feeling better?"

The door closed behind him. I wasted not a second. Out I sprang, closing the wall and nipping down the corridor. I guided myself with my hand against the stones, afraid to use the lamp lest I be discovered.

When I reached a door, I stopped and listened. What would I say if someone were to see me? How would I explain not having shown myself to Mr. O'Shay?

I leaned against the door while slowly twisting the cold knob. The door was heavy but swung easily, and then I was in the stillroom. The door was camouflaged with stocked shelves to look like the other crowded walls. Up three steps and I was in the wine cellar. Up six more and I was outside the servants' hall.

Again I listened tensely at the door before tugging it ajar to check the room, which, to my astonished relief, was deserted. Out I shot like a captive butterfly from the hand of the oppressor, and just as confused as to direction of flight. I had no clue where I was. Then, from the sunlight on its panes, I spotted the exit.

After hastily dropping the lamp behind the espaliered apple tree to the left of the kitchen door, I sat by the dairy well to calm myself. Beside me, several dozen clams in a bucket of water and cornmeal cleaned themselves for our dinner. Their presence eased me back into the real world.

As I rounded the orangery, Denvers was working on the patio, trimming the pleached hawthorn with nail clippers.

"Is Brian with Ambrose?" he asked.

"I've no idea. Shall I go look?"

"Didn't he come back with you?"

"No. Should he have?"

"Yes, of course. I sent him to the stable with two umbrellas when I saw the rain. I gave him a key to the cottage, had you not been able to reach here in time. Didn't you see him?"

"No. I never saw Brian. Excuse me. I must go change."

"I don't know what to do about that boy. He's becoming more eccentric every day. Don't be late for tea, Robert."

He turned his attention back to the stray hawthorn branches. I crossed the patio and entered the house through the library, assuming my portico windows had been closed (and probably locked) before the storm. I wanted to closet myself with my frenetic imaginaton to have it out once and for all.

"It was *Brian* in the cottage . . . not a cow or a poacher. But who is Ruby? It's none of my business who Ruby is! If I don't stop snooping, I'll spoil everything."

I opened the door to my room.

But what about the spider mum? And what about the portrait?

I quickly forgot those questions. Large boxes emblazoned with my name were piled around my sitting room; shipping crates from Wanamaker's containing more clothing than I ever imagined one person owning. Wherever I requested two or three, Denvers had ordered six, and in some cases, twelve ("Much more attractive groupings"); where I had thought one sufficient, he had demanded two ("If one gets soiled or torn?").

I unpacked two full-length black mackintoshes with velvet collars. *Two*! Six caps! A dozen cardigan vests in various colors. Two calf-length chesterfield coats (herringbone: one brown, one gray). Two caped traveling ulsters. Three four-button double-breasted suits (one blue, one brown, one gray). Two all-white flannel summer suits (I'd passed them up as impractical). A dozen different pairs of trousers in all kinds of materials. And shirts! Dozens and dozens of shirts: chambray shirts, linen shirts, percale, cotton, and flannel shirts; soft shirts, stiff-bosom shirts; shirts with and without collars; polka-dot shirts, burgundy shirts; blue, white, yellow, and green twilled sateen.

Sitting on the floor, surrounded by shirts, I touched one after the other while Cael sniffed and stepped from one to the other. I started to laugh. Denvers called my name. Scooping in an armload of shirts with Cael in the middle, I went out to the portico.

"Robert, I forgot to tell you! Your—"

"Denvers! All these shirts! I've never seen so many beautiful shirts!"

"I'm glad you're pleased. Now you can dispose of your old drugget. Come down to tea."

After tea, I found Brian collecting my empty boxes to cart away.

"Brian, I'm sorry I missed you at the cottage. Do you forgive me? Look at my new clothes!"

He smiled and nodded. Spotting a gray herringbone cap, I grabbed it up and placed it on his head before he could speak.

"A perfect fit! We have the same size head! It looks great with your hair."

He walked to a mirror, adjusted the cap, smiled with pleasure at his jaunty appearance, and took it from his head to return to the pile.

"No! You must keep it. I want you to have it."

He looked confused, then became as delighted as a child just presented with a sweetmeat. Back he went to the mirror to reexamine himself in that cap. I picked up a similar one in blue and shared the mirror with him. When he saw the blue one, his smile disappeared; he eyed it warily.

"Which do you prefer, Brian? The blue or the gray? You can have either, you know. You can have *both*."

He chose the blue one.

I tugged on a mackintosh, flipping up the velvet collar.

"Try on the other one, Brian. See if it fits. We could have used these today."

"I have one."

"I'll bet it's not as nice as these. *These* are the very latest. Charles Mack himself is probably wearing one of these. Not to mention Donough Gaylord."

He lifted the second coat and fingered the velvet.

"How old is yours?"

He shrugged, then held up three fingers.

"Good Lord, man! Has it a velvet collar like this?"

He shook his head.

"That settles it! Three years old *and* no velvet collar? Send it to Teddy Roosevelt!"

It fit him better than it fit me. His shoulder muscles were more developed; he filled out clothing better than I.

"Happy unbirthday, Brian! You've just gotten yourself a mack to go with that smart cap. Don't argue, Brian! It's *yours*. I want you to have it. Now, how about some shirts. . . ."

He was gone. I studied myself in the mirror. I was pleased. I looked like a fashionable gent from a magazine. I was also delighted to share some of my good fortune with Brian; he wanted for nothing, but it was amusing that we wore the same size, because he looked much bigger than I. (In actual fact, it was much more than amusing. It was to prove itself a lifesaving coincidence.)

After examining the rest of my finery, down to the hose, underwear, nightshirts, and dressing gowns (one silk, one wool, one cotton), I put everything away piece by piece, fondling each before allocating it to the bureau or closet. Then I gathered the boxes and lugged them down to the kitchen for Ambrose to store.

"That's fine gear you gave young Brian. When 'e came strutting in 'ere, I thought it was you! 'What's Mr. Robert doing below stairs?' I asked myself, and myself 'adn't a clue! I took 'im for you, I did! Fancy that!"

"We're the same size, Ambrose; you'd never think it, but we are. If you were my size, I'd invite you upstairs to choose something, too."

"If I was your size, I'd feel only half-growed. Ta very much. I took 'im for you, I did. Gave me quite a turn to see your lovely 'air gone funny red."

I left the servants' hall by the same door used earlier. The lamp was where I'd left it. I picked it up and headed for the portico, but as I approached the patio, I heard Denvers laughing with Brian about mistaking him for me. I hastened to the front of the house and used the main staircase. I loathed sneaking around corners, and vowed to mind my own business from that day forward. It proved much easier said than done, but it might have prevented my undoing.

At eleven that night, Brian brought me warm milk. Before saying good night, he apologized for not having been at the cottage. He explained that Mr. Harrington needed help rubbing down Anita because his son had sprained an ankle playing with Cael. I said I knew about the ankle. I said good night. I don't know how I said anything. I was so stunned I could not blow out my light. Who in God's name was in the cottage?

Eleven

DURING THE SECOND WEEK OF NOVEM-
ber, the cold set in. I had planned to view the coloring
leaves, surrounded as I was by so many arboreal species,
but the cold was suddenly too severe to saunter out, the
wind too chafing. I found myself virtually house-bound.
It was then Denvers decided to teach me the rudiments
of whist; I would be able to complete a foursome when
Goodbody and Mortimer arrived. We had received word
that Donough was bringing them for Thanksgiving.

As we huddled in the library those first "blowy" days
with Cael asleep on the hearth, gardeners scurried about
the grounds carrying cloches to prepare the less hardy
perennials for winter. The delicate tree roses, long since
wrapped in tarpaper with their round crowns tied in bur-
lap, were like mummified guardians outside the newly
sealed and draped windows. The wind soughed in the
chimneys; radiators hissed and banged. In other rooms,
carpets were being laid and heavy curtains hung. Cumu-
lus clouds scudded across the darkening sky as Denvers
chatted about *Othello* and other passions.

"Ah, nature! So unpredictable. So deficient. Always in
need of judicious assistance. I should be more diligent in
overseeing their work, but I've other things, far more
pleasant things to do. They know best what needs doing.
I hope they've covered the strawberries with straw. Robert,
your turn to play. You play like Donough, safe and
slow."

"Is that bad?"

"Bad? No! Dull. There is *never* a surprise. The only
person who ever played cards with verve was dear young
Cormack. He campaigned, pillaged, and destroyed! He
knew the power of the conqueror. It was delicious. He
never composed his behavior or suppressed his discontent.
He was rude as a savage. He was magnificent. Your move."

My typewriting was improving. I had memorized the
finger placement and dutifully repeated letter exercises,

but according to my journal, I frequently employed my left hand in place of my right, which is a thing that never happened at the piano keyboard. My music lessons were regular. Even when he was not at table, Keyes would be waiting in the music room each morning at eleven. We would run through my lesson until he, at my side, was satisfied with my performance; then he would motion for me to remove myself to a seat opposite the Steinway for his daily "program."

Since it was too cold to breakfast on the patio, we moved indoors to the orangery. Originally a hothouse for young Cormack's orchids that still fill one side of it, the hexagonal room has seven glass walls with a glass roof ("like the cell of a bee") and is the storage space for the second Cellini satyr. Brian grows his morels and his bonsai here, and koi swim in their private pool. Roses bloom year-round and tropical ferns lend an exotic tone to the simplest repast. On a frigid morning years before my arrival, it seems Denvers awoke with a touch of bursitis and announced "warmth, a touch of rhodon, and a lusting satyr" were what the doctor ordered. I always found it a bizarre, disturbing enclosure for a breakfast nook.

The satyr terrified me. Unlike its playful mate in the front hall, this bronze holds no benign flute, but extends its right arm to capture and violate with its engorged sex clutched in its left hand. The figure's face is distorted by rage. ("*Lust*, Robert, that's extreme need!") He does not dance, he waits. Denvers found it provocative. "He reminds me of Steven. The two have similar charms."

"Who's Steven?"

I LIKE IT AS MUCH AS BEING S.

"Cormack, the elder, once owned an assistant named Steven Ramsay. He was a common sort who made unnecessary demands."

"What happened to him?"

"He was dismissed. I detested him. He nearly destroyed Gaylord. He was clever, I'll give him that much. Almost as clever as you are."

"You didn't hate him for being clever?"

"No, of course not! He lacked perspicacity. I nauseate cupidity."

And then there were the orchids. I discovered on my

first morning in the orangery that I am not fond of orchids.. There is something disturbing about them. Denvers thought it a delightful congruence that the flowers with the heaviest sexual connotation should bloom in such profusion around the mythic fertility symbol. Not comprehending, I stared vacantly.

"Remember your Greek, boy!"

I remembered my Greek and blushed.

"It was Cormack's proficiency in Greek that initiated his interest in orchids. Most of these blooms are Brian's hybrids now, but if I am not mistaken, that pale green clone is still a pure genus . . . *Brassalova*, I think. Those hideous spiky thingies behind our heated companion over there are *Odontoglossum* from the Andes; I'm quite certain of that. I recognize cymbidium to your left. I must say, you don't seem overexcited by this nature class, Robert. Why not change the subject while you pass the toast?"

"Did you sleep well?"

"*That* will not do, my friend. The bad always sleep well. In future, if you wish to breakfast in silence, stay in your room. I'm at my rosiest now, and you should take advantage of my company! Try again while you pass the preserves."

We both laughed. Ambrose snorted. Cael bit into a mauve cattleya.

"Brian's bonsai are very beautiful."

"Ah! Strawberry preserves inspire you! Ambrose, make a note of that!"

"Do it yourself! What the bloody 'ell do I look like?"

"Exactly what you are: an old fart! Try the white epidendrum, Cael, mauve was never your color. Where were we? Ah, yes, Brian's landscapes. The grouping in the hollowed lavastone is my favorite. It represents the pond and the pond garden."

"How long has Brian been doing it?"

"Since his accident. It was what maintained his sanity the months he could not walk. Donough taught him."

Cael curled between the spread legs of the satyr. Ambrose departed for another pot of tea, leaving the door between the orangery and the servants' hall ajar.

"Tell me about the boating accident."

Denvers lowered a piece of toast. He sat motionless,

staring at the bread as though expecting to find the answer to my question scrawled in the jam.

"Robert . . ." he began tentatively.

Brian ambled into the room carrying a coffee cake. Ambrose followed with a pot of tea and began speaking very loudly: "Such a darling cake, I said to meself. Brian should take a bow, seeing 'ow good 'e is at taking bows. Don't you agree, Denvers?"

Ambrose and Denvers exchanged quick glances which I immediately read as conspiratorial. What was going on?

"Yes, I do indeed! How thoughtful of you, Ambrose. Dear Ambrosia! Brian, join us for cake. Robert was just now admiring your bonsai. Were you not, Robert?"

I stared at Denvers for a few beats before nodding. Then, turning to the delighted Brian, I asked him to teach me the art. I spotted Cael stalking a koi in the stone pool.

It was to be months before the mystery of Brian's accident was solved. Answers came from a totally unexpected source, someone whose presence was unknown to us all that morning in the orangery, someone I would regret meeting for the rest of my life.

Those mornings after breakfast, before sitting at my typewriter, I would detour into the old washroom: a dark closet off the kitchen. Wasps had built a nest, a pastrylike cornucopia, against one of the windows; if I stood beside the pane, I could safely observe their behavior as clearly as if I had opened their nest in a laboratory. The passages surrounding the full egg chamber resembled a vertically halved artichoke; the eggs resembled pearls.

"Remember," I lectured myself, "stumbling around in other people's affairs is like removing this pane of glass and pushing your face into the heart of the hive."

In the afternoons, I worked with the books: carrying, sorting, ordering, arranging. After tea, I read Herodotus and Saint-Beauve with Denvers, and Zola alone in my rooms before bed. I wrapped myself in my new apparel against the inclement weather to wander among the shrubbery or along the beach. The wind burned my cheeks. The leaves flew about in cyclonic patterns. Fall surrendered to winter with one long freezing sigh. I grew depressed as the grounds became inaccessible, tyrannized by winter's contumely as I was being tyrannized by nightmares.

The dreams excoriated me. Unbidden, a hostile image

from the depths erupted in perverse visitations. I wished
to name it ghost, but it was not of that hallowed order.
It fluttered around my bed in three dimensions, whispering
my name and touching me lasciviously. The fear it induced married the panic engendered by the nightmares
and locked me into my rooms for entire days. That an
image seen in a portrait should take form and walk was
madness. I agonized in my journal that the Whyte legacy
was fulfilling itself. I believe that had I not Donough
Gaylord's visit as a lodestar, I would have become irrevocably lost. On mornings after these apparitions, Cael,
too, seemed to suffer from a torpor that kept him within
stroking reach. His purring warmth calmed me and at-
tenuated the distance between me and my beloved.

Enervated, I dreaded mealtimes. I was incapable of
maintaining coherent conversations; each time Denvers
snarled at me for inattention or the absence of vital life
signs, I was devastated out of all proportion to his rebukes.
And when he saw my confusion, he responded with barbed
cruelty.

"You reflective types," he drawled contemptuously,
"you're all the same. You can't deliver in a pinch. A
little pressure and you snap. Your brains become like
windows dimmed by frost. Give me a man of action any
day or night, summer or winter. The good die young because they drain the cup of life. *They* don't sit moodily
staring into it with their mouths hanging slack and their
muscles soft."

I forced myself to visit nature and was comforted. I
walked among the birches and sat among the oaks; seeing
them surrender to the barbarous assault of winter, I was
less frightened by my soul's dark nights. I accepted them
as my fate. Everything was changing; it was a stressful
time for me. I would not allow my fears to control me. I
vowed to make my days manageable by not allowing my
nights to shadow them. The dreams would pass. I would
bear them as the trees and the other animals bore the
frigid cold. I shouted to the waves that I would not be
defeated. I shouted to the stars that I would be happy. I
would conquer myself. I would triumph.

I awaited Donough Gaylord's arrival. Each day I
marked off the day gone, the day that had surrendered
to time's relentless transitions. They sped along as they
do for the young. My typewriting improved; the simple

skill was acquired. I began to comprehend the piano and the mysterious connections among note, sound, and player. I waited in vain for a second letter from my father. I did not expect a letter from my mother, although I wrote several times. In my journal I noted that I was not responsible for her illness, that I could not heal her wounds, that each must find his own way.

As if a phantom caressed me
I thought I was not alone walking here by the shore. . . .

I read books on the subject of twins. I was possessed by Cormack and Donough Gaylord on my treks up the beach. I imagined perfection as they merged into one flesh. Where my Donough feared to tread, Cormack would rashly charge and carry me away.

"Carry me away?" I groaned, uneasy with the excitation such dime-novel notions evoked.

To be snatched up and run with had a mysterious attraction. Would Donough ever try? Having lived with an image of self who *did* what he dreamed must have inhibited. I imagined living with an extraverted me, with someone who dared soar while I remained securely earthbound. How long could I tolerate vicarious pleasure unless the stakes grew progressively higher? I would grow to resent his freedom as he would grow to resent my security.

I HATE AND I LOVE: ASK HOW? I CANNOT TELL,
BUT I FEEL IT AND I AM TORN IN TWO.

The holiday arrived. I awoke as I awoke every day, with Cael by my side. His winter fur was thicker and fuller; he looked and felt larger, and his extravagant ruff made him appear round. He lay on his back. I stroked his stomach. He awoke, yawned, stretched, and rolled over, before sitting up and becoming attentive, sensing my excitement.

"They come today, puss," I said, squeezing him in a hug, "they come *today!*"

I bathed, dressed, breakfasted, practiced my typewriting and piano, lunched, walked, worked, took tea, read, bathed, and waited. They had not yet arrived. At dinner, I was frantic with excitement.

"Do we keep you so poorly amused that you can barely contain yourself at the arrival of guests?" asked Denvers with amusement in his eyes.

"Yes . . . you know, dear, we are getting on."

"Yes, Keyes, ever onward. Pass the peas."

I heard the horses. Rising from the table with a hasty "excuse me," I hurried into the foyer. I could hear laughing outside. Ambrose appeared, lamp in hand. Cael sat on the landing, ever curious. I lurked behind the dancing faun. The door was opened before a knock sounded. Bearing leaves like harbingers of good tidings, the wind swept into the foyer and frisked me where I stood.

Donough Gaylord was the first to appear. Wearing a sable hat and a long sable coat, he stopped on the landing to remove his gloves. Timothy Goodbody, tall as Donough but pale and thin, with an oval face and thick blond curls, followed, wrapped in brown fur; laughing, he glanced over his shoulder at Eugene Mortimer. Taller than the other two by a head, Mortimer was encased in Persian lamb dark as his skin; his exquisitely honed features were contorted in a grimace at something one or the other had said. He sighed. He spoke. His voice had a basso timbre that turned the landing into a stage.

"As always, Cael greets us first."

Ambrose took their things.

"*Cher* Ambrose, it's good to see you again. You are well, I hope!"

"It is always a pleasure to see you, Mr. Eugene. Welcome to Gaywyck, Mr. Timothy. The others are at table. Will you be joining them, Mr. Donough?"

"Yes, we will. Bring us some brandy, Ambrose, please. Robert, come out from behind that thing and greet my friends."

While the men removed their coats and handed them to Ambrose, I crossed to be introduced. Both guests smiled as I approached.

Mortimer raised his right eyebrow and chuckled. "So this is the new librarian you've been so eager for us to know! I don't wonder at your delight. But then, I have a predilection for alabaster cherubs."

Goodbody laughed. Mr. Donough grinned and blushed. I said how pleased I was to meet them. Goodbody descended the landing steps, extending his right hand in greeting. "Don't mind him, Robert. Not many folks do."

Mortimer chuckled again as he moved down to take my hand. "More's the pity. Lead me to the brandy, young man. Tim and Donnie will follow. Is it not boring for you here?"

He clasped my arm with his enormous hand, turned me around, and led me ahead of the others toward the dining room.

"What a beastly trip! Only the bouillabaisse kept me from slipping over the edge. I'm exhausted! Have you ever thought of going on the stage?"

"No! Never! *Me*?"

"Yes! You could make your fortune in no time at all. We have a client who is a prodigious producer and always on the lookout for a face like yours."

"But I don't think I have any talent."

"Nowadays, no one on the stage has any talent! What about becoming a partner in our law firm?"

"I don't know anything about the law."

"Neither does Goodbody. Look how well *he's* done!"

Mr. Donough, walking close behind, guffawed. I turned to see excited eyes flash in his rubescent face. He had his arm around Goodbody's shoulder.

"You're drunk!" I said, laughing happily, having just caught the joke.

"You might say that. Mightn't he, Eugene?" Goodbody asked in his light smoky voice.

"Yes, Timothy, he might. *I* certainly would not censure him for doing so. Would you, Gaylord?"

"Censure Robbie? *Never*! It would be like censuring a narcissus."

"Or censuring veltheimia for bearing *pink* flowers."

We reached the dining room.

"Whose veltheimia is bearing pink flowers? Have you brought it here for us to see?" asked Denvers, rising from his seat to shake hands with the visitors.

There was uproar all around. Keyes literally shrieked with joy and ran into Mortimer's arms.

"Oh, my *dears*, I am thrilled to see you both again. Will you play for us? Please? You *must* say yes."

"Keyes, let him rest awhile. We have had a tiresome, foul journey."

"Yes, Keyes, of course I'll play. We've brought you a special present."

"Some Mahler songs?"

"Yes! Some new ones just out here."

"I feel faint. I must sit down." Goodbody sighed. He has round indigo eyes. He wore a silk scarf tied around his throat in the style of a French bohemian.

"You *will* play them for me . . . do say you will."

"He'll play them, Keyes," promised Goodbody, reaching for an orange. "We've been practicing all week for you."

"Must you give away *all* our secrets?"

"What are friends for, Mortimer?"

"I hadn't realized you two had any left!" Denvers laughed.

"Oh, dears, I vibrate with pleasure."

"You play the piano?" I asked.

"Better than *I*, dear Robert," shouted Keyes.

"No one plays better than you, Keyes," Mortimer softly corrected. "I play *adequately*, Robert."

"I'm learning. Keyes is teaching me."

"So Donough told us."

I smiled shyly, gratefully, at Donough Gaylord. He gave me a shy inebriated grin in return. Ambrose brought the brandy. Brian carried in cake, ice cream, more fruit, nuts, and coffee. M. Henri and Taio appeared briefly to say good night. Then we all sat around the table.

Goodbody made a toast, winging the words into the air as he raised his glass. "To a marvelous Thanksgiving!"

I lifted my glass, convinced it would be nothing short of sublime.

After several more toasts and two pots of coffee, we retired to the music room, where we settled with some anticipation around the piano. Mortimer had gone ahead to locate the music in his baggage, and while in his room had changed into a peacock-blue velvet jacket that shimmered softly in the light when he sat down to play. Goodbody stood behind him to turn the pages (I thought). After a few aery chords, he opened his mouth and the strange, dry tones of his speaking voice bloomed into a crystalline tenor sound.

Through six gorgeously dolorous songs, the two of them fused into one; it was a most moving experience. Keyes went limp in Denvers's arms and was guided to his rooms. Donough sat in silence. With few words, we parted for the night. Goodbody, Mortimer, and Donough Gaylord returned to the first floor; shyly I drifted to my own quarters.

I could not sleep. I wanted to go for a walk, but the wind was howling and my sense of adventure was exhausted; only my mind raced. I could not calm myself. I took a very hot bath. I paced the sitting room. Goodbody and Mortimer joined in Mahler songs had stirred me too deeply. Goodbody, so blond, almost as fair as myself, was obviously deeply attached to Mortimer, a man as dark as his shadow and almost as beautiful as Donough Gaylord. I had seen Negro men in upstate New York, but they were laborers with sorrowful eyes and callused hands. Denvers had told me of Mortimer's princely Haitian heritage, but that had not prepared me for this exotic, graceful creature. Having such a royal friend revealed my employer.

And there was Goodbody. While he sang, he had expressed such passion, such sorrow, such longing, and such joy. It was evident: his tall, lithe body was fused with an extraordinary soul. Both these gifted men were lodged in rooms next to mine; they would be my companions for the next four days. It was too much to bear calmly. I continued pacing the sitting room. I missed Cael, too, but I knew he would be spending most of his time with Donough, who came first in his heart.

"I need something to read . . . something soothing!"

As I stepped into the hall, I realized from the flickering brightness that the door to the next apartment was ajar. I could hear two sweet, rumbling voices exchanging words too softly to be intelligible. I quickened my step so as not to overhear ("like an ear pressed to a keyhole"), when Goodbody mentioned my name. I stood still.

"Robbie *is* lovely-looking."

"He seems *tellement doux*, as well."

"Looks a bit like Donnie."

"A *bit*! The resemblance is astounding!"

"Merely the eyes."

"Yes, but that's more than enough, *mon cher*. Men *kill* over eyes like those. He is well shaped, too, which is *toujours gai*. Beautiful hands, wrists . . ."

"You were very observant tonight."

"One notices . . . unless one is unwell; and *à-propos* Robbie, one must be dead not to notice, and I, *mon cher*, I have never felt better in my life. Come here. . . ."

There was a pause. I heard the rustling of satin. Moving closer to the door, I peered into their sitting room. The two men stood side by side in front of the fire, their backs to me. Mortimer wore only a red bath towel tied around his waist. Goodbody, in a blue robe, stroked his friend's bare back.

"Donnie loves him."

"Yes, thank God . . . at long last. . . ."

"Do you think he knows?"

"Which *he*?"

"Either he!"

"Neither knows. *Naïfs*. That's why they get on so well."

"And *our* excuse?"

"I love you."

"That will do nicely."

"It's served these twenty years. . . ."

At that moment the red towel fell to the floor. The naked Mortimer sat, chuckling. Goodbody, shedding the robe, knelt uncovered beside. The two kissed and caressed. I left them to each other.

Back in my rooms, alone, under my quilt, I was happy.

They are wrong, I thought. I know I love him. I would die for him. Love makes us equals.

When I awoke the next morning, the room was unusually bright. The air seemed phosphorescent. Recognizing the glow, I leaped from the bed to open the drapes. The world had been transformed by a heavy blanket of snow. There were drifts on the portico, and the sea looked like a silver platter. No wind disturbed the icicled yews; the fluttering sunlight danced in their boughs like a dove. Donough Gaylord, Goodbody, and Mortimer were walking toward the house from the shore; I could chart their course from the footsteps in the snow. I rushed to dress for breakfast.

We ate in the main dining room. While we talked and laughed, devouring omelets, wondrous strange smells wafted from the kitchen: Henri and Brian had begun preparations for our Thanksgiving celebration. Plans were formulated, discussed, dismissed or accepted, according to this or that whim. We all agreed on ice skating after breakfast. When Donough announced he planned two hours' work following luncheon, Goodbody threw a roll at him, threatening to follow with the compote if he didn't immediately change his mind. He relented. A sleigh ride was seconded by Keyes. The Eranus was referred to; I requested more information.

"Each contributes something to the banquet."

"I can't do anything."

"I somehow doubt *that*!"

"What Mortimer means, Robbie, is each does the best he can."

"As in life. . . ."

"Not at breakfast, Denvers. No metaphysics before vespers."

"Well, dear, that takes care of you for today."

"Pass the toast, Keyes? And do me a favor? Hum Vivaldi's 'Winter Music' without making any sound."

Mortimer booed.

"And as for you, my black prince . . ."

"I cannot wait."

"*Tu parles.*"

"Far too much and far too often, if you ask me."

"Sensibly, Goodbody, no one has."

"Pass the compote . . . *gently*, please."

We skated on the portion of the lake closest to the cottage. It took but a moment for Lonnie and Joshua to clean away the loose snow; and while Denvers and Keyes made a snowman, we others skated in circles, overlapping and crossing one another. Brian arrived at eleven, bringing hot chocolate, red apples, and gingerbread. Long icicles hung from the wych elm; we snapped them free to form wings for a snow angel. We took turns pulling one another on a brightly painted sled, and laughed so merrily that Joshua had to run to the main house for a key to the cottage and "the facilities." Clumps of snow dropped from the golden raintree, its silvered branches raised in joyous witness to our pleasure.

By noon the conversation turned to Thanksgiving dinner. Henri had announced on a beautifully scripted menu card: hot turkey *ballotin* stuffed with a French *pâté* dressing, and the usual holiday trimmings. We returned to the main house, which was deliciously warm after the hours out-of-doors, and we agreed to postpone the sleigh ride until the next day. After luncheon (*consommé madrilène* and *rognons sautées*), we retired to our rooms for a nap ("and meditation") before assembling in Li-

brary I at three. While I nervously practiced my selections
for the musicale, I could hear Mortimer and Goodbody
laughing over some privity.

At three, refreshed, we five convened. Keyes, in a burst
of communal spirit, suggested we devise an entertainment.
Denvers stood, commanded our attention by clapping his
hands thrice, and recited:

> *What wisdom stirs amongst you? Come, sir, now*
> *I am for you again. Pray you, sit by us*
> *And tell's a tale.*

I responded, knowing the play—the scene by heart—it being a favorite of my father's.

> *Merry or sad shall 't be?*

Denvers, delighted, continued, making it clear to the
others by nodding and silently clapping that I was on the
mark.

> *As merry as you will.*

I smiled, proud of myself, and pleased to be the one to
declare:

> *A sad tale's best for winter. I have one*
> *of sprites and goblins.*

Denvers sat, regally commanding while lovingly as-
senting:

> *Let's have that, good sir,*
> *Come on, sit down. Come on, and do your best*
> *To fright me with your sprites, you're powerful at it.*

I whispered:

> *There was a man . . .*

He spoke with me:

> *Nay, come, sit down, then on.*

I sat by him.

> *Dwelt by a churchyard—I will tell it softly*
> *Yon crickets shall not hear it.*

I pointed to the other three, much to their merriment.
And he concluded:

> *Come on, then,*
> *And give 't me in mine ear.*

Only Mortimer could not name the play. When told, he
shrugged and said in a haughty manner with a suddenly
acquired stage French accent, "*Merde!* Shack-*spear*? Not
a point on our Molière!"

We formed a circle and read the play aloud. I had recently collected all the volumes of his plays; distributing
five copies of *The Winter's Tale* took but a moment. My
efficiency drew favorable comments from my employer.
I was pleased everyone noticed how seriously I was taking
my position. It *was* my first job; I was proud to be doing
it well.

At five we returned to our rooms to prepare for dinner.
I bathed, practiced my pieces, and for the second time
donned formal attire with Ambrose's invaluable assistance.
I was still anxious about that musicale. Everything was
going so well; I dreaded making an ass of myself. While
he struggled with my tie, I fidgeted, absently raising my
hand to scratch my nose. He slapped my wrist.

"You are not paying any mind, Mr. Robert. This is
the fourth go at your bloody tie, and it still looks like you
slept in it."

I apologized. He grunted. I stood rigidly to attention
and, statuelike, thought of Hermione. We succeeded.
After a meticulous going-over with several brushes and a
comb, I was anointed. Scented, I was permitted to descend
to the sitting room, where we were to gather at six for
"cocktails." When I entered, buffed and shining, all the
faces turned and smiled.

"A perfect entrance, lad." Mortimer chuckled, dubbing
me the fairest ("the better angel is a man right fair").
Considering the competition, I was truly honored and
told them as much. Goodbody, raising his glass, solemnly

intoned: *"Gaudemus igitur juvenetum idem."* Donough Gaylord stood alone, lost in thought by the piano, stroking the languorous Cael.

Taio called us into dinner at 6:30; we finished at ten. It was a feast as baroque as anything in Huysmans. Every dish contained an exciting surprise for me, including the turkey. I was puzzled during the carving until I realized that the bird's skeletal framework had been magically removed. When I voiced my amazement at its not collapsing, there was a toast to the "winged wonder," and another refrain of Goodbody's paean to youth.

We took pumpkin pie and coffee and liqueurs in the sitting room. Keyes promptly fell asleep. We discussed the route of the next day's sleigh ride. I watched Goodbody and Mortimer affectionately touch one another casually and frequently during the course of the conversation. At one point, Mortimer called Goodbody "dear," inflecting the word as Keyes never had. Bewildering thoughts I'd not confronted surfaced; I could not mask them.

Their relationship went beyond the classical ideal of "perfect friendship" that I had envisioned between myself and Donough Gaylord. Their love seemed passionate, like that of a man for a woman. The image of them together, naked, skidded across my mind, merging with the drawings in the cave. I glanced at Donough Gaylord. I wanted to touch him, to hold and be held by him. If Goodbody and Mortimer could exchange their expressions of love openly, why could not we? Was something wrong with *me*?

Standing abruptly in the middle of a story Goodbody was relating, I could not catch my breath. I walked to the window and stared, unseeing, into my own reflection. I was confused by my thoughts and feelings. If they guided me to him and I denied them, there was nothing but the sorrow of a barren life devoid of truth. I could not believe *he* desired any life but a truthful one, yet each time I touched him, he recoiled. He could not love me as I loved him. Goodbody and Mortimer were wrong to think so. Perhaps it was for the best? He did not need someone whose demons governed insensate fears. But when he was with me, I never knew bad dreams.

"Robbie, are you all right?"

I turned to him enveloped by the loving warmth in his voice. I wanted to rest my head on his shoulder. I wanted to ask him why he didn't love me. I wanted to ask him if there was anything I could do to make him love me.

"Yes, Mr. Donough. I'm fine, thank you, sir."

Denvers suggested some exertion on our part. Keyes, waking with a start, was the first to exit the sitting room and the first to enter the music room, where a great fire had been lit and where brandy, poured into ornate crystal decanters, awaited our pleasure.

We drew lots to see who would first perform. I won. Walking to the piano, I announced in an even voice that my Chopin nocturne would be followed by a recitation of Whitman's "When I Heard at the Close of Day." There was a buzz of anticipation which I found encouraging. I sat in front of the open keyboard and arranged my music, all the while drawing deep breaths.

I played very well: few technical blunders and with enough musical intelligence to inform the piece and carry it above an exercise in fingering and *tempo rubato*. The applause went as much to my teacher. My audience was so pleased with the Whitman poem, they demanded another. I recited the only other one I knew. When I reached that last, bitter line: "Have you no thought O Dreamer that it may be all *maya*, illusion?" my voice nearly broke. There was silence afterward. I remembered the agony that poem had engendered in me, and could not look at anyone as I resumed my seat. The pain swelled anew.

"Dear Whitman!" Denvers sighed. "No one understands as well as the poet how everything we do is instigated by an illusion. Do you agree, Mortimer?"

"Of course! Only when we know our illusions can we find our truths."

"So the poem is not a warning," I asked, "but a statement of fact?"

"More a definition of terms," Mortimer offered. "The terms of love's contract between one fallible mortal who knows his frailties and another whom he begs to understand and not expect what cannot be given."

"I see. . . ."

"Who's next?"

Donough stood. As he did, Cael sprang from his lap and followed him to the piano, where they shared the bench. Donough played two toccatas from memory, one by Galuppi and one by Scarlatti. I was amazed at his mastery of the form, and at his dramatic power. His offering excited me; I told him so. He laughed and claimed the company inspired him, but he was very pleased and did not attempt to conceal his pleasure. I was touched by his honesty. I wondered, again, where I was making my mistake.

Goodbody and Mortimer performed together. They sang a group of operatic arias by Puccini, Verdi, and Bizet. Not only was Mortimer a wonderful pianist, but he also possessed a rich baritone which he displayed in two duets with his friend, one from *La Bohème*, and one from *Les Pêcheurs de Perles*; the latter, with its ravishing melody, was repeated upon request, and we all hummed along ("like Cio Cio San's dawn companions").

Denvers caused great merriment with two Gilbert-and-Sullivan "patter songs." "A Private Buffoon" was enchanting. As the song finished, he shuffled from the room, returning to sit at the piano and "pound out" three rags by Scott Joplin with perfect rhythmical "swing." Donough bounded to his feet and danced the length of the room with a startled Cael in his arms. He moved splendidly, swaying to the music. I gaped. Mortimer clapped in time and hooted with glee, poking me into joining him.

"*He* should go on the stage," I shouted.

"Don't think we haven't tried. He's a brilliant actor, too!"

When the music ended, Donough looked exhilarated and not the least embarrassed by his spontaneous display. He was radiant, and I loved him again, and more, for several new reasons.

Then we took a short interval for refreshment, while Keyes prepared himself for his contribution. It was part of the ritual that he was last. We settled into our chairs as he took his place.

"Mahler's Resurrection Symphony," he announced.

And so it was. Lush and complex as a Liszt transcription, his performance would have enthralled the great Viennese maestro himself. I sat suspended between terror and exaltation while he led me into the very presence of death, then swept me outside time into an eternity of love and salvation. I was enraptured. It was the eternity of my childhood.

Before the last chords had faded, Keyes, hugged by

everyone, was helped to his room by Denvers. Silenced, we kissed one another good night and parted fulfilled.

In my room, I was surprised by the clock. Keyes had played for over two hours. I undressed and got into bed immediately. I tried not to think of anything that would deflate the sense of elation. Something miraculous had occurred. I would never be the same again. Death, my own, everyone's, was defeated. Comforted, I slept.

The remaining days passed too quickly. I scan my journal in an attempt to grasp them, but they fragment into bright moments like a handful of luminous stones flung wide.

The next day we took a sled, pulled by raven-black bays, to Sterling Harbor. The weather, calm and cold, was held at bay by thick fur blankets and flasks of hot chocolate and plum brandy. The two fast friends sat in front holding the reins; Donough Gaylord and I sat together in the rear.

"I've never been so happy," I said, "not in my whole life."

"Your life is just beginning, Robbie."

"May it never end!"

"I'll drink to that!"

"Mortimer, you'd drink to Dr. Quackenbos."

While we walked along the beach the next afternoon, those two in front, we two behind, I thanked him for taking me into his home. He was the grateful one, he said; there hadn't been such peace at Gaywyck for years. I took him at his word and was catapulted into a spiraling joy. I wanted to hug him. Instead, I knelt, collected flat stones, and skidded them across the rippling surface of the gray sea.

I told him about the letter from my father. He responded hesitantly that he had looked into my mother's condition and wanted my permission to move her to a private nursing home.

"Your father has already given his approval."

I was speechless with gratitude, far beyond words.

"Will that help, sir, do you think?"

"It will be more pleasant for her. And it can't hurt."

"Is it the same place your mother stayed?"

"No," he answered after a pause.

I detected his discomfort and changed the subject.

Has there ever been a kinder, more considerate friend?
I wondered, looking out across the still-rippling surface
of the sea.

We played whist, we talked, we read aloud, we walked,
we made music, we told stories, we shared four days, four
short days. And then they left. I was grief-stricken. I felt
abandoned. They had made me a part of themselves: they
had listened to me, they had sought my opinions, they
had respected me as an honored peer.

> *But shall we wear these honors for a day?*
> *Or shall they last, and we rejoice in them?*

I sat by the still-flickering fire in Goodbody and Mortimer's sitting room, Shakespeare open on my lap, Cael by
my side. I sat in that place because it had sheltered virtue
and tenderness. My tears fell. In the flames, I fancied
images of limbs entwined, and heard whispered sighs.

At the center of myself, a bubble of sensation formed,
rose, and burst, flooding me with warmth. For the second
time in my life, passion erupted. Now I knew it by its
name.

Twelve

THE FIRST DAYS WITHOUT THEM, I ENdured the anxiety of separation. Keyes appeared at none of the meals. Denvers was silent at most. Mr. O'Shay served up leftovers ("a pity to waste all that fancy food"), and no one complained. Brian, too, was subdued, baking whole-wheat loaves and plain pound cakes for tea. He was experiencing the loss as intensely as the rest of us. Donough had managed to spend hours with him, transplanting orchids and starting an herb garden in pots. Only Ambrose welcomed the peace: "At my age, so much excitement is 'ard on the kidneys."

The snow, at first exhilarating, was now like so much sand packing us tightly into the house. I devoured Dumas novels, one after the other, while Cael slept unmoving on the bed by my side.

I resumed my work in the libraries. I finished grouping the books according to language and subject, prose and poetry, and was ready to begin my filing cards as soon as I collected the stray volumes from the rooms that did not have special collections. It was a pleasant task. It took me into those apartments I had not visited since my first tour with Denvers, giving me the opportunity to look at the paintings again.

The house was mysteriously silent as I made my way down the dim corridors. The snow outside muted sound while heightening color. Though it was early morning, I carried a lamp. The heavy winter draperies were drawn. I collected seven volumes in the second-floor left-wing rooms from bureau drawers and closet shelves where guests had deposited them many years before.

Stuck into a leather-bound collection of Poe's poems was a letter written in a large, sprawling hand, dated 24 July 1884:

My dearest Pim:

Alas! All is *not* well in this kingdom by the sea in fact things could not be worse and you were lucky to stay out of it this year. I wish I could manage my money better because this is really hard on the spirit and too hard a way to earn it (money I mean not spirit). She is worse then ever if you can believe it. He should put her away but why should he care, he never sees her except for an odd Saturday and Sunday when he spends his time in the ocean with those monsters and snooty Steven, whose as bad as ever. The weather is beautiful. It is a relief to get out of that stinking city. I can't tell you how awful she is, not that I need to. If I ever go crazy, no moddlycoddling for me. But I'm not rich I don't have anything to worry about, right Pim? They are calling me to play crokay. God help me. The really rich are really different, I have to say that. The food is tops, but its pretty hard to swallow with Ophelia talking to the mashed potatoes. (I'm only fooling its not that bad.) The good news is we are doing Twelfth Night and I'm Orsino. The monsters are the twins (clever huh?) and Denvers is directing. Its gonna be good. The rehearsals are the best part of the day. It is fun to learn some lines again not that its been all *that* long but you know what I mean. If you are free maybe you can come out and see me? We are scheduled for the first Sunday in August. Herman is coming out to do the set and Brooks is supplying the costumes like last year. It isnt 14th Street but its better then nothing. Did you get the part in the new Belasco? They are all screaming for me. I've got to go. More later. I miss you.

XXXXXXX,
Margie

I wondered what happened to Margie. I wondered what happened to Pim. The guests/relatives were paid actors. I crumpled the letter into my pocket, planning to feed it to the first fire I happened upon.

"Did Cormack play as well as Donough does?" I interrupted my lesson to ask a sleepy Keyes.

"Cormack had perfect pitch. Donough has a touch of
the poet. If I played a piece through twice, Cormack
could play it back. He lacked discipline, dear. He could
not practice. He was mercurial. Each reading was different. One minute he was happy, the next sad and
gloomy. I often thought he had no form of his own. It
was what made him so ravishing. You could shape him
into anything you desired. Of course, dear, that was all
maya, illusion. And dangerous to boot. They were themselves but needed each other the way goldfish are separate but need the sea. Poor analogy. Sorry, dear. I'm old
and very tired of all this. Being malicious is a terrible
strain."

I blinked at the non sequitur. He appeared flustered
and closed the piano. I was cursorily dismissed.

It took me the rest of the morning to gather the books
scattered throughout the right-wing rooms on the second
floor and the left wing of the third. After lunch, I
planned to finish the search and begin typewriting the
cards. When I returned to my closet to prepare for luncheon, I discovered Margie's letter in my pocket. Instead of
burning it, I flattened it into my journal.

It started snowing after luncheon. Denvers excused
himself immediately to resume work on his project. I
wrote in my journal for an hour before walking through
the remaining rooms as I had intended. I expected to
spend only a short while in the right wing; most of the
area was Library II, the art room, and Keyes's quarters.
I found one stray, then went into the art room to peruse
those shelves for misplaced miscellany.

I felt guilty being there. The case full of lepidoptera
attracted me, as did the black metal cabinet marked
"Photography," but I was uncomfortable and wanted to
forget my transgressions in that room; yet I was determined not to leave books scattered about like leaves after
a windstorm. So I continued browsing the shelves, con-
centrating intensely on titles to avoid wondering what
Ruby was doing on the other side of the wall in a room
accessible only by means of a spiral staircase hidden in
the basement, a room with windows sealed closed by
Boston ivy.

I looked about the room. A large door with a brass key
in its lock was centered in the connecting wall between
me and Ruby's quarters.

I walked directly to the door and without hesitation tried the knob.

"May wasps swarm and hornets rage," I mumbled, yanking it open to reveal a storeroom. "Sneak and ye shall find a closet, my smart young snoop," I added guiltily.

I could see a small stack of books on a shelf too high for me to reach without assistance.

"At least I haven't disgraced myself for nothing. I can lie and say I did it for the books. . . ."

Taking a low stool from beside the photography cabinet, I stepped inside the closet below the back shelf. I stretched my hands up for the books, unaware that the door behind me was quietly closing, until the key turned in the lock with a deafening click. I spun around on the stool. The shock of the sudden darkness and the realization that someone had just locked me into the closet made me lose my balance. I fell backward, slamming my head against the shelf, but not, thank God, tumbling to the floor. Overcome by nausea from the blow, I sat down on the stool. Was this someone's idea of a prank? I was not smiling.

I must have sat there collecting my senses for fully five minutes before realizing I was no longer in the dark. Glancing over my right shoulder, I saw that the walls no longer formed a corner; in the fall my head had opened another secret door! Swiveling on the stool, I peeked through the crevice. A diaphanous white fabric hung in front of my face. Using my left hand, I pressed the walls farther apart. The purdah rustled. The space on the other side was crowded with white dresses. Squeezing in among them, I peered out into a room bright with winter light, warmed by a crackling fire, and colored completely in cheerful pastels.

Stretched out on a divan, her back toward me, a silver-haired woman reclined in the sunlight. She fidgeted nervously with a white shawl, which I assumed had been recently removed from the closet in which I now stood. She'd left the door ajar, and the light had shown me the way to her. This was her sitting room. A stunning Fragonard took my attention. I took two paces toward it. She turned to face me.

No one word can express what I felt at that moment!

Rested, calm, drenched in snow-heightened sunlight was the face I had seen in the mirror! The face of my mother, yet not her face. The face ravaged by the merciless claws of time and by unspeakable memories. The face of my mother, not as I had last seen it, but as I would see it perhaps in twenty years time. I gaped in stupefied amazement. Was this an illusion, the product of a deranged mind?

She smiled at me. She spoke in a soft, high-pitched voice with only the vaguest timbre resemblance to my mother's sound. She spoke without surprise at my presence in her sitting room.

"I thought you would never come! I am pining for you. The birds were discussing us this morning, which was what brought you to mind, though you are never far away. Will you stay to tea? If you don't, I shan't be able to mention your visit. The last time I spoke of Cormack to Ruby, she became quite cross."

"Don't tell her I was here, please! Don't mention it to her."

"Very well, but I *am* weary of this secrecy. It reduces one so."

"When will she return?"

"She left for the tea things a moment before you arrived. Didn't you pass her in the hall?"

She opened her eyes very wide. They were my mother's eyes. I had to sit down. I walked shakily to the chair opposite her.

"Don't fret! We'll hear her at the door. Why have you cut your hair so short? Mama will be very angry. Did *they* make you do it?"

"Who?"

"The Gypsies, of course! Come, sit here beside me and tell me all about it. I never tire of hearing it, you know."

"Did I wake you? I'm sorry if I woke you."

"I wasn't asleep. I never sleep."

I moved to her side on the divan. She took my hand in hers.

"It's such a trying life here. I do my best, but Mary Rose would be grateful for your help. Cormack has that evil Steven. Are you coming to live with us again?"

"No! I can't! Not yet."

"Well . . . I will content myself with an occasional visit from you and the boys. For one as weak and as delicate as I, too much strain is not good either. I *am* happy to see you."

The resemblance was uncanny. She was more breathless and fluttery, more traditionally "feminine" in gesture and behavior, more agitated, "high-strung," and tense, with noticeably more cultivated manners and style; yet, there was a flickering half-smile, an overall shape to her presence and the structure of her body to confuse my senses and convince me the similarities were more than coincidental. I barely heard what she said.

"Why are you staring at me like that? Has my hair come down in back?"

"No. Forgive me. You remind me of someone. I didn't mean to stare. I don't mean to be rude."

"I remind you of someone? How glorious! That's always so delightful! Who *is* the fortunate being?"

"I can't recall . . . which, I guess, is why I was staring." She became distracted suddenly, and I feared she was going to cry.

"You must be happy when the vines shed their leaves," I said, clutching at a distraction. "The sunlight is wonderful."

"Yes, but it makes me sad. It's like a net. The years literally blow away. You understand?"

I said I did. She seemed relieved. I asked after her health. While she spoke, I wondered if, like me, she had no other place to go. How had she come to Donough's attention? She became involved in a convoluted explanation of her invalid state; straining to follow, I did not hear Ruby until a door slammed in one of the other rooms. I stood to take my leave at a run, placing a fleeting kiss on her forehead.

"Please come visit, dear."

"I will. I promise. Soon, I'll stay for tea."

Rushing into the closet, I yanked the door closed just as Ruby's voice was heard praising Mr. O'Shay for another extra-special tea: crumpets! Crumpets? Scenes from Dickens and Thackeray rose before me. I ceased struggling with the clothing that entangled me, and was tempted to reconsider the specter's offer, but thought better of it. I groped my way back to the wall and passed to the other side, grateful her shoes were kept elsewhere. I pressed the wall nearly shut, taking great care not to lock it.

Sitting on the stool, I pondered my predicament. How was I to get out of the art-room closet? If I became hysterical and shouted for assistance, Ruby would hear me. If I stomped my feet against the door, Keyes might hear me and think a thunderstorm was approaching; Beethoven, of course, would notice nothing. Perhaps when I didn't appear for tea, Denvers, alarmed, would organize a search? Led by Cael?

As if materialized by my thoughts, Cael howled outside the door. Stooping to peer through the keyhole, I saw him sitting in front of me, distress evident in his round eyes. He howled again, demanding entry.

"Cael, trust me; I would if I could, but I can't."

I pressed my mouth against the keyhole, planning to instruct him to go for help (knowing better, but hopeful nonetheless), when the door sprang open. I toppled out like so much baggage, bruising my nose when it thudded against the wooden floor. The cat bounded backward, horrified; not entertained, he scurried from the room.

The door had been unlocked. The key had been removed. Had I not looked through the empty hole? Whoever locked me in now held the key in his possession.

This is a problem, I thought, still sitting on the floor. "Whenever I visit her, I'll risk incarceration. Well . . . that is the chance I will have to take."

So saying, I went down to tea, hungrier than usual. A letter waited by my place. A letter from Timothy Goodbody. With Denvers's permission, I opened it at the table. It was a short note written on legal yellow-pad paper.

> My dearest Robbie:
>
> The district attorney is making his opening statement to the jury. As he reiterates the "moral" question at every trial, I can write now without fear of missing anything crucial. Mortimer is paying attention. Believe it or not, this is the only place I can steal time to write. How much I enjoyed my visit with you at Gaywyck! You must come to New York soon and visit with us. Again, thank you for your companionship.
>
> Fondly,
> Goodbody

A postscript in a different hand was appended:

> P.S. Ditto here. Love, Mortimer.
> P.P.S. He has such a way with words. TG.
> P.P.P.S. Must always have the last word. EM.
> Now we have done it! The DA is all excited. He hasn't seen such animation at this table since our first day in court. He thinks his rhetorical brilliance has generated this note passing. I find that endearing. Don't you, TG?
> Yes, EM, I do. However, the court awaits our pleasure. The show must go on and on, and the State vs. Imre, remember? Good-bye, Robbie. Thanks again! TG
> He's right, as always. Good-bye for now, new friend. EM

When I finished the note, I gave it to Denvers. He, too, had received one, more restrained than mine, but warm and very affectionate. We laughed over their antics, but he insisted that despite their levity, they were two of the finest, most successful lawyers in the city.

The day after Thanksgiving, I had found myself alone with them in Library I. I felt comfortable and had no compunctions about asking personal questions. I managed several leading ones; they showed no reserve with their answers.

Goodbody and Mortimer were introduced practically at birth. Their fathers were Wall Street financiers who owned neighboring houses on Fifth Avenue and belonged to the same club. Their boys played together and, at age five, visited Gaywyck for one week during the summer of 1874. Never having seen a black child before, the twins were fascinated by Mortimer, who also spoke several languages, and they readily accepted his wiry blond friend. The four formed an amiable team from the first.

Cormack sensed the strong bond between the two visitors; he treated them as equals. He rarely became violent or unpleasant, restraining himself from any overt acts of hostility, for the two of them (they could not be separated) were stronger than he alone; and Donough, sensing their combined strength, always sided with them. The visits were a continued success. During the annual Christmas recess in the city, the twins lunched with their friends at one house or the other, and spent a day in shared amusements. When they reached puberty, the visits abruptly ended.

"Cormack was too demanding, too aggressive. And ferocious when refused! We'd go back to town unnerved. Then he hurt Tim's left eye. We were just kids: curious and excitable."

"Cormack was *never* a child, Eugene. We found that out the hard way. He never played a day in his life; he didn't know how to play. He went for the jugular when he was crossed. I doubt if Donough ever refused him anything. I know his parents never did. We are probably the only ones who said no to him, and *I* paid for it!"

"In the cave?"

"Yes . . . in the cave."

"You know the cave?" Mortimer asked.

I nodded. There was a hesitation.

"What did he want?" I asked, seeing the cave crowded with the four young bodies.

"What he always wanted! What he couldn't get enough of: love. I said no. I loved Mortimer. He hit me so hard with his fist, I had to wear a patch for nearly a year."

"What happened after that?"

"There was no *after that*. We never came back. Our parents sent us to school together that fall and we were always too busy in the summers, and not available in the winters. We wrote to Donough, even arranged secret meetings with him in town over Christmas vac for a time, but he could never lie convincingly, and the whole thing was too hard for him. We drifted apart, but we loved him too much to ever lose him completely."

Mortimer interrupted. "After Cormack's death, we saw as much of him as we could manage. While we were in law school, we spent our summers with him in Paris. He's our dearest friend."

"Here is where Keyes would quote the old sage, son of Sirach: 'A faithful friend is a sturdy shelter; he who finds one finds a treasure.' And, he'd be right! That's the way we feel about Donough."

When I asked about Mary Rose Gaylord, they stalled before Mortimer answered: "She's dead, you know."

Then Goodbody added, as though sharing his thoughts, "I liked her. She was gentle and loving; at least, that's how I remember her. She had a difficult time. . . . Gaylord was a remarkable man. I loved being with him; he was easy and kind. He'd play with us for hours. I think he was the most beautiful man I have ever seen."

"More beautiful than Donough?" I asked incredulously.

"No," Mortimer answered, chuckling. "Perhaps not."

I nodded, relieved, unable to visualize a more perfect form.

"Well . . ." Goodbody continued, "*as* beautiful, Gene, but darker and bigger."

Mortimer laughed, about to reply. Then he glanced at me and changed his mind. Instead, he said, "I always thought he was the perfect father."

"Donough says he *was*, for the most part."

That surprised me. I imagined him aloof and removed from his two sons, unable to communicate with them and too self-absorbed to try. I had imagined him locked away in his study with Steven, always unavailable. I had imagined him the image of my father. Evidently I had been wrong.

Holding their amusing letter in my hands, I reread the last words over and over: "Good-bye for now, new friend." I knew they were speaking from the heart and I was happy. Denvers sat opposite, sipping wine, engrossed in the *New York Times*. I had a surge of affection for him. As though conscious of it, he glanced over the top of the page and smiled at me. I folded the letter. Friendship engulfed me. And the dearest friendship of all, I knew, would soon be mine.

We were served crumpets.

"Ah," Denvers said, "now we are certain winter has come."

Two days later, I received a letter from Donough Gaylord. It was the first he had ever written me. I hold the gray, monogrammed stationery in my hand now. I remember the words:

Dear Robert,

If you think you would find it to your liking, please consider a visit to Gramercy Park for Christmas. Ponder and send your decision—I will inform the household to plan accordingly.

I dined with Goodbody and Mortimer last evening. They send their regards.

DG

Ponder? I had no idea what he thought I would need to ponder. When I asked Denvers, he shrugged and suggested I wait several days before responding.

"Then Donough will be convinced you've thought over what he expects you to think over, and you've decided on a visit in spite of, or because of, or whatever. God knows *what!* Ponder, indeed. . . ."

I nodded and waited two days before replying in the affirmative.

At first I had some qualms about leaving Keyes and Denvers and Brian for Christmas, but when it was explained that the holiday was treated as just another excuse for an elaborate meal, I started counting the days until the twenty-third of December when I would board the train at Sterling Harbor. As with every other emotional upheaval, it took nearly a week for me to identify the uneasiness I felt regarding the impending holiday. I spoke to myself: as always, the exchange was brief and to the point. (It was belabored later in my journals.)

"They said he loves me. I heard them say he loves me, *finally* loves someone."

"But they don't know how difficult it is for him. How secretive and mysterious it has to be."

"No. But he and I know. I'll change all that."

"Oh?"

"My love will transform him."

"*Yes!*"

I hadn't read so many novels without learning something. I felt better, quieted. Trusting to the healing powers of love, I inhaled deeply, savoring the sensation swelling at the core of my being.

"So this is love?" I pondered, pleased.

During the month that followed, I altered my routine to include regular visits with the sequestered woman in white. Only once did she visit me. That night, I jolted awake knowing I was not alone. She stood by my bed holding a silver knitting needle as if it were a dagger. I wondered how long she had stood by my bed, but that was not the first question I framed when I was able to speak.

"What's wrong?" I gasped, moving to the far side of the bed.

"They're dead. I've killed them."

"Killed *whom?*" I shouted, leaping out of her reach.

"It had to be. God will forgive me if he saw. Cormack is free! If you had not been lost, my dearest, we would have found another way. We were reckoned clever before they buried Mary Rose."

"My God! Give me the needle! Whom have you killed?"

"Denvers is mad. He's tormenting Cormack. I think he's jealous."

"Have you killed Denvers?" I whispered, staring at the needle for signs of blood.

"Cormack isn't Donough, and never forget it! That's why they send him away. No one knows he visits me."

"*Who* visits you? Have you mentioned me?"

She sped away. Horrified, I followed. Like Cael, she seemed to see in the dark. Her white figure led me to the art room, where I watched her negotiate my secret passageway. For her safety and mine, I resolved to lock the wall. I sneaked into Denvers's rooms. Though his snoring reassured me, I was awake the entire night. Had she murdered Gaylord and Cormack? The next afternoon, I found the spring mechanism and closed the doors behind me.

I conjecture in my journal who the woman could have been. Her resemblance to my mother was stupefying, and the mystery frightened and stymied me. Reader, I was as one lost in a foreign country. Voyagers both, we haunted Gaywyck. As with the other conundrums, I listened to my heart. It bade me be still and wait.

Four weeks after posting my acceptance note, I left for Gramercy Park. I packed enough for a two-*year* stay, because Brian insisted he knew better than I and he helped me with an excitement equaling my own. We prepared for every emergency, including midwinter spring, which he posited might arrive without warning the next morning. He dogged me, making certain I was not stuffing suits into hatboxes or tossing shoes into dressing cases. When we finished, I sat exhausted, toying with Cael.

"Well, Brian, I can now survive the flood, the freeze, the frogs, the flies and even hail and boils, but the famine still has a chance. . . ."

I laughed. He frowned. I knew he was irrationally contemplating a tin of biscuits for my gladstone. To distract him, I threw a pillow at his head. We ended the last afternoon with some raucous laughter and my threatening not to "fill his order" if he didn't desist. We produced such a noise that Denvers appeared in my doorway to see what *exactly* was going on.

"I warned Brian I wouldn't bring all he wants back from town if he doesn't stop throwing things."

A pillow shut my mouth. I grabbed Brian by the waist and tickled him until he broke free and ran, laughing, from the room.

"He's going to miss you, Robbie. We all are."

"I'll be back soon."

"Yes . . . and the peace and quiet will do us all good, and tomorrow the lilacs will bloom again, and Thursday Christ will come to tea with his comrade John the Baptist. . . ."

The train departed Sterling Harbor at eleven in the morning. We left Gaywyck at 10:30. Brian held the reins of the sled; I sat by his side. I asked him if he ever thought of visiting New York. He said no: the noise was too great, the people too many, and the smells made him ill. He did, however, enjoy the ferry; to compensate, Mr. Donough took him on a birthday steamboat excursion each May 21. I told him that in exchange for that yearly ride, I, too, would forego the pleasures of the metropolis. He asked to see his shopping list. I produced it. He was happy to see, he said, how reliable I was. His officious, condescending manner amused me. Putting my arm around his shoulder, I called him the truest of friends. He laughed and admitted he liked me, too.

"When you first arrived, I took you for a prig. But I was wrong. Even Ambrose likes you, and he doesn't like anybody. He says you're *slow*, but he shouldn't complain."

Taio awaited us on the platform. He was not alone. By his side stood a young man, a curious-looking young man with large ears, a pug nose, brown hair cropped without design, ferret eyes, skin not too clear, and more curiously, a frame smaller than his Japanese companion's.

"Mr. Robert," Taio addressed me with cool formality, "this is Pryce Jones. He will assist you on the journey."

I noticed a distinctly acerbic tone. I smiled at the new person. He smiled in return, revealing the most perfect set of white teeth.

"Take the gladstone, Pryce Jones," Taio ordered as we boarded.

While he struggled with the heavy bag, I said good-bye to Brian, who was grinning idiotically at the youngster's difficulties.

"I am training him," Taio explained, settling me into the carriage. "He is a good little chappie, really, but I do not want him to get funny ideas. You see? He is Welsh, he says. I do not know any Welshmen. I have no idea what to expect. Mr. Donough wants him to take over the train journeys. I am pleased. It is a good job. I hope he is up to it."

"He seems willing and eager."

The sound of Pryce Jones cursing as he tumbled down the steps interrupted our colloquy. Taio emitted a guttural expletive in his native tongue and hurried to the window.

"I hope there is nothing breakable in your gladstone, Mr. Robert!"

"Actually, there are scent bottles and—"

"Goodness! Hold yourself there, Pryce Jones! I will assist you. I will send him in to see if you require anything."

Pryce Jones? I wondered if he were any relation to the murdered Mr. Jones. I could hear Taio berating him, saying his name as if it were one word.

The train started. Taio reappeared. A tremendous racket came from the carriage in front of us.

"Goodness!"

"Taio, I think you had better go see what just fell on Pryce Jones."

I shouldn't have laughed, but I did. I wouldn't be laughing for long.

Luncheon was worse than awful. Poor Pryce Jones's natural clumsiness was not aided by the twitching and jerking of the railroad car, or by Taio's tutting and sighing for each error of form committed by his new assistant. I did all I could to help (even refusing second helpings), but my very presence complicated matters for the neophyte. He trembled violently, tracking venison blood across my lap and sliding a buttered bean into my vest pocket. My brown tie remained unsullied until dessert. That mishap was partly my fault: the chocolate ice cream would have rolled down my back if I hadn't turned when Pryce Jones yelled.

"At least, sir, it's the same color, sir, as the tie, sir."

"I don't believe you said that, Pryce Jones. Tell me you didn't mean that, please?"

He was instantly banished by Taio, who noticed the bloodstain on my trousers. He whimpered, then cried aloud as I produced the green bean from my pocket. He called after the fleeing boy to open my valise; a change of costume was required. Then, growling, he gave chase.

When he opened the carriage door, waves of my scent wafted through the air. I shook my head in disbelief and began undressing. Taio screamed in several languages. Mr. Tibbs reappeared to inform me Taio was too distressed to serve me, and would I like my coffee now? Half-dressed, I sat before the fire. As he left me, I caught a few obscene phrases in Taio's high-pitched voice and another cloud of my scent. He closed the door; another one, farther on, slammed. Then there was silence. The sudden silence was more worrying than the fracas.

After a tense fifteen minutes, Pryce Jones entered, his nose and eyes red from weeping. He carried a wooden tray, where he deftly stacked the dirty plates and the remains of my luncheon. I watched him work, and wanted to comfort him.

"You'll get the hang of it in no time, you know."

"I've got the hang of it now, sir, if that chink would leave me to it. Staring at me! Making me do everything wrong! If he'd stop poking at me like I was muck . . ."

He stopped. His words caught in his throat. Tears spilled onto the tray.

"He's Japanese," I said softly, unable to think of anything else.

He shrugged eloquently; to him there was no difference.

"He told me," I said soothingly, "that he thinks you're a good chap. He doesn't want you to get any funny ideas, that's all."

"The only funny ideas I got, *he* gave me, and if I carry them out, he won't be around to dance at my hanging, 'cause he'll be the cause of it!"

I smiled. He stopped crying, sniffed heartily, and laughed, baring those perfect teeth of his.

"If he thinks *me* a problem," he added, "wait till he meets Seth!" The rest of the journey unfolded without incident. I stepped down from the train rigged up in a different traveling outfit, but only Taio seemed upset by the change.

Pryce Jones looked glum until he caught my eye; then he winked boldly. I liked him and for the second time wondered about his background. Where was he from and who was Seth?

I was to learn the answer all too soon. Taio accompanied me to the waiting carriage. Our eyes met. I saw his distress, and realized he was not angry at Pryce Jones but deeply mortified at what he considered his own failure.

"As for the ice-cream stain on the tie: I said, 'At least, sir, it's the same color, sir, as the tie, sir!' "

He laughed and waved. I felt better. That first night at Gramercy Park, when everything was grand and strange, he had treated me as one who belonged. If Donough came to me about it, I would laugh a great deal about the Pryce Jones mishap. All would be well, I would see to that.

The snow had turned to slush on the streets of New York. It was too cold for the windows and I drew the curtains and huddled under the lap rug. At the ferry, I stayed where I was. On the seat, I discovered the copy of *Là Bas*.

When the carriage started to roll again, I could no longer read. Only my destination interested me. I did not even care for the hubbub outside. The horses' hooves sounded on wood, then on concrete, then on freezing cobblestones. The noise heightened as we slowly swung into open traffic. I pulled the lap rug tighter. Would he be in his study, or in the sitting room downstairs? What would his first words be?

A comfortable journey?
What tidings of home?

Alighting from the carriage, I glanced at his second-story window, expecting to see his face and form. The window was in darkness, as were all the others. The sidewalk was recently shoveled, though a few footprints marred the thin layer of newly fallen snow. Carriage tracks crossed clearly in the whitened streets. The drifts on both sides of the shiny black door and against the red-brick house were pristine and beautiful, protected by the tall black wrought-iron fencing. A great Christmas wreath hung on the door, elegant and seasonally perfect as something on the cover of *Collier's Magazine*.

Mr. Moore took my coat and showed me into the front parlor. I glanced affectionately at the large arrangement of winter flowers in the foyer, then at the Van Gogh over the fireplace. A note was placed in my hands. Still standing, I read:

> Robert:
> I have been called away on business. I shall be back as soon as possible. We will be spending Christmas Eve and Christmas Day with Goodbody and Mortimer. I've planned shopping for gifts tomorrow with the opera in the evening. Will that suit you?
>
> DG
>
> P.S. If I am not returned for dinner, Taio, has been instructed to serve you in your room.

Not returned by dinnertime? I was stupefied that business took precedence over me. I sat before the fire and felt tears welling. It seemed I had a great deal to learn.

Taio led me up to my room. While he ran a bath, I sat at the desk studying the arrangement of white spider mums. Utamaro's women imparted their mysterious longings, infusing the space with their beauty. I reread the note.

After dinner I made a lengthy, ponderous entry in my journal; suddenly I began to cry. I was astonished by the torrent, but continued writing as tears fell onto the page and coursed downward, connecting the lines with tiny streams of ink. The page is illegible. It became so as I wrote. Yet, I continued.

"I never learn by my mistakes. What difference does it make if I can or cannot read them?"

I knew disappointment did not warrant such an outburst. Whatever love is, it is not rational. I closed the journal unblotted, and climbed into bed.

Taio knocked. He asked if I wanted tea or hot milk. I did not. I began making plans for the morrow in case a note awaited me apologizing for his immediate departure on important business in Persia.

There was another knock.

Donough Gaylord, looking exhausted, appeared in the doorway. Without entering, he spoke.

"Put out your light, Robert; it's very late and we've a full day tomorrow. You will need your rest. Go to sleep. Good night."

He closed the door. I listened to his steps recede. He spoke a few words to someone before a door opened and closed.

As ordered, I extinguished my light, but the sight of him had excited me beyond sleep. I lay awake, alert with the quick pulsations of love. I whispered his name over and over, a sweet litany, praying he would visit my dreams.

The streetlamp illumined the white flowers across the room.

Be patient, I thought. There is time. There is an eternity for loving.

I rose and removed one of the mums from the vase, placing it in the water glass at my bedside.

"One step at a time, Robert Whyte. One small step at a time," I murmured, suddenly happy.

Thirteen

THE FIRST WORDS DONOUGH GAYLORD spoke next morning startled me. He entered the breakfast room engrossed in a piece of the morning's post. Barely glancing at me, he nodded a silent greeting and took the place opposite as Phillips served him tea. Laying aside the letter the moment we were alone, he smiled shyly.

"I'm sorry, Robbie."

I looked up from my porridge. The light from the sun embraced him; his skin was a delicate amber. He wore a dark blue suit and a white shirt with a high white collar as crisp as a eucharist wafer.

"I'm sorry I was so cross last night. I looked forward to your coming all week, then at the last moment was called away to business most unpleasant. I had no dinner, and I involved Goodbody and Mortimer, ruining their entire evening."

"Hmmmm," I said, not wanting to pretend I hadn't been disappointed. "What was wrong?"

"You met Pryce Jones yesterday?"

"Yes. I liked him. Did he get into some difficulty?"

"No, not him. His younger brother."

"Seth?"

"How did you know?" he queried, raising his eyebrows.

"Pryce Jones mentioned him."

"In what context?"

He seemed alarmed. Why had I not kept silent?

"He said he had a brother," I replied nervously.

Mr. Donough looked satisfied. I felt guilty, yet could not keep my mouth shut.

"Jones? Is he any relation to that man who was murdered?"

"You have a good memory. He's their father."

I wondered when he had started parting his hair down the center instead of brushing it straight back from his forehead. I envied his thick, black Irish hair. I decided to let mine grow.

"Why does this involve you, Mr. Donough?"

"Jones was in my employ."

"What did he do?"

"He was my foreman at a mill in the Bronx. It's a dreadful mess! There are union problems at the mill and . . . I feel somehow responsible."

"Why?"

"Because . . . he was against the union, thinking I would be pleased, even though I'm sponsoring it. He couldn't understand that I wasn't planning to fire them all. He was a thug, playing both ends against the middle. His throat was slit."

I shuddered. "Are you giving this Seth a job?"

"No. As far as I'm concerned, he's too young. He's just turned thirteen."

"Could you send him to school?"

"He wouldn't last a day!"

"What else can you do?"

"I don't know yet. I'll find a solution."

"Where is he now?"

"In the custody of his married sister."

"Why can't he stay there?"

"She won't have him. I can't blame her. He's a wild urchin. Lived on the streets from age five when the mother died! Thank God, he's the last one."

He asked if I had ideas about my Christmas gifts for Goodbody and Mortimer. I did not know what he meant. He wondered if he had not made himself clear in his letter.

"Not very."

"Not to worry. I rarely do. We'll find something."

I thought it odd for me to bring them gifts, then I thought it odd of me to think it odd: *Good-bye for now, new friend.* If I was to be a part of their holiday festivities, how could I not exchange gifts?

After breakfast, he ordered the carriage. Wrapped in scarves and wearing wool mittens, I went outside to wait. During the night, more snow had fallen; the air was cold but exhilaratingly clean, sharpening sight. Traffic moved slowly; horses, wary of the icy streets, proceeded gingerly.

We headed up Third Avenue by sled to the "Ladies' Mile" on Broadway. Our carriage, like all the others, was decorated with bells and ribbons and holly, extending the holiday festivities from the shop windows into the streets. The traffic of both humans and machines was stupendous. We decided to forego the shopping expedition and buy everything at one emporium. He abruptly ordered us back downtown to Louis Tiffany and Company on Fifteenth street. We nearly collided with a Lord & Taylor delivery van, and almost ran over a woman who sat on the curb selling wooden toys from a basket. A gigantic policeman in hat and white gloves cleared the way.

Donough was very patient with me as I browsed from counter to counter. I was completely unaware that he was guiding me past certain glittering cases. I chose a silver fountain pen for Denvers, a tiny pair of gold shears on a chain for Goodbody's thin Havanas, a bookmark in Nubian ebony shaped like a clef for Keyes's manuscripts, a dozen miniature porcelain birds for Brian's bonsai, and a slim silver flask for Mortimer's brandy.

It was a pleasure shopping with no money changing hands (except once); I pointed and he signed pieces of paper. There was something fantastical about the entire experience. I felt as if *I* owned the store. When I came upon a glass paperweight in the shape of a chrysanthemum the color of pale fire, I used the money Denvers had advanced me from my salary. With the complicity of a highly competent salesman, I managed that transaction without uttering a sound while Donough hovered over me, greeting the elegantly attired people who called him by name and wished him Merry Christmas.

In his favorite men's scent shop, I found exactly what I wanted for Ambrose: a very dry fragrance redolent of lilies. In a nearby haberdashery, I discovered an item on Brian's list and made a great display of checking off one article of the fifteen. He laughed until he saw the variety of requests.

"Taio will take care of that, Robbie. He'll enjoy a day 'on the trot,' as he calls it. You can check off the signals for his set of trains; I've sent them in my Christmas package. Put Henri's name beside that pastry pin; he'll know right where to find it. I'll give this to Taio later."

Taio! I had forgotten to buy something for Taio! Glancing to the rear of the shop, I spotted the perfect gift. Donough could not understand my delight in finding a silk tie the color of chocolate ice cream.

A black silk cravat reminded me of my father. My father! My mother! I bought the cravat for my father, and asked if we could go to the bookstore. The bookstore! Miss Grimmond! Did Annie still live with her? And what about Aunt Emily? I bought a pair of black fur-lined gloves for Father Howard, remembering that his hands were delicate and finely shaped. One recalls the oddest things!

"I'm starving," I said aloud.

He suggested we return home. I hesitated, feeling the thrill of the hunt. He reminded me Henri was expecting us. I acquiesced. On our way to the sled, my head swiveled, tracing the most marvelous smell. An elderly man stood at the curb beside a stove on wheels grilling slim sausages and boiling sauerkraut in a caldron. I asked what the things were called.

"Why, hot dogs, boy!"

"Robert! You'll ruin your appetite!"

"But, I've never tasted—"

"I don't know if they're safe to eat. You might contract ptomaine poisoning or Ermengem's botulism."

"I'll chance it."

"Then I shall have one with you."

After proper luncheon, I suggested we walk to the Ladies' Mile. When he informed me that many workers were liberated at one o'clock on Christmas Eve, adding several million more to the crush, I insisted. He laughed excitedly and confessed he had never shopped during the rush. We hurried to dress.

The first stop was the bookstore. I introduced myself to the proprietor, Mr. Cullam, who showed me a package he was preparing for Miss Grimmond. I added *David Copperfield* with a note bearing seasonal greetings and eternal gratitude. Then I purchased a splendid edition of *The Winter's Tale* for my father. I hesitated at the moment of inscribing it; instead, I enclosed a card.

We made our way easily through the serried ranks of shoppers. People were very pleasant, nodding and smiling and wishing me seasonal greetings as if we were upstate in a small town. I told him I thought Manhattan's reputation for coldness and brutality (a favorite theme for magazine articles) was unjustified. He told me to keep close tabs on my wallet.

I stopped frequently to give small coins to begging children and to examine the multitudinous wares street sellers offered from nearly every doorway and street corner. A circle of dogs yapped around a man carrying a placard advertising Macy's emporium. I spun around to ask if we could; he shook his head, drawing the line.

"It's like a fair," I called to him while buying a bag of cooked chestnuts.

He nodded wearily. I could see his enthusiasm waning. I hurried into the first ladies' glove shop sighted on Twenty-first and Broadway to select a pair of short black leather gloves (two buttons only) for my aunt. He pointed to green suede, ivory snaps, elbow length.

"Buy something *cheerful*, Robbie," whispered Donough. "These are very fashionable. She can wear them to church. She'll love them!"

"I'm sure!" I said, smiling sweetly. "But I doubt if her mother superior would approve."

He blinked, paused a beat, then sauntered away with flawless comedic blankness. When I laughed, he glanced slowly over his right shoulder, raised an eyebrow, and projected monumental indifference before disappearing into the assemblage of glove buyers. While I was paying, he reappeared waving a white handkerchief. I laughed again, reading the gesture as one of surrendering to despair and fatigue, and said I was finished, but he mumbled, "For Annie . . . not *too* fancy . . . perfect for Annie," and then vanished again. He was very right: I purchased it, admiring the delicate lace and the discreet letter A embroidered in a corner.

I found him outside leaning against the shop window smoking a cigarette. He gestured with his head for me to follow. Leading me several shops down Broadway, he turned into one specializing in woolen goods. It was overly stocked with frenzied shoppers, but he grasped my hand and elbowed us to a particular counter. Triumphantly he pointed to unbleached wool shawls from the Aran Islands.

"Perfect!" I exclaimed.

He nodded, very pleased with himself.

"Hurry this along if you can. Believe it or not, it's practically teatime."

Expecting to meet him on the sidewalk, I found him

sitting in a cab at the curb, finishing the last of my chestnuts. All the while, he'd been making purchases of his own. The seats were crammed with packages; one box was larger than I. I thought I heard it speak!

"What's in there?"

"Two charming elves to wrap all of this. Let's go home!"

We were greeted at Gramercy Park by a full Victorian high tea as close to Mrs. Beeton's "movable feast" as I had ever imagined. While the Darjeeling steeped, he recited Cowper's lines in wonderful mock-serious tones:

> Now stir the fire, and close the shutters fast.
> Let fall the curtains, wheel the sofa round,
> And, while the bubbling and loud-hissing urn
> Throws up a steady column, and the cups,
> That cheer but not inebriate, wait on each,
> So let us welcome peaceful evening in.

We took that Christmas Eve tea in the main parlor. A full fire blazed; snowflakes fell outside; carolers sang in Gramercy Park; and, on the table before us: deviled eggs, caviar in aspic, oyster bisque, tongue-and-ham salad, lobster thermidor, mimosa salad; on a sideboard, between flowering poinsettia plants (their brilliant red bracts a celebration in themselves), Henri had balanced *petits-fours, mille feuilles, gâteau moka,* and *dacquoise* on long-stemmed silver cake servers.

"Henri loves the holidays." He chuckled in the Mortimer manner while preparing a plate for me. "They are coming here for supper tonight after the opera. Last week, Henri posted his menu. Goodbody told me when Mortimer read it, he vowed to fast until the hour. They sent me this."

He handed me a large card on which had been affixed the piece of sheet music of an original song in six-eight time entitled "Dr. Johnson's Rag":

> I look upon it that he
> Who does not mind his belly
> Will hardly mind
> Anything else.

Our laughter was interrupted by Phillips.

"Mr. Eugene on the telephone, sir."

"You take it, Robbie."

I was thrilled. I'd never spoken over a telephone before. I followed Phillips into a closet off the dining room where the instrument was kept. I took a deep breath and shouted, "Hello?"

"Donnie? Why are you screaming? I haven't done anything yet."

"No! It's Robert."

"Oh, Robert! Listen, you needn't shout! Just talk in your normal voice and I'll hear every word. How are you? Merry! Merry!"

"I'm fine! Thank you! Merry Christmas to you, too! How are you?"

"Couldn't be better. When are you coming?"

"At seven."

"Too late! Come now! Is Donough there?"

"He's inside. I'll get him."

"No! Don't bother! *Bring* him *now*! His immense package just arrived. Goodbody can't possibly wait until tomorrow to open it; he's coming down with fever from the excitement already. Tell me what's in it. I won't tell anyone, I promise."

"I don't know."

Screaming and yelling at his end interrupted us, then spilled over into the telephone.

"My good God! A cockatoo just arrived! Is he out of his wits? A *cockatoo* as big as I am and whiter than Goodbody's . . . *Mon Dieu*! Put that bugger on the phone! Drag him if you must!"

"Just a minute."

Donough refused to take the mouthpiece.

"He won't talk to you."

"Robbie, tell him he's got forty-five minutes."

"He wants to know what will happen if we're late."

"Everything! Tell him *everything* will happen."

"He says we'll be right there."

We walked directly up the stairs to bathe and dress.

"I don't know what's happened to me this year, Robbie. Normally, I detest Christmas."

First Christmas, I thought, then . . .

"I love Christmas," I said.

"Mortimer and Goodbody don't add up to eight years old between them. Wait until you see their tree. They have a collection of glass ornaments from around the world."

"What did you send them?"

"A screen they admired, and toys for their cats."

"They have cats?" I asked, pausing mid-step.

"Seven! They share their house with seven, all relatives of Cael."

"Seven cats and a cockatoo?"

"Oh, Christ! I never thought of that! Get dressed as quickly as you can."

On my bed was a new evening suit. I bathed and found Taio waiting to help me dress.

All the clothing was new. On the desk was a small mound of white boxes which we emptied, one by one: studs and links of jade and onyx, a white silk tie, a white silk muffler, gray kid gloves, a black silk top hat, and a key. A key?

"To that closet, Mr. Robert. But first let me brush your hair."

"I never use that closet."

"We couldn't be certain of that."

I unlocked the door. Inside hung a dark blue melton overcoat with beaver lining and collar. A Christmas greeting was pinned to the right sleeve. I pulled the coat off its hanger and moved toward the door.

"Did you place my gift for him where he'll find it, Taio?"

"I placed it on his pillow and instructed Phillips accordingly."

"Thank you, Taio. I'm fine, now, thank you."

Crossing to the desk chair, I presented him with his gift. He was honestly surprised by my gesture. If the tie was a *faux pas*, the thought behind it would lighten my gaffe.

Then I rushed down the hall to Donough Gaylord. I knocked. He bid me enter by name.

"How did you know it was I?"

"You are the only member of this household who runs."

I blushed. He called me to him. Placing his hands on my shoulders, he thanked me for the paperweight. His eyes were full of affection.

"May I ask one question?"

"Yes, sir, of course."

"How on earth did you manage it?"

We both laughed. I thanked him for my beautiful pres-

ents. He said they weren't really presents, but necessities.
I laughed louder.

"It's true, Robbie! They are really just things you need.
This is your Christmas present."

He handed me a small velvet box. I stopped laughing.

"What is it?"

"What an absurd question! Open it and find out."

Inside was a silver watch on what resembled a tiny
belt, with a silver buckle. I recognized it immediately
but, dumbfounded, said nothing.

"It's a wristwatch, Robbie! The newest thing! I went
with Goodbody when he bought one for Mortimer, and
then with Mortimer when he bought one for Goodbody.
It was very funny! While I tried to keep them from buying the same one for each other, I convinced myself to
take one for you and one for me. It's a wonderful idea
for a timepiece, don't you think?"

He showed me his; it was the same as mine. I managed
a nod.

"Yes! It's the one I liked best. I hope you don't mind."

I started to cry. I wanted to mask my startling response
to his generosity by sitting down, but every space was
covered with elaborately wrapped boxes. I crossed the
room and stood, my back to him.

"What the devil are all these?" I sputtered, alarmed by
the sobs I felt rising in my throat.

"They're mine . . . from business associates, friends,
employees. . . ."

I saw his reflection in the mirror approaching me from
behind. He looked glorious, a beneficent angel. I turned.
He opened his arms. I fell against him. My tears spilled.

"What's wrong? What have I done?"

"Happy . . . I'm so happy. . . ."

He hugged me to him.

"You're too good to me," I whispered, calming. "I'll
never be able to love you enough."

He stiffened. I could feel his entire body remove itself
from mine. I straightened, freeing myself from his sup-
port. I read reproach in his cold gray eyes and waited
for him to speak, repenting what I had said, fearing he
would cease to respect me.

"I'll help you into your coat, Robert."

It took fifteen minutes by sled for us to reach our destination. During the ride to Thirtieth Street, on Murray Hill at Lexington Avenue, his mood lightened; the introspective tension gave way; the sweet temper of our shopping expedition was restored. Feeling the moment, I apologized for embarrassing him.

"Your candor startles me, Robbie. It always catches me off guard."

"But why are you *on* guard?"

"It's the way I am. It's the way I've always been."

"It's a fascinating style."

Catching my relieved grin, he smiled and took my hand briefly to squeeze it. The sudden pressure forced me into a clenched silence as tears of gratitude threatened again.

I must not rend the tender calm in his eyes. . . .

The front door of the brownstone house was opened by Goodbody himself. He wore a red-and-green velvet smoking jacket, and a sprig of holly was stuck in his blond hair.

"Thank God you've come! I've given my all to keep him from shredding the wrappings. Hello, Robbie! Welcome!"

"How is he?" Donough asked, amused.

"Gnawing holes."

"Has he discovered anything?"

"Only that you've wisely had everything double-wrapped. The Black Prince is having a nervous collapse!"

"On the telephone, he intimated *you* were giving way to fever."

"*I*? Imagine!"

I handed him packages beautifully wrapped by Taio, and he giggled like a young boy, thanking me several times before turning us over to Cato, a tall black servant who divested us of our winter trappings while his employer closely examined my gifts for clues.

An unearthly, high-pitched voice screeched welcome several times as we entered the front parlor.

"He has quite a working vocabulary," Donough said to me enthusiastically. "He comes when called. He sings. He dances. He laughs. He—"

"He's beautiful!" I interrupted, quite sincerely.

A great white cockatoo perched in an enormous metal cage on a table near the fireplace. On overstuffed Victorian red velvet settees and on the American antiques that covered shelves and tables, seven Persian cats with various markings sat at degrees of petrified attention around the ivory-colored room. A child's-fantasy Christmas tree, bedecked and twinkling, stood to the right of the fireplace. Dozens of gifts littered the room, most bearing a huge G or a huge M. One of Monet's "morning" Rouen cathedrals hung over the mantel. An elaborately wrapped bundle, large as the celebrants, stood in the alcove in front of the bay windows. Mortimer, garbed in a blue silk Japanese kimono, waited.

"Greetings, friends, seasonal and otherwise. Those aren't more gifts in your grubby paws, Goodbody?"

"They're from Robbie."

"Thank you, *petit*. As always, you look superb!"

I thanked him. There was a long, calm silence. This was not at all what I had expected. Goodbody offered us a drink. We accepted some port.

"It is certainly *big*," I said, eager for some fun, nodding in the direction of the alcove. Donough settled on the couch, between two cats.

"He's been *crazed*," Goodbody began, sighing. "It's been an agony."

"*Fou? Moi?*"

"Hello! Hello! Hello! Drop dead! Ha! Ha! Ha! Ha! Ha!" Donough apologized for the bird's rudeness.

"We can't keep him, Donnie. He's gorgeous, but we can't."

"What a shame!" I exclaimed to Donough. "Then there's no point to the other gift."

"I'll have it picked up in the morning," he answered softly, while our hosts gaped at one another. "May I have more port, please?"

Each time the bird twitched a muscle or fluffed a feather, the cats stirred. When he opened his coxcomb, one began to growl.

"I'll take the bird," Donough continued.

"*You'll* take him?" Goodbody asked, amazed.

"Yes, I'll take him. I've always wanted a cockatoo."

"Why haven't you bought yourself one?" I asked, wondering if he always took such an indirect route to satisfy his desires.

He shrugged, verbalizing as an afterthought: "The staff has enough to do. . . ."

"Awk! Sod you, you bloody bugger! Awk!"

The cats went into a frenzy of activity: growling, hissing, and changing stalking positions. We all guffawed and nervously made certain a cat was not within climbing distance of us.

"Where did he ever learn *that*?"

"Possibly from Mortimer while he was attacking your gift."

"Speaking of your gift . . ."

"In a moment, Eugene! Let me introduce Robbie to the boarders."

"Can't that wait?"

"Wait? Wait for what?" I asked, wide-eyed.

Mortimer sat on the floor near the package and started singing a Christmas carol. Goodbody continued, ignoring the reveler, "Normally, we'd have to wander all over the house collecting this clowder, but thanks to Feathers, here, they've all gathered near our happy hearth. From left to jolly right: Doniel, Petahel, Zarazag, Xomoy, Bethuael, Chermes, and Rugziel . . . angels, all."

"Those two look like Cael."

"His brothers, Doniel and Xomoy. Zarazag's his sister; she and Xomoy produced Chermes and Petahel, who managed the other two beauties."

"*Now* can we open?"

"I've no idea why you've waited," Donough responded.

Mortimer whooped. Goodbody climbed over a chair to join him. With much hilarity, three layers of multicolored paper were removed to reveal a sewn cloth casing. Their moans of disappointment and confusion drew the servants, who joined in the festivities. The cats, intrigued by the flying bits and balls of paper, gamboled around them.

"Get stuffed! Get stuffed! Ha! Ha! Ha! Ha! Ha!"

Cats flew to resume their positions around the bird. Cato presented Mortimer with a pair of scissors. Among the gasps, the "oohs" and "aahs," the hisses, growls, and squawks, a gilded coromandel screen was unveiled. Mortimer cried *"Bon Dieu!"* spun around twice and tumbled into the wrappings, where he rolled and squealed with glee. Tremblingly Goodbody opened the ornate screen. The servants applauded. Donough bowed his head, graciously accepting their praise. I squeezed his arm to congratulate him. Rugziel leaped to the mantel and stalked the cockatoo eye-to-eye.

"This is *the* most divine gift I have ever received!"

Rugziel pounced, upsetting the cage, sending six cats in as many directions, and freeing the bird by springing open the wire door.

"Help! Help! Ha! Ha! Ha! Ha! Ha! Help! Sod you bloody buggers! Awk!"

Donough leaped to his feet. The bird swooped down and landed on his shoulder. The cats, as though pulled by wires, reversed themselves and moved in for the kill. I had a terrified vision of Donough scaled and clawed by seven rampaging cats. Goodbody, sharing my vision, screamed instructions from across the room: "*Everyone grab a cat!*"

I caught Rugziel, the ringleader. Goodbody chased Petahel and Xomoy behind the Christmas tree, which began to totter. Mortimer scooped up the furious Doniel. The able Cato clutched the hissing Chermes. The housekeeper scurried out of the parlor chasing Bethuael. A valet grabbed Zarazag's tail.

Rugziel bit my hand. I shouted and dropped him. He squeezed under the couch. Zarazag clawed the valet, who persevered, still holding the tail. The housekeeper reappeared, proudly hugging Bethuael, now whining. Mortimer slapped a hissing Doniel. Goodbody separated Petahel and Xomoy, and lifted them at arm's length one from the other. Donough caged the laughing, clucking bird and carried him from the room, closing the door behind him.

I stopped poking for Rugziel when the others released their hostages. Ignoring me, he squeezed out from under the couch and grouped with Xomoy and Petahel to attack the library door where his cohorts massed, howling for entry.

"This is *horrible!*" Mortimer groaned. "Do something, Timothy, *anything!* They are disgracing us!"

"What can *I* do?"

"I've already done it," announced Donough, reentering the parlor. "I've called Taio. He's sending the carriage for the bird. Please forgive my damnable stupidity."

"Nothing to forgive, Gaylord. A little excitement is always delicious."

Once cajoled (and tugged) away from the library door, the cats quieted. One by one, they reappeared to collapse over the arm of a settee, across the mantel, or on a tabletop. Rugziel curled in my lap. Xomoy stretched on the back of the couch behind my head.

Goodbody and Mortimer opened the rest of their gifts and presented us with ours. They thanked me profusely for my trinkets, and took us upstairs, with great glee, to hang on their bedroom wall Denvers's addition to Mortimer's Americana collection: a first printing, dated 1 January 1863, of the broadside of the Emancipation Proclamation signed by Abraham Lincoln. They saved their own gifts, one to the other, for a later, private time.

In a large hatbox, Donough found a model of an automobile.

"It's a miniature of the one awaiting you in Hanley's Garage on Twenty-third Street."

Donough Gaylord sat silent and still. I watched his color rise.

"Goodbody, he hates it."

"It was your idea, Eugene. I should have known better than to listen—"

"I think he's overcome," I said quietly.

"Robbie! Do you really think so?"

"Ask him."

"Donnie, are you overwhelmed, or undone?"

He remained silent, holding the toy in his hands.

"Maybe we can get our money back?"

"Is the garage open now?" he asked almost inaudibly.

"What did he say?"

I repeated his words.

"I don't know, Donnie. Is it, Eugene?"

"How should I know? Do *I* frequent Hanley's Garage?"

Donough rose and began pacing the room. "When will it open? Please call and see if we can have the machine for a ride tomorrow!"

"It's after six," I said, glancing at my wristwatch.

"Eugene! Look what Robbie's wearing!"

We all compared wristwatches. It was the one gift they had exchanged as Christmas Eve presents. Donough chatted with the cats.

"I think," Mortimer whispered, "he wants his automobile *now*."

"I'm so relieved!" Goodbody sighed. "I knew it was a good idea."

"It was my idea!"

"Then *you* call the garage."

Mortimer made an appointment for one o'clock on

Christmas Day. Opening another large box, he presented us each with a pair of goggles. Phillips arrived for the cockatoo and we all wrapped the cage in woolen blankets to guarantee Donough's pet would not be carried off by pneumonia. Donough sat in front of the fire, grinning like a child, caressing the miniature automobile.

I opened my gift from the two friends. It was my turn to be delighted. I had always wanted a camera. I told them so.

"Everyone says that when they hate their gift. Blame it on Gaylord."

"Don't thank *me*! I had nothing to do with it."

"Do you no longer take photographs, Gaylord?"

"I never did."

"I thought *you* took that wonderful naughty one of Gene?"

"Which one is that?"

"The one at the waterfall at Gaywyck."

"I never took photographs. Cormack was the one with the camera."

A thick, uncomfortable silence settled, as palpable as the curtain of snowflakes outside the windows.

"Forgive me, Donnie. For what it's worth, I don't believe I've ever made that particular error before."

Donough shrugged. "Not to worry, Tim. You two had better dress or we shall be late."

I was amazed by the extent of their embarrassment.

"How in God's name could I have been so stupid?" Goodbody continued. "I think it's because I love that photograph so much. I want *you* to have taken it. How could I have forgotten? I've just blocked it out, I guess."

I fondled the camera in my lap. The two friends left Donough and me to our port. We didn't speak. I could see that the slip had distressed him. I left him to his thoughts. Mortimer returned briefly to hand him another package.

"I had it sent from Vienna," he said softly. "Merry Christmas, Donnie."

It was an unbound manuscript. I read the German title page over his arm: *Die Traum deutung*, by Dr. Sigmund Freud. Mortimer remained long enough to say that Dr. Freud was causing quite a stir, then left us again. My friend began reading. I sipped my port.

He was withdrawn for most of the carriage ride to the opera. Goodbody and Mortimer discussed where the coromandel screen would be shown to best advantage, and then drew him into conversation about the unconscious, which I found stimulating. The subject was obviously very important to Donough. When Goodbody asked if he ever heard from Dr. Mesmer, Donough became quiet again and solemnly shook his head. To lighten the mood, I clumsily dropped the non sequitur that *Faust* would be my first opera. Instantly I became the center of attention. All else was forgotten.

"All that matters, Robbie, is that you have a good time."

Mortimer flashed his new silver flask and winked at me. "I'll drink to that!" he exclaimed.

"You'd drink to Jefferson Davis!"

The number of carriages at Thirty-sixth Street was so tremendous that we four alighted from ours to walk the three blocks to the Met, joining the glamorous tide drifting toward the "Faustspielhaus." New York "society" people were far grander than I had imagined. We walked in a cloud of variegated scent. I felt giddy being in their legendary midst. Goodbody whispered in my ear, "You ain't seen nothin' yet, kiddo." He was right.

Our box was in the parterre. The auditorium was full. I thought the theater beautiful and Donough agreed, calling it "one of the loveliest interior spaces in the city." When we took our seats, people everywhere acknowledged us. This famed "golden horseshoe" was crammed with waving, nodding, laughing people, exhilarated by the prospect of hearing the celestial Melba, I assumed, until Mortimer assured me they were more interested in seeing and hearing one another. Someone shouted seasonal greetings to Donough from an adjoining box. He nodded in their general direction and under his breath demanded that the opera begin.

"All these noisy fools are making my head ache," Goodbody moaned. "*Everyone* is here!"

"Put up the *cordon sanitaire!*" Donough whispered, laughing.

I tried to read my program but could not concentrate. I looked around me, realized anew where I was and laughed aloud in excitement as the lights began to dim. My heart was pounding in my ears.

I shan't hear a thing, I thought when the conductor appeared. Distressed, I glanced at Donough Gaylord. He looked at me and smiled, reaching for my hand.

"Just *feel* the music, Robbie," he whispered.

I nodded, grateful and reassured.

I felt the music. I *rode* the music, its swelling and breaking reminding me of the ocean at Gaywyck. I had no difficulty following Faust's bargain with Mephistopheles, and I spontaneously applauded the student's song, which pleased my friends, because the young man, making his debut, was an acquaintance of theirs. I was so exhilarated by the end of the first act that I said I had to walk or jump up and down. I understood why there was such fuss over opera. It had everything: music, drama, spectacle. I asked if we could come again. They laughed, reassuring me there were more nights planned.

Out in the corridor, an elderly matron with silver hair called Donough Gaylord. We stopped walking and turned in her direction. She waved him forward with her fan, and before we were close enough for words, began scolding him for refusing her holiday invitations. She introduced him (as well as Goodbody and Mortimer) to her three nieces huddled behind her.

Her nieces seemed embarrassed. Mortimer, sounding "silly," introduced me as Robert, Lord Wight. I thought I'd misheard.

The matron paused in her harangue and eyed me suspiciously. Had *she* misheard?

Mortimer clarified for everyone. "The island, Mrs. Bingham, off the coast of Sussex—in England. His mother."

She composed her face and curtsied. The young ladies curtsied. I smiled wildly. Donough turned away in horror and disbelief.

"Oh, your lordship," she said, "how long do you stop in New York?"

I could not say a word.

Mortimer took command. "My cousin is here for the holidays."

"Is there any possibility . . . ?"

"None, regrettably. Good night to you. This way, your lordship."

I nodded. The women curtsied again, and one of the lovely nieces glanced at me with a knowing smile that suddenly informed the charade with gaiety. We four fled down the grand staircase.

"We would *never* have freed ourselves from her," Mortimer explained.

"You *think* yourself clever, Eugene," Goodbody sighed, "but now every grande dame will be queuing up for an intro to his majesty here."

"*We* shall manage," he replied haughtily, stressing the royal "we."

"I hope they wait till the intervals," Donough said, smiling in spite of himself.

People to the right of us, the left of us, ascending and descending on both sides of us, nodded or spoke to my friends. Men and women stopped to exchange greetings, invite them to gatherings, or congratulate them on some recent success. Each received a kind, courteous word in response.

"You're celebrities!" I said. "I'm bedazzled!"

"Mortimer, get his grace, your *cousin*, some champagne."

It was the same at every interval. As the last chords sounded, we were out of our seats to perambulate in those splendid corridors and foyers. By the third intermission, after Melba's triumphant "Jewel Song," I was soaring with excitement and managed the hordes of eager mothers as graciously and efficiently as if I were to the title born. By the fourth act, I, too, was a celebrity.

Maurguerite's agony at her undoing moved me immeasurably, and at the conclusion of the act I paused to calm myself, causing us to be swamped by visitors. The onslaught nearly ruined the evening for Donough. I thought the lights would never go back down, and when the fifth act was finally under way, I noticed, as he handed me the binoculars, his hands were shaking. I asked did he feel ill. He returned a look expressing such discomfort that I hardly heard the last act of *Faust*. I could not wait to leave.

Riding home, it was obvious that he was upset. When I asked what was wrong, he shrugged and said, "If one becomes as rude and as stupid as they, one can only blame oneself."

The decorated Christmas tree in the sitting room at Gramercy Park, a gift from Goodbody and Mortimer, lifted his bruised spirits. The cockatoo's cheer returned us all to a festive mood.

Merry Christmas, Donough Gaylord!
Ha! Ha! Ha! Ha! Ha! Ha! Ha!
Merry Christmas, one and all!

M. Henri's supper triumphed. I could not believe the beauty of the *poularde à la Neva*, a white-glazed bird, ornately decorated with truffles and green scallions. on a silver tray large enough to skate on. We drank many toasts and sang Christmas carols until dawn.

The event of Christmas Day was the ride in the automobile. We gathered at the garage and at precisely 1:10, according to our synchronized watches, drove into the street. A horse, pulling a barouche landau from the opposite direction, became hysterical, reared up, and neighed. The driver and gentleman passenger cursed us as we rocketed by at eleven miles per hour. Donough handled the machine superbly, having studied exhaustively the maintenance and control of an automobile. We jerked and jolted along the snowy streets. Holiday sleighers waved and cheered us on as we caused merry havoc among the horses with whom we shared the avenue. I was concerned about the speed and the noise until a fire engine tore past.

We rode around the block twice. A crowd of spectators gathered in house windows and on the pavement. When we had ventured two blocks from the garage, Goodbody and Mortimer—pleading the "giddy vapors"—asked to be carefully deposited at the curb.

Donough and I motored up to the southern end of Central Park and back down to the garage in just over two hours, leaving a highly entertained populace in our wake. I waved and laughed and all the while sustained a monologue on the glories of progress, pausing only once, when a rearing horse threatened to kick me into an early grave.

Back at the house, we found Goodbody and Mortimer seated in front of the fire anticipating Christmas dinner. I burst uninvited into their midst, interrupting a discussion concerning Melville's passion for Hawthorne, and babbled about the ride as *the* most exciting thing imaginable.

."For you, perhaps, my dear Robbie," drawled Mortimer,

"for whom the acquittal of Lizzie Borden was *the* most exciting—"

"Come, adventurers," ordered Goodbody, "sit by the fire with us!"

The eleven days of that sojourn burn fiercely in my memory. We attended the opera three more times. Nordica as Norma was sublime, with her ravishing *"Casta Diva."* I needed to know everything about Bellini. Donough and I sat in the study until dawn playing selections from the Sicilian's other works. The *Trovatore* was riotously exhilarating. The last evening, *Tristan und Isolde*, proved the greatest for me. Lilli Lehman's *"Liebestod"* left me unable to speak or move. Alone with him that night in the box, I could do no more than glance in his direction and raise my hands in helplessness, struggling to catch my breath. Understanding my turmoil, he dismissed the carriage and suggested a walk.

In silence we reached Central Park. He led me to the large pond. On its arching bridge, we stood side by side in the moonlight as the stars shone above, looking more like Doré's sparkling circle of the heavenly host than the familiar constellations. He spoke of his loneliness.

"You need someone to love," I said softly, boldly.

"I can't. I am unable. . . ."

"You loved your brother."

"Yes."

He looked at me and smiled, his eyes awake to the love his heart denied.

"I think," I said, "in each of us is Tristan and Isolde. I think we all can be . . . are able, if we dare . . ."

After a pause, he spoke one word, more for himself than for me.

"Yes."

When you are ready to know your love, to be transported beyond the confines and the supports of life, then let me be beside you, I said without saying.

He looked down to the frozen surface of the lake where the silver winter moon appeared captive. Large snowflakes began to fall. I leaned close to him and spontaneously placed a kiss on his warm cheek.

"That's the second time you've kissed me."

"May it not be the last, sir."

He studied my face. I laughed, amused and stirred.

"Why do you laugh?"

He looked puzzled. Smiling, he encircled my shoulders with his right arm, and declared the evening ended. We walked in search of a cab, neither of us speaking. Our chilled breaths merged.

We went to the theater, dined out—with and without our friends—visited museums, galleries, landmarks, and other places "of interest to the young and inexperienced." Goodbody and Mortimer, who shared a passion for New York City, had made lists coded by different-colored pencils as "musts," "perhapses," and "we-like-its." The two of us walked for miles, talking ceaselessly about countless things, all somehow relevant to ourselves and to our friendship.

New Year's Eve arrived and a new century loomed. As the clock in the parlor at 15 Gramercy Park struck twelve, we four friends toasted one another. A roar from the streets drew us to the windows. Donough pulled the drapes open eagerly. Outside, thousands of souls danced and sang, hugged, and kissed while bells of every quality pealed. We grabbed our coats and joined the revelers.

Reaching the pavement, I clutched Donough's hand and attached myself to a passing line of people skipping in a chain around the park, chanting amidst the raucous tintinnabulation: "Happy New Century . . . Happy Great Century . . . Long Live the Century . . . Happy New Century!" We danced with the others, intoxicated on the sense of Time Present as Time Eternal. The circles broke, reformed, and broke again. Suddenly connected with Goodbody and Mortimer, we formed our own circle and danced our private jig. For the third time, I kissed Donough Gaylord. It was a riotous party! After we ebullient four reclaimed our fire, the indefatigable celebrants continued for hours to tumble by our windows, singing and laughing and cheering their good fortune in witnessing the dawn of the twentieth century.

I returned to Gaywyck on the second of January. Pryce Jones, alone, made the journey with me. There were no problems. Brian met me at the station. He was delighted: Taio had done a yeoman's job on his list. He talked at a clip of the wonderful time they all had even though I wasn't there. I hinted at some "goodies" in my trunk. Frenchie's quickened pace flung us backward into our seats.

I found Denvers in the Della Francesca study. He was

not alone. A brutishly ugly young man with large ears, the small eyes of a rodent, a spotted complexion, and a mass of lank dark curls, sat to his left.

"Robert, I would like you to meet Seth Jones."

"Jonesy!" the boy snarled. "I call myself Jonesy!"

He smiled a mean, tight smile, revealing crooked broken teeth.

"Very well, *Jonesy*," Denvers retorted in evident distaste. "Meet Robert Whyte. Now, get out of here and leave us to ourselves. We've a great deal to discuss."

The boy stood, looked me over from top to boot, and smirked; his beady eyes remained impassive. Then he walked out. Denvers stared after him with a face that expressed cold nothing. I had to repeat my question twice.

"When did *he* arrive?"

"Soon after you left," he said softly.

"Why?"

"Donough thinks we'll be a good influence."

"For how long?"

"He didn't say."

"What's he like?"

"The meanest cur walking upright on two feet."

We laughed. But not for long. The catalyst had arrived. The die was cast.

Fourteen

"I WAS PETRIFIED LAST NIGHT. I EX-pected to be violently borne away."

My secret friend fanned herself in the overheated room while freezing rain pummeled the windows. Her old-fashioned white organdy gown covered my lap and most of the chaise.

"Aren't you used to storms by now?"

"There are certain things one *never* accepts. The boys were born during a storm, you know. Mary Rose tried to drown herself, they tell me. Foolish woman! *Ah, perfido!* Cormack saved her. Denvers *adores* Cormack. Everything begins there."

"You think so?"

"Absolutely! Nanny Welles said just the other day that if you look into anything you will see Denvers. She's right! This morning, I saw him in my egg cup."

I nodded. A key turned. A lock clicked. I rose, kissed her extended hand, and moved quickly into the open closet. Tugging on a certain coat hook, I released the spring and quietly passed to the other side. Methodically I locked the passageway. Since the arrival of Jonesy, I was apprehensive of carelessness. My nightmares had ceased and I was alert to possibilities.

Once standing in the art room, I heard Jonesy struggling with his piano lesson next door. He had begun soon after arriving, and as the lessons were scheduled for just before tea, Keyes became a permanent fixture at the midafternoon table, accompanying his always ravenous pupil from key-board to sideboard in the small dining room.

The boy played clumsily and learned slowly, which was not surprising; we were amazed to find he could retain *anything* from lesson to lesson. Totally illiterate, he was no use to me in the libraries, and none as a companion for more than the shortest periods: he was incapable of uttering a kind word about anyone or anything. Denvers considered it his "Christian duty" to teach him to read, and Keyes seemed activated and challenged by the presence of *l'enfant sauvage*. I left him to them.

"Wasps attract wasps," Brian commented. "Go visit your friends in the laundry-room window. You won't find any butterflies in their midst, except laid on as a main course."

One afternoon I found our guest in my rooms when I returned from my music lesson to dress for luncheon. Instinctively I glanced to my journal on the desk. I felt a spasm of anxiety before remembering the grinning fool's handicap, and Denvers's recent quip concerning his mental constipation.

"What are you doing here, Jonesy?"

"I come to walk you to lunch."

"That's kind of you."

"I thought you'd like it." He leered.

I wanted to clout him. Then I imagined how disappointed Donough would be, and contented myself with a heavy frown before going into my room to dress. The chiffonier drawers were open.

"Jonesy, were you podging around in here?"

"No! What the fuck would I do that for?"

He'd learned early that a well-placed obscenity could distract from the issue at hand, but I'd learned quickly how transparent most of his attempts at manipulation were. I didn't even pause to reprimand him.

"Next time you're snooping, close the doors and windows afterward."

There was a pause. I waited for a hotly phrased denial.

"I'll remember that one, thanks!"

"I'm sure you will. A little more time with us, and you may become domesticated."

I had not been surprised to find him sprawled on my sofa. He had a knack for being just outside when a door opened suddenly, and next to a room occupied by adults engaged in private conversation. He dawdled at table after meals and was always the first seated, lest any chat be missed. He lurked around corners and at bends in stairwells. He also disappeared for hours, regardless of the weather, and I dared not speculate on his wanderings because, as I now understand, I was afraid to know. Something told me he was eager for "trouble." Something also told me he would find it.

Leaving the art room after the visit to my secret friend,

I avoided passing the music room by taking the small stairs at the end of the hall. I hurried along the second-floor corridor, pausing before approaching the main staircase to listen for footsteps or conversation: the piano above had quieted; I did not wish to collide with Keyes and Jonesy descending. There was silence. I hastened to my rooms to prepare for tea.

A dramatic change had come over Keyes since the advent of Seth Jones, and I pondered its manifestations as I sat watching the aged music master that evening at dinner. Beethoven was laid to rest soon after his second pupil began lessons, and almost instantaneously the teacher transformed himself into a fop, a dandy, an overdressed, overscented, overmannered, arch, coy, silly, giggling spectacle replete with lace handerchief and overzealous applications of the curling iron and the rouge pot. The ultimate folly, however, was a pair of white linen gloves which he wore during dinner.

Appearing at each meal, he achieved by degrees the extraordinary disguise he wore *in toto* at dinner. It was as if each morning he forgot where he deposited this mannerism or that curl, rediscovering them during the course of the day under this sofa or that sheet of music. He maintained an appropriately animated conversational style, but he frequently rested his fluttering eyes on the grinning Jones whelp. I thought of Molière and wanted to share the observation with Denvers, but he, too, had changed, albeit more gradually and more subtly. For several days he absented himself from the evening meal, then began dressing in elegantly tailored clothing I had never seen before.

"We must all join the game, Robbie. *He* won't look quite so absurd if we all 'up the ante.' Meanwhile, is there *ever* any fool like an antique one?"

I could not decide which evenings were worse: when Jones sat grinning dumbly, vacantly, eating in silence, causing Keyes to chatter incessantly and Denvers to counterchatter, or when Jones himself nattered throughout the meal, spewing food in every direction, all the while demanding (and receiving) our undivided attention. I would stare at him, appalled and slightly frightened by the power he had over the two older men.

"I met a sweet little lass today. Have any of you lads got your peg up her? I told her it was a slammer, this

house, and I was starting to envy my goddamn brother
riding back and forth on that fuckin' choo-choo. She ran
away, and that dumb, fat-ass cook—"

"Mr. O'Shay," Denvers corrected.

"Yeah, O'Shay, he chased me outta the kitchen with a
fork!"

He would ramble on in his ugly, raspy voice, pausing to
snort and guffaw at his own feeble jokes, usually joined at
those moments by Denvers and Keyes—now become
Tweedledee and Tweedledum. Occasionally I would inter-
rupt him and try to divert the conversation to more fertile
ground, or I would boldly charge him to "belt up"; but
since neither of the other two seemed to object to his
blather, I eventually surrendered and stopped listening.
Every now and then I studied him to fathom his appeal,
but I could never see beyond the squat troll, more man
than boy, with his vulgar, whining sound and dirty, crenel-
lated fingernails—a creature of malicious cunning.

I was not alone in my dislike of Seth Jones. Brian refused to acknowledge his presence. And if ever the inter-
loper entered a room where Cael was, the cat, ears pressed
back against his head, would dash out. Unseen from the
orangery, I once watched while the boy tried to feed the
cat some tidbit; with narrowed eyes, Cael remained rigid
in a crouched position until the irritated Jones tossed the
offering and stomped away. For several weeks I observed
a concentrated effort on the boy's part to woo Cael; all to
no avail. Working in the library, I watched puss awaken
from a deep sleep and hiss with claws extended when Jones
approached.

"Leave Cael alone! You're wasting your time."

"Mind your own business! I never waste my time."

"Cael is *my* business. Leave him alone!"

When I next discussed Jones with Denvers, I came away
from the interview puzzled by his ambivalence. He professed boredom with the "runt," yet spoke of him with
great admiration (close to old-fashioned zest).

"He is a despicable, callous little monster, society's
Frankenstein *thing*. But perfection is not of this world. . . ."

According to Brian, only Denvers and Keyes accepted
the boy. The staff despised him. Mr. O'Shay sent his niece
home ("until the time when that rascal is gone"); and
Ambrose refused to serve him ("a nauseating slob"), but

Denvers turned livid ("a guest of Mr. Gaylord's," etc.), and the old man acquiesced, hurt and angered by the charges of elitism and negligence.

Donough Gaylord wrote to say how pleased he was that everything was working out so well. (Denvers had written, detailing the boy's progress.) While the tutor read "our employer's" reply aloud at tea, I silenced my discontent, aware more than ever (as was intended) that I, too, was a guest at Gaywyck. Wherever I happened to be, Cael was nearby; I called us "the fugitives." As long as I could arrange my day without interference, I made no more complaints. Then the order of life began to change.

Jones slept late in the mornings; breakfast was shifted to 9:30. Jones no longer found Denvers's study comfortable for lessons; they commandeered the downstairs library, causing me to alter my morning routine. Then, the question of tea arose: four o'clock was too late for the "growing boy"; it was shifted to half-past three. I was distressed until I discovered my secret friend would also be affected, but by then my complaints had angered Denvers, who imperiously accepted my apologies as though betrayed. I was furious with myself for fearing his anger. The entire Mad Tea Party—as Brian and I dubbed the mess—was a true domestic crisis and removed me even further from Denvers's affection.

Then came the matter of food. Jones loathed chicken, accepting it only "Southern-fried." Jones despised stews. Jones abominated veal. Macaroni made him "puke." Fish gave him "gas." Sauces brought him out in hives. Only white bread was "actual." Vegetables, *all* vegetables, were "glop." Salads were for rabbits and "sissies." I only half-heard his complaints, until I began missing the foods he railed against, while growing overly familiar with the ones he praised.

"This is the third time this week we've had roast beef," I muttered to Ambrose, who held the platter for me.

"I love roast beef," Jones snorted.

"So do I, but enough is enough."

"I eat all the *shit* you like, Robbie-boy!"

Keyes giggled. Denvers sat silent. Ambrose banged the serving dish down on the sideboard and fled the room. I reached down to pat Cael, then realized it was Jones's white napkin that Ambrose had accidentally tracked to my side while handling the beef platter. I rankled. Cael was no longer allowed in the dining room; Jones had complained: white hairs were everywhere. The cat hadn't fussed over the decision; even under my chair he wasn't safe from pieces of creamed "glop" or low-flying chicken bones.

"Denvers"—I chose words carefully—"why can't we eat as we always ate, letting Jones take only what he wants while we eat what we want?"

"We must endeavor to make everyone happy, and a growing boy needs a balanced diet."

His frown warned me I was nearing perdition. I nodded, waiting for the approved mashed potatoes. Ambrose appeared with a great crystal bowl of broccoli hollandaise. I caught his eye as he placed it before Jones. There was mischief there, and I glanced away.

"Ambrose!" snapped Denvers. "I ordered the vegetables served ungarnished with sauces separate!"

"Since *Mr.* Jones don't eat broccoli, I thought it would make no matter with broccoli, since *Mr.* Jones says broccoli looks like trees, and people don't eat trees."

"Did you say that, Jonesy? Aren't you a clever dear!"

Denvers ignored Keyes's chirping.

Koala bears eat trees, I thought. Jones looks like a koala bear.

"Ambrose!" he commanded, again. "Remove that broccoli and bring it to us with the sauce in a gravy boat."

Ambrose stood unflinchingly, obviously enraged and eager for the confrontation.

"Did you hear what I said, *Am*brose?"

"I ain't washing no cooked veg for nobody."

Denvers slowly pushed his chair away from the table. Keyes stopped chirping. I felt ill. The pale line between master and servant was now frighteningly clear. Denvers rose.

The door to the kitchen opened. Brian entered carrying two crockery bowls: one held broccoli, the other sauce. He thumped them on the table and with an extended gesture whisked the offending course back into the kitchen.

Denvers sat. Ambrose repeated in a dull, flat voice, "I ain't washing no cooked veg for nobody."

He left us sitting in silence.

Jones was the first to speak. "I hate trees, with or without white slush."

Denvers glared at him across the table. "Shut up, Jonesy!" he said impatiently. "No one cares about your preferences."

"I wouldn't bet a penny on that one!"

Denvers and Keyes laughed. I reached for the broccoli. Smothering it with sauce, I finished my meal without looking up from my plate.

That night, when I was comfortably in bed with Cael settled on the pillow over my head, Jones paid me a visit. He wore only a robe, with no covering on his feet.

"What do you want?" I asked without moving, forcing him to curl on the bottom of the bed. I noticed his legs were hairy, his toenails blackened with grime. Cael stopped purring.

"I thought I'd make sure you were all tucked up."

"Nice of you. Good night."

"Those two nearly had a set-to at the table tonight. I was ascared for a minute there."

"*You* were scared! You caused it!"

"I know." He laughed. "You and me are the only sane blokes in this house. We should be friends. If you knew what was good for you, you'd jump at the chance. Say! I'm cold out here. Let me under the covers."

"If you're cold, go to bed . . . your own bed."

"I can't . . . not just yet, anyways."

"Why not?"

"I got my reasons. If we was friends, I could tell you things would make your pretty blond hair stand on end!"

"My pretty blond hair is happy right where it is. Go to bed, Jonesy."

He slid off the bottom of my bed and ambled to the top, placing his hand on my head. Cael hissed.

"You ain't called me Jonesy in a long time. Let me under the covers, Robbie-boy. I'm freezing my butt off out here."

I hadn't called him Jonesy in a long time because those other two had converted it into a term of endearment.

"Go to your own bed, *Jones*!"

He removed his hand and shrugged.

"Good night, *Jones*!"

"You're making a big mistake. You'll be sorry."

"Are you threatening me?"

"I don't need to threaten nobody. I'm too smart for that

mucky shit. I'll tell you one thing, though: when I get what I want from this place, you'll be the first to know."

"Good! Write me a letter, if you've learned to hold a pen by then."

Smiling, he put his fingers to his forehead in the gesture of Donough Gaylord's salute.

"I won't have to write no letter. I'll just leave you my *journals*. It's funny the way everybody in this cockeyed house writes everything down in books. It's enough to make a body want to learn reading."

I sat up in bed. Cael grunted.

"Good night, Robbie-boy. Pleasant dreams!" he taunted, repeating the salute and leaving me alone.

I leaped out of the bed, felt the chill immediately, and bounded back. There was no point in my going after him. I was angrier at myself for believing his claim of illiteracy than I was at him for snooping in my journal.

He's a sneaking, lying mongrel, I thought. I was right! He's vermin, and I'll never trust him again for an instant.

Seth Jones telling me he could read was a serious tactical error. I had no idea what war he was waging, but he had made a blunder. I knew it. He knew it. The next morning, after breakfast, he sought me out in the upstairs library.

"Robbie-boy, I'm sorry for what I said last night."

"I'm not."

We looked into each other's faces. He smiled, revealing those crooked, rotting teeth of his, somewhat improved since his sojourn with us and his introduction to a toothbrush. I did not smile. I tried to appear stern rather than angry.

"I just want my share," he said softly. "You got the big fish, can't I have the small fry?"

For the first time in my dealings with him, I was speechless. I could not believe I'd heard him correctly. He went down to his sham reading lesson with Denvers. I walked to the window and stood watching the gray waves fanning the shore. After a good ten minutes of brooding, I forced myself to resume my work.

The next morning, I found a black orchid in my water jug. Sometime during the night, a visitor had stolen into my room. I assumed it a peace offering and said nothing. I awoke to flowers regularly in the coming months. Once, after a snowstorm, I opened my drapes and discovered footprints on the portico outside my window with an orchid resting on the banister where I was certain to see it. Another day, the shape of a drift where an orchid was planted clearly demonstrated a person had stood for a considerable time peering through the drapes watching me sleep. It was a game I found charming. I should have recognized it was not in the style of Seth Jones. Again, I did not remember my Greek.

Three mornings later, Brian woke me with a cup of hot chocolate in one hand and a saucer of fish for Cael in the other. I made room for him to sit by my side. He was excited and threw open the drapes before alighting on the bed. Midwinter spring had come at last. It was time to go out and take pictures with my new camera. Soon after my arrival from the city, he had helped me clean out the old darkroom off the laundry room. He checked the chemicals, reordered the ones no longer usable, and prepared the room for my first experiments in developing. Together we read through the collection of photography manuals. Alone, I had picked through the photographic images assembled by Mr. Gaylord for Cormack to study and "appreciate"—the art-room cabinet held hundreds of such images; the shelves housed dozens of albums by Brady, Daguerre, Muybridge, and Niepce.

I had proudly displayed my Eastman's Kodak Detective Camera at tea, and babbled on about an article I'd read years ago in *Harper's Magazine* by Mr. F. C. Beach on the taking of instantaneous pictures. Suddenly Jones expressed interest, whereupon Keyes announced directly he would instruct us in "the correct way to approach the science." Denvers forthwith communicated a desire to share his knowledge of "the accidental art." At that point, Brian and I became conspirators; it was "us" against "them."

He wanted an image of the mud flats.

"Cormack photographed them superbly," I said, sipping my chocolate.

"I don't care what *he* did."

"The pictures are wonderful, Brian. Mine should be half as fine. He had a painter's eye for line and perspective."

"I don't care what he had! They were always fighting about his pictures. Once, his mother wanted him to photograph her and he wouldn't. He took pictures of everyone swimming instead. She cried. I hated him for that."

"When was that? I didn't see any of anybody swimming."

"A long time ago. Before my accident. The plates are in the storage bin downstairs. I saw them when I was cleaning up. Everybody's naked."

I wanted to question him further about his accident, but somehow didn't dare.

"I wonder what else he photographed that's not upstairs?" I asked, remembering Mortimer's mention of the waterfall image.

"He photographed his brother . . . and his naughty father."

Brian and I were startled by the sound of Jones speaking from the doorway. When we didn't respond, he continued.

"I heard you chattering away like a polly bird, and I couldn't figure who was with you. I thought *he* was a dummy!"

He laughed his sneaky, dirty laugh. I hated him.

"Leave us alone, Jones!"

"I just come in to answer your question, Robbie-boy."

"Which question?" I asked, victim again of my own curiosity.

"Cormack's pictures, all line and perspective! He photographed himself. And his holy brother. If you're good to me, I'll give you one of his pictures of his brother. You . . . yeah, you, *especially* you, Robbie-boy, will be real glad to have one."

He laughed again, the meanest laugh imaginable, before turning himself out of the room.

"I hate him," Brian muttered.

"He's the *lowest*—"

"Not the lowest. Cormack was lower."

"Thank Christ I never met *him*!"

"I wish *I* never had!"

The photography was more than fun. It was, from the first moment I looked through the eye of the camera, *the* most exhilarating creative experience of my life. All of my instincts for form and balance asserted themselves, directing me and the machine. I felt an immediate affinity for the visual exercise. (As proof, I offer the fact that one of the nine plates I exposed was exhibited at my first show in New York in 1914.)

With Brian's expert assistance, I carried camera, tripod, plates, and a small basket of foods around the grounds, photographing the main house, the cottage, the ocean, and the mud flats (with Brian standing center, arms extended, head thrown back laughing self-consciously). We had a wonderful afternoon, and were looking forward to spending the next in the darkroom, but an incident occurred that put all ideas of pleasure out of my mind. My wristwatch disappeared.

I had purposely removed it before going out with Brian. When I returned to my room, it was not where I had left it. I distinctly remembered placing the treasured gift in the large white clamshell on my dresser top. Frantically searching the apartment, I looked inside everything that opened, underneath everything that lifted, and behind everything that moved. The watch was nowhere to be found. I went to Brian and asked for his advice. Together we went to Ambrose who insisted the staff scour the rooms I frequented.

"It won't do no good, you mark my words!"

We glanced at one another, not willing to speak our minds. If we could not censor our thoughts, we could keep from uttering the damning accusation and sowing more discord.

At tea, Jones's loquacity annoyed me. I studied him while he babbled about the splendors of Gaywyck, and did not flinch when he showered bits of cheese on my arm in his raptures over the dolmen, where he had been sitting for most of the afternoon with Keyes. All this struck me as building an alibi. "My watch has misplaced itself," I suddenly announced.

"You mean you lost it, Robbie-boy?"

"No. I mean it is . . . *gone*."

"Mislaid?" Keyes queried, eyes wide.

"Perhaps. . . ."

There was a chorus of concerned noise. Everyone promised to recover my precious trinket. At the dinner table that night, it transpired that a search had been conducted but uncovered nothing resembling my watch, though Keyes discovered a long-lost cuff link and requested we add its mate to our list of lost treasures. I was not angered by the charade, having expected little else from them. Late that night when I turned out my light, I had two visitors.

The first knocked gently on my door. Denvers entered, evidently deeply distressed. After mentioning the loss of my watch, which he claimed prevented his sleeping, he casually asked, after a very tense pause, if I thought Jones might have taken it.

"I have no proof."

"I speak not yet of proof."

"I have suspicions."

"You don't like him."

"No . . . I've never tried to hide my dislike for him."

"Could that have any influence on your suspicions?"

"What do you think?"

There was a hesitation. His lamp began to smoke. He extinguished it and lit the one on my bedside table, exchanging it for his. I noticed his trembling hand.

"He's a desperately lonely, sad boy. He's not like us. He needs so much."

"Are you saying I should let him keep my watch?"

"I'm asking you to be patient with him. His needs are so great. We can never control another's needs; it's difficult enough controlling our own. We can only hope to accept them and understand their power. And what is love but need?"

He was talking to himself. I was moved by the force of his distraction and the thoughts he spoke aloud. I had never equated love with need, love as the gratification of needs.

"Be patient with him, Robert. Please, for me, be patient!"

"Why for you? For Keyes I could understand, but why for you?"

There was another silence, charged with the stillness of truth.

"I love him."

Passion needs small evidence.

What could I say?

"I love him," he repeated in a stronger voice. "I love him and he allows me to love him. Forgive me, Robert, but here I stand, his slave. A poor, infirm, weak, and despised old man."

He began to weep. Sitting on the side of my bed, he turned his face away from me.

"Denvers, I never thought . . ."

"You never thought *what*? That I was fit to love or be loved?"

"I never imagined . . ."

"I love him, and want you to treat him decently *for me*. Please!"

"Yes . . . yes, of course, I will."

He rose and walked to the door, wiping his face with a handkerchief. I called him back and handed him the lamp. He thanked me and slowly returned to the doorway, where he paused and asked without turning, "Has he been visiting you at night?"

"No. Once he did for a few minutes. Why?"

He was gone. I settled back under the covers and tried to grasp the import of what had just passed between us. A sneeze in the other room warned me the evening was not yet ended. Jones appeared barefoot, carrying no lamp. He curled on the bottom of my bed. Cael stirred. I pulled my legs away from him, into the circle of warmth where Denvers had been sitting.

"Well, Robbie-boy, what did old Denny have to say for himself?"

"Something tells me you have a very good idea."

"Oh?"

"Why did you steal my watch?"

"I never touched your fucking watch!"

"Go to bed."

"I can't right now. In a little while."

"Why?"

"Can't you guess?"

"No."

"You are a blind ass. And you think you're so smart, that's what kills *me*."

I shrugged my shoulders. I was not comfortable with this conversation.

"Robbie-boy, I'm going to tell you something for your own good."

"I don't want to hear it."

"I'm gonna tell you anyways."

I groaned and thought: "*By the pricking of my thumbs/ Something wicked this way comes. . . .*"

"I know *just* what I want, Robbie-boy! I been poor like you can't never imagine. I wanna be rich and I know how I'm gonna do it."

"Nobody has any money here."

"No, but *he* does."

"No one tells him what to do, Jones," I sputtered, sitting up.

"Someone did before," he said, laughing at my consternation, "and someone will again."

"Are you saying *you* will?"

"I'm not *saying* anything, Robbie-boy. I'm *telling*, for your own good!"

He took a brown envelope, legal size, from inside his robe.

"Here's a present! Something to paste in your journal and use on cold nights to heat yourself up!"

I waited for him to go before opening the envelope. In order for me to see the contents clearly, I would have to go into the sitting room for a lamp. I did not move. I was afraid to see what that evil runt had dropped upon me. I took Cael into my arms and hugged him closely.

In the morning, I hid the unopened envelope. At breakfast I was aware of Jones observing me; I pretended not to notice. We managed to get through the meal with no nasty complications.

I went for a long walk after breakfast. I thought about Denvers and then about my own position vis-à-vis Seth Jones and Donough Gaylord. I decided I was dramatizing the entire meager incident; nothing the guttersnipe could do would ever harm my employer. If love was need, then that explained so much.

After luncheon, Brian and I developed my photographic plates in the darkroom. One, an image of the left wing of Gaywyck taken from the back lawn, was perfectly composed, but ruined by a smudge on my bedroom window.

"That's no *smudge*!" Brian corrected. "There's a woman standing in your bedroom window!"

Rushing to the library, we found a magnifying glass on my desk and held it over the photograph. I was electrified by what I saw. Brian paled. Framed in my window stood the Rossetti figure! And like the canvas in the attic of the cottage, the figure had no face: in front of her head she held an open fan. I pretended not to recognize it.

"Who is she, Brian?"

He shrugged and mumbled he did not know. It looked familiar, but he could not place it. He opted for a ghost. He had always wanted to talk to a ghost.

"Oh, dear sir, I would not speak to a ghost for the

world." I quoted *Otranto*'s Bianca, trying to sound playful.

"I've *seen* her before," he whispered excitedly.

"Where?"

"I don't remember."

"She's too *tall* to be anyone we *know*."

"Ghosts should be big."

"Not when they are standing in *my* room!"

We looked from the photograph to each other, then back to the photograph. I was confused and frightened but also relieved to see my nightmares based on an objective reality. A ghost was an attractive alternative to madness. I lunged at any possibility and clutched the photograph to me. We decided not to mention the apparition because there was no one with whom we wished to share it. It was our secret. (Later, it became our *mistake*, and we shared the consequences.)

I left him and returned to my room, tucking the new photograph into the envelope with whatever Jones had given me. There was an ominous aura of the fearsome and accursed about that packet.

Again, Jones came to my room. I wanted to lock my doors but knew Cael would never tolerate it. I could handle a nocturnal visit from the pathetic snake across the hall with his delusions of conquering Donough Gaylord.

"Did you like your present? If you want seconds, just let me know. I picked that one 'cause it's funny, you know, and I wanted you to have a laugh. The other ones I got are more serious . . . *worth a lot more*. . . ."

"Get out of here, slime! I don't want you stinking up my rooms again!"

He slid off my bed and patted my hair. Before I could move away, Cael clawed him. He leaped back, whining.

"I need a friend, Robbie-boy. I guess you ain't him. Too bad!"

"I hate you!"

"Now, now, Robbie-boy! Don't blame *me*! I didn't do nothing! *I* didn't take those dirty pictures! *I* didn't cut the old man's fingers off! *I* didn't hack off baby Brian's pecker when he wouldn't roll over!"

"You *bastard*!" I hissed and punched him in the chest, knocking him to the floor, where he sprawled, laughing at me.

"You're a devil!" I said, leaping out of my bed on the

side farthest from him and holding a growling Cael in my arms.

"The old man says this place is consecrated to the devil. Hey, ya think he means me?" he asked, grinning, rising to his feet. "I don't wanna hurt you, Robbie-boy, but you're a fucking idiot and if you get in my way . . . Get back into the bed before I beat you bloody."

The rage in his voice made me nauseous with fear. I did what he ordered. Before I could phrase a retort, he was gone. I remembered how peaceful life was before his arrival, how safe and comfortable. I was tormented. I wanted all change to be pleasant. Now the peace was irretrievably gone. Like so much else, it slipped through my hands. I should have gripped it more tenaciously. I should have . . .

Horribly wakeful after Jones left me, I lit the lamp and took the journal from its new hiding place. I could not write a coherent line. In my heart there was a churning. Suddenly I knew what had to be done.

"I have decided to leave the cloister," I wrote to Donough Gaylord, "and would be pleased to accept any type of employment in your office."

There was no need for me to invent some baroque excuse. I stated simply that I had acquired a taste for New York City after my successful Christmas visit; Gaywyck bored me. I concluded with: ". . . the time for solitude has ended and I am tired of seclusion." I sealed the letter, planning to mail it from Sterling Harbor the next day.

They would manage very well without me, I reasoned. In a few weeks, Denvers would come to his senses; his needs fulfilled, he would see Jones for the garbage he was. Keyes, too, would survive this absurd infatuation, which surely involved no more than a little lace and too much rouge. Was it so harmful their pandering to Jones when love was involved? Used to the streets, he would overplay his hand, underestimating the intelligence of his fellow players. Everything would—in time—clear itself up, disentangle, go away. . . .

I felt restored. Still too restless to sleep, I decided to read. During the previous days, I had been gripped by Darwin's *Voyage of the Beagle*. After my walk along the shore, I had retreated with the book to Library II where I'd left it. Lighting the old rush lamp I used late at night (preferring it to the glare and the bulk of the newer lamps), I made my way silently into the hallway. Cael walked beside me.

The door to Jones's apartment was open, and the sound of a stifled scream held me in mid-step. I heard gasps and moans coming from the bedroom. Its partially opened door cast a narrow path of light, which I followed. Sprawled on the bed, the disheveled blankets revealing his naked back and thigh, Denvers muffled his hysteria by burying his face in the pillow. With a sense of scarlet shame at invading such a private moment, I returned to my room. Needing the book more than ever now, I set out again, after reassuring myself that the missing Jones had not tampered with my sealed letter.

Once I held the Darwin, I blew out the lamp, knowing the brightness of the moon would light the way back down. Stepping gingerly into the upper hallway, I hurried to the shallow stairs at the end. My shadowlike presence in the small landing's mirror was suddenly clarified by the opening of a door behind me. Pressing against the wall, I watched the reflections.

Seth Jones, naked, pranced slowly into the square of golden light emanating from Keyes's bedroom. A hand thrust his black robe after him. Dreamily the boy turned, took the garment, and laughed when the hand dropped to grope between his legs. Tossing the robe over his slender shoulders, he sped down the hallway with the silken fabric floating like shimmering bat's wings above his pale form. The door closed slowly, unwillingly. I stood gazing into the darkened mirror. They say vampires don't reflect, I thought grimly.

Once back in my room, I tore up my letter to Donough Gaylord. There was more falseness and more cowardice there than I cared to acknowledge. I did want to return to New York, but not from boredom; I wanted to go because everything seemed fine and good there, the way things had been at Gaywyck before Jones arrived. I wanted to escape from Gaywyck.

I brought out the envelope Jones had given me, and overcoming my fears, opened it. Behind my own photograph of the house with the mysterious presence in the window, I found a sheet of white paper with a note scrawled in crude lettering: "There is more hidden. Only

I know the place." Then a short paragraph followed that made me cry aloud. It was obviously from Donough Gaylord's diary! How had Jones gotten it?

The selected portion read:

2 September 1882

There are secrets in this house to bring down the stars, secrets to make Lucifer weep for having brought light to the likes of us.

I looked at the photograph. I heard Jones repeating over and over and over again: "I picked that one 'cause it's funny . . . the other ones I got are more serious . . . worth a lot more . . . worth a lot more . . . a lot more. . . ." In the photograph, a young Donough Gaylord, naked but for the flashing ring on his right pinkie, took the pose, successfully, of the Cellini satyr in the orangery. About the same age as Jones when the image was made, Donough Gaylord looked as ferocious and as sexually violent as the statue he mimicked. I could not connect the brutally perverse nakedness with the placid, natural wonder I had watched bathing in the moonlight that Indian-summer night.

Cael leaped onto the desk and sat on the photograph. When I touched him, a purr burst from his throat.

"Cael, I won't leave. Donough needs me. I must do battle with his devils."

After burning the picture in the fireplace, I dressed and went outside into the predawn light, where the night was dying and the day was not yet nascent. I walked down the back lawn to the beach and along the beach to the jetty. There was no wind, not even a breeze; the calmness of the sea reassured me. I clambered up over the rocks. At the jetty's end, I waited for the sunrise.

Months before, I had stood in the same place at the same ghostly hour, between night and day. But similarities ended there. The previous time, I had been troubled by lies; now I was troubled by truths. Then I had resolved to fight for my own peace; now I was resolved to fight for his.

Whatever our souls are made of, his and mine are the same. . . .

The light from the sun's first rays tinted the oval window, investing its depths with life.

"Polyphemus, I will know what secrets you are guarding. . . ."

The light on the panes grew brighter.

"Rage, Polyphemus, rage! All the terrors of the earth shall not make me weep! *I* will bid the thunder-bearer shoot!"

Cael scampered over the rocks. I gave chase. Laughing, I greeted the sun. Feeling its equal, I was ready to vanquish the dark and rescue with love all living things.

ination During the ride to Thirtieth Street — Murray

Book Three

Fifteen

On THE INSIDE COVER OF MY JOURNAL for 1900 I boldly printed: "Love Allows No Compromise." I did not understand that one must never attach clauses to love. What is loving but compromise!

Midwinter spring, 1900, lasted for thirteen days. My journal shows a preoccupation with walking and tracking animals over the wonderland the snow had made of Gaywyck. The willow trees, their branches resembling a frozen cascade, inspired me to take more photographs; the results were as disturbing as my first efforts. Instead of an unidentifiable female figure, I captured a male specter in the second-floor window of the cottage among the branches of the wych elm.

I developed the plate after discovering that someone had cut out the eyes from prints hung up to dry, converting head shots of Brian and me into ghoulish death masks. I gasped aloud and quickly destroyed them, but a frisson of terror skidded down my vertebrae. That malicious act was more disturbing to me than the second apparition, whom I christened Whitman, the poacher-poet.

The calm with which I accepted the ubiquitous poacher should have warned me that I was becoming dangerously blasé and mindlessly overconfident.

The most obvious course of action, I reasoned, was to become "friends" with the despicable Jones, and to find out precisely what his villainous plans were, and *then*—at the eleventh hour—to flamboyantly expose him. For our first encounter, I charted his path and fell in with him. Lacking inventiveness, he usually made for the small pond when he went for a stroll after tea. He was skirting pebbles over the frozen surface as I "happened" upon him.

"I can't wait for this fucking thing to melt so I can swim in it."

"Aren't you interested in the ocean?"

"You gotta be bonkers to go in there!"

"Can't you swim?"

"Good enough to keep up with you! I took a leap into the East River every summer. It'll be fun not keeping my mouth shut and my eyes on the look-see for floating shit! You ever have to do that?"

"We'll never become friends if you continue to be so hostile."

"Who said anything about us being friends?"

"You did, Jonesy."

I realized from the look he shot me that more art was called for. I wondered if I should thank him for the orchids.

"You coming over to the winning side?"

I shrugged quickly, the way he often did.

"Or you decide when Tammany Hall falls down, you ain't gonna be left with nothing but your stiff peg in your fist?"

I shrugged again. He was impossibly vulgar. I tried not to look shocked.

"You think you can change my mind?"

I shrugged again, sensing this was getting out of control.

"Or maybe . . . maybe *you* want what the others are getting?"

He guffawed. I know I looked shocked. That was one variation I had not expected.

"No, Robbie-boy! I read enough of your journal to know what you got in mind. All that hearts-and-flowers crap! It don't work out *ever*, no matter the setup."

"Why did you lie about reading?" I asked the obvious, hoping for inspiration.

"Why'd ya think? The less you can do, the less they ask. People get slow when they think you're stupider than them. Take you, Robbie-boy. You left your journal on the desk beggin' for it. From you I learned about *his* journal. You smart alecks all make me laugh! You think everything you see, everything you hear, everything you say and do and think is so fuckin' important, you gotta write it down so you don't forget it."

"We write in journals to try to understand things."

"And you wanna know something else?"

No, I thought.

"What?" I said unwisely.

"Oh . . . so now you wanna know things from me, huh?"

I shrugged. His mood was changing, and I had no idea

what direction it would take. I thought: Run. But didn't. I should have.

"I'll tell you, Robbie-boy! When I get finished with *you*, I'll make Cormack look like a fuckin' angel with that big tool of his."

Then, without changing the expression on his face, he punched me in the stomach. I toppled to the ground, gasping.

"That's for the other night in your room. I don't forget nothin'. Good-bye for now, *new friend*!"

I tried to catch my breath while I watched him disappear in the direction of the mud flats. The burning sensation in my middle made me feel sick. I didn't see Brian until he stood by my side nudging my shoulder with his knee to get my attention.

"Why didn't you hit him back?"

I shrugged, employing a gesture that was quickly becoming a habit.

"I deserved it. I was trying to be his friend."

"I heard."

"Where were you?"

"Behind the wych elm."

"What were you doing there? It's not like you to hide behind trees."

"I was coming from the stable. I saw you two and—"

"How long were you there?"

"Long enough."

I turned away. The pain in his eyes was more than I could bear. He poked me again with his knee. "What did he mean by Cormack's tool?"

I lied: I shrugged.

"Has he told you anything about me?"

"Yes, Brian, he told me Cormack attacked you. He said Cormack cut . . ." (I could not say it; I forced a synapsis.) ". . . Denvers's fingers off, too."

He sat down beside me. I took his hand.

"Robbie, how did he find Donough's journals?"

"I don't know. He must have searched his rooms."

"When I gave them to Donough, he said he was going to burn them."

"When *you* gave them to Donough?"

He nodded. I had a feeling one of my questions was about to be answered.

"I went to the art room to call you to tea. I saw you reading them. I hid in the music room. After you left, I took them to him. There's a set of keys to all the rooms hung in the pantry. He said he was going to burn the books."

"What did you tell him?"

"That he shouldn't leave them lying around. Why didn't he burn them?"

Sentiment had overtaken reason. I understood that.

"What is Jones going to do with them?"

"I think he plans to blackmail . . . somebody."

"I hate him. I could kill him."

I looked away from his rage. Two squirrels scurried across the frozen pond. When I turned toward him again, I was startled to discover him silently weeping. I put my arm around his shoulders.

"Brian, I *am* sorry."

"Why are you sorry? You never do anything mean. You even tried to be friendly with Jones!"

We laughed. He continued speaking, very softly, while wiping his eyes with his mittened hands. "I'm glad you know. We couldn't really be friends until you did. I was always afraid you'd find out and not want me around."

"I love you, Brian. How could I ever not want you around?"

He leaned against me. I hugged him closer. We sat together for a few moments before a snowball smashed into my head.

"I'm watching you, boys!" Jones shouted from the other side of the pond.

His was not the only pair of eyes upon us that afternoon. Unaware of the other set, we took our leave of only his.

The morning brought two surprises. When I opened my eyes, I gazed up at the painting of the twins! During the night it had replaced the Crevelli Madonna. By my head, a scrap of paper was folded on the pillow. It bore the printed words "Look to thyself." Brian helped me return the painting to Donough's bedroom. It was outlandishly heavy; we had to rest many times in the corridor. We conjectured who or what had managed the switch without awakening me. The following morning, the two sets of matching eyes stared at me again! There was a second note, repeating the pithy message of the first. And there were two drops of blood. Whoever was playing the game had been clawed by Cael. I clandestinely viewed the hands of everyone, but no one displayed the talon wound. I assumed it covered by a sleeve.

I left the painting in my room. Every morning, it was the first thing I saw. Every night, it was the last. In the presence of the twins, I felt blessed by endless love. They were an icon. For hours I stared up at them and imagined what they must have sounded like in their most private conversations. I reinvented them like a novelist his characters. I ached for a twin soul from whom I would keep no secrets because he would read my mind. I knew if I had been their friend, everything would have turned out differently. I would have saved Cormack Gaylord as I was soon to save his brother. We three would have become one.

My next conversation with Jones produced a detailed account of Brian's accident. The year was 1884; Brian was twelve. Cormack had taken him fishing in the cove. They stripped for swimming. Cormack made "demands." When Brian refused, he was "doctored."

"Cormack was a fucker. And you think *I'm* a bad lot!" observed Jones, winking and leaving me to my agitated self. In my bed that night I found thirteen headless bees.

My last experiment with him was equally unpleasant. He discovered the collection of dime novels in Library I and, to Denvers's delight, spent hours comfortably curled on the sofa in his sitting room. I interrupted his concentration with an offer of chocolate, a sweet I knew he fancied. He neatly dispatched me back to my own territory.

"A tale of 'retribution' I'll give you today, Robbie-boy. Have you ever wondered about Denvers's hand?"

I lied and shook my head.

HE SAYS HE WILL PUNISH D.

"Cormack took it for his journal!" He roared at his own drollery. "He cut fingers off for being where they shouldn't, if you get what I'm saying, since you're so pure and all. The twins would change rings and make believe they were each other. Denvers thought he was in bed with Donough, but it was *friendly* Cormack all the time. One night he grabbed for it and lost his touch!"

"Have you been practicing this in front of a mirror?"

I snapped, unable to tolerate what he mistook for a clever narrative style.

"A question I been meaning to ask you about something else."

I walked out of the room, but he called after me. "The old man never found his fingers, *friend*. If you run across them on one of your adventures, I'm sure he'd like 'em back again, though he does okay without them."

I was convinced that any plans I had involving the churl were unrealistic; he was scum and incapable of posing a threat to anyone.

The morning following, Brian handed me a letter as I entered the orangery. Ever since the Welsh intruder had revealed his true colors, all letters were personally delivered rather than set by our place at table. That letter, coupled with an unexpected visit two days later, catapulted me away from the intrigue at Gaywyck, into a state of emotional dishevelment that lasted beyond Jones's mysterious disappearance, and beyond Easter.

The letter was from my mother. Written in her own neat and simple script, it was more a note than a letter, but it was sufficient to show me she was recovering what the doctors called her "wits." She was pleased with her new surroundings. She thanked me for taking such good care of her, and hoped I was well and happy. She sent love from herself and from my father.

I was so excited that I sought Denvers, who was in his bedroom sleeping off the effects of "too much of the grape" the night before. To the best of his out-of-sorts ability, he told me that our Donough had moved my mother to a private home "for such things" (which I knew), and there had informed all that I was handling the arrangements, "monetarily and otherwise" (which I had not known). After breakfast, I wrote a heartfelt letter of thanks to my benevolent employer and dear friend, which I took to Sterling Harbor that afternoon with my reply to my mother and a short letter to my father.

Two days later, after luncheon, I was astonished when Donough himself walked into the library where I was working. I rose from the typewriter to shake hands with him and to chide him for traveling all that distance just to acknowledge my charming, thoughtful letter. When he did not smile, I became puzzled. When he asked me to sit by him in front of the fire, I grew apprehensive. Had something ghastly happened with Jones? Had I done something wrong? Was I to be banished from Gaywyck, exiled from him?

My father, he said, was dead. A heart attack, he said. A cable from Father Howard. He'd come immediately to tell me. I thanked him. Of course, he would go with me, he said, taking my hand in his. We were to leave as soon as possible. The train was waiting.

He helped me pack. He wrapped me warmly. He carried my bags. He helped me into the sled and out of the sled. He guided me down the icy platform and into the car, which we did not leave until, together, we stepped into Father Howard's landau. The train was moved from one rail to the other, across two rivers and around Manhattan Island by private ferry, avoiding intrusion on my privacy. He offered me soups and cups of tea. He banked the fire. He sat quietly, leaving me to my thoughts. And when the time came, he held me while I wept.

"He died angry with me, Donough. We can't ever be friends now. I was certain someday he would understand why I did what I did, but now he'll always hate me."

"He didn't hate you. When I saw him—"

"When did you see him?"

"When I moved your mother to a private sanatorium, I visited to discuss arrangements. I was unable to spend much time with him. The train could not be held for very long."

"What did he say . . . about me, I mean?"

"He said he had come to realize that your life was your own. He said he would write you. I wanted him to tell you himself."

"Yes, yes, I see."

"Try to sleep. Stretch out on the chaise."

"I'm afraid."

"You must sleep sometime. The dreams can't be postponed indefinitely." He had understood me precisely. There was silence before he spoke again. "For years after my father died, he visited me in dreams. I knew he came with questions."

"What were they?"

"He never said. For years he came to say good-bye, until I was able to say it. Releasing, saying good-bye, forgiving oneself and them for resolving nothing, and accepting that one won't ever, not with them or with anyone else. After a death, one begins anew, diminished by all that has not happened."

"I fear this pain will never lessen."

"It will. It loosens. It takes different forms and we call it by different names. With the death of a parent, a terrible solitude is born."

I started to weep. He drew me close to him.

"Cry, Robbie, cry. It's the only thing one can do. *'Comfort's in Heaven, and we are on the earth/ Where nothing lives but crosses, cares, and grief.'* "

Father Howard met us at the station. He informed me that my Aunt Emily, Sister Josepha, had arrived from the convent the previous night; from my sense of relief, I realized how much I dreaded returning to my empty house. He also supplied details of my father's death: the attack had occurred at school; it had been sudden and irreversible.

"Strange, Robert, he never mentioned any pains to anyone."

"Nothing strange about that, Father. He rarely mentioned anything to anyone."

"He and I spoke of many things, Robert."

"Yes, Father, I'm sorry. I know you did."

"Perhaps, Father," Donough interjected, "there weren't any pains. There frequently isn't any warning at all."

"Yes, Mr. Gaylord. I pray that was the case with Andrew."

My aunt greeted us at the door. She looked frailer and very tired. The smell of freshly baked apple pie warmed my spirit. After a few pleasantries, she told me without emotion that my father's body was laid out in the front parlor, if I wished to pay my respects. The whole village had been in during the afternoon. I did not want to see him, but I knew I had to overcome my fears. When I rolled back the double doors, I discovered another Sister of Charity saying the rosary beside the plain wooden casket. She turned to me, smiling. She appeared younger than I; her radiant oval face with large brown eyes was suitable for framing in a Renaissance headpiece.

"You must be Robert," she said softly, rising to her feet. "I'm Sister Theresa, your aunt's traveling companion."

"Good evening, Sister."

"I'll leave you, Robert."

The doors closed behind me. I turned to see if anyone had come into the room. Alone, I walked toward the body of my father. He wore his black suit. I wondered who had dressed him. Contrary to what I expected from books, where corpses were described as looking asleep, he looked dead: sallow and still, like a cut flower beginning to wilt. His nails were white. His left eye wasn't completely closed. I thought of Cael peering out from under barely open lids, but I knew the body inside the wooden box in the center of the front parlor was dead.

He's dead, I thought, expecting acceptance. If I touch him, he'll be cold.

I touched his hand. It was cold. From within, I observed myself worrying, waiting.

If I strike him, he won't respond. If I kiss him, he won't pull away or look embarrassed. He's dead. If I cry, will it be for him? My father is dead. I'll never have a full-brother or sister now . . . not that it matters. . . .

I looked at him closely, and suddenly felt a gash of pain in my heart. He looked so vulnerable. Anyone could do anything to him. He could no longer defend himself.

Always so defensive . . . even in death you can't close your eyes all the way. Papa, why couldn't we be friends? We were both to blame for that. Papa; I love you. I always have, Papa. I love you, Papa.

I put my hand on the top of his head.

You have such beautiful hair, Papa. I never told you how much I admired your hair. When you came into my room to help with my schoolwork, I'd watch your hair shining and falling in front of your eyes. I never could have told you how much I wanted to touch your hair, Papa. If only . . .

Leaning forward, I pressed my lips to his hair.

The doors to the parlor rolled open. I turned. Donough asked with his eyes if all were well. I answered with a nod. He entered, followed by Father Howard and the two nuns. We knelt and said the rosary. I heard none of it. I was staring from a great distance at the awesome profile of my father's body forever out of reach, a barren landscape beyond the coffin's rim.

When the prayers were concluded, Donough touched my shoulder. I rose and followed them out of the room. In the hallway, I paused and drew a deep breath as the walls dropped into place around me. Donough held my arm at the elbow; he led me, behind the others, into the kitchen. A knock sounded at the front door. Sister Theresa went to answer and immediately returned to inform Father Howard that he was needed at the rectory. He took his leave, promising to return at nine for another rosary.

When we sat to dinner, I did not feel hunger, but my aunt, the cook at her convent, had prepared an aromatic mutton stew that piqued my appetite. Between visitors, she had spent the afternoon in the kitchen baking bread and making pies.

"After we prepared the body, there was nothing to do but cook, which is, as the good Lord knows, what Sister Theresa and I do best in this world. Robbie, I'll be eighty years old next month! Your sainted aunt is getting on, in case you haven't noticed. I haven't much time left, God willing, but I am grateful he has seen fit to send me not only a superb student but a fine friend as well! Theresa is a true *fidus Achates*!"

Sister Theresa laughed, obviously proud but slightly embarrassed by the lavish praise.

"Your father was a good man," my aunt continued, "may he rest in peace, but he was a stubborn man and a stern man, too. He never learned to laugh at himself. I said as much when he came to celebrate my eightieth two months early, then behaved as if he'd committed a grievous sin! He told me what you and Mr. Gaylord are doing for your mother. He was mighty pleased with you, Robbie, dear."

I looked into her eyes. She stretched her hand across the table and patted mine.

". . . mighty pleased with you, dear. Isn't that so, Sister?"

Sister Theresa smiled and nodded.

I felt calmer.

My aunt made a toast. "To my good brother! May he rest in peace!"

There was a jocularity in her manner that we emulated. Dinner commenced, not shrouded in silence as one would expect from a group of mourners, but alive with laughter and pleasant conversation. It was revealed that Sister Theresa was educated in private schools in Switzerland and had a passionate interest in modern French literature. (Donough began speaking of Balzac and Dumas *fils*, but she was much more concerned with Huysmans, Verlaine, Rimbaud, and Mallarmé.)

"I would not have imagined—"

"Fortunately, Mother Superior does not read French. She recommends me to my conscience. Friends send books, barely enough, and never what I would choose for myself. People assume the role of censor. They think I park my brains at the convent gate and they behave as though I were an impressionable innocent!"

Josepha snorted loudly and sent me a wink. Donough promised to supply Sister Theresa with whatever books she wanted, as well as the journals when he finished with them. Smiling serenely, she thanked him. I caught a flash of rapture in the glance she gave my aunt.

"Your beauty, Mr. Gaylord," said my aunt, "is matched by your generosity. God has been good to you, sir!"

A blush was his response.

After coffee and apple pie, we savored a small glass of brandy. As we were finishing, Father Howard returned and we retired to the front parlor to say another rosary. Arranged around my father's coffin, the five of us prayed for his soul's repose. The dark, warm voice of Donough Gaylord played a perfect counterpoint to the light, sweet voices of the Sisters of Charity as they prayed the responses:

> . . . Holy Mary, Mother of God, pray for us sinners
> Now and at the hour of our death, Amen.

I knelt in silence, numb and achingly separate. Their words had little meaning for me.

Papa, soon, when this is all over, I know I'll be able to mourn you. . . .

> . . . Holy Mary, Mother of God, pray for us sinners
> Now and at the hour of our death, Amen.

Papa, I will mourn and feel whatever I should feel. I promise, Papa, I promise. . . .

> . . . Holy Mary, Mother of God, pray for us sinners
> Now and at the hour of our death, Amen.

Father Howard asked me to remain with him when the prayers were completed. He placed his hand on my shoulder and guided me into a far corner.

"Do you wish to make your confession, Robert?"

I said no, that I had nothing to confess. He asked if I intended to receive communion the next morning. I said yes.

"Robert, there is something I want to say to you."

"Is it about my father?"

"Yes. I hadn't planned to say anything, but your comment in the carriage this afternoon . . ."

"I'm sorry about that, Father, I was—"

"No, I understand. I want you to know because I think . . . I hope it will help you."

"Help me, Father?"

"Yes, Robert. Help you forgive him."

I looked into his eyes. They were filled with tears. I looked away.

"Andrew and I were very close, Robert. I knew everything about him. I felt great affection for him and he for me. He was a deeply tormented man, Robert."

"Tormented, Father?"

"He loved you, Robert. You *must* believe that. I cannot bear to think you never felt his love. He was too full of love. He thought he loved you more than he should. I would tell him, over and over, that it was never possible to love someone too much, but he was so afraid. . . ."

The priest began to sob. I moved close to him and put my hand on his arm. With great heaving gasps, he started to cry. I felt him moving away. I clutched his arm and placed my free hand on his far shoulder, turning him toward me.

"Afraid of what, Father?"

He could not answer me. I stepped against him and put my arms around him. I could feel his attempts to restrain himself, then his surrender as he tumbled headlong into his grief.

"I cannot imagine my life without his friendship," he said, inconsolable.

I glanced at my father. Why had I never noticed his love?

As there were only two beds in the house, it was arranged that Donough and I would share the one in my former room, and the two religious would share the one in my parents' room. Donough unpacked my bag and laid my nightshirt across my pillow. We undressed by the flickering light of a small yellow candle. I got into bed first. He blew out the candle. Once under the covers, I began to shiver. Sister Theresa had warmed the bed, but it was cold. I called for a hot-water bottle. He laughed and said our body heat would suffice. The bed seemed enormous. He was nowhere to be felt.

"Where are you?"

"On my side of the bed."

"You seem in an undiscovered country."

He laughed again. Stretching out my hand to reach for him, I touched his bare chest.

"Don't you have a nightshirt?"

"I never wear them."

"What do you wear?"

"Nothing. I'm wearing my undershorts tonight."

"Why?"

There was a pause. "It's very cold. Try to sleep."

"I don't know how I ever managed to leave this house. I feel ten years old here."

"Go to sleep."

"Yes, sir. Good night, Donough."

He reached across the wide expanse of bed between us and gave my hand a gentle squeeze. "You'll be fine," he whispered.

"I feel fine."

"Good! Go to sleep now."

Obediently, I went to sleep. I don't remember having a thought after Donough's words, but no sooner had I dropped into sleep than I stood looking down at my sleeping friend. The comforter had slipped away, exposing his muscular chest; I raked my fingers through the thick, coarse hair before drawing the blankets up to his throat.

The cold pummeled me. I crossed the room to close the bedroom door. The floor in my room was covered by a thin film of ice. It was snowing heavily in the hallway; my bare feet left no prints. I knew I was dreaming and felt a certain relief. The door to the front parlor was rolled open. My father waited. Inside the room, he was kneeling beside his coffin.

The windows there were open. Drifts of powdered snow were in corners, against the legs of chairs, on the bookshelves, and on the side of my father that faced the wind. A gust tore off my nightshirt. Naked, I approached him. He stiffly embraced me and effortlessly lifted me into the coffin. Snow covered me. Encased in the freezing white,

I sensed him reclaim his place in the box on top of me. I watched a lid slide over the box, nailed into place by a weeping Father Howard in a white robe. The snow around me hardened. I could no longer breathe. I screamed in desperation and then awoke.

Donough wrapped his arms around me and drew me close to him. I trembled, suddenly exploding with grief. The force of the pain made me cry out again. He hugged me tightly. His warmth enveloped me. I wept, penetrated by his tenderness. Pressing my face to his chest, I could feel his heart beating, which calmed me more than the gentle words he was whispering. Opening my hands, I flattened my palms against his shoulder blades. Moving my feet, I settled them on his warm ankles. Curled against him, breathing his musky firmness, I felt my own weakness and cried for many things:

> . . . that thou didst know how many fathoms deep I am in love! But it cannot be sounded. My affection hath an unknown bottom, like the bay of Portugal.

I then slept a deep and dreamless sleep.

I awoke at 7:30 to find him dressed and standing by the bed holding a cup of hot milk. While I sipped the milk, he banked the fire, laid out my clothing, and then went to the kitchen to fetch hot water for my bath. Ordered out of my nightshirt, I stepped into the metal tub which he'd set up in front of the fire. The bath was a perfect antidote; I felt able to face the day.

The nuns served breakfast. Sister Theresa and Donough had both risen at dawn. Finding themselves together, they had shared the time talking of Paris and London, a conversation they continued over the morning meal. Sister Josepha was quiet, reflective. I was foully depressed. Listening to the two of them discussing places my father had always dreamed of visiting made me sad. *He* would never feed the peacocks in Holland Park. *He* would never see Bernini's Louvre. And why? Because he never had the courage to lead his life as he wanted. But what was it he had wanted?

The carriage arrived for us, and a hearse for my father. Miss Grimmond, having offered her carriage for the two nuns, was present to ride with them. We all gathered in the parlor to pray and to pay our last respects. Then we waited outside, huddled together, while Mr. Teale and his son fastened the lid to the coffin. The sound of hammering quieted any attempts at conversation.

Donough and I rode with Father Howard. The Mass was suddenly a burden to his heart; his grief made everything seem complex and unmanageable. There was no one to play for the service. My father was the church organist; until that morning Father Howard had not realized Andrew Whyte would not be playing at his own Requiem Mass. Miss Grimmond volunteered, but panicked and retracted her offer. Donough saw no problem. He would play.

"It is a Low Requiem, Father?"

"Alas, yes, Mr. Gaylord. Securing a deacon, subdeacon, and choir is as impossible here as it was in the Middle Ages. Andrew never tired of drawing parallels."

"My father would prefer a Low Requiem, Father."

"Yes, Robbie, I know. I take comfort in that."

I patted his arm affectionately. I noticed he wore the gloves I sent him for Christmas.

My father claimed he maintained his connection with the Church because as schoolmaster it was a "necessary obligation," and because it was the only opportunity he had to play the organ. Now I realized it was for his friendship with Father Howard as well.

The priest left us the moment we arrived at the church. Neighbors had gathered to assist us from the carriage. The mayor, the sheriff, and members of the school board lifted my father from the hearse. Father Howard appeared in his black cassock and white lace chasuble on the church steps to give us the greeting at the door. He solemnly intoned:

> Come to his assistance, ye Saints of God. Come forth to meet him, ye Angels of the Lord, receiving his soul. Offer it in the sight of the Most High.

My aunt, Sister Theresa, and I followed the casket down the center aisle. To my surprise—why was I surprised?—the church was full. I remember very little of the service. Father Howard moved gracefully through the ritual, and the nuns on either side quietly recited the responses with the acolytes.

I remember the music. At one point I began brooding over the image of my father, Andrew Whyte, the soul of the faithful departed, being delivered from the pains of hell, from the bottomless pit, from the lion's mouth, and from eternal darkness by the Holy Standard Bearer Michael, when the sacred music brought the archangel into our midst wearing wings of fire. His sword, a rainbow of sound, illuminated the air as clearly as the sunbeams that pierced the colored windows.

"Your father is most fortunate in his gifted organist," Sister Theresa whispered. "Fauré's music will carry his soul to heaven directly."

After the final benediction, the priest walked from the altar to the bier and commenced the Absolution and Burial Service. He spoke of judgment and verdict. Then he sang of the day of wrath; he sang of fear and terror. He prayed my father was not handed over to "the enemy" since he (my poor father) had believed in him and had hoped in him and (theoretically) merited everlasting joys rather than undergoing the punishments of fiery hell forever and ever and ever.

"*. . . through Christ, Our Lord . . .*"

"*. . . Amen,*" we all answered in unison, voices dulled.

"An end," I wanted to shout at them all. *An end* to your fear and fire and terror! An end to your tigers and lions, to your Abraham and Lazarus and Jerusalem!

In a rage I started to cry for my father, helpless in that black-draped box, having this ritualistic outrage perpetrated over him, sprinkled upon his head, his heart, his groin, his feet. Then the music soared and carried me with it. My rage was dissipated, my fury quelled. I felt a peace as serene as the sacred music that consecrated the ground we all occupied. I returned to myself.

Sister Theresa touched my hand. It was time for us to leave for the cemetery. I gazed into her beautiful face. How could this wonderful woman believe in all this hideous nonsense, give her life to perpetuate it? Then Denvers's voice echoed in my head: "And what then is love but need?" More. *Much more.* I watched my father's coffin being carried up the aisle. I surrendered to the rush of Donough's music. Stepping from the pew, I followed obediently.

Large wet flakes of snow fell on us all at the graveside.

*. . . Take away out of their hearts the spirit of re-
bellion and teach them to see thy good and gracious
purpose working in all the trials which thou dost
send upon them. . . .*

"Thank you, God," I prayed as they lowered my father
into the ground. "Thank you for showing me your good
and gracious purpose, and my good and gracious purpose.
To love and be loved is *all*. Nothing else matters, God.
Life is too short for more than one goal. Oh, dear Papa!
We are leaving you in that hole. Don't leave me, Papa.
I'm *sorry*, Papa!"

Donough took my arm and led me back to the carriage.
The snow stopped and the iron-gray sky brightened.

"Good-bye," I whispered as the sun appeared. "Good-
bye, God! *Non serviam!*"

When we reached the house, there was a surprise awaiting me in the front parlor. My mother, accompanied by
Dr. Anders, sat in the sun-soaked chair near the open
windows of my dream. I approached her slowly. From the
doorway she appeared to be asleep. I did not want to
frighten her. Hearing my footfall, she looked up from her
meditation and smiled. She had aged greatly and her resemblance to my secret friend was astonishing. Surely
Donough saw it?

"The doctor thought the service would be too great a
strain, but I wanted to see you and the house, and pay my
respects to your father as best I could."

I kissed her. She rose slowly from the chair. Holding
my hand, she walked me to the sofa.

"I am much better, thanks to you and Mr. Gaylord and
Dr. Anders. Soon I'll be able to come home. Isn't that so,
Dr. Anders?"

Dr. Anders, thin and nervous-looking, nodded.

"I'd prefer your not selling the house right away, dear."

"Mother, the house is yours, not mine! You can do
with it what you will."

"No, Robert, dear, the house is yours now. Mad people
may not own property. Isn't that so, Dr. Anders?"

Dr. Anders, seemingly thinner and more nervous-
looking, nodded again.

"As far as I am concerned, Mother, this house is yours."

"You won't sell it?"

"No. How can I sell what isn't mine?"

"Then I'll keep it. You've grown so, become such a man!"

"Good!" I mumbled, pleased but embarrassed.

"How was the funeral?"

I shrugged. What could I say?

"I never could understand how your father tolerated Roman Catholicism. It must have been his fondness for guilt. My mother always said I would never be happy with one of them. I could not have been happy with one of anything. I was never happy with myself."

She continued to chatter happily. I continued to listen and make the appropriate responses, but all the while I was aware of her love for me; and I marveled how she had nurtured in me the need to love and be loved. I wondered if she were aware of the great gift she had given me. Across the room, Donough Gaylord sat talking with Miss Grimmond. I had never seen her so comfortable with anyone before. Just at that moment, she lifted her hand and gave it to him.

"I always thought you were the best-looking man in the world, son."

"Oh?" I said, grinning. "And *now*, Mama?"

"Now I think the golden apple must be shared with Mr. Gaylord."

"Gladly, Mama, gladly!"

"The eyes are remarkable. Dr. Anders?"

"Yes, Mrs. Whyte?"

"Do all beautiful men look alike?"

"I shouldn't think so, Mrs. Whyte. Why do you ask?"

"I wanted a professional opinion, doctor."

Then she laughed, the same soft, warm, throaty chuckle that always made me laugh with her.

"He's convinced I'm one endless non sequitur. It gives me pleasure not to disappoint him."

I glanced at Dr. Anders. He was smiling to himself. He caught my glance and winked at me. I realized he wasn't the nervous-looking one. I was.

Sister Theresa offered me a sandwich. I ate it, then rose to get another. Detouring, I approached Miss Grimmond, who shyly extended her hand to me.

"Robert, I'm sorry we have not had time to talk. Next time, perhaps?"

"You owe me a letter," I said.

She nodded, and promised to write. Again, I was grateful to her: she had agreed to accept responsibility for the house until such time as my mother would inhabit it again. I thanked her for her kindness. She said it was the least she could do.

It was time for my mother to leave. Everyone gathered around her. For a brief while, as the center of attention, she looked young again. My heart swelled with a particular sadness for her and for myself and for each who had seen her beauty eroded by her bruising sorrow. She clung to me and whispered in my ear.

"Take good food and rest, my little boy. Be happy with yourself. Love yourself. And love me, if you can. Forgive your Papa. He drank, you know."

Is that what she thought his guilt was?

She and Dr. Anders left. Father Howard, distant and removed, offered to drive Donough and me to our train, scheduled to arrive at 12:42. Miss Grimmond and Sister Theresa ordered the room, fluffing pillows and collecting sandwich plates. Sister Josepha took me into the kitchen.

"Write to me, Robbie!"

"Yes, I will. I promise I will. I'd like that."

"So would I, dear."

"You look exhausted, Auntie Em."

"You know, I am! I look forward to getting back to Our Lady of Good Counsel. In case you haven't noticed, I'm getting old. Eighty next month, if God spares me. Give me a kiss."

I kissed her on the cheek. She smelled of sweet powder.

"Your father was a good man," she said, hugging me. "We had our differences, but he was a good man."

I had forgotten he was dead. How could that have happened? The weight in my heart was identified anew. I blushed for my crassness.

As if reading my mind, she continued, "Each of us reacts to death differently. While I was cutting the sandwiches, I actually forgot why I was here. I never could get a grasp on death."

I looked confused.

She laughed. "Even Jesus had trouble comprehending death when His time on the cross came. If it proved a mystery to the Son of God, who am I to understand it? I accept it as His will. Is there any other way?"

I shrugged. I shook my head.

"I pray for your father's soul, Robbie. It helps him and it makes me feel better. I wish there were something to make you feel better."

"I'll be fine, Auntie Em. I'll be just fine."

She scrutinized my face, then hugged me with all her strength.

"I know you will, but I'll pray for you anyway. You may not want me to, but I will. It will help you through the difficult times ahead, you'll see."

"Of course I want you to! I need all the love I can get."

She hugged me for the last time.

"Loving is easy," she whispered. "It's living that's hard."

Saying my good-byes to Sister Theresa, I was moved when she kissed me on the cheek.

"Take care of Donough Gaylord," she said.

"It's he who takes care of me, Sister."

"Well, then, take care of each other."

We laughed. I was struck again by her loveliness, and promised to write.

From the carriage we waved to the three women in the doorway. As we drove away from the house, I felt a wrenching grief in my stomach.

"I don't know why it's so hard to leave. It's no longer my home."

"Home is always home, Robbie," Father Howard said. "You grow older and make your own life, and you have more than one, that's all."

"Auntie Emily was right."

"What did she say?"

"She said loving is easy, it's living that's hard."

"For some of us," Donough replied, "neither comes easily."

The train was waiting when we reached the station. I had taken several boxes of my father's books, packing them hastily after the conversation with my aunt in the kitchen. Sister Theresa had been reading the copy of *The Winter's Tale* I'd sent him for Christmas; she found it by the bed and carried it into the kitchen. Seeing it convinced me that I wanted something belonging to him: the books we both loved seemed the most appropriate. I had gone up to his study and randomly selected ones he had shared with me. In the right-hand drawer of his desk, I uncovered the journal for the last year of his life. I took it. Frightened

and grieving, I took it and placed it safely on the bottom
of one of the boxes.

We were barely settled on board when the train began
the long journey back to New York City. Throughout the
afternoon, during tea, while the sun blazed orange and the
sky shifted from dove gray to lavender, until the train
reached Hoboken, Donough Gaylord and I talked together
of ourselves, our thoughts, our feelings, and our dreams.
I was stirred anew by his goodness, his gentleness, his
intelligence, and his compassion. He blamed no one for
his failings. He praised everyone for his strengths and his
blessings. He spoke of his love for his mother and for his
father with such candor, at times expressing feelings so
akin to mine that I frequently interrupted him (and he,
me). He would smile as if to say: "I knew that all along."
I admired him and respected him and loved him. I prayed
our time together would be for all time; I knew not to
what or whom, but I did pray.

I stayed the night at Gramercy Park. I was exhausted.
Following a bath and a very light supper, I said good
night. We had not discussed how long I would stay in
town, but I assumed it would be for several days.

Next morning, descending for breakfast, I heard a
woman's voice inside Donough's study. It was a lovely
voice, velvety, and beautifully modulated. I stopped on
the landing to listen to its cadence, which suddenly faltered
and was halted by sobs. The door opened; Donough appeared in the corridor. Sighting me, he requested a glass
of water *pronto*. I rushed back to my room and quickly
returned to the corridor, but he was gone and the door
was closed. Should I knock? The sobs began again. I
knocked. He called for me to enter.

Seated in a chair in front of the fire, dressed in a plain
brown frock devoid of all adornment, was the young
woman. Her brown hair was carelessly piled on top of her
bowed head. Seeing me, she forced a smile. I recognized
the face as a Jones face. I was pleased to see she had
Pryce's teeth, white and square, rather than the other's.

Gratefully she took the water. I moved to exit, but she
spoke. I stopped, thinking it was directed to me.

"I can't accept your money," she said, which most
certainly was not directed at me, but when no one asked
me to leave, I stayed.

"I'm not offering it to *you*. I'm offering it to your children."

"It's the same thing, Mr. Gaylord. I don't want your charity."

"It isn't charity, Mrs. Davis. Gwyllum worked for me."

"Four years ago, for two months! They fired him because he was drunk all the time!"

"Makes no matter! He was an employee of mine."

"I won't accept it, and *that* is an end to it!"

"What will you do?"

"Get a job. What everyone does."

"And the children?"

"I don't know. I *can't* take your money, Mr. Gaylord! It isn't like father! Gwyllum's death was nothing to you. Why don't you leave us alone?"

"You and your family are my responsibility."

"Nonsense! I won't *ever* be dependent on any man ever again!"

"All right, Mrs. Davis. You can work for me at Gaywyck!"

I nearly shouted at him. Luckily I remembered my place and clenched my diaphragm, extinguishing all sounds.

"*What?*" she exclaimed for me.

"You and your family can live at Gaywyck. Denvers is always in need of good help. In the fall, the children can begin school in the village. The country will do you all good."

I expected her to protest. Instead, she rose and walked silently to the window. I waited breathlessly. The very thought of three urchins careening up and down the—

"I'll have to think about this, Mr. Gaylord."

"By all means; take your time. I'll continue with Gwyllum's pension until you decide."

"But this is absurd!" She spoke very softly, no longer arguing. "Mr. Gaylord, it was a blessed hour when you crossed our path. The only day God was ever on our side. Thank you, sir. You are a splendid man!"

When she turned toward us, she was smiling. Very like her brothers, but her features were smaller and cooperated without tension; she was remarkably pretty in a vixenish way. Donough sighed. He had won. I felt ill.

Running in and out of rooms, I thought, miserable. Screaming and fighting . . . breaking things. . . .

Donough introduced me to Margaret Davis. Excitedly she crossed to me, extending her hand, which I took, dazed by her exuberance at meeting the librarian.

"I'm very pleased to know you, Mr. Whyte. Pryce says you're a wonderful fellow, *really* decent and good. He thinks the world of you. Says your gift to Taio made all the difference for him."

"Nonsense," I corrected her, charmed. "He made all the difference himself."

We all walked down together. She would not stay to breakfast; she had parked her children with a kind neighbor, and did not want to impose on anyone. Over our first cup of tea, he suggested lunch at his club and a few hours at his gymnasium to keep ourselves "in shape."

"Gymnasium?"

"I go three times a week, to swim, to box, lift the weights, and play tennis with Goodbody when he's free."

"Does he play well?"

"He was varsity champion at Yale."

"Does Mortimer play, too?"

"Not well. He prefers throwing pigskin to hitting a ball over a net with 'paddles.' Football is his game. He was varsity captain at Yale."

"Good Lord!"

"If you intend to keep up with us this summer at Gaywyck, you had better begin preparing now. I'll set up a gym for you there. You *must* keep fit! I'll have the equipment brought down from the attic to where it used to be, across from the art room. There's even a shower head in that bath to make it official."

He laughed at my obvious fright. Well, I thought, fifteen minutes a day before tea would not hurt. I looked across the table at the breadth of his shoulders and remembered the musculature of his chest and back. All the years of dreaming had not made me grow tall and muscular; perhaps some concentrated effort wasn't a bad idea.

We lunched at his club, a mausoleum off Fifth Avenue where a dozen men interrupted our meal to ask questions about business matters. (Each man appeared old enough to be his father.) We then went on to his gymnasium, stopping in a sporting-goods shop to outfit me. I was terrified, convinced I'd make an ass of myself and disgrace him in front of his friends.

He was very patient, introducing me to the men who were in charge of the different sections, and explaining nonchalantly that this was my first visit and guidance was in order. They examined me, testing my skills and my strengths, before directing my attention to the various simple implements designed to aid my healthy growth. All very scientific. And I had nothing to be ashamed of. My body was in excellent condition. I had always eaten properly; since living at Gaywyck, I exercised vigorously: walking and swimming and riding Anita regularly. I was complimented and encouraged to develop my "possibilities" in jargon reminiscent of Horatio Alger.

The kind man in charge of the iron weights was the sternest. He warned I was not to endanger my "natural physique" by becoming "muscle-bound." I agreed, making a mental note to ask Donough how lifting lumps of iron could hinder the digestion. He demonstrated how one develops one's musculature without "bunching," how one adds firmness and "tone" but no "unsightly bulk," how one limbers but never hinders the body's singular movement. The man was an artist. He pointed to Donough Gaylord as the perfect example of a vigorous, healthy, virile specimen. I watched my protector exercise with small weights, systematically stretching the toned muscles of his bare torso. I committed myself forever to physical fitness.

In the pool and the showers, surrounded by naked men, I felt uncomfortable until I took my place among them. Full-length mirrors lined one wall of the aquatic sports room. Standing at the edge of the pool with him by my side, I looked at myself in relation to him. I was no longer a child. The lines of my body had hardened, and the heavy blond down on my legs, chest, and buttocks was rapidly darkening in patterns similar to his. I was no longer skinny. I was no longer small.

"I've grown," I said, stretching taller.

"Yes, you have. The change is remarkable."

"I may get to be as tall as you! And wouldn't that be fine!"

He nodded, puzzled, obviously not understanding my pleasure at the thought. He dived into the water. I remained at the edge, looking at myself in relation to the other male bodies reflected. Most of them were far removed from the classical ideal. Though young, they were paunched and flabby and soft; they waddled like gulls, and except for the hair that sprouted in all the same places, they had the pudgy form of newborn babes. The exceptions, the godly men, were not all classically perfect, but had grace and took pleasure in their beauty. I stared boldly, embarrassing several. There *is* more to love than need, I thought as I dived into the water, highly amused by the techniques naked men employ to avoid appearing to be looking at one another. I felt exhilarated. There is something very special about male bodies, something very *Cézanne* in all those planes and angles.

The pool was refreshing. It was instructive as well. Donough Gaylord worked furiously hard. For two solid hours he put his body through the most grueling exercise, and as I floated lazily in the warm water, he swam with a trainer clocking his time. He joined me, pleased with his performance. We swam together, pausing to play when I pushed his head under the surface. The staid gentlemen did not approve. Donough said we had to behave "like adults" or *they* would not renew his membership.

We swam the length of the pool twice, like proper strangers, then headed for the showers. I contained myself. I wanted to tell everyone that the man by my side was my comrade; it was natural for us to frolic in their pool. I contented myself with touching his arm and asking him to write Denvers about my gymnasium immediately.

That night, I fell asleep the moment my head was comfortably settled on the pillow. I don't know how long I slept, but there were many convoluted dreams before the one involving my father. He stood by my bed, leaned over, and kissed my hair—his face in the darkness outlined by a halo's glow. I reached to embrace him. He vanished, yet the halo remained, floating like a golden ring of smoke. I groaned and woke with a sickening jolt.

I heard the bedroom door open and footsteps approach. Donough, in a gray satin robe the color of the morning sea, stood by my bed.

"He came to say good-bye," I sobbed.

He sat on the bed and gently stroked my face.

"Please come under the covers and hold me."

There was a rustle of satin as the robe slid from his body. I felt the bed shift and the cool air touch me as he settled beside me. Then he wrapped me in his arms and I pressed myself against him.

"Where's your nightshirt?" he asked roughly.

I started to explain that I was following his example and not wearing one any longer, when my particular sorrow, with the unexpected violence of Jones's punch, threw me into a fit of convulsive weeping that stopped ten minutes later only because I could no longer sustain it. Limp and exhausted, between sighs and mild hiccups, I told him I loved him.

"I love you, too, Robbie."

There was barely time for another sigh before I fell asleep, as deeply as if a potion had been administered. When I awoke, he was gone. One of his embossed gray envelopes was propped against the lamp on my bedside table. Inside was a note:

> My dear Robert,
>   I am called away on business. I think it best if
> you return to Gaywyck on the morning train. If
> possible, I will visit for Easter.
>
> DG

He said he loves me. That's more than I expected.

Rising, I dressed and went down to breakfast. Before leaving, I wrote a very short note, just two words: "Thank you." I signed it: "Love, Robert."

Brian met me at the Sterling Harbor station. He wore a black band on his right arm for my father, which touched me more than he could have guessed. I kissed him in greeting. After pulling away in amazement, he returned my kiss and added a hug.

"I missed you, Brian. I love Gaywyck."

"You're an idiot!"

"Why?"

"Denvers and Keyes had a terrible fight."

"Over Jones?"

"No!" he exclaimed. "Over Cael!"

"Cael?"

"He's gone."

"Gone?" I shouted. "What do you mean, *gone*?"

"He's gone! No one knows where he is. Denvers swears Keyes killed him."

"Keyes?"

"Beethoven's back."

I could not catch my breath.

"I knew you'd be upset, Robbie. Don't worry. We'll find him."

"Not back ten minutes, and *already* the descent into chaos begins! How could Cael be gone?" I shouted over Frenchie's hooves pounding on the frozen road. "Who would hurt Cael? Jones! Jones did it! That ugly bastard has killed my Cael!"

It cannot be any other way, I thought. There was no room for doubt.

How could I have been so blind?

Sixteen

Cael's disappearance had disrupted the entire household. Ambrose greeted me with a circumspect glance and a short question: "Brian told you?" I answered with a nod before asking: "You've looked everywhere?" He responded with a nod and remained silent. In the carriage, Brian had assured me the house was searched and the surrounding grounds explored foot by inch.

"Has Donough been informed?"

"No."

"Why not?"

"We're waiting to be sure. No one wants to tell him. No one wanted to tell *you*."

At tea I waited the arrival of my three companions. After a decent interval I ate alone. Ambrose grunted, annoyed, when I demanded an explanation.

"They're looking for that feline, if they know what's good for 'em!"

It was a dreadful time for me. Everything white in my peripheral vision was Cael. Every soft sound was Cael. Every bang, thud, scratch, or bird twitter was Cael. At night I missed the pressure of his body against my head; I'd hesitate before moving or stretching or turning, forgetting there was no risk of his being squashed. *I* was in danger without my guardian angel. A black orchid appeared in my water jug. The picture of the twins was turned to face the wall, as though they were being punished. A chair was moved closer to my bed, where someone had sat for how long? A gold ring was tucked under my pillow.

I wore the ring on my right hand when I visited my secret friend before tea on the third day.

"Shall I wear one, too?" she queried. "Then everyone will be able to tell *us* apart. Mary Rose *adores* Denvers's idea! Gaylord thinks it a silly joke. He laughed in the poor man's face. He takes *pleasure* in humiliating him.

Nanny says *that* is behind everything. She's usually right, dear. I will admire, laugh, rejoice, exult when Gaylord is in the darkest abyss."

Removing the ring, I went to Denvers after tea. "Who saw him last?"

"We *all* did! He defiantly sat in your empty chair during dinner."

"Maybe he's run away?"

"You can't believe that! Gone in search of you? I'm certain Keyes is responsible."

I went to Keyes.

"He's jealous of me, that nasty old seven-fingered toad! *He* did it! Who else would be so . . . so . . ."

I left without pursuing anything. I did not want to know. All I wanted was Cael back on my pillows. I sorted the information. What could they have overlooked? The cottage? He may have got locked into one of the rooms. The stable? He may have curled into a corner. For five days? What about Mr. Saunders? Perhaps Cael was bested by a testy raccoon and was laid up on the hearth of the gatehouse? It was time to find out. I sent Joshua on the errand.

I visited Jones. He answered my soft knock immediately. Sprawled naked on a bear rug in front of the raging coal fire, he lay glancing through a sporting paper. Scattered towels suggested a recent bath.

"You should don a robe, Jones. You'll catch a cold."

"There are lots of things I can catch in this position, Robbie-boy. A cold ain't one of 'em. Wadda you want?"

"I wonder—"

"Fuck off! If it's about that goddamn cat, save your breath!" he shouted, leaping to his feet and flinging the paper over the sofa. He stood with his hands on his hips. He was practically hairless, and though slight of stature, was nicely proportioned, with well-defined muscles.

"You like what you see?"

I tutted lamely and said good-bye.

Retrieving his paper, he settled again before the fire, calling after me provocatively, "You're welcome anytime, you know, Robbie. There's a lot I could teach you. Might be handy someday."

I closed his door and opened mine. To my astonishment, the sight of him in front of the fire, the flames coloring his white flesh, stayed with me. I thought of the men in the gymnasium, then of Donough Gaylord; the images surged and excited me. The mind plays a great role in this, I thought. Perhaps greater than the senses?

Joshua returned with a message from Mr. Saunders. Cael often rested on his hearth after a journey from the main house, but he had not been seen for several days. I tugged on a coat and went to question Mr. Harrington. If he had no answers, I would request Anita for a morning ride to the farm. On the way, I stopped at the cottage to see if any windows were open. Nothing! I had much better luck at the stable. I found Cael.

"I spotted him this afternoon, Mr. Robert. I don't know how long he's been hiding. He started to whimper from hunger. As soon as my son got back from school, I was going to send a message to the house."

While tending to Cael, Mr. Harrington found broken bits of shell and seaweed in his matted coat. Several ribs were badly bruised; he doubted they were broken. A visit to the veterinarian was in order.

"What happened?"

"He either *fell* off the rocks, or was kicked."

Wrapped in a large wool blanket, Cael woke and struggled free. He hobbled to me, leaning his bandaged body against my leg. I patted his head, afraid to lift him. Mr. Harrington laughed, said the cat was fit to travel, and arranged him comfortably in a wicker basket for me to carry home.

During the walk, I decided not to make an issue of the incident. What was the point? I'd only stir up the hornets in our nest, initiate a sting fest, then be universally loathed for the action. I had my Cael back, that was enough. I promised to keep a sharper eye on him in the future.

February was a cruel month, locking us into the house together. The delayed response to my father's death came in the form of an immense depression. I withdrew, ignoring everyone, taking meals in my room. One afternoon, during a ferocious winter storm, I dared open my father's journal. I read as if it were addressed to me. Often I stopped, closing my eyes to answer him, to reassure him, to promise him I would not make the same mistakes with my life that he had made with his.

Father Howard's word, "tormented," had not been an exaggeration; my father experienced agonies at finding himself in that house without love, without tenderness.

He blamed no one. He struggled to understand. He lived without hope and prayed for death. He allowed himself neither joy nor solace in his love for Michael Howard. He never questioned his feelings; yet when he wrote of his friend, a sense of peace informed his language.

I read quickly, eager to see if he ever recognized the quality of their relationship and the nourishment available to him. But he never wrote of it. I pictured him sitting *with* Father Howard, feeling bereft, all alone. I closed the book, wanting to believe he had not murdered his heart. I needed to believe he accepted the truth and had not written it down.

Following my thoughts, I never heard Jones enter. The overview of grief and hopelessness in my father's vision crushed me. Covering my eyes with my arm, I called his name and cried for us both. Jones gently stroked my head. I gasped at his unexpected touch.

"When my dad died," he said consolingly, "I cried for months. And I always thought I hated him!"

"I never knew my father."

"Like Denvers says, who does?"

February passed snowbound. I worked tremendously hard, achieving more in the month than all the months before. Besides my journal, the piano, and two hours a day in the gymnasium, I began a correspondence with Donough Gaylord that sustained our intimacy. The letters were extensions of my journal. I shared with him almost without reservation.

Our correspondence grew from the letter I wrote expressing my gratitude for his understanding, his kindness, and his tenderness. I told him he was right in assessing the pain of saying good-bye. I thanked him for being my friend. I did not expect an answer, but answer he did; a long letter arrived. He said how much my letter impressed him, how rarely persons share their feelings simply and directly, without embarrassment, and how pleased he would be if I occasionally wrote, could I "find the time," because he missed me. He was lonely in New York, and he wished me nearer. He closed with thanks for my friendship, and regretted my having said it first, my having "gotten the jump" on him.

And so it began and continued twice a week until Easter. At first he wrote of superficial things: his evenings, for example. Descriptions of various operatic performances, concerts and musicales, of theatrical events, the "doin's" of Goodbody and Mortimer, filled the pages, bringing his fantastical imagination and outrageous sense of humor into play. Often his observations made me laugh out loud. I was already aware of his quiet wit; I was delighted to discover a blazing satirical touch as well. Most of the funniest statements were attributed to one Osric, the cockatoo with a difference, the bird-about-town.

Then his letters took a more private, more personal turn. It was after I mentioned the delight I took in the lower garden. I'd written that walking down the old, broken stone steps into that enclave was exciting and mystical, a bit like loving. I felt at peace by the ancient dolmen, eternally safe. I felt hidden from all shocks there.

He answered immediately, and in one sitting. (Normally his letters were composed over several evenings, like a diary.) First he asked a question: "From what are you hiding now?" Then he confessed:

". . . the lower garden is my favorite place at Gaywyck, even dearer to me than the oakstand. Nothing unpleasant ever happened there. I cannot imagine why—it seems created for just such a purpose. When I enter there, I feel like an innocent—pure, untouched, and unused—a stranger to the devil. . . ."

I asked if he were now a companion to the devil. He answered: "And who is not? Except maybe you, who *are* good!" I sent him a short typed note:

I see what you are, you are too proud.
But, if you were the devil, you are fair.

By return post I received the rest of the quote:

My lord and master loves you. O, such love
Could be but recompensd, though you were crowned
The nonpareil of beauty.

I responded by admonishing him for harboring dark thoughts about himself and for believing that I, in my "ethereal sanctity," would have any love for the Devil!

The fact of our love had effortlessly entered our letters as naturally as the salutation "My dear Donough" replaced "Dear Mr. Donough," and the word "Love" replaced "Always," which had replaced "Sincerely" at the closing. We often wrote of love as an emotion and an absolute. It was he who clarified a fundamental truth. I had written in a gush of romantic fervor that I dreamed of loving someone more than I loved myself. He chastised me. I copied his words into my journal. (Later, much later, I remembered them, but by then it was too late.)

"Robert, one must always love oneself first, never hurting or betraying oneself, I think. One must strive to live *with,* not for or through. . . ."

Another time I mentioned how difficult it was for me to overcome the feelings of isolation and of loneliness. He wrote of similar pain.

"I overinsulate myself. Too much self-control. I am afraid of suffering. I've never thought suffering natural, as Cormack did, but as punishment for some error of judgment. I will do anything to avoid it. Often I lock myself away. I think I am now more frightened of living my life alone, however. It is awesomely difficult to change."

March was one continuous downpour, "one long piss," as Jones put it. I had never experienced so much wet. Although fires were constantly burning in most of the rooms, the damp was maddening; it seemed to seep through the walls into everything and everyone. And for the few hours free of rain, we had mists as dense as wool rubbing against the panes. The sea, viewed from my windows, resembled a boiling caldron. One morning over breakfast, Denvers requested of God that he move his production of spring to another county.

As a group, we did not thrive on the rains. Denvers and Keyes barely exchanged a civil sentence the whole month long. And if Beethoven had not entertained after tea, Keyes would never have survived dinner. Denvers worked diligently in his study most of the day. Jones sulked. When not sulking, he complained loudly and assiduously of boredom. When not bemoaning his fate, he drumbled and yawned noisily; fortunately, he slept almost as much as Cael. The only one who seemed undisturbed by the deluge was my secret friend.

"God's watering his garden!" she'd say in her *féerique* manner, over and over, on each of my clandestine visits. "I requested he pay special attention to Mary Rose's beloved tulips, and he promised me he would."

"Aren't you worried the bulbs will drown?"

"Bulbs don't drown, dear. Only people and animals and

insects drown. We pay our gardeners to tend to such things. Proper drainage is essential to healthy flowers and shrubs!"

"Uh-huh."

"I am happy to see you wearing your ring, dear. Tonight at the masquerade ball I shan't be wearing mine, of course. I'm going as the Rossetti. I wish I could show you my costume, but Lucy is pressing the skirt. It's an *exact* copy! I'm to win the prize. Mary Rose will be unhappy. Unhappiness is her morphine. Cormack doesn't love her anymore. Love is not a tender thing. It pricks like thorns. Give liberty to your eyes. If Love be blind, Love cannot hit the mark! Blind is *his* love and best befits the dark. Why not come tonight as Juliet?"

She magnified my sense of isolation. Entering her cloistered universe, with the boundaries of time and space no longer extant and androgyny rampant, removed me further from reality. Living in a mansion on the edge of the land imposes a solitude like none I had ever experienced. Time dissolved. Weeks evaporated. The sea became our guardian, sternly ever-present, ever-changing, yet always the same, and relentlessly tapping on the shore to keep us cognizant of ourselves as perishable in the elements.

The only consolation was Easter's rapid approach, the moon being obligingly full early that month. I wrote to Donough warning that Gaywyck might be adrift before his arrival. He answered I was not to worry: " '*He that has a house to put 's head in has a good headpiece.*' I am an expert celestial navigator. Wherever you are, I will find you."

In spite of the rains, I took long walks. Warmly wrapped in my Aran Islands sweater and my mackintosh, my cap (earflaps down) and a pair of fishing boots, I stalked the grounds from the oakstand to the farm, from the seashore to the gatehouses; Gaylord's domain became mine. I watched winter wash away. I watched the dark brown branch pale, preparing to shoot forth leafage. It was the beginning of the cycle, and I felt attuned as I had never been before. I anticipated. I drew parallels; I constructed metaphors. I wrote poems, the best of which I sent to him.

He praised my sense of rhythm and facility for locating the "eccentric" rhyme, admitting he preferred the bunch of violets I shipped the same day via Pryce Jones. In an accompanying note I said I was pleased they had not "withered all when my father died," because he had always loved their fragrance, and sighting them had returned that memory to me. Later, when I learned from Ambrose that the twins would go violet gathering every year under those exposed gnarled roots of the great elms, I was grateful to Donough for allowing me the sentimental self-indulgence; of late he had been less patient with my flagrant romanticism, regularly warning me of its inherent dangers.

The violets brought gaiety to our table that night. Donough observed that I rarely wrote of my companions. I was not purposely avoiding the subject; they had become sensitive areas because of my feelings about Jones. And I had grown to suspect they hated me with the excess loathing they had for each other and themselves. From then, I made a point of mentioning something innocuous about them most of the time, such as Keyes using the violets in his bath powder.

I dared to say to him that I knew sex and love were closely related, that sex was the direct expression of love and ideally should not, perhaps, be encouraged on its own, divorced from emotion. (I dropped that into other random thoughts about Plato's notion of passion being directed toward good. More honestly, it belonged in a paragraph about my infuriating envy for Jones's sexual experience.) Donough, of course, agreed with me, though he knew for most people the two were not always fused. I valued my innocence because I knew it was something Donough Gaylord loved. With trepidation, I asked if he thought goodness and innocence one and the same—a concept I had grown weary of; he said no, definitely not! I was profoundly relieved. I wanted to be good always. I did not wish to remain always innocent.

The tulips poked through the soil and the rains moved to another county. It became April! I wrote detailing the marvels of Gaywyck, hoping to hasten him on his pilgrimage. In a week they would be arriving for four days. With the warmth of the sun, everything changed.

Gardeners appeared, clipping, pruning, and unwrapping, raking and prodding in every corner. I learned their names and helped in small ways. My body pulsed with an overabundance of energy. Before breakfast each morning I started racing my shadow several miles along the beach, along the curving, ragged edges of the sea. I had begun that particular exercise accidentally while playing with

Cael; it was so exhilarating that I continued. Wearing only gymnasium shorts, I sucked the cool, ripening air into myself and leaped as Cael had done the first dawn we had played together in the surf. I collapsed into bed hours earlier than usual. My appetite increased alarmingly. And I grew two and one-half inches! I was exactly six feet tall, and weighed one hundred fifty-five pounds. (Donough was still four inches taller and forty-five pounds heavier.)

My sequestered friend inquired after the tulips each day. I assured her they were thriving, like everything else. I tried never to reflect on who or what she was and who or what she believed me to be. I knew I would have answers soon enough. In the beginning, I figured she thought me a Gypsy; an unflattering assumption: those nomads had inhabited the environs of every major city in her youth and were never regarded as anything but evil. Then it was clarified: she thought me escaped from Gypsies. Then I passed it by.

Poor Ophelia
Divided from herself and her fair judgment,
Without the which we are pictures, or mere beasts.

The visits were necessarily brief, and one never seemed connected to the other. The time was cheerily spent in greetings and observations on the state of the natural world. When she segued into an incident involving "him" or "them," I allowed myself to become engrossed, ever greedy for gossip about the past.

"Cormack loved playing with knives. It was a fascination I objected to strenuously. First, he decapitated Mary Rose's tulips! Then, he cut up Denvers's hand! Cormack tells me Denvers wants him incarcerated in a boarding school. Revenge, he says, for taking Gaylord's love. I said to Cormack, I said, Cormack, you cannot go around cutting off people's fingers, dear. It will make people want to send you away. Denvers knows what he is doing. He sees quite clearly. And *he's* not happy!"

The visits, though unsatisfying in many respects, were important to me. Spiritually they kept me close to my mother.

Six days before Donough arrived, the windows were unsealed. The spring air charged through the house, filling the rooms with a palpable cheer. We four sat down to dinner in good spirits. Denvers complimented Keyes on a shorter hairstyle, and did not go shades of puce when Jones proudly claimed the credit for it.

Five days before he arrived, I finished the card catalog for Library I. I took a long walk to the farm after burying a dead rabbit that Cael had killed and left on the hearth. When I walked by the waterfall, I was amazed to see Jones splashing in the pool. To my touch the water was freezing, but had it been bath-warm, I would have refused his invitation. I could not have undressed before him; he made me feel self-conscious and embarrassed by my body. (Recently he had joined me in the gymnasium. There were never any conflicts, but the clean, heated smell of him made me uncomfortable.) I read Stoddard's *South-Sea Idyls* and concluded there was more to love than "chumming." I dreamed that Osric bit the small finger off my left hand; I awoke inordinately distressed and read Dowden for three hours.

Four days before he arrived, the tulips opened. My friend claimed she heard them part their petals. Their brilliant colors burned the retina like sunspots. I walked briskly with Cael for two hours along the shore, humming the new Chopin ballade (in G Minor, Opus 23) that Keyes had selected for me that morning. The first thirty measures seemed deceptively simple; then the form became clear and the staggering demands apparent. The coda taxed me and made me resent my small hands yet again, but Keyes was especially pleased with me; he literally dragged me back to the music room after lunch to work on the piece until past three.

"*Why*, Robbie, dear, don't I love *you*?" said Keyes quite suddenly. "You are nearly *too* beautiful and you are quite, quite gifted. Why don't I love you instead of him?"

I sighed eloquently.

"He is a Welsh mongrel, Robbie! He hasn't a glimmer of intelligence under all that cunning, and he will *never* make music."

"Does it matter?"

"It most certainly ought to matter. But, no, of course it doesn't matter. You see how wise you are? Why *don't* I love you?"

I turned and looked upward at the Botticelli Madonna. She had green eyes.

"Denvers adores him, too, Robbie. Not that *that* con-

firms or denies anything! My Welsh rabbit swears he will
have only me. He swears Denvers hounds him. He swears
—not that I believe him, of course. Jones is my Atlas. He
holds up the globe of my life. I want everyone to be happy.
You can take him away now, if you must, as long as I can
have my Sweetness."

Take him away? I thought, recalling my first meeting
with Keyes. He was afraid I planned to remove Donough
from his life. Why should he think that?

"*Amo, amas, amat!*" he sighed melodramatically. "Who
would have suspected *me* capable of such a love?"

I turned back to the keyboard and began at the beginning. I could not imagine why Keyes had taken me into
his confidence. The binding power of music? I suddenly
felt implicated in some way, involved. To change the subject, I purposely devalued several notes, which instantly
shifted his attention to where I wished it.

Before dismissing me, he played through the ballade
once, then, without a hesitation, plunged unannounced
into Liszt's Sonata in B Minor. He played the swelling
melodies and impossible beauty as a passionate, lucid
afterthought to our conversation, pounding his irrational
joy into its shape and design. Afterward I sat in silence.
Putting my arm around his shoulders, I hugged him to
me and kissed him on his tearstained cheek.

I hurried down the central staircase. The strains of the
Liszt sonata, Keyes's ringing tones in its cantilena, chased
me. Through the oval window, the sunlight paved a path
on the surface of the sea. I wanted to leap upon it and
dance a crazed jig to its end beyond the horizon. I felt
Donough's presence in its golden warmth. I remembered
having kissed him for the first time on that landing.

Three days before he arrived, the leafless cornelian
cherry trees flowered yellow. A young man unwrapped the
rose trees outside the open windows while I sat at my
desk reading a letter from *him*.

". . . if my father taught me aggressiveness and com-
petitiveness, you are right to perceive he also taught me
courage and independence. . . . I do not know where the
error lies. I do not pretend to set people right, but I do
see that they are often wrong."

I walked to the farm to watch the plowing and inhale
the fragrance of the furrowed earth. On the way back, I
left the beach to check Tristan and Isolde, the swans, on

the pond; their mating ritual had been continuous since mid-January and I was eager to view the cygnets. (One year, Brian told me, there were seven!) On top of the compost heap behind the cottage, I saw a dead gull. From a distance the creature appeared to be a small eruption of bubbling water, so great was the activity on its corpse. I stood mesmerized, aghast, appalled by the sight. Countless white maggots undulated, encasing, enveloping, ingesting.

" '*Within be fed, without be rich no more,*' " I quoted, attempting, but failing, to distance myself. For an instant I pictured my corpse teeming with similar creatures.

"Good Lord!" I moaned, stepping away, repulsed and shaken by the violent mound. It appeared a misshapen, pulsating chrysanthemum.

Two days before he arrived, the shadbush blossomed white. I strolled across the warm meadow, beyond the budding jam pot, to get a closer look at the trees. I discovered a patch of scarlet columbines. As a child, I had always considered them the most bizarre flower. I remembered the stairwell of Gramercy Park, and made a mental note to ask Donough why he had chosen them. A large colony of maroon wake-robin drew me farther. I sat on a stone stile admiring the mahogany-red flower and absorbing the heat of the sun when someone called my name.

Jones, disheveled, balancing atop the crumbling wall, was walking toward me. He wore only trousers rolled up to his knees, and carried in his right hand his shoes, stockings, and shirt. His hair was wet and he had curling tendrils of red-violet wild flowers entwined in it, around his neck, and dangling from his left hand.

"Guess what I've been up to?" he shouted gleefully.

"Don't tell me! I've just finished eating."

He laughed so loudly and so long at my weak joke that I had to smile.

"You've been swimming in the ocean!"

"How'd ya know? You been spying?"

"No! Your head's wet, you're draped in beach pea, which grows in the sand at the end of this pile, you're coming from the water, and now that I see you up close, your eyes are red. An educated guess, Jones."

A robin flew overhead. Forgetting Jones completely, I watched it disappear into the woods.

"You really think you're smart, Whyte. You think I'm stupid?"

I looked at him and rose to go. He was annoyingly repetitive. Obsessive. He stood dividing his attention between me and untangling his gold chain with its pendant dragon that had knotted in his pocket. I wondered which of the two old fools had given it to him. At one time, I had contemplated stealing it but had refused to stoop to his level. He leaped from the wall, blocking my way. Slipping the chain around his neck and centering the gold dragon on his breastplate, he giggled, stalling for time. He wasn't very good at playing confrontation scenes. He lacked a strategy; his aptitude for the practical precluded cogitation.

"I know a lot you'd never guess . . . a lot nobody would!"

He looked like a rat tangled in weeds.

"Good for you, Jones."

I moved around him. He caught my arm. I braced myself. This was his moment to throw down the gauntlet. I wrenched myself free of him and forced an insouciant smile.

"Your gossip, Jones, ain't worth the time of day."

"Maybe not. But the story of how Cormack killed his father and then himself *is*!" I blanched. He grinned. I strained for bravura.

"You're worse than stupid, Jones. I think you're insane!"

"You oughta know, friend. You're an expert on that subject, ain't you?"

I wanted to smash him in the face, but I didn't. To my credit, I turned and walked away, leaving him alone to trample the wake-robin. I tried to put the scene out of my head. I knew Donough had nothing to do with any of it. Cormack was dead. More than that I need not know.

Brian, crossing the meadow, caught my attention. He was carrying a basket. I ran toward him.

"What are you looking for?"

"Morels. Want to help?"

I live in terror of mushrooms. My mother was an anthologist of stories about people mistaking death cap for the edible field mushroom or the common puffball, and perishing quicker than by spontaneous combustion. "Their heads fell into the stew!" was her favorite tag line. We ate mushrooms cultivated by local farmers, and even those she cooked with a penny in the pan and onions to make doubly sure. Neither ever turned black, but she persisted in warning us that the fleshy fungus was brother to the mold and sister to the slimes. She served them only because my father insisted. I still bore the psychic scars.

"They grow near mayflowers," Brian said.

"I know!"

He laughed. Everyone at Gaywyck knew of my fear. Whenever the mushroom was served, a joke would be made and a reference to place of origin (the far meadow, the lower garden, Brian's crop, etc.). An evening of the previous fall, after eating one he could not name, Denvers slid off his chair, crashing to the floor! When Ambrose and Keyes shouted with glee, Denvers rose, bowed, and explained he hadn't dropped his head into the stew because of the wash and curl he'd given his hair that very afternoon.

"Do you want to help?" Brian repeated. "I'm making mushroom cookies for Mortimer. I make them for him every Easter. He loves them."

I was certain I had misunderstood him.

"Butter, brown sugar, eggs, vanilla, almond extract, chocolate, flour, baking soda, salt, sour cream, *amaretti* crumbs, and mushrooms."

"I don't believe it!"

"So don't!"

We gathered morels. I had to admit that nothing looks like a morel but another morel, which gave me some peace. It was fun rooting among the mayflowers. Since my arrival at Gaywyck, I had indulged my inhibited taste for the mushroom's strong, earthlike flavor; I was curious to sample the cookies. Before Jones, mushrooms had been a common sight at our table.

"Brian, how did Cormack die?"

"In a fire, saving his father. They died together."

Revisionist history? I wondered.

"How did the fire start?"

"Everyone says it was a kerosene lamp. Mr. Gaylord was drunk. He knocked it over in his bedroom."

"What was Cormack doing in his bedroom?"

"He ran in to save him, I think. Why? Have you been talking to Jones again?"

"Ummn! He's such a pig!"

"I wonder if piggy is any good at finding truffles?"

We laughed. The sun had grown hotter. I was perspir-

ing heavily from stooping and traipsing among the mayflowers.

"Jones has been swimming," I said, weighing the possibility.

"I went this morning."

"Did you? I tried two days ago after racing on the
beach, but the water was too cold."

"It wasn't too cold this morning."

"Let's go swimming. We've got enough morels to open
a bakery."

He hesitated, flustered. If he refused, I was not going
to pursue it. If he did not feel able to let me see . . .

"Yes," he said. "All right."

"Good!" I shouted, excited by his trust.

I ran in the direction of the jetty, unbuttoning my
heavy cotton shirt. He followed at a slower pace, frowning. At the rocks, I stripped quickly, sat, and immersed
my feet. The water was freezing.

"This water is *freezing*, Brian!"

"It warms up once you're in it."

"Uh-huh," I grunted, unconvinced. Standing to lean
over, I wondered about my heart's condition.

"See?" he snorted, as he shoved me into the sea.

I howled, flailing and sinking with a gurgle. When I
surfaced, he was beside me.

"You can die from that!" I sputtered.

"Uh-huh," he mimicked.

The water was icy, only just bearable if we danced
briskly and splashed energetically, which we did, to each
other's great amusement. *He* spotted the high dorsal fins
about one hundred yards offshore. I had just butted a
wave when he calmly directed my bleary-eyed gaze. I
howled again and shrieked: "Sharks!" springing toward
the shore.

"A gam of *whales*!" he corrected, as the three awesome, twenty-foot mammals with their white chins and
white eyepatches turned and rolled, displaying white
bellies. One broke free and did four back flips. Brian applauded. They were frolicking, he explained. I was not
smiling. I'd read that those killer whales shared much
with their cousins, the porpoise, but that did *not* include
a pleasant disposition.

I raced to the jetty, demanding Brian follow. Clamber-
ing to the front, I watched the three traveling companions

shoot up out of the water and gracefully bound one over the other, performing, it seemed, for us. I thought of Jonah. It suddenly seemed feasible; they were bigger than my bedroom. One paused mid-turn and got an eyelock on me. A feeling of direct communication tingled down my spine: I knew there was no danger. Spring was theirs as well as mine. They turned several more complete flips, then submerged and disappeared.

I sensed Brian behind me. Glancing over my shoulder, I saw him standing, watching for the fins to reappear. In his excitement, he hadn't covered himself. I saw his wound. To my tremendous relief, he had not been destroyed. He caught my glance.

"What's the matter?" he asked defensively.

"Jones told me you had nothing left."

"Almost."

"That isn't true!"

"It's ugly," he whispered, turning away.

"You could never be ugly, Brian. Jones is ugly." I thought of the thirteen headless bees. "Does it . . . ? I almost asked if it *worked*, as if I were discussing a fountain pen.

He sat down, facing the opposite direction from me. I felt he wanted to talk to me about it, even if he couldn't look me in the eye. I listened hard.

"Yes," he answered. He confessed he didn't know from personal experience, but all the famous doctors had promised it would function efficiently, though the damage had been extensive and irrevocable. No one but Donough Gaylord had ever seen him unclothed.

"He doesn't think I'm ugly, either."

"He never lies."

"I know."

"Which is more than we can say for Jones!"

The day before Donough's arrival, it turned cold. I was worried for the hundreds of daffodils that carpeted the edge of the rise around the yew trees, but my secret friend assured me they and her multicolored tulips would look newly minted. I collected a large bouquet of wild flowers for Donough's study: dandelions, forget-me-nots, iris, spiderwort, and blue violets. I wondered if he knew the old lore and could read the message of the flowers; I thought of writing it out, but rejected the notion as vulgar and overstated. Engrossed in arranging the flowers; I only knew Jones was behind me from our reflections in the glass shielding the Manet.

"You are *so* talented, Robbie-boy! You and Steven would have hit it off very good."

I did not look at him. I groaned loudly and theatrically.

"You are so *tiresome*, Jones. It's a curious talent being as tiresome as you. It's a kind of miracle, really. I *know* who Steven was, Jones."

"How do you know?"

"It's all in Donough's diary. I read it in Donough's diary. Did you miss that part in my journal?"

He looked stunned. It was my turn to laugh. He shrugged and walked from the room, leaving his nasty aura behind. I walked around Donough's desk and opened the window. The sunset was in triumphant progress. The hovering clouds sat motionless in a sky that shifted from bright blue into green. The sea was burnished copper; the air soft with silent expectation. The stillness! This spectral moment, brother to the dawn, was mine! I felt blessed and alive with grace.

They arrived. Suddenly Mortimer was hugging me and Goodbody was telling me how robust I looked. Suddenly Donough was handing Ambrose their coats and I was grinning at the glorious sight of him. We shook hands, like old friends, and walked into dinner side by side. He said I was larger than he remembered me. I thought his eyes seemed paler gray. When he laughed, I was made restless by the beauty of the sound. He touched my shoulder. Short black hairs grew above the knuckles on each of his fingers.

During dinner, we often exchanged glances across the table. When he said the carrots were splendid, I took a second helping. When he asked for local news, I nearly said nothing had happened since I left him at Gramercy Park, but Denvers began discussing the farm; Donough's eyes told me he understood what I was thinking. I told about the whales. I wondered if his neck had always been so sturdy. I wanted to stretch across and fondle the deep black curls that twisted behind his ears. When he laughed at something Goodbody said, I laughed as well, though I hadn't heard a word; I trusted his judgment. As he listened to Keyes tell a story, he lifted his right hand to his forehead and brushed back his tousled hair. For gestures like that, I thought, one falls hopelessly in love for a lifetime.

I looked around the table. Goodbody loved Mortimer.
Keyes and Denvers loved Jones. I loved Donough. Love
held us all. Love bound us together. Everyone looked
happy and good. My secret friend was right!

Nothing evil will ever happen to us, I thought. Too
many of us are motivated by love. Love changes, love
inspires, love heals. . . .

Jones said something that upset Donough. I hadn't been
listening to the conversation, but I felt the pall descend.
When I attempted to assemble the pieces, it was too late.
Jones was gone. Donough was outraged. Denvers was embarrassed. Keyes was offering excuses. Mortimer and Goodbody were noticeably silent. I returned to their midst.

"What happened?" I asked.

Donough looked at me with a stunned expression on
his face; then he laughed. I grinned stupidly and said
something about being preoccupied with private thoughts.
Mortimer said he knew that country well. Keyes started
to relate the events to me; Denvers interrupted, saying it
wasn't worth the effort, but apologies were certainly in
order. I offered my apologies. Everyone laughed.

There was no singing that night. Donough excused
himself from the table. Mortimer and Goodbody followed,
retiring to their rooms. I dallied with the notion of asking
Denvers or Keyes what Jones had said, but decided it
would be "stirring the pot," as my mother used to say. I
went to my rooms, intending to bathe and read more
Carlyle. I must confess, for the first time I was actually
pleased to find Jones sprawled on my sofa.

"What took you so long?"

"What do you mean?" I asked, removing my jacket.

"Everyone shot off soon after I did. I was out of my
head down there, Robbie. You're right. I'm an idiot."

I stared at him. Though he looked quite acceptable in
his new dinner suit, the tone of his voice bade me beware.
I put my jacket back on and sat in a chair beyond his
reach.

"I don't know what you said down there. I wasn't
listening."

He gave me a squinting, unconvinced glance. I felt
threatened.

"I wasn't! I was thinking."

"About Cormack's death?"

"I *know* how Cormack died."

"Nobody knows how Cormack died but me and Keyes."

I shrugged. Denvers knows everything I thought. Keyes is a proud fool. There was a long pause. I wondered how I could get him to tell me what he had said at the table.

"I thought you was just being polite."

"Polite about what?" I asked, thinking I'd missed something again.

"About what I said."

"No. I really didn't hear you."

"That's good! It was stupid. I'm sorry I said it."

"You should apologize."

"I know! I ain't gonna, but when I ask to talk to him tomorow, he'll think that's what I want. Won't he be surprised?"

"Good night, Jones."

He raised his eyebrows. I stood up.

"A bit early for bed, ain't it? Or should I say early for *sleep*?"

"What do you want, Jones?" I asked, sitting, still hopeful the conversation could be turned backward.

"I came to say good-bye."

I looked dumbfounded.

He laughed, delighted with himself. "You heard me right."

"Where are you going?"

"That's my secret."

"Why are you leaving?"

"Because my plan's all set. Everything's ready. I need to see Gaylord, and then I'm off. Fuckin' goddamn! You think it was easy with those two? I'm only sorry you and me never became friends. There's still time, you know. I ain't goin' till tomorrow."

"There'll never be time enough for that, Jones."

"Your loss, Bob Whyte. Bob*white!* Bob*white!*"

He repeated my name loudly, expertly mimicking the song of the bird. I laughed, amused. He smiled.

"Don't it annoy you?"

"No! You do it well."

"I do everything well, Robbie-boy!" He laughed charmingly.

I felt compelled to believe him, but not to tell him so.

"I never took your watch, you know."

"Uh-huh! Good night, Jones."

"Good night, Bob*white!*"

He stretched to his full length, then stood. He crossed toward me. To my credit, I did not flinch.

"I have a long day tomorrow, Rob. I need my sleep, too."

Before I realized his intent, he swooped down and kissed me wetly on the mouth.

"You're such a pretty lad, Bob Whyte. If I was even half as pretty as you . . . But, what the fuck! I'm doin' real good just as I am!"

"Good night, Jones."

"Good-bye, Robbie-boy."

He closed the door quickly and quietly behind him.

I was overwhelmed by a presentiment of doom. I wanted to warn Donough, but I had nothing tangible to offer besides palpitations. I decided to leave the entire situation in his capable hands. I decided to take a hot bath. While the tub filled, I imagined what Jones could have said at dinner.

Seeking distraction, I looked out the window. A star fell. I wondered if Donough had seen it.

Seventeen

IMAGES OF DONOUGH IN HIS WHITE caftan standing amidst a caterwaul of seagulls stirred my waking moments. Sharp knocking sounded. Sleepily I called entry.

"Robbie! Get up!" Mortimer ordered. "We need your smiling presence *tout de suite!*"

"What's happened?"

"The tulips! Someone's decapitated all the tulips!"

"Oh, my God!"

"And where *was* Madam God?"

"Asleep, obviously, as I was."

"Donough is very upset. Cormack once—"

"I know. I'll be right down."

He left, using the portico stairs. I dressed as quickly as I could. If anything spoiled this day with my friends, I would be miserable. By the time I reached the back lawn, a fragile calm had been negotiated. Five gardeners huddled between the rose trees, silent, bewildered, waiting for orders. Mortimer and Goodbody stood in the library windows conversing quietly. Keyes, in tears, sat alone in a garden chair. Halfway down the lawn, Denvers walked with Donough; a white piece of paper flapped in his hand. I noticed the different-colored tulip blossoms scattered on the trim green; they looked like jewels dumped from Donough's box.

Brian called me from the other side of the pleached hawthorns; an eerie disembodied voice, his. I could barely see him through the tightly knitted budding branches.

"Jones did it."

"You frightened me! I didn't know you were there! Why are you hiding?"

"Jones is gone."

"I know. He told me he was leaving."

"He didn't!"

The pleached trees shook. I half-expected his head to burrow through.

"Would I lie? He told me last night, but he never mentioned this."

"It's a farewell present."

"Charming! How do you know?"

"He left a note explaining."

I looked out at Donough and Denvers. Their white paper simplified matters nicely. I wanted to read it.

Mortimer whispered in my ear, "Robbie, dear, why are you gnawing the hawthorns?"

"I'm not! I'm talking to Brian!"

He laughed, beckoning Goodbody. "From over there it looked as if you were nibbling the leaves. We were worried about you."

"Mortimer?" Goodbody queried. "Is it what we feared?"

"No! He claims he was talking with Brian, who has taken to concealing himself. Not that I blame him this morning! Thank you, Brian, for the cookies."

There was no answer.

"He's gone," I said, peering through the hedges.

"Strange boy." Goodbody sighed.

"Wouldn't you be?" I snapped, suddenly annoyed.

"Sorry!" Goodbody offered sincerely, making me feel ashamed.

"Don't feel ashamed, Robbie! Timothy was behaving insensitively. You were correct to show impatience."

I wondered if my emotions were always so transparent.

Donough called me. I excused myself from my companions. Denvers passed me, clutching the note, and we nodded at each other without speaking. Donough was walking toward the sea. By the time I reached his side, he was standing pensively among the daffodils. His eyes were dark with rage. He spoke softly. "Let's go for a walk along the beach, Robert."

We did not speak until we reached the jetty.

"Would you like to swim?" he asked.

"No, Donough, the water's too cold for me."

"It will warm soon enough," he said, smiling, moving close to put his arm around my shoulder. We turned and walked in the other direction.

"Jones left you a note?" I asked.

"No. It's addressed to Denvers."

"He explains about the tulips?"

"No, he never mentions them. Why?"

"Curious. What does he mention?"

"Only that he's leaving."

"Didn't he tell you that himself?"

"When?"

"Didn't he see you before he left?"

"No! Was he supposed to see me?"

I related my last conversation with Jones.

"I don't understand any of it," he muttered, turning us around to walk again toward the jetty. "Why didn't you write me about him?"

"I didn't want to bother you. I imagined we could manage him."

"I should never have sent him here. It's made things difficult."

"Well . . . it's *complicated* things."

"Were you friendly?"

"No. I hated him."

"Why?"

"He lied about everything."

I dreaded becoming involved in some distressing conversation about Jones's fabrications; the tulips had caused enough trouble for one morning. We passed the boathouse.

"Donough, where are we going?"

"There's someone I want you to meet."

"Who?"

"A friend of mine."

Four fishermen sat on the beach mending their large net, torn by a jagged piece of driftwood. Their boat was beached a little beyond. Seeing Donough, they stood and tipped their caps. We stopped to discuss the damage to their equipment. He asked if the whales had bothered them, remembering a time when a boat had been accidentally overturned and an elderly fisherman drowned. They assured him there had been no problems, except for the "critters" eating several tons of their fish.

"Luckily it was driftwood in your net!" he said as a parting pleasantry and we all laughed in agreement.

We continued on our leisurely way. I needed to ask about his brother's death, and other unanswered questions. I wanted to tell him about Cael's disappearance, about his diary and my watch, but he started humming "*Una fortiva lagrima*," while gulls circled, and I surrendered willingly to the warming day, and the pleasure of his company. Falling in with his brisk stride, I accepted the inevitability of only casual exchange. As my blood quickened with the exercise, I thought to tell him of my progress with my physical regimen.

"Robbie," he interrupted, "I've been meaning to talk to you about your mother. Let's sit for a minute."

"Is there anything wrong?"

"No."

We sat on the grass growing up the dunes.

"I thought maybe a relapse. I worry. . . ."

"I know. I worry, too."

I did not look at him. Staring at the sea, I searched for dorsal fins. I felt something weighty was about to be dropped.

"Robbie, how long have you been visiting her?"

I knew he meant my secret friend. She must have told him.

"A long time . . . months."

"How did you find her?"

"Through the closet in the art room. I was searching for misplaced books."

I wanted to ask how he knew, but I was ashamed of myself.

"She told me she enjoys your visits."

"Oh?"

"I'm sorry I didn't tell you the truth."

I studied him. What did he mean?

"She's my mother."

I gaped at him. "You told me she was dead!"

"I'm sorry, Robbie," he whispered, looking grief-stricken in the lie.

"You said she was dead!" I repeated as an excuse for my not having guessed. "I thought she was a foundling like me."

"You aren't a foundling!" He laughed.

"She speaks of herself in the third person. She thinks everyone is alive. *Are* they? Is Cormack alive, too?"

"No! No, I swear."

"Your *mother*? Why does your mother look like mine?"

"I haven't a clue. Tell me about your mother's past."

"She was raised a Quaker on a farm near my father. Her parents died soon after they married, and I don't think she had any living grandparents. She never talked about her family. There has always been something furtive in her manner. I guess that's where I get it from . . . sneaking around in other people's closets!"

We both laughed. He took my hand.

"Her parents are not dead, Robbie."

"But, why . . . ?"

"I don't know. Do you mind if I look into all of this? There are too many coincidences."

"*Mind*? No, of course not! Donough?"

"Yes?"

"I'm starving."

"Good! She'll be delighted."

"Who?"

"My friend."

We continued walking. The day was going to be sublimely beautiful, one of those late-spring days presaging summer. He spoke of his mother. Her announced death was the decision of his father; it was "cleaner" and easier that way. Mental illness bore heavy stigma, and he had done it for his sons as well as for himself. Nothing was to interfere with their making "good" marriages. Like most wealthy men of his era, a fascination with European nobility was awakening; the idea of his sons as titled gentry motivated him. He wished to keep the family's facade in good repair, although he was wise enough to know the power of his money and aristocratic Europe's tolerance for properly concealed "cracks." The funeral was a simple one.

"My father loved the theater. He staged the event, personally filling the coffin with stones."

About one hundred yards ahead, a narrow path appeared in the sand dunes. Donough veered in that direction. We followed the narrow walk as it curved and dipped, then climbed into a small wood. I could hear children laughing. Before us, in a clump of daffodils, a young boy sat holding a green ball. Behind him, two young girls were skipping rope, counting each turn. An unadorned one-story stone house with an ivy-covered slate roof appeared at a bend where the path widened into a cultivated yard filled with (unmolested) tulips. In front of the cottage's open door, a tiny child was curled up asleep in a puddle of sun.

"Is this a school?" I asked, charmed.

"The best in the world!" he whispered, approaching the door, grinning and slightly flushed.

We stepped over the threshold. The cottage was tiny.
From the central doorway we could see the bedroom to
the right and the parlor to the left, with the kitchen behind it. The rooms were simply but elegantly furnished
with lustrous sturdy wooden furniture piled high with
brightly covered cushions and cluttered with beautiful
figurines of delicate china. A dado decorated the four
parlor walls: the lower half green, the upper periwinkle
blue. In the kitchen, by the open back door, an old woman
sat rocking a sobbing child, all the while making sweet,
comforting sounds. The child, calmed, slid from her lap
and ran in our direction.

"My Donnie!" the old woman exclaimed. "Is it *really*
you?"

"Yes, Nanny, it's really I."

I remember everything about our first visit to Nanny
Welles. In particular, I remember the change that overtook Donough in her loving presence. He was relaxed
and loquacious. He was sweetly childlike with attitudes
I cannot describe precisely. Smiling radiantly, she rose
and hurried toward us. She was *very* old and seemed no
larger than a child herself. We both towered over her.
When he introduced us, I could hear in his voice how
important this occasion was to him. (Perhaps that is
what I mean by childlike: his thoughts and feelings
seemed transparent.)

"Hello, Robert," she greeted me, with a singsong Irish
brogue. "I'm ever so glad to be finally making your acquaintance. Donnie's been talking of little else but the
good fellowship at Gaywyck since you came there. Thank
God, I say, and you *are* right about the face, Donnie!"

"The face?" I asked, confused.

"Have you lads eaten?"

We said no.

"Then follow me into the kitchen and I'll remedy that!"
The face, I thought. Not just the eyes—the face!

> Thou art thy mother's glass, and she in thee
> Calls back the lovely April of her prime.

We sat in the kitchen at a large round oak table, and
she prepared a huge breakfast of porridge, eggs, bacon,
blood pudding, scones, jam, and tea.

"I prefer this tea to any other, Donnie," she announced,

pouring a cup before sitting beside him. "It's from County Kerry, you said, did you not?"

"Well, Nanny, actually I said the man who sells it is from County Kerry."

"I don't think tea grows in Ireland," I said importunately.

She looked appalled. I was willing to compromise.

"I can tell *you've* never been to Ireland!" she said. "*Everything* grows in holy Ireland."

I apologized profusely, admitting I had never been abroad. She seemed appeased and instantly took me into her confidence.

"I come from Ireland, Robert, dear, and I know much of the sainted place. It's coming up fifty years since I immigrated, and I miss it as if it was but yesterday."

"If Nanny had her way, every house would have a dado like hers to sing the praises of Ireland."

"It was the first thing I did upon arrival at Gaywyck: I painted Ireland in the nursery. No place ever needed it more."

"*And* threw away all the mousetraps!"

"How old were you?"

"Nanny Cruickshank was with us nearly four years."

"When I think . . ." Nanny Welles began, stopped, shook her head, and resumed sipping her tea.

"What hapened?"

"My father dismissed her."

I wanted more information, but he changed the subject rather than risk disturbing Nanny Welles further with unpleasant memories. Why did I know nothing of this woman beyond her delight in one of the whimsical boats built for the pond?

"Was she dismissed because of the mousetraps?" I asked on the walk home. "Did you complain?"

"No. I wasn't quite four and had no idea Nanny Cruickshank wasn't the way of the nursery world."

"Well, how did Nanny Welles come here? Did your father know you were unhappy?"

"No. When we saw Mama and Papa, we didn't want to talk about awful things like Nanny Cruickshank. We wanted to be happy with them. Besides, they were very distant from us then . . . especially Mama. She was a great, beneficent soul who was fun to be with and who put lots of butter on our bread and gave us cake *and* jam.

Once she stuffed Cormack with macaroons and made him sick. Nothing like that ever happened with Nanny Cruickshank. Mama had no power over us, no power over anything. We knew it and Nanny knew it; she was often savage and brutal without worry of reprisals."

"Why didn't somebody do something?"

"You don't understand, Robert. We weren't people, we were *children*, toys, showpieces, as children in wealthy families tend to be. In midafternoon on Sundays and on Wednesdays, we were brushed and scrubbed and properly dressed for presentation at tea in the adult world of shiny mahogany that smelled of beeswax and flowers. Few suspected how ill Mama was. For us she became a goddess, the antidote to Nanny Cruickshank."

"So how did your father find out about the mousetraps?"

"The mousetraps were the least of it. They were benign unless provoked. Nanny Cruickshank beat us for no reason at all. There were literally dozens of rules to be obeyed, some invented solely to justify a punishment: silence at all meals, no playing on Sunday or for one hour after eating, no books except by special permission, 'please,' 'thank you,' 'may I,' 'yes, Nanny Cruickshank,' 'no, Nanny Cruickshank,' 'I'm sorry, Nanny Cruickshank,' 'forgive me, Nanny Cruickshank.' She set timetables that had to be followed precisely. She had converted the nursery into a prison, so uncomfortable, so impossible an environment that I honestly don't know how we survived it.

"She was a Calvinist from Scotland. She stood six feet tall, was as thin and as quick as a switch. She was superstitious and gloomy, dour at best, telling us tales of terror that provoked monstrous nightmares. One tale of a butcher who made meat pies from the 'tails' of naughty little boys, still makes me sick. Cormack insisted he wanted to be good so his tail would grow big and strong and hairy like Father's. She beat him and dressed him in a shift, forcing him to stand in a corner for a whole day. She professed tremendous love for us, and repeatedly reminded us that her actions were to prevent our heads getting 'swollen' or our becoming 'spoiled' or being 'show-offish.' "

I had never seen Donough so volatile. He slowed his walk and frequently stopped, accompanying his story with wild gesticulating.

"She hated Cormack. He radiated a sensuality, a physi-

cal energy that she feared. She hated him for it and for
the contempt he never hesitated to display. She rarely let
him out of her sight. She never rewarded him. She would
rage and then beat *him* for raging. She would 'discipline'
him by holding his head in the lavatory and pulling the
chain, or by shaking him violently to rattle the devil out
of him, or by screeching at him and dragging him around
the room by the arm, knocking him into furniture."

Donough was shaking. His voice had gotten dark, husky,
as though strafed by the weight of his words.

"At tea, she took the best cakes for herself. She wanted
us to eat nothing but starches and rice pudding twice a
day—no fruits, no vegetables, no lean meats; they were
not intended for children, she'd say. To this day, I cannot bear to be in the same room with 'ricey pud.' 'Eat it!'
she'd shriek. 'Eat it *up*, or you'll have it for dinner, and
again for breakfast, and again until it's moldy and we use
up all the agains in this world!' Cormack would steal the
food off my plate, leaving his unfinished; then he'd laugh
while she shouted her agains and agains and disciplined
him. She always answered to a 'higher authority.' "

I took his hand.

"Once, when she was shaking him, he bit her ear. She
made his nose bleed. Once he hid under the bed; she
prodded him out with the hot poker and washed his mouth
with brown soap. He started blowing bubbles from his
nostrils. When I laughed, she turned and punched me in
my chest. He picked up the poker and threatened to kill
her if she ever made me cry again. And another time he
played with the poker after she had ordered him not to
touch it; she heated it and forced him to grab it."

"She was *mad*!" I exclaimed angrily.

"Cormack always took the psychic brunt of her. 'I'm
stronger than you,' he'd say, comforting me when the
lights were out. She abused us continually. I pretended
it wasn't happening, or fantasized a world without her.
Cormack fought against it. I had frightful nightmares. He
would cradle me in his arms to quiet me. I would spend
afternoons in terror of the approaching night."

"Couldn't anyone hear you?"

"We were in a separate part of the house, in the rooms
above you, a nursery world apart from everything else. I
always believed we were responsible for our troubles—
whatever they were, they were our own fault. She re-

peated *ad infinitum* that children are born evil and need to be 'shown to the righteous path,' and how some never could be, some were damned from the beginning. Who knew otherwise? We believed her."

"How were you freed of her?"

He sighed and detoured toward the dunes. I sat beside him. Sliding down the hill, I rested my head in his lap.

"She hated everything, but she hated two things in particular. She hated sensuality and she hated 'dirt.' All sensuality was evil, and only for the married; the magic of that ceremony somehow made the abominable bearable, but only for God's purpose of procreation. I was not yet four when she tied my hand behind my back for immodestly handling myself. She once tied Cormack's hands to the bedstead because she was convinced he was 'up to no good' at age three and a half! Then, 'dirt.' All of the bodily functions came under that heading. Dirt was for the chamber pot, 'the article' as she always called it. We had a flush toilet, but she preferred 'the article' because she could watch us perform the rite. Every morning after breakfast, we had to move our bowels. Is this upsetting you?"

"Only because it's upsetting you."

"You're certain?"

"Yes. Please go on."

"For one-half hour we would be forced to sit if 'nothing happened,' with one-half hour off before another half-hour on the article. Then, it was syrup of figs or Gregory powder. Occasionally she would make us sit, bottoms numb, until something happened. When she grew impatient, she'd force her fingers inside us to make certain we weren't hiding anything from her, or she'd grease her thumb and use it as a suppository when she wasn't slamming the actual thing up, or she'd give us an enema with hot, *hot* sudsy water. Cormack insisted it was one of the reasons he was the way he was! Like everything else, I accepted it and did my damnedest to oblige. He finally found a solution."

"What did he do?"

"He started hoarding."

I assumed I'd misheard him and asked him to repeat himself. I had not misheard.

"Do you want me to stop?"

"No! I want to hear everything *now*!"

"Actually, it was the only way. The woman was obsessed."

"He stored them? Where did he store them? How?"

"It was wonderfully simple. Whenever something happened, we would bring her the article for her to see and approve before emptying the pot into the toilet. Cormack swiped one of the large nursery jars and put it on the roof outside the lavatory window."

"Instead of flushing, you saved for less fertile times."

"Yes."

"And during your half-hour off the pot . . ."

"Yes."

"All right. Now, how does this combine with sensuality to get her dismissed?"

"One summer afternoon, we all went on a family outing, a picnic, if you will. Nanny, of course, brought the article. A little while before that—I don't remember when exactly, but not more than a few weeks—she sealed each of us into a German *korsett* to prevent our handling ourselves with evil intent."

"What were they like?"

"A *korsett* is . . . was a metal suit of armor designed for precocious little boys."

"I don't believe it!"

"It's true. They were quite popular."

"For four-year-olds?"

"That's precisely what my father said. On top of everything else, they were damned uncomfortable. One could not sit without feeling clasped—more like bitten. My father asked why I was standing idly, not playing or reading."

"Reading? At three?"

"We both read at three. Papa taught us. If you don't stop interrupting, I shall never finish."

"There's so much I want to know about you."

"We have eternity, Robbie."

"I know . . . but I'm impatient."

"Don't be. Where was I?"

"Reading at three. Actually, you mentioned before that she wouldn't let you read. I didn't pick it up then."

"Yes, reading. Or, rather, *not* reading. Papa asked Nanny why she hadn't brought any books. Cormack said we weren't allowed to read all month, I don't remember why. 'Not allowed to read?' he shouted. 'It's not good for young boys; it gives them bad ideas,' she replied. 'Better bad ideas than no ideas, Nanny!' She ignored his tone and started unpacking. Out came the article. 'What's that thing doing out here?' he boomed, still angry about the books. 'They must behave themselves, Mr. Gaylord! I only want them to be good.' 'She only wants us to be *dead*,' Cormack said aloud to me. Papa glared at him, then reached across the blanket and tugged him into his arms. I thought Papa was going to spank him; I moved to defend, but Papa grabbed me, too, and hugged us very hard. 'Try to spank us!' Cormack taunted. Papa squeezed us and felt the chastity belts. He asked what we were wearing. Nanny told him. He became enraged. I'll never forget his screaming: 'self-pollution? At age four? You must be daft!' I remember it was a hot day. He took off all our clothing and let us run naked in the tall grass. When we returned to the blanket, she was gone. We never saw her again. This morning, I could still hear Cruickshank calling Cormack a mean, selfish liar who would burn in hell for all eternity, and I could hear him speaking of himself in the third person the way he did when he was upset: 'He's no good! Why can't he be good like Donnie?' Or, 'He's hungry,' and 'He's tired.' It breaks my heart to this day.

"He soon forgot all about Nanny Cruickshank. I brooded and brooded. He flung himself into whatever was next; I always held back, preferring the fear I knew to the fear of the unknown. I take after my mother, I think. I remember one afternoon in Manhattan when we were thirteen. She was better and we took the sled across Twenty-third Street to see the Statue of Liberty's arm in Madison Square Park, where it was set up as an attraction. Papa was on a committee to have the statue assembled on Bedloe's Island, and had helped to have the huge copper arm brought from Philadelphia to generate some interest in 'Liberty Enlightening the World.' We walked around the arm and climbed the spiral staircase to the torch. Mama glanced around at all the people, obviously threatened by the multitude. It was a glorious day; the crowd was milling in the park and shopping on the Ladies' Mile.

" 'It will become a beacon to the world!' Papa was saying. 'It will welcome all the immigrants and become a great symbol of liberty and justice for all!'

" 'Would you give all of these people complete freedom? They all look so strange . . . and different.'

" 'There are only two kinds of people, my dear, those who love and those who do not. Everyone is equal and everyone is extraordinary.'

" 'I mean—'

" 'I know what you mean, and I think it's all nonsense. *We* set the standards, we make the rules, and then we claim them either God's will or nature's way. Rubbish! Every individual is entitled to his or her personal freedom, to live as he or she desires.'

" 'I am free to disagree, of course?'

" 'Being Irish and Catholic, you can't but do otherwise, nor can you ever be free to do anything.'

"Father always said mother 'broke' because she wouldn't bend to the storms of the human heart. Everything was always so simple for him, and for Cormack, too. 'What about male and female?' I asked. 'There are more similarities than differences.' Mama tutted in disgust and descended to the sled. She was silent the rest of the day. She was always the pragmatist, my mother. When I asked her where we came from, she said she bought us at Tiffany and Company!"

I guffawed; he joined me.

"You were never cherubs?"

"Oh, of course. But whenever we misbehaved, she couldn't very convincingly threaten to send us back to heaven!"

After a pause he added, "Papa always said there would be less confusion between the sexes if Shakespeare were taught in grammar school. That was Nanny Welles's genius, I think. She never expected anyone to be what he was not. She always let us be ourselves, and didn't try to mold us into her own image. 'That isn't loving the other person,' she'd say, 'that's only loving the part of ourselves we find in them.' Cormack comprehended all of it. He was wise and passionate; I was always reserved and temperate. He understood instinctively the tyranny of love."

Maeve Elizabeth Welles arrived at Gaywyck one month to the day before the twins' fourth birthday. She was forty-three, and immediately felt she had found her true home.

At age thirteen she ran away from Kenmare, Ireland.
She hiked around the Ring of Kerry and over to Limerick
to avoid starving with her nine younger brothers and
sisters on a farm where nothing grew. Not liking the
looks of Limerick, she hiked over through Roscrea and
on to Dublin, which was too noisy and seemed as poor as
Kenmare. She continued to Kells, where the earth seemed
more inviting than the rocky, fallow fields of her father's
Kenmare. Stopping at the first large house she deemed attractive, she asked for employment of any kind. Just
sixteen hours previous to her ringing at the back door of
the Brennan estate, the nursery maid in that household
had run off with a stablehand. Maeve Welles was hired.
After two days, she said, she found her calling.

All her life, she had been caring for children. Her
mother was constantly pregnant, continuously unwell,
but fortunately Maeve had a natural way with babes. She
enjoyed sewing, cleaning, and comforting. Of course, as
nursery maid for the Brennan children, she spent her entire day fetching for Nanny Keene—food, coals, water—
but, being bright and quiet and quick to see what needed
doing, she soon made herself invaluable. In three years, a
new nursery maid was hired when she was promoted to
undernanny.

The five Brennan children adored her. She was small
like one of them, gentle and patient, but always con-
sistent and loving. "Patience and perseverance brought
the turtledove to Dublin," she would say with her unerring
instinct for dispensing comfort and encouragement at
precisely the correct moment. When Nanny Keene died,
she became their nanny at twenty-one, helping to ease
their grief by her loving, continuous presence.

She stayed until they were grown, then followed the
eldest daughter, Eileen, who had gone to Kent, England,
as Lady Lowell. She raised the four titled children; then,
as with her first "brood," she followed the eldest married
daughter, Rachael, to her new home; but instead of
crossing the tumultuous Irish Sea, she crossed the vast
Atlantic, for Lady Rachael and her wealthy American
husband, Mr. Markson, lived in a mansion on fashionable
Fifth Avenue at Thirty-second Street in New York City.

In September of 1873, with each of Rachael's married
sons eager for Nanny to take over his nursery, and little

David's departure for Exeter imminent, she was called to the front parlor. It was a hot, oppressive day. David, recovering from scarlet fever, was distressed about leaving home. As she walked down the main stairs, she brooded; she was certain the summons was to discuss her future plans. How could she ever choose one of her boys over the other? She was surprised to find a gentleman with her mistress in the large front room.

"Nanny!" Rachael exclaimed, rising from the plush chair to take her hand. "Nanny, dear, this is Mr. Gaylord."

So it had begun. Before discussing his situation, he asked with honest concern after David, and was relieved to hear the child was nearly well, commiserating with them on the scarlet fever's having kept them from their country estate. Then he told her candidly of his wife's illness. He detailed the disastrous experience with the first woman to whom he had entrusted his two boys, and offered her the position of nanny in his household. He asked that she decide quickly. He expressed a sincere gratitude to his business partner's wife for considering him worthy to be interviewed by Mrs. Welles. Then, with little formality, he was gone.

Nanny Welles liked the man. She liked the polite way he addressed her, using the honorary "Mrs." She liked the way he gazed forthrightly into her eyes and did not shy away when she held his attention in the same direct manner. She liked his gravity, his evident strength and concern for his boys' welfare, but most of all she liked his fierce, proud beauty, which recalled the dark, sad father and lost grown brothers of her native Kenmare. She liked, too, the idea of a house by the sea. Even before he was gone, she had decided in his favor.

Rachael detained her after Gaylord departed.

"Nanny, I know how difficult it's been for you to choose between our boys. When Mr. Gaylord spoke to me last night at the opera of his desperate need for a good, loving woman to look after his twins, how could I not think of you? If you decide to leave our family, everyone will understand."

Later in the day, when Rachael arrived to take tea with David, it was evident she had been crying. She sat next to Nanny and frequently rose to kiss her former nursemaid. By the next afternoon, it was all arranged. David was leaving for Exeter in six days; Rachael planned to leave for the country at that time. In six days, Nanny Welles left for Gaywyck.

The journey was made by steamboat. Mr. Gaylord, having offered Mrs. Welles a choice (rail, road, sea), was pleased when she preferred the water route, but his plans did not sit well with his sons. The twins had been bedded on the ship the previous night for a dawn departure from Gaywyck. When the ship arrived in Manhattan, only Donough was aboard, his twin having absconded sometime before sunrise.

Gaylord was enraged by his son's perversity. Nanny Welles reassured him: all children were mischievous at that age but always had good reasons for doing what they did. Gaylord was convinced it had been done primarily to provoke him, and Nanny agreed that was a possibility, but insisted there might have been other motivation as well. The parent grudgingly nodded, appeased by her not equating his son's disobedience with his own failings as a father. She requested he show her his lovely vessel.

During the exchange, the boy in the white sailor suit stood watching and listening from behind and around a book. He was amazed she had not automatically assumed his brother guilty. He was impressed by the way she had mollified his father. When she extended her tiny hand to him, he willingly took it and walked by her side, touring the steamboat under her white umbrella.

After luncheon, the two sat on the upper deck under a pale green awning the color of celery; it fluttered in the cooling moist breeze. The sky and unrippled sea seemed all of a piece, she said, and gilded by the hot sun. The boy was immersed in thought. She left the child to himself. Gaylord was below, working with an assistant in his cabin.

"You were right," the child spoke, suddenly. "My brother had good reasons for doing what he did."

"I thought as much. We all have our reasons for doing what we do. It's what makes life sad sometimes."

"I understand."

"I'm sure you do."

"He was afraid you'd be like her," he offered after a long, deep silence. "Like the one before you."

"I hope not," she responded matter-of-factly, as though the thought had never crossed her mind.

The child nodded. He felt he had made his position clear and had been accepted on his own terms. The new experience exhilarated him.

"He told me he was afraid he'd start to cry in front of Papa if you were. He makes believe he's braver than he is."

"Many of us do, dote. There's nothing wrong with that as long as we know what we're up to."

"And up against."

"Yes," she agreed, "and up against."

"May I tell you a secret?" he whispered.

"Yes, of course, dote, if you would like to."

"I'm really Cormack."

"Oh!" she said. "Hello, Cormack."

They both laughed. She looked closely at the little boy sitting by her side. If he could fool his own father . . . During lunch, a dollop of lobster salad had dropped on his left sleeve; his overreaction, verging on distress, ruined the meal for her. She had ignored the incident, but even now he sat with his right hand covering the stain. Her heart ached for him. She said a quick prayer for Nanny Cruickshank's newest charges.

"The sun looks like a juicy plum," she said.

"It frequently does," he answered, unsettled by his having revealed himself to this small creature so quickly, or at all.

There were many changes in the nursery the first days of her life at Gaywyck. All their pleasant sense memories began with Nanny Welles. Her first official act was to have the baroquely patterned wallpapers removed and washable paints applied in colors of their choice ("You live here, too, you know.") The dado in the sitting room she discussed with them and would not have commissioned without their approval. All the mousetraps were removed ("God's little creatures are precious, too! We'll get a cat, a fat fluffy one"). A huge overstuffed sofa was introduced in front of the fireplace, where all three sat (or sprawled) comfortably, to read or play at going to sea or simply to talk at night before bed, sipping warm milk with the drapes drawn and the kerosene lamp turned low.

"You don't want to eat, dote? Don't eat!" she said sweetly, early on, leaving Cormack stunned and speechless. "You don't like cauliflower? You've plenty of time to learn to appreciate cauliflower. You know, Cormack, it's like nothing else on God's green earth. Vegetables are a bit like people: every one is different and every one is good. You may not like them all, but you should give each a fair shake."

Suddenly they inhabited a warm, embracing, private place. She brought with her a way of life rich in tradition and luxury—from the clear, amber-colored bars of Pears soap to the Huntley and Palmer biscuits and plum puddings in their bright tins. Two English collapsible tubs replaced their hated gray metal one, and the chamber pots were used as planters. ("When you need to use the toilet, lambs, you know where it is.") By the packing case, she ordered playing cards, picture puzzles, cutouts, armies of toy soldiers (British and American), stuffed animals, and with Gaylord's assistance, a library. When asked about her rules, she said she suspected they recognized a transgression and, except for the basic rules of civility, "all the other malarkey" could be dispensed with.

One of the other changes was the relation between the nursery and the staff below stairs. Tension eased. She paid a call on Mrs. Morgan, the cook, and her assistant, niece Lucy, to smooth over the rumpled feelings. She had sent a note to Mrs. Morgan via the nursery maid, Geraldine, requesting permission to make the visit. Cook, knowing her place, had offered to journey to the third floor, but Nanny insisted and Cook acquiesced, pleased and flattered. They met in the servants' parlor, over teacups and chocolate-chip cookies.

"I understand, Mrs. Morgan, that my predecessor had a special menu for the boys, with special mealtimes."

Mrs. Morgan nodded stiffly. Niece Lucy sat silently, a witness to her aunt's good behavior, should the encounter turn ugly.

"Well, there'll be no need for such stuff and nonsense any longer, I can tell you. We'll take luncheon with the others, so you'll be preparing only the one meal for us all from now on,"

Mrs. Morgan nodded less stiffly. Niece Lucy smiled, relieved but slightly disappointed, as she reached for her fifth cookie.

"Breakfast, however, seeing as the dotes are up so much earlier, at the crack, if you will. . . ."

"I understand, Mrs. Welles. Breakfast was never a

problem; I must be out of bed early, too. It was lunch and tea that drove me wild. Are you devoted to rice pudding, Mrs. Welles?"

"Can't abide it, Mrs. Morgan. I do believe the boys have had their fill of the stuff, too. Fresh fruit will do nicely, raw will suffice. I leave it to your judgment. Your niece looks fine, a healthy girl. Whatever you feed her, I'm sure will do nicely."

"Thank you, Mrs. Welles."

"You're welcome, I'm sure, Mrs. Morgan."

The nursery had the finest teas from that day forward, with Mrs. Morgan as a guest of Nanny Welles every so often to explain to the boys how food was prepared and to answer any questions they might have on the subject. Each night, when the twins were bathed and safely in their bed, the two women sat and talked together in the sitting room, sipping hot cocoa. The light shining warmly under the door, the chattering female voices in soft, harmonious whispering like the breaking waves of the calm eternal sea, gave a comfort to the children that eventually soothed away bad dreams.

"She never learned to read," Donough added, removing his shirt to take the sun. "We read to her every night before going to bed. She had great shelves built around the room so everything was always in the open, accessible at any hour. As we grew taller, our books moved up in the world with us. Cormack liked that best, I think. He rarely tried to hide anything from her or fool her; when he did, it was usually from a sense of fun. And she never mistook one of us for the other. 'You look like two different people to me!' she'd say, unable to understand the business with the rings, or how we fooled the others. 'Two different people, which is as it should be, dotes, seeing as that's what you are!' "

We scrambeld to our feet and started to walk toward the house.

"What did you read to her?"

"Stevenson, Dickens, later Shakespeare. She loved a good story. She's a simple soul, a very happy, gentle woman who sang hymns to herself while she sewed and rocked."

"Hymns?"

"Yes, hymns to her beloved, sweet Jesus. Closer, I may add, to Wilde's Christ than Rome's! I think she never insinuated religious ways because she set a good example which she expected us to follow. Even in the middle of Cormack's blackest rages, she never mentioned the devil, but only his need to govern himself. She considered his foul temper a part of him to be tamed, not an outrageous or disgusting extremity to be eliminated."

She was as different from the first one as summer from winter, or a caterpillar from a butterfly, I thought, as Cael bounded up the beach in our direction.

"It's odd how clearly one remembers," he continued, stooping to greet Cael. "She loved blue and violet and dark gray. Every day she would change from a morning white cotton frock to a dark cotton print for lunch, emerging for tea in one of her many bombazine dresses. The rustle of that fabric still makes me think of bread-and-butter 'fingers' dipped in egg yolk, or peeled and seeded grapes. Cormack once described her nursery as the most successful realization on our planet of the Platonic ideal of civilization."

We were nearly at the top of the wooden steps, and could hear Goodbody and Mortimer arguing amidst the yews.

"Don't be so snarky!" Mortimer demanded.

"I am not snarky! I'm *never* snarky! But how can you stand there and tell me to be objective? How can one be objective about the past when one is always at the center of the present?"

Mortimer seemed relieved to see us.

"Did you two have a lovely walk? I feared we'd lost you!"

We both nodded and muttered affirmative replies.

"Good! I have had *the* most trying time with this item. If it isn't objectivity complications, it's the monadic systems."

"I'm hungry," Goodbody growled.

"Or food! I neglected to mention *food*."

We went in to lunch. The four of us were alone at table, and had an interesting conversation regarding objectivity, or the absence of it, in our lives.

"In the first place," Goodbody insisted forcefully, "we spend all our time in the middle of what happens to us, always at the center of our own landscape. We never learn how to *see*, never mind see *objectively*."

"One of the things that enraged Cormack was people seeing us as one and the same."

From the momentary pause following Donough's statement, I could tell how surprised the friends were to hear him speak so directly of his brother. I knew it to be a continuation of our previous conversation.

"Precisely!" Goodbody agreed. "People see what they want to see."

"Or need to see," Mortimer added.

"The difference being?" I asked, making certain I understood.

"*Need* implies compulsion; *want*, choice. We may be predisposed to a particular need by learning and circumstance, but ultimately everything must pass through the mind for review and decision. Ideally, we should lead our lives by choosing: one choice gracefully leading to the next, guided by *need* in harness."

"One foot in front of the other."

"Thank you, Mortimer. There's something primitive, I think, about living one's life according to need *alone*. Don't you think so, Donnie?"

"Yes, of course I do," he said, frowning. "But I think we tend to malign our feelings or inclinations. We tend to make them subservient to our reasoning processes. I think the one should instruct and be instructed by the other. Used alone, reason can lead to chaos. On that point, Nietzsche is right."

"You equate feeling with need, reason with want?"

"Yes. It's grossly simplistic, I know, but, yes, for our purposes, I do. I also think there is more to heaven and earth than is dreamt of in our philosophy, but not in Dr. Freud's. . . ."

"Yes! I expect chaos is the only way we appreciate the dichotomy, and strive to bring the two together."

"Or go mad!"

"How does one tell need from want?"

"Honesty. Observation. Hard work."

"Which could be just other words for objectivity. . . ."

After lunch, I went for a walk alone. Donough had work to do, he said; and Goodbody and Mortimer, following his example, locked themselves in Library I to frame a brief. It had turned sultry, the air scented by cut grass and the mulch-covered undergrowth surrounding the house. I strolled through the birch grove, directing my steps on the

longest route to the waterfall by passing the pond to
check the swans. I had decided to swim and swing dry in
the hammock.

Stripping, I stepped under the cascade, then dived into
its pool. It was icy, but I enjoyed the plunge and swam
to the far end. As I swung around, a figure appeared behind the shimmering curtain of water, moved through it,
and stood bathed in sunlight on the ledge for a moment
before diving.

"I thought you had work to do," I teasingly called to
the submerged, approaching body.

I watched him swimming toward me below the surface.
I moved backward, but he grabbed my legs and pulled
himself up by wrapping his limbs around me like a giant
squid. I shouted gleefully, expecting to be released as soon
as I saw his face; but he retained his tight clasp while the
water flowed from his hair into his eyes, and he laughed
aloud at my ineffectual struggling. He squeezed me hard.
I opened my mouth to protest; he covered it with his and
ran his tongue over my lips. Lifting me, he carried me
to the hammock with the gentleness of summer in his eyes.

At last! I thought, fear rising. But what. . . . ?

Swaying in the warm air, I responded beneath him,
eager to know. When he stroked me, I started trembling
and squirmed to escape—suddenly shamed by the violence
of my excitement and frightened as it expanded beyond
recall, until I felt his passion rise and pass mine, leading
me forward. Restraining me with tender words, slowly
and carefully he pressed me further into the blind force of
pleasure, the appalling pleasure of love. I nearly tossed us
out of the hammock. He grasped me, pulling me back to
him. I shouted. He held me securely, whispering his need
for me.

That was *easy!* Wonderful! I thought, relieved and
ecstatic.

He kissed the tears on my neck. I opened my eyes and
looked into his. They were wide with love and clear as
dawn. I saw passions there that I never knew existed.
What had suddenly awakened him? He was perspiring
heavily. He smiled at me. I started to laugh, a deep, loud,
raucous laugh.

"What's so funny?" he asked, confused.

"I don't know! It's so silly . . . absurd, and so *wonderful!*"

"No sadness?" he asked quietly.

"Why should I feel *sad*?"

"Some people do."

"Not me. Do you?"

"Sometimes."

"Maybe next time!"

I lunged to hug him, successfully toppling us to the soft, mossy earth. He scrambled to his feet and stood straddling me—a searingly erotic image. I thought of the Cellini satyr.

"Sadness?" I asked, grasping his calves.

He grinned the shy, sweet grin I loved. Lowering himself to my side, he let me handle him and fondle him until the urgency of his body propelled me into passion. When he separated us and splashed into the pool, I lay giddy and disoriented, but bizarrely calm. I did not see him leave, yet I knew he was gone.

At tea, I ate ravenously. Sitting opposite, Donough brushed a damp curl from his forehead.

"Did you enjoy the sea, Donnie?" Mortimer asked.

"Yes. It's splendid this time of year. You should have joined me."

"Were you with him?" Goodbody asked, disbelieving the word "splendid."

"Not in the sea, no. I was at the waterfall."

I glanced at him for approval. He was cutting the mince pie.

That night I waited for him to come to my room. We had a riotous evening in the music room (my Chopin was a success), and upon retiring, I had boldly, softly kissed him on the lips. Taking my hand, he had lovingly pressed it to his warm cheek. I felt certain the change in our relationship was for all time. When the clock chimed 1:30, I impatiently extinguished my light, pulled on my robe, and barefoot, hastened to him.

There was no light under his door. I knocked. Receiving no answer, I returned to my room, unwilling to invade his bedchamber uninvited. Perhaps he was swimming? I went to my windows. Goodbody and Mortimer stood on the portico in quiet conversation, their arms around each other. Furtively I opened the windows a crack to hear.

"I don't know, dear," Goodbody said sadly. "He seems very confused by it all. Do you think he's ready?"

"He's ready for a love affair, but not for love."

"Would he?"

"No! Of course not!"

I closed the window and climbing into bed, left them to their speculations. They were wrong, but I certainly was in no position to correct them.

The next morning, I awoke slowly from deep, restful sleep, dreams forgotten but a tantalizing sense of indomitable delight remaining. Flowers were everywhere: dandelions, forget-me-nots, iris, spiderwort, and blue violet. A black orchid was on my pillow. I was crowned with tendrils of wild flowers. At breakfast, he was playful and warm but never betrayed our new intimacy. I studied Goodbody and Mortimer for telltale signs; there were none.

While he and Mortimer enthusiastically tossed a football on the shore, Goodbody and I walked and talked. I turned the subject to love.

"I love him," I confessed at the first opportunity, thrilled to be telling it.

"I know you do. It's quite obvious."

"I mean, I *love him* as you love Mortimer."

"I know what you mean."

"And he loves me."

"Yes, Robbie, he does. He loves you very much. He never thought . . . I mean, be patient. He isn't like the rest of us. Love is *tristesse* for him. Do you understand? He's just beginning to accept. I've never seen him so happy."

I grinned, keeping the secret. I was violently happy.

After lunch, I hurried to the waterfall. Undressed, I waited for him in the hammock. He appeared in the foliage, naked, moving toward me as confidently as a wild animal in its natural habitat. I reveled in his power over me.

He's like Adam, I thought. He looks newly formed by an overgenerous God. . . .

Twice I laughed tumultuously. I apologized the first time, thinking perhaps the seriousness of our love was affronted by the peal of joy. He said my laughter was a most beautiful denouement and proceeded to provoke it a second time.

At tea we discussed Spinoza's belief that timidity is an emotion one must struggle to overcome. I resolved in the future to invade his bedroom.

The next two days were magnificent. When we were

not together at the waterfall, we were with our friends: walking, riding, playing tennis and football on the rear lawn, or talking about his family and mine. Once we went swimming, but the sight of him reduced me to a stuttering timorousness, then unexpectedly inflamed me with lust; I fled the spot, blaming the temperature of the water for my discomfort, but inwardly furious and shamed by my intemperance. At the waterfall, when I gave him my real reason for leaving the group, he laughed and ordered me to practice self-discipline.

"... or everyone will know."

"And what is wrong with that?"

"Not yet. There's time enough for that."

Saturday night he came to my room in the middle of the night, waking me with his strong hands and licentious kisses. His hair was wet and smelled of the sea. He was anxious lest we awaken Goodbody and Mortimer. I could understand his preference for the waterfall as he nervously checked his wristwatch, fearful of sleeping into the light.

"Rosy-fingered dawn," I whispered, annoyed, "is no friend," drawing him back for a humoring, parting kiss.

The last morning, Easter Sunday, we met before breakfast and I cried in his arms at the thought of losing him. We met again after lunch and after tea, but he seemed distant, and I feared my tears had been melodramatic and excessive, yet I still managed to utter: "I'll never be lonely again! I'll fill every corner of your life with my love!"

"We're always lonely," he responded brusquely. "Love makes it bearable, that's all. Fill every corner of your own life. I'll take care of mine."

At six they left for the train. When Donough took my hand, I smiled at him and told him to hurry back to Gaywyck. He said yes. I said I would be waiting. I kissed him to upset his composure and test my power over him. I could feel his muscles tense under his clothing.

I wrote in my journal until dawn. After watching the sun rise, I tried to sleep, hugging the cat, pretending Cael was he come to ease the quaking sense of desolation.

Everything is different now, I thought, trying to convince myself, unable to accept the inability of love to keep away fear.

"... *Fill every corner of your own life. I'll take care of mine.*"

He doesn't understand, *yet*. The power of love will change things. When he loves me as I love him, perfectly, completely, everything will be fine. Love is both needing and wanting to need. Love is . . . love is . . . the tyranny of love. . . .

Eighteen

As is the way with deep and dreamless sleep, my heart's discords were resolved into harmonies. I reached the breakfast table in a vigorously positive humor, but Denvers managed, with a sharply raised eyebrow and a tight smile, to repress my spirit's flow, instantly inducing a torpor akin to catatonia. By his plate were two tomes bound in purple leather, their titles stamped in silver on the spines. He lifted *Roman History* as if it were buttered toast, and handed it to me.

"I've been reading Dio Cassius," he said lethargically, "and Spartianus's *Historia Augusta.* I think it might profit us both to study the texts together."

He handed me the second volume with a little more enthusiasm. I noticed a bookmark slipped between the pages and opened to the *Life of Hadrian.*

"I've been reflecting on Hadrian."

"Oh?" I said, struggling to fit Jones into the Mondragone image of the willful and brooding Antinous, who sacrificed himself at nineteen and was made divine. They both had broad faces.

"*Humanitas, libertas, felicitas,*" I added aloud.

"Yes, but I am more concerned with love."

"Uh-huh."

"Antinous has always intrigued me."

"I blame Hadrian for his death."

He raised both eyebrows. I asked for the jam, wishing I were somewhere else.

"May one know why?"

"Well . . . I've always thought Hadrian's grief and guilt well-founded. It seems rather careless of one so brilliant not to have seen and comprehended the boy's intentions."

"And if the secret was too well-concealed to defy augury?"

"I don't think that's possible. When two people love, each ought to know everything about the other."

"A sixth sense?"

"Uh-huh."

He stared at me as though my brains had atrophied. He spoke after a measured pause.

"We'll begin with Dio Cassius this afternoon after luncheon."

Late that morning, the sky blackened and the wind rose and the sea abandoned the sandy shore to spill over the rise, spreading its waves around the yews. Like a ghostly shadow, I moved in the great dark house, awaiting the rain. The wind's howling agitated my nerves. Pacing my corner rooms, where it seemed loudest, exacerbated matters. I was lonely for Donough. I tried to write a letter but was paralyzed by shyness and love. I ached for his hands, and when I closed my eyes to clear my senses, I saw him approaching through the foliage, parting the thick, budding branches. I heard us in the moaning wind. I could not write of other concerns because there were none.

"What a hardy breeze!" Keyes offered at lunch. He seemed calm. "Here's a day pities neither wise man nor fool! Give us a thought, Denvers, on the doin's outdoors."

> Blow, winds, and crack your cheeks! Rage! Blow!
> You cataracts and hurricanes, spout
> Till you have drenched our steeples, drowned the
>   cocks!
> You sulfurous and thought-executing fires
> Vaunt-couriers to oak-cleaving thunderbolts,
> Singe my white head! And thou, all-shaking thunder,
> Smite flat the thick rotundity o' the world!
> Crack nature's molds, all germens spill at once
> That make ingrateful man!

We applauded Denvers with gusto. I was relieved to see him in such good humor; it boded well for Dio Cassius. I looked at him closely. The loss of Jones had marked his face: great circles darkened his eyes, and his lips drooped at their corners. He looked old and tired. After the burst of energy that had brought Lear into our midst, he faded and shrank like the light at dusk. Not even a second bottle of beer restored him.

In Library I, with the book between us, he revived again. We read aloud, pausing to discuss and elaborate.

Hadrian was a hero to my father, who had always been fascinated by the Roman concept of truth. He maintained a belief that good, like evil, became routine, the temporary became permanent, and the mask endured as the face itself.

"Do you accept that wisdom?" Denvers questioned.

"Yes, of course," I answered defensively. "I believe in the leprosy of lies."

"You must teach Donough."

"What?"

"I never could. He lies. He always has and always will."

I could not look at the man. Hatred seethed in every word, leaving me shaken and unable to reply.

"That's been the problem here. Even now without Cormack to cover for him. The leprosy of lies, indeed!"

So much for Antinous and love, I thought, bounding up the stairs to my rooms. Although it was absurd, I felt threatened, and the weather certainly wasn't helping. The storm was positively gothic. Doom darkened the oval window. I needed the security of my own bed, with Cael within hugging distance. As I ran, the sound of rain eased my tensions, but the rumbling of thunder presaging oak-cleaving bolts was horrifying.

I retreated to my darkroom, planning to pull the black drapes and ignore the world outside. Turning the lamp to a pinpoint, I entered. The moment the door shut, I sensed something horribly wrong. My knees locked. Standing still, I allowed my eyes to adjust. Under the sounds of the storm there was an unfamiliar buzzing. A breeze brushed my neck. The darkness was infested with spots that rose and fell. Something alighted on my cheek, on my hair and my hands. I shook my head. In a second I was covered with wasps! They roared over me. Petrified, I dared not breathe. Wasps crawled on my face. I closed my eyes in horror. I did not know what *not* to do! Wasps explored my ears. I saw my father burning a nest, warning me of their sting.

One stung my hand. I jerked. The lamp top dislodged and dropped to the floor; the shattering stirred the swarm. Wasps were inside my clothing. Another stung my wrist. One moved into my nostril. Gripping the lamp's key, I rapidly raised the wick. The sight of the room filled with frenzied wasps was a nightmare. Using the lamp as a torch, I carried it to my face. Wasps fled. Moving the flame in a small circle, I managed to clear my head of them. With my free hand I turned the knob. One stung my thumb. Instead of slowly backing from the room, I bounded, crashing into Ambrose, who rescued me by chasing the more tenacious killers. He packed the stung areas and sent me up to my room after scolding: "We shoudda burned those buggers months ago!" Someone would have been disappointed had we done so. Someone had carefully removed the pane of glass, releasing the deadly swarm.

I peeked through my bedroom drapes. The wind pounded the house; lightning illuminated the tumultuous sea. I shut out the chaotic heavens, shouted when thunder boomed, then lunged for Cael, who stretched into view from under a chair. Looking startled, he fled back under the chair. There was a knock at the door. I hoped it was not Denvers with more bizarre behavior. Brian stood grinning and holding a package. I joined him in the hallway, closing my door to prevent Cael from abandoning me.

"What's so amusing?" I asked sullenly.

"I thought this would cheer you up."

"I'm cheered," I mumbled, taking the package.

The house shook and groaned; the gale raged. I winced.

"Were you hurt by the wasps?" he asked. "You took so long answering the door."

"No. Just scared. The wind must have broken the darkroom window. What is this?"

"A small package."

"I can *see* as much, Brian!"

"Then why ask? How should *I* know what's in it?" he whined, mimicking Jones's tone superbly. "*I* don't open other people's mail."

My laugh was frenzied.

"Are you coming in?"

"No. I have a crust in the oven. I'm making a custard tart for tea."

"Fuck tea! I'm not interested in *tea*!" I informed his departing person, but I wasn't heard: the wailing wind swallowed all civilized exchanges.

I pounced on the sofa in front of the fireplace. I could not believe the uproar in progress outside. Would it never desist? Nearby a shutter had blown loose and went on banging and banging. Where was everyone? The rain bashed the portico. The wind screamed like an operatic

chorus doing scales *sforzando*. The house quivered, and
for one mad instant I pictured it blown from its foundation, to become a ship bucking the air currents.

I opened the package on my lap. Under the brown wrapping was the familiar gold of the Gramercy Park Book-
shop. A small white envelope inscribed to me was attached;
in it, a note: "Thought you might enjoy this—D." Undoing the gold paper, I stared perplexed at the book in
my hands.

A book for tots? Is he trying to tell me something?

Brian called me for tea. I was engrossed in the book
and had not gone down. He had grown "concerned."

"What *could* have happened to me, Brian?"

"Anything can happen to people with weak hearts!
What's the book?"

"*The Wizard of Oz*, by someone named Baum."

"Donough gave me *Tales of Mother Goose* two years
ago for Christmas. We both love it. Are the drawings by
Deneslow?"

I nodded. Outside the oval window the sky was lighter
but not friendly. The storm carried on without me.

"May I read it after you?"

I nodded again.

"What's it about? More tales?"

"One long one. A kind of saga."

"Like the *Odyssey*?"

"Yes." I laughed, attending fully. "It's a lot like the
Odyssey. Dorothy Gale's trying to get home to Kansas.
She has three friends with her: a lion looking for courage,
a tin woodman looking for a heart, and a scarecrow looking for brains. All the heroic elements! And there's a fab-
ulous witch, the best witch *ever*!"

I hurried tea, eager to return to Oz. Nature's din made
conversation awkward. We three huddled over our plates,
nodding and going through the motions of the late-
afternoon meal. We agreed to dine in our rooms. I was
pleased. I felt uncomfortable with Denvers; he was obviously grieving for Jones, and had spoken in senseless
anger. He looked old, broken.

Mundus senscit, I thought, foolishly forgetting the incident after entering it in my journal.

I finished *Oz* before dinner. Enchanted, I barely noticed
the storm abate. I thought the book immensely rich, full
of good and true populist ideas. I began a letter to Don-

ough, completing it near midnight, as the wind decreased to a distracting rumble. I knew why he had sent the book. It was what he believed: know yourself, seek and you will find the crucial virtues within *yourself*.

"Ah, love!" I whispered to the dying embers, thinking of the four comrades sharing their strengths, loving, overcoming all odds including a potent witch.

With my cocoa and biscuits, Brian brought a letter from Donough that had arrived on the evening train. It was a response to my yet unposted one, extolling the wisdom of Baum's triune, and it brought me glorious news: Donough planned to spend July and August at Gaywyck! Instead of resignedly sweltering in Manhattan, he would be spending "as much time as possible with you, dear friend."

I had a dreadful time sleeping. The sighing wind reminded, tormented, provoked. The bedclothes pressed and rubbed and twisted like heavy, heated limbs. I dozed and dreamed of my friend as the Tin Woodman. Awake, I pronounced my dream precise: he wears his love like armor.

An orchid was in my water jug. Had Jones returned? I had come to accept the flowers as his calling card.

Untangling myself from the crumpled bed, I went to the windows. Opening the drapes, I pushed wide the panes. It was a clear, warm, billowy dawning—soft blue and mauve, with the diffused, gaudy light that only exists on the edge of land after a storm. Bathing nude in the morning air, I recalled a Mahler theme and drifted into a reverie. I saw Donough and me in Ireland, riding donkeys along the cliff of Morah on his estate. Suddenly sensing I was not alone, I turned to discover Denvers standing by my bed. A keen, inquiring look was on his pale, gaunt face. Reaching for my robe, I muttered embarrassed apologies. He assured me there was nothing whatever for which I need apologize.

"But do get dressed in any case," he concluded coldly. "There is something on the beach I wish you to see."

Before I could frame a query, he was gone. Alarmed, I dressed hastily, dread rising. From the landing, through the oval window, I saw him pacing impatiently by the yews. Passing out the main parlor windows, I ran to him. The lawn was strewn with debris: pieces of shingle, branches, hedges, flowers. When he spotted me crossing from the house, he descended the wooden steps. The daffodils were decimated; I was grateful Donough had seen them fresh and whole. The steps were blanketed with damp sand embedded with shells and draped in weeds.

He moved at a brisk pace toward the cove. The storm had radically altered the physiognomy of the beach: the sand was flat and hard like a heavily traveled road; mud flecked its dark surface. The sand shrubs were gone, replaced by huge pieces of driftwood, uprooted trees, beams exposing rusted nails, colored bottles, and hundreds of shattered shells. Dredged-up clumps of sea verdure encrusted with purple mollusks were drying in the moist sunlight; stranded, they floated in pools of trapped seawater where small fish darted and crabs crawled—all fated to die when the pools evaporated, unless rescued by the rising tide. One willow had toppled inward.

Upon reaching his side, I saw he was ashen and rigid with contained rage. I was frightened into silence. Ahead, a group of men gathered surfside to the winding green chain of sea debris that outlined the outer limits of the water's encroachment during the night. Like great birds resting, the men slowly shifted positions, and the cause of their convening was suddenly revealed. I went cold with horror. I stopped walking. Denvers grabbed my arm and yanked me forward. A twisted, naked male body lay in a heap, like a dropped string puppet, whiter than the sand that buried its feet and right arm. With a nauseating jolt, I perceived the form as Jones.

A human moan set the air vibrating with grief. Sitting in a fold of sandy dune, Keyes was convulsed by sorrow. Beside him sat Brian, holding his hand.

"*Look!*" Denvers commanded, pointing at the dead boy. "You said Donough saw him last!"

Transfixed, I stared at Jones. Seaweed and seascum were tangled in his matted hair. His bulging, colorless eyes were seemingly detached from the rest of his glabrous, swollen body. They stared back at me. Forcing myself to concentrate, I was able to comprehend that his head was not where it belonged. Snapped free of the spine, it rested on his chest like a flower dangling on its broken stem. A sea spider slowly emerged from his open blue mouth, while the sun glinted on the chained gold dragon embedded in his flesh. Sickened, I turned away.

"I never said that, Denvers. He told me he was planning to see Donough. That's all I know."

Removing myself, I walked back along the shore, hugging the surf. Coming toward me from the house was Cael, leading Dr. Anders; some others I had never seen followed. Claiming Cael, I nodded to them and continued walking, passing the stone jetty, passing the boathouse, walking in the clean air, trying to erase the numbing image of watery death.

"He must have gone swimming after leaving me, which is why he never saw Donough," I reasoned.

But there was something wrong, something out of order. I could see nothing beyond the bulging eyes and the voracious sea spider deserting its putrefying host. This horror added monstrous ramifications to Denvers's claim that Donough was a stranger to the truth.

The sea was unclean, heaving its churned bottom onto the cluttered shore. I walked in a wavy line, following its scalloped, lacy edge until turning up a trodden path into the dunes. In a few minutes I stood at the door to Nanny Welles's cottage. I heard her welcoming Cael before expectantly calling Donough's name. I called out my own and entered as she bade me do. I could no longer contain the grief I felt. I started to sob. She led me to a chair, where I proceeded to break down completely, able only to mutter a broken litany of "Poor Jones . . . poor Jones . . . poor Jones . . ."

"The arrogant pup was out way over his head," she said. "Just like him!"

"You knew him, Nanny?"

"Denvers brought the scamp to tea. Had some hold over the old fool—the usual one, I presumed. Always favored the rough ones, he did. He loved Cormack best, but to the end kept insisting it was Donough he treasured. That was the cause of the trouble, it was. I didn't take to Jones at all, I can tell you!"

Oh, poor Jones! I thought. Had he no friends but those clawing old men?

During breakfast, I tried to pry more information from Nanny Welles about Denvers and Cormack, but she became guarded and uneasy. I changed the subject, leaving soon after the meal's conclusion. I was devastated by the death of Jones. On my way back to the main house, I passed the wall where he and I had talked about Cormack's death. All his clever plans had come to nothing! I remembered him vibrant and smiling, draped in sweet pea; then, this morning, draped in seaweed. I had to sit on a stile to calm my pounding head.

There I remembered other things. Jones coming along the wall from swimming in the salty sea, untangling his beloved gold chain and pendant dragon, kept dry and safe in his trouser pocket. That chain was his most precious possession. He would never *willingly* have gone into the water with it around his neck; yet, his corpse wore it. I could see it glinting in the sun with the sea spider. . . .

I rose and ran back toward the house, taking deep breaths to keep down my sobs. I refused to draw any conclusions. I did not want to know.

A troop of gardeners and laborers were cleaning the back lawn and the surrounding gardens. I joined them to pass the morning until Donough arrived. I learned the body had been taken to the doctor's office for a surgeon from New York to perform the autopsy. I worked furiously hard, avoiding contact with anyone from the household until Brian sought me out and insisted I stop for lunch. He had packed some sandwiches. We walked to the gazebo, but several men were removing the dead willow. We walked to the pond. The swans had four cygnets in their wake. I smiled for the first time that day.

Brian spoke in a whisper. "Denvers says Donough did it!"

"That's absurd! How could he! Why?"

"Blackmail. He says Donough killed him."

"I don't believe it!" I shouted, starting to rage.

"I think they're both crazy! I always have."

At three o'clock Donough arrived, with Goodbody acting as unofficial counsel. They had gone first to Dr. Anders, and then to Sheriff Rooney to organize an inquest, at which time the autopsy report would be heard. While we three friends sat alone at tea, Sheriff Rooney appeared to inform us the inquest was arranged for ten the next morning in his office.

"So soon?" I mumbled, feeling light-headed from the image of Denvers, like Hadrian, fondling the plucked heart of his dead Antinous.

"The sooner the better!" Goodbody snapped officiously.

I excused myself and went immediately to my rooms. I had a headache and wanted to rest before I made myself too ill to attend the inquest. I drew a hot bath and liberally scattered bath salts. Thinking myself safe from everyone,

I took a headache powder and submerged my stiff back in the tub.

Brian was the first to visit. He came to apologize for having upset me, and to borrow *Oz*. He repeated his opinion of Denvers and Keyes. He told me not to worry, Donough would take care of everything.

Then Goodbody appeared wishing to make certain I was in order. He had thought me "strange" at tea.

Then Denvers tapped at the door. He looked worse than I felt. I told him of my sorrow over his loss.

"I came to make certain you were speaking at the inquest."

"Yes, of course I am! If anyone wants me to."

"*I* do. I may have a great deal to say and I may want your corroborating evidence."

"Uh-huh?"

I looked away from his glazed eyes. I could say nothing. After he left, I forced myself to wash with a coarse cloth to improve my circulation, but it did nothing for my head and little for my disposition. I resolved to visit Donough. I would share this growing alarm with him.

"May I come in?" he called from the bedroom.

"I was just coming out."

He tossed me a towel and with another began rubbing my back. Noticing the tension in my shoulders, he spread his warm, strong hands across them, massaging the muscles there. He insisted I recline on the bed, where he continued to massage the tightness from my back and neck and legs in silence until I spoke.

"I can't believe Jones is dead."

"Why are you so upset by this? You told me you hated him."

"Yes, but I didn't want him *dead*!"

"I'm sorry, Robbie! Forgive me, I'm . . . It will soon be over."

"Denvers thinks you killed him."

"*What?* What are you saying?"

He stopped massaging my calves but did not remove his hands.

"I think he's going to tell them at the inquest."

"Why would I . . . ?"

"Blackmail. Jones was planning to blackmail you."

"There are no grounds! I've done nothing wrong. Nothing *that* wrong."

I stared at him. He had flushed scarlet. His profound confusion shattered my concentration. He released my legs and sat on the edge of the bed. I put on my robe and sat close by him.

"What about Cormack's death? Jones said he knew the truth about Cormack's death. What is the truth?"

"He died in a fire with my father."

"How?" I took his hand. "Please, Donough, tell me the truth!"

He lay back across the bed. I leaned over him, touching his expressionless face. I kissed him on the mouth. He did not respond. Without moving, he began to speak very slowly.

"Cormack started the fire. It was an accident. He didn't want to die. He'd found my father drunk, and soaked the room with cognac to teach him a lesson, I suppose, or maybe from anger. He hated my father's drinking. So did I. My father was an ugly drunk. He slipped with the lamp. They both burned to death while Cormack was trying to drag him out of it."

"Who told you this?"

"Denvers and Nanny Welles. They heard the screams and were there at the end."

"Where were you?"

"I was asleep in my room. How could Denvers think that I could . . . ?" He hugged me to him.

I kissed him again. "He's not well, Donough. He's not himself. He's crazed."

"But why?"

"He loved Jones. They were . . . involved."

He pulled away and sat up. "He won't say anything to hurt me."

He already has, I thought.

The inquest was a horrid business although it took less than half an hour. The men who found the body were present, as well as Jones's sister, several officials, the doctor, and the five of us from the house. Denvers did not speak; he sat rigidly throughout and never uttered a sound. Only Keyes wept. The doctor reported a great quantity of water in the boy's lungs that confirmed death by drowning. Jones's sister offered a letter as evidence from the boy that he wished to leave Gaywyck. I was a key witness. If the boy was leaving of his own free will and under no duress, as I swore, then there could be no question of doubt: his demise was ruled a misadventure.

Goodbody left immediately for the train but Donough remained at Gaywyck until the following morning to make certain all was well. Denvers had visited Nanny Welles; she managed to appease his wrath. Donough wanted to speak with his tutor but the distraught man refused to see him.

After luncheon, I went to the waterfall. The laborers had finished with that area and were now working among the fruit trees; the paths were cleared, and I detoured to the pond to visit the cygnets with crusts of bread.

He was waiting for me in the hammock, wearing only his wristwatch, reading Gray's *Anatomy*. We did not speak.

"I love you," I sighed afterward.

He nodded, squeezing me very tightly before disengaging himself and silently taking his leave. I called to him. He turned and smiled; my heart rocked with joy.

"Stay!" I called after him. "Please, stay?"

"Stay," he echoed with a fleeting smile. " '*I prithee tell me what thou think'st of me,*' " he recited laughingly. " '*I am not what I am.*' "

" '*I would you were as I would have you be!*' "

" '*Would it be better, lad, than I am? I wish I might, for now I am your fool.*' "

"I love you," I said, and he smiled wider, fuller, exposing his beautiful teeth. Then he was gone.

Stretching my full length, I relaxed. For the moment, I was satiated. The scent of his body clung to me. My muscles felt him still; his caresses hovered, outlining my self. Springing from the hammock, I dived into the water. While under the cool surface among the water-lily roots, I imagined drowning and was afraid. *His* lungs had been filled with water. Diving from the rocks, had he broken his neck, perhaps, and drowned? Or had a cramp disabled and drowned him—his broken neck a result of the storm's tearing, pulling currents. I scampered up the rocks and sat under the waterfall. I still had my doubts, but no one to pin them on. Poor Jonesy!

Donough and I had tea in silence. He was exhausted and depressed. It started to rain; instead of our planned walk, we settled in the small downstairs study, making desultory conversation until the clock rang six. I suggested a hot bath before dinner. We separated, meeting again to

dine in silence. I had never seen him so withdrawn. Over
coffee, in front of a fire, I offered to read to him. He
smiled gratefully but said no. I sat back in my chair and
left him to his thoughts, hoping they were of me. The
clock struck nine. I suggested we go to bed. He did not
argue.

We walked up the central staircase, pausing to look at
the moon through the oval window. The rain had cleaned
the sky of clouds. He stood by my side.

I love you, I thought. The first time you held me was on
this staircase. Do you remember?

He took my hand. "I don't know how I've survived
without your love, Robert. Just give me a little more time."

I've given you everything else, I thought. Why not time
as well?

"All my life," I said.

He raised my hand to his lips and kissed it with such
sweet reverence that a quick tenderness vibrated through
me.

"I love you, Donough."

He closed his eyes and nodded. The moonlight covered
his face like a silver mask.

"Please try to understand," he pleaded, suddenly weeping.

"There is no reason for you to cry."

"No reason? My life isn't reason enough?"

He turned from me and ascended the steps. I called to
him. When he turned, he smiled. My heart swelled with
joy.

"I love you," I said.

He nodded and disappeared into the shadows. I went
up to my room. I wanted to go for a walk, but instead
ran another hot bath and sprinkled it with a scented
powder. I wanted to understand his pain; unless I could,
I knew I would never understand him.

". . . Love is *tristesse* for him. Do you understand? He's
just beginning to accept . . . beginning to accept . . .
accept . . . accept. . . ."

He *must* accept, and quickly, I thought, growing impatient. "The mask endures as the face itself."

Dried and powdered, brooding, I strolled naked into
my bedroom and was startled to see him sitting on my
bed. He wore a silver silk Japanese dressing gown. Distressed and disheveled, he looked in the grip of torment.

I felt shy, suddenly shamed by my nudity when he nervously glanced away from me. Scurrying under the covers, I waited for him to speak.

"Donough," I said, patience ending, "will you come into bed and hold me the way you used to do?"

"I'm far beyond such innocent play," he said huskily. "I can't breathe in here!"

"Open the windows."

"Yes! Yes! I will! Thank you!"

He crossed to them and pushed one fully open. I noticed his bare legs with their delicate ankles, so slim for such a large, muscular man, like a fine Irish stallion. I felt nervous and frightened, uncertain of what words might soothe him: I felt angry and impotent over my inability to take his pain away from him. My love seemed useless. Suddenly, speaking loudly and adamantly, he said without looking at me, "I cannot live with the world's disapprobation."

I was stunned. This reality had never occurred to me.

"Must we acknowledge it, Donough? It's like your father said: there are only two kinds of people, those who love and those who do not."

"That was fine for my father . . . and for Cormack."

". . . and for Goodbody and Mortimer, and for millions of others!"

"But, not for *me!*" he whispered, leaning against the open French window.

We'll continue as we are, I thought. My love will change all this.

I called to him, stretching out my arms. Crossing to me, he allowed an embrace, then pulled quickly away; his robe fell open, revealing his familiar need, but he drew together the ends of the silk garment and hurried from the room. I did not sleep again that night. I wrote in my journal, then paced the length of my apartment weeping for us both.

The next morning, on the sod beneath the hammock, he was more frenzied and wild than I had ever known him. There was a violence that twice caused me to cry out in pain. Both times, he cradled me in his arms, apologizing between fervent kisses and whisperings: he wanted to give more pleasure than I had ever known; he wanted me to forgive him for being weak, frightened—the cowardly animal he was.

Instantly he left me, to dive into the pool. He always waited for several minutes, continuing his gentle caresses while provoking teasing, grateful kisses. I sat up and watched him swim to the cascade, where he stretched under the shower (calling Cael to mind), before disappearing into the cave. Inside, he stood studying the drawings.

"Do you like these?" he asked.

"Yes," I answered shyly, barely glancing at the coarse pornography. "At first they frightened me. Now . . ."

"Now?"

"Now they excite me."

"Which one frightened you?"

I pointed. He smiled. Pulling me to him, he pressed me down to the ground.

"Why should this frighten you?"

When we could speak sensibly again, I said foolishly, "If only *your* fears were as pleasantly dismissed!"

As soon as I spoke, I regretted it. He stood and strode under the falls again. He disappeared, and I shouted his name in a panic. He stepped back toward me, the water coursing down his body, making paths in its thick, curly hair.

"It's best during the day, when we're alone like this," he said, kneeling by me. "I think I can tolerate anything with you. I love you, Robert. Who gives a damn about the world's approbation?"

I nodded. He looked amused, then laughed to prove it. His laughter echoed eerily in the confines of the cave.

"I understand."

"No! No, you don't, Robert."

I knelt opposite him. He put his hands on my shoulders.

"Don't ask any questions, Robbie. Be grateful for what *you* have, my darling."

I started to weep.

"Why are you crying?"

"You see, no one ever called me 'darling' before."

He laughed again, and kissed me.

"But," I said, "what about what *we* have?"

That sounds like a question, I thought, closing my eyes, listening to him leave.

He decided to stay one more day. I was determined to ask no questions. We walked along the shore talking of love. He told me about Steven, his father's last protégé, the one passionate love of his father's life.

"What happened to Steven?"

"The week before the fire, they had a fight. He left here in the middle of the night. My father followed, but the last weekend he came back alone. Cormack rejoiced."

"Why?"

"Like Denvers, he hated Steven. They hated everyone my father loved, often including me. That last day, when Cormack asked after Steven, my father said he went to Europe."

"Were there many protégés?"

"Yes. And guardians ostensibly for us, but actually for my father's pleasure. Steven lasted the longest, nearly ten years. I believe he really loved him. The night I was born, my mother found my father with a protégé in his study. She tried to drown herself. He saved her. Often I wish he had not. . . ."

We were together constantly. He wanted to talk; I was content to listen. It drew us closer. He held my hand, touched my face, and kissed me spontaneously, often, throughout the day. After lunch, we rode the horses and exercised in my gymnasium, showering together. After tea, we walked to the white oaks. On the wrought-iron bench at sunset, he kissed me with such loving tenderness that a thousand ecstatic couplings by the waterfall were not worth its beauty. After dinner, we sat on the dolmen in the sunken garden studying the sky.

"Denvers is a fervent admirer of Aratus with his descriptions of the Greek sky. Somewhere there's a copy of Bayer's *Uranometria* . . . somewhere . . . there *was*. Is there still, my sweet librarian?"

"Yes. All fifty-one plates extant. The astronomy books are now grouped in Library I."

He laughed, delighted, as though I'd done something extraordinary.

"Cormack was convinced everything is in the stars. He felt crushed by the enormity of it all."

He pointed to the Corona Borealis and related Ariadne's betrayal on Naxos by Theseus, finding similarities between the Minotaur and Baum's Wicked Witch of the West, both incarnations of fear. Chance seemed everywhere. If Ariadne had not seen Theseus arrive in Crete? If the pail of water had not been at Dorothy Gale's hand? If Antinous had had no grandfather in Nicomedia? If Father Howard had not known Father Collins?

"But occurrences are eternally recurring."

I felt awed by the heavens, but not by the weight of circumstance. I could choose which move to make. Love grants us freedoms.

The next morning I rode with him to the train. I had never indulged myself in that pleasure before, but this morning was different. We had joined deliriously at the waterfall before breakfast; he had wept for love of me.

"I feel scorched," he said.

"Did you think your heart asbestos?"

"I thought myself immune to happiness, and therefore to burns."

After the train departed, I sat in the rear of the carriage in anguish. I felt as if I were hollow, as if my rational parts had gone with him. I craved him. My mouth felt dry. My heart pounded. My hands were trembling. I began to perspire heavily.

This is love? I wondered, bemused. I'm more like an opium eater.

I tried to force a laugh, but nothing was funny. I felt ghastly.

"I want him."

That did not explain it.

"I *need* him."

That was closer to the mark.

"But at least I've *chosen* my opium, Mortimer!"

I believed that? I felt worse. Even I could see the transparency of the lie. I realized with a chill that I was being untruthful to myself. It had never occurred to me that I might lie to myself! The mask *had* endured as the face itself.

"There is something wrong."

I began to regain control of myself. My reason warned me. Obsession was repulsed for the moment. I admitted doubt. It was the beginning of my awakening. It was worth my life in the coin of the heart's realm.

Nineteen

IT ANGERED ME THAT OUR LOVE HAD not yet reached the healing stages. Its magic powers needed prodding, and among the doubts that occasionally tweaked my euphoria was an old new one: What am I doing wrong? I was impatient for my rewards. I wanted my happily-ever-afters *now*. True, he needed a great deal of concentrated effort, but my impatience gave rise to a new doubt: Could love survive life?

I reread *Wuthering Heights*. This was not the time for temperament or flaring nostrils. Death was not an attractive alternative. *Dum spiro, spero* became my motto (and with *every* breath, I hoped). There were the glorious summer months ahead. Maybe he would retire and we could spend our lives loving? Since I never had a share in the working world, relinquishing it was no problem; and it was easier still for me to give up Donough's share. (Nothing could be easier than giving away what belongs to someone else.) I probed for *his* truth, and became more determined to find it for him—thinking it lost, not merely unrecognized.

My dreams returned to terrorize me. The apparition taunted me, and were it not for Cael's talons, would have physically harmed me. I was too dazed the next mornings to remember clearly. Gifts of seashells and wild flowers decorated my bed table. The paintings of the twins returned to my wall after mysteriously journeying back to Donough's for his visit. I attempted to fetter my fears. I resolved to write Donough and mention these unnerving games.

A restlessness seized me. I could not read. I could not catalog. I could neither write letters nor rant in my journal. Keyes locked himself into his rooms, which ended my piano lessons. I dared not play `the instrument for fear of seeming disrespectful to the memory of Jones (too soon departed), and for fear one of the old men would slam the cover on my knuckles. So I exercised for hours in my gymnasium. I worked with the gardeners. I swam with Brian. I tossed a football with Brian. He and I played table tennis, the latest gift from Donough, or took photographs, or made bonsai. He tried to teach me to cook, but I lacked the patience for all that chopping and waiting; I had always found chemistry tedious. My only accomplishment was a growth of one and three-quarter inches.

The fourth morning after Donough's departure, Denvers appeared at breakfast. He looked well, I said placatingly. He raised an eyebrow and noted it was time I learned to observe rather than to judge. There was nothing I could say to that; the truth stung, and I remained silent.

"We'll resume Dio Cassius after lunch," he commanded.

"Uh-huh."

"And do *cease* those annoying grunts!"

"Uh-huh . . . *sorry*! I mean—"

"Eat your eggs."

"Yes, sir."

He sighed and rested his head in his hands. Lowering his arms, he looked steadily at me, then smiled gently, eyebrows level.

"Have you grown taller or are you sitting straighter?"

"Taller."

"You grow larger and I grow smaller. I believe everything is a decision of the mind, but there are some things . . ."

". . . written in the constellations called chromosomes?"

"Yes, exactly!" He laughed, handing me a book of poems—the actual peace offering, I assumed.

"Thamyris?"

"One of the first to write of love between comrades. The world's disapprobation is easily won, Robbie. Another type of growth will soon take care of it. Do eat your eggs."

That explains it! I thought, hopping to conclusions. He's worked everything out with Donough. Thank God!

The discipline imposed by Denvers that afternoon made the resumption of my other duties easier. His erudition inspired me, though his occasional flashes of black impatience—stinging jibes at my youthful "romanticisms" —reduced my brain to the "dark and soggy place" he labeled it. Two days later, while we sat over our books, Ambrose interrupted with the news that two gigantic packages had arrived. Donough sent Brian and me De Dion tricycles. The lightweight, air-cooled, single-cylinder affairs soon replaced Anita as my mode of transportation; but since they made so much noise, we agreed to keep them at the gatehouse, far away from Denvers, using the road outside the estate walls for our races after raising red warning flags to inform the villagers and their nervous horses that we were operating our machines.

Donough wrote of plans to build a garage near the gatehouse, and sent a packet of brochures advertising the latest automobiles for me to examine. We decided on a Mors Petit Duc for the two of us and a British Daimler for crowds. He also announced plans to bring electricity to Gaywyck, overriding Denvers's long-standing objection.

"If we are to live there," he wrote, "we will live comfortably and well, full members of the twentieth century's family of man."

My interest in the cottage revived. Getting a key from Denvers, I began to catalog the books there. My work in Library I was completed; I was not comfortable in Library II: the silence in Keyes's apartment was positively ominous. Frequently, when working with my back to the door, I glanced over my shoulder to reassure myself he wasn't approaching armed with a harpoon. That morning on the beach, when Jones lay dead between us, he had paused in his keening to fire at me a glance of hatred sharp as shrapnel. I was afraid of him.

"Denvers, is Keyes all right?"

"No. He'll get over it."

"Are you sure?"

"No."

"Shouldn't Donough be notified?"

"Whatever for? What can *he* do about it? The old fool's quite mad. His grief has eclipsed his reason. If we need Donough in a hurry, Brian will telegraph for him. It's why he was taught to use the thing."

"Brian never mentioned—"

"Did you ever ask?"

"No."

"Your sixth-sense asleep? How do you think he sent for Donough last time? Where were we?"

Daily, after my reading with Denvers, I stopped in the kitchen for crusts, then walked directly to the pond, forbidding myself a detour to the waterfall, that environ now claustrophobic with secret harmonies. I worked until tea-time.

Denvers and I resumed *Roman History*. One after-noon, finished at the cottage, I discovered it was raining. The warm day, overcast and misty with the sun a diffuse white brightness amid the gray, could have held until evening. Long Island weather was never reliable, but I was beyond lamenting its dampness and perversity. With-out hesitation I decided to use the connecting tunnel; I had no attractive alternative: getting wet was not amus-ing, and waiting out the downpour would cause me to miss tea. Besides, I reasoned, what the hell is a tunnel for!

With the help of a borrowed lamp, I made my way without incident until I reached the nail-studded door at the far end under the manor. There, against the wall on the near side, I found a suitcase. It was a beautiful bag of soft brown leather with the initials CG engraved on its gleaming gold clasp. Without a qualm, I opened it—or *tried* to. It seemed locked, but with a concerted effort I managed to press the bulging sides together and free the jammed clasp. It fell open, immediately revealing the identity of the packer.

Jones had thrust Donough's diaries in last, at the pen-ultimate moment, which had not been the case with my two cashmere sweaters or the caftan Donough had given me. When I removed everything else, I discovered them on the bottom. A side pocket held a gold brush and a medieval French silver ladle for heavy cream. Another pocket was crammed with Donough's precious stones: I fondled the purple amethyst, the color of Denvers's grief. A third housed an indiscriminate clutch of Greek and Etruscan coins and, ironically, one Hadrianic coin bearing a likeness of Antinous. Wrapped separately, in a mauve silk scarf, was the small signed drawing of the crucified Christ by Da Vinci—one of the most valuable pieces in the entire Gaylord collection.

At least you paid attention to what people told you, Jones.

I went through everything carefully. A photographer's large gray envelope—similar to the one he had given me, but packed to bursting—I put aside. On top of it, I placed the three diaries. I returned my own clothing first; then a pair of filthy undershorts from which I removed the ivory and jade cameo he'd pinned to the crotch. I rifled through the other articles of clothing piece by piece, discovering a jeweled Medici dagger in a pair of socks and a black-lacquered box from Heien Japan which contained Donough's diamond studs. But no wristwatch!

I arranged the valuables neatly, delicately handling the diaries and the photographs (not wishing to damage them), and closed the bag. I carted it back to the cottage. Choosing the second-floor room overlooking the wych elm, I stashed it in an empty closet. Outside, it was still raining. I was chilled. I retrieved the case and opened it for a sweater. This time I kept the envelope and the diaries aside. Crossing to the windows, I sat in the dull, murky light and extinguished the lamp.

I opened the envelope first. There were seventeen prints inside, all in superb condition but for one. Each had been carefully notated with subjects, dates, times, and places, except for one. The two exceptions were not the same photograph. The first, a damaged print, was folded down the center; the face of Steven, who sat entwined with a very supple Mr. Gaylord, had been neatly excised. (With a shudder, I thought of the Rossetti portrait.)

The second exception, unannotated, was of me and Donough Gaylord! It had been taken in my room—*my bedroom*; the Crevelli on the wall above us attested to that as it gazed upon our rioting forms. How could it be? I was stunned. I looked through the other photographs: there was one of the twins: "1-6-83 2 P.M. Lib[rary]"; in another, "CG and K[eyes] 25-5-83 11 A.M. K-Bdrm." There were four more of the twins together, posed. One of Mortimer at the waterfall, sunlit, flaunting his gifts: "18-4-81." Two of "D[envers] and C[ormack] 11-11-82 4 P.M. D-Bdrm." Five of Mr. Gaylord (unidentified) and Steven, all blurred by their carnal activity, all focused on the rampant priapic nature of the two of them. And one of Mr. Gaylord and Cormack: "3-8-84 9 A.M. St[udy]."

I put them aside. Never having seen their lascivious like before, I experienced a profound, dizzying concupiscence that annihilated me. I had to stretch myself out flat on the wooden parquet floor and think of other things.

After several deep breaths, the blood returned to my head. I stood and walked around the room. I am a very visual person. Those images seared into my brain, and like the learned notes of a Chopin ballade, they automatically flexed the appropriate muscles. I felt ill with a dry, nerve-scraping tension. I wanted to look again; I wanted them gone forever. The turmoil they engendered was catastrophic. I started to cry. A part of me (the innocent part of me) believed what Donough and I did together was unique. I did not understand sexuality, my own or anyone else's. If people loved one another, why was some of their love acceptable and some not? *Why* was I crying?

Suddenly, inexplicably angry, I snatched the top diary. Undoing the tie, I opened it. A sheaf of lavender papers fluttered around me, dropping to the floor. I sat in their midst. The scented, folded pages were covered with Keyes's majestic, florid hand; they were love notes to Jones, *billets-doux*, lewd verse, and several sonnets. I read a final couplet:

> *Be not self-willed, for you are much too fair*
> *To be death's conquest and make worms your heir.*

"How *à-propos*," I muttered nastily, "if a trifle derivative."

The extent of the passion expressed in the notes was shocking. He had loved the boy, undoubtedly *still* loved the dead boy, with every atom of his being, beyond all reason, to the grossest excess. I read every line enthralled and horrified. The last was a short note:

> You cannot leave. I forbid it. Before I lose you, I
> will kill you. You know the strength in my hands.
> Do not play with me. You are my life.

An immense scrolled K, like a crumpled spider, filled the lower half of the page.

It was as I expected. The boy had been murdered. After leaving me, he went to Keyes, who lured him to the sea and murdered him—strangled him, or snapped his neck in a crazed frenzy of despair. I knew all along that Donough had nothing to do with it. Like summer heat lightning on the horizon, the photographs flashed at the edge of my mind, distracting, disturbing. I put aside the loose papers and opened the diary.

C IS OBSESSED WITH PAPA. HE HAS TO KNOW
EVERYTHING. HE SPIES ON HIM THROUGH A
HOLE IN THE DRAPES AND THROUGH THE

MIRROR. WE STILL TAKE TURNS BEING PAPA.
I CAN'T WATCH THEM. IT EXCITES ME TOO
MUCH. C SAYS THERE IS NO SUCH THING.
THERE ARE TOO MANY THINGS C DOES NOT
UNDERSTAND. FOR HIM, SEX IS ALL. FOR
PAPA TOO. I WANT MUCH MORE.

I flipped to the last entry.

C IS DEAD. I MUST DIE TOO. HOW CAN I
LIVE WITHOUT PAPA AND C?

I opened it to the center.

C IS NOW WITH PAPA AND S OFTEN. I HEARD
PAPA TELL D IT WAS TO MAKE C MANAGEABLE.

I closed the book, tied the leather thongs, and put everything into the suitcase. The irregular tapping of the rain
on the leaves told me the downpour had abated. I carried
the suitcase to the closet and hurried out into the dusk.
I had missed tea but I wasn't hungry. I felt weighted down
by sorrow. Not even the sight of the swans with their
cygnets cheered me.

The photographic images came to life in my head: a
series of sighs, moans, and animal gruntings. But no joy.
No laughter. Behind the lies and secrets of Gaywyck there
lurked only shadows groping and grasped. All was grief.
All was sorrow.

"*Their* sorrow," I repeated aloud. "Why is *their* sorrow
suffocating *me*?"

No sadness? he has asked by the waterfall.

"No!" I wanted to shout to the heavens. "*I* have no
sorrow with my sexuality and I don't want anyone else's!"

The male swan rose from the water, shaking his body
and spreading his wings. I laughed, understanding the act
and needing to do the same. I felt fiercely alive and buoy-
antly free. I ran around the pond, intending to swim in
the cove—a place I had assiduously avoided since Jones
surfaced there—but the rains had soaked the mud flats,
converting the arid acre into soft, welcoming "primal
ooze." Stripping off my clothes, I slid and flopped and
rolled in the satiny-smooth, warmly enveloping earth.
Shouting with happiness, I fell into the surf, loving myself
and my life, and wanting nothing to be different, *ever*.

I returned to my room to bathe before dinner. Ebulliently happy, I liberally sprinkled the bath powder. To my delight, suds rose above the rim like alpine peaks. Cael settled himself on the sink to observe, looking like a snowy owl. I immersed myself and was distracted by lost soap, when suddenly the lamp was extinguished. Before I could rise, two hands grabbed my head and pushed me under the water. I flailed and splashed, but my assailant's grip was so well-judged that I was unable to right myself and was on the verge of blacking out when I was released. Sputtering and gasping for air, I climbed from the tub to the sounds of a demented Cael. His paws were bloodstained and his fur was puffed up as it had been the first time I met Keyes. His growls were deep-throated and his tail flicked with rage. The cat had saved my life. Wet, bloody footprints ended halfway through my apartment. The game had gone too far. I would leave Gaywyck in the morning.

Denvers and I dined together. We shared a piece of sirloin, some kale and mashed potatoes ("very shanty Irish, this"). The meal went well after a rocky start: a very angry Ambrose had questioned us about Brian.

"Has anyone seen Brian?"

"I never see Brian," Denvers mused, "not even when he's directly in front of me."

I glanced at him to see if he were joking; he decidedly was not. I shook my head and asked how long he'd been missing.

"Since right after luncheon," Ambrose whined. " 'E's gone off!"

Denvers sniffed the sirloin nervously. "What's gone off?"

"That's odd," I said, unable not to say it. "He hasn't done that for the longest while."

"Could your magic be losing its potency?" Denvers asked with the tiniest half-smile twitching upward at the corners of his slack mouth.

I filled mine with mashed potatoes to avoid risk.

There was much wine to lighten the mood. Afterward he invited me into the small study for a brandy. He stood under the baroque mirror in front of a fire, as he had my first night in the house; but his was the only face above me, a face pale and aged, ravaged by time, weary, loveless, and revealed. I thought of Mary Rose Gaylord, es-

caped from her locked chamber, peering through the
window-mirror at both of us. I made a mental note to ask
Donough why such a mirror as this existed at Gaywyck;
pieces of a conversation describing the house as a stop
on the Underground Railroad came into my head when
Denvers spoke.

"I'm tired," he said, "desperately tired. Old age is
hideous. Life is grotesque."

"I don't agree," I said firmly, holding steady as his
eyebrow slowly lifted.

"After what you've discovered here?"

"I think the only thing hideous and evil here has been
excess."

"Thank you, Socrates. Are you immune to excess?"

"Good intentions are my only protection," I said defensively, wanting to flee but mesmerized by curiosity. I
felt beyond his reach, as though the glass of brandy in my
hand was as potent as Dorothy Gale's pail of water.

"The road to hell is paved with good intentions." He
grinned mockingly.

"I don't believe there is a hell."

"Love is hell."

"Only if we allow it to be. Thinking makes it so."

"You've learned your lessons well."

"You are the best of teachers."

"I don't live by what I teach."

Several retorts, but no contradictions, came to mind. I
remained silent. The use of "don't" instead of "can't"
made his position clear. I wanted to continue the conversation; sudden exhaustion forced me to end it. He walked
me to my rooms, pausing there a moment to whisper:
"We two alone *have* sung like birds i' the cage," then,
turning, departed without a good-night. I fell into bed, too
spent to read, barely able to undress.

I was sucked from my sleep by a voice sweetly chanting my name. Disoriented, slow to awaken, I was buoyed by
warm currents, yet there was a heaviness in my extrem-
ities as though pulled by aqueous roots and tendrils. From
the corner of Jones's mouth, a sea spider peeked. Lewd
images torn from photographs aroused me. The cooing of
my name consoled like stroking, loving hands. I tumbled
in a grinding wave before touching earth.

I opened my eyes. A noose of anxiety tightened around
my throat. Devoid of peripheral vision, I peered into a

funnel. At the open window, the woman from the Rossetti portrait glistered and billowed, beckoning me to follow.

We met at a masquerade party and similar dreams, I thought. She knows the way back.

Her blue dress twisted flamelike in the breeze. Around her, moonbeams refracted, momentarily blinding me. I moaned. Why had Donough lied? He *had* been in my bed. The eye of the camera saw us in my bed. Keyes saw him leave. I closed my eyes and slept. Again I was called, but this time less gently: hands yanked the coverlet away. I sat up. The figure drifted from the room, gliding across the portico. Unwillingly I followed. Awake, asleep, the two states coexistent, I walked in darkness but for her luminous presence, hung like the moon in my eyes.

The night air chilled. On the lawn below, the coruscating figure fluttered toward the ocean. Unafraid, I descended, crossing the dew-soaked grass in pursuit. At the yews, I stopped. She had taken flight: high behind scudding clouds she drifted.

"Robbie! Rob-bie!"

The wind raised and carried me down the slanting wooden steps to the sloping shore. On the soft sand, balance eluded me.

"I'm cold."

"Warmth this way!"

Through the lapping surf we splashed toward the jetty. Where is Cael? I wondered. Why didn't he come to my room tonight? My rescuer. She hummed Albinoni. Her extended arms moved in the air like butterfly nets.

"Where are we going?"

"To peace and quiet," she sang.

At the base of the jetty, confronted by that pile of rocks, strength deserted me. I was dizzy and numb. A sourness filled me.

I'm going to throw up! I thought.

"I can't go any farther."

"Just a *little* more. Come up to the moon with me, Robbie!"

I called for Donough. I wanted release from this dream.

"Come up to the moon with me, Rob-bie!"

I climbed the rocks. She was already poised at the far edge, gazing out to sea like a figure on the prow of a ship. I advanced. She was gone. The earth spun too quickly;

the moon swirled, and light sparked like spray from a wave. I stood at the edge, surveying the unsteady sea, expecting to sight her gliding over its surface. The rocks rose and fell with the pull of the tide.

She called me from behind. Swaying with the moon in my eyes, I pivoted, tilting. She approached. Her outstretched arms were huge. I balanced on the edge, crumbling to my knees with fright. Closer she came, hands larger and larger. On my back I felt spray from the impatient sea.

This will be the end, I prayed. Or must I fall and awaken screaming?

Donough's voice bellowed my name. It was the last thing I remember before surfacing in my bed twenty-four hours later. . . .

When I awoke, my tongue was swollen; I could not speak, could barely swallow. There was a pain in my head above my eyes that banded my skull, making it difficult for me to move. My neck was stiff; my stomach clawed; my extended gut radiated soreness; a rigidity cemented my toes together and produced the sensation of adamantine fingers; but, most horrifyingly, a spasm knotted the muscles of my left side, causing me to cry out in pain. Donough leaned over me, softly murmuring comforting words. He looked heavy with grief, oppressed by his dark, secret attachment to me. Who called love "a pleasing plague"?

I closed my eyes. When next I opened them, all my physical difficulties were present but lessened, the only addition being a smarting in my lungs that hindered the free flow of breath.

Jane Austen, I thought, without knowing the reason.

The clock struck three. From beneath the drawn drapes a seam of yellow light lay along the floor, confirming my sense of unnatural dusk. Gimlet-eyed, I noted a fire, Cael by my hip, and Donough Gaylord hunched in a chair near my hand's end.

"Psst!" was the only sound I was able to produce and project.

Donough instantly leaned forward. "Don't try to speak," he whispered. "You *must* sleep! You're safe now."

"Uh-huh." I nodded, suddenly feeling nauseous from the movement. I wanted to tell him that before he could openly love me he would have to clear the barriers from his heart; the old affections with their untoward grief

needed his acceptance first, his acknowledgment. I wanted
to tell him many things that seemed wonderfully clear to
me. He leaned farther and kissed me on the lips. I sighed,
content. He kissed me again. My heart revived. Raising my
hand, I touched his unshaven cheek. Had anyone else ever
felt the coarse stubble?

"I love you," he said.

I ventured another nod, swaying internally as though
swinging in our hammock.

"Go to sleep, Robert, please."

I frowned. Go to sleep! I was thirsty. I needed to use the
bathroom. I felt gummy and uncomfortable and I smelled
foul. Only in novels can people sleep for days, ignoring
all bodily functions. I was annoyed *someone* had not considered this. I grunted instructions. I was in a very bad
temper, bitterly aggrieved by my inability to ask pertinent
questions and by no one *offering* explanations. Safe, was
I? Safe from what? Safe from whom?

Brian was called, a chamber pot located, water heated,
and soup administered. I was not a good patient. I whimpered a great deal. I had difficulty swallowing the soup.
I began to sob, which brought on another spasm in my
left side, which instigated my pushing Donough away. His
surprise and hurt mortified me. I felt wretched. I fell
asleep.

I awoke feeling sanguine. There was a nub of stiffness
in my back and thighs, but the debilitation was gone. Brian
slept soundly in the chair by my side. Cael was away. It
was night. Slipping from the bed, I walked quietly to the
bathroom. I was wearing a mint-green flannel nightshirt.
A fire burned, although the windows were open and a
warm breeze fluttered the drapes. The clock read midnight. I was nearly back in bed before noticing a form
standing motionless in the shadows. Wrapped in a full
black cape, his hair dripping from the sea, my lover
beckoned.

"You've been swimming?" I whispered, not wishing to
awaken Brian.

"Yes. How do you feel?"

"Fine. I'm well. What happened to me?"

He motioned for us to go outside.

"What happened?" I repeated on the portico, leaning
against him.

"Keyes tried to kill you."

My jaw dropped in disbelief.

"He dressed in the Rossetti costume of my mother's fancy ball and took you to the sea. He drugged you first. He's been drugging you for months. The bedlam's dead. He's hanged himself."

I felt sick. I did not want to believe him. Questions arose, causing greater pain in my mind than had recently been in my head. Keyes *dead*? Murder *me*? Was he the mysterious image in my photograph? How had he drugged me? How was Donough there to save me?

"Come walk with me, Robbie. The balmy air will do you good."

Opening the cloak, he revealed himself naked beneath. I pulled off my nightshirt and stepped within the circle of his arms. His warmth and musky scent quickened my senses. With our arms around each other, we walked down to the sunken garden and along the narrow path that linked it to the sea. There was a summer stillness and a cloudless, star-bright sky.

The tide was out. The black jetty looked like a beached whale on the vast sand reef formed by the storm. Separate lakes shimmered where the shallows should have been. I felt disoriented. He dropped the cape. Taking my hand, he led me. We walked and waded out to the skipping, foaming, distant surf. Somewhere a bobwhite trilled. One moment the water swirled at my ankles, the next around my chest: the bottom had dropped from under. My feet sank into soft sand. With a hefty stroke, I was out of my depth but calmly swimming beside him. He surged ahead, his muscular arms pulling him effortlessly through the water. I was able without strain to keep within calling distance; the absence of tension or fear gave me greater energy and speed. Stretching every muscle, I darted, passing him with a shout: "Turn left, then straight to Galway Bay!"

He caught my leg and gently pulled me to him. With short, thrashing movements, he drove his body beneath mine, making himself an island of warm flesh on which I could shelter. I reversed my position to kiss him on the mouth. When I glanced over his bobbing head toward Gaywyck, I was astonished by our feat: we had swum a tremendous distance.

"You are a man one can lean on," I said, laughing at my silliness.

I reversed my position again to continue our swim, but from under the tender waves his body's wonders distracted me. Perched on him, I managed to delight and be delighted.

"I *love* you," I shouted gleefully, thrashing and flailing, repeating it, howling at the stars.

I rolled overboard, surfaced, and climbed on top of him, planning to kiss his eyes, his ears, his neck, but was halted by the sound of sobs.

"I nearly lost you," he explained hoarsely, withdrawing into grief. "It will happen soon, now, and I cannot bear it."

"I'll never leave you, Donough, you must know that!"

He reacted as if I had stabbed him, wrenching his body in pain. Suddenly I wished us alone in the world, shipwrecked, in sight of Elysium. He had begun to shiver, less from chill than from profound distress.

"Make for shore, Captain Gaylord," I ordered, adding in an attempt to distract him from this sorrow I thought familiar: " '*What country, friend, is this?*' "

I answered myself, abstracted, eager to be landed: " '*This is Illyria, lady.*' "

He whispered, his deep, mellow voice caressing the verse: " '*And what should I do in Illyria?/ My brother he is in Elysium.*' "

" '. . . *Perchance he is not drowned,*' " I continued. " '*What think you sailors?*' "

Encircling me tightly with his arms, he began kicking his feet, propelling us toward shore. I could feel his heart pounding. I spoke the next line, wondering how much of the text I remembered: " '*It is perchance that you yourself were saved.*' "

He continued, hoarse again, overwhelmed by his sorrow. I could feel the words vibrating in his chest, echoing in mine: " '*Oh my poor brother. And so perchance may he be.*' "

Enraged, he shouted his own name, and without breaking the rhythm of his movements, rolled over, submerging me. For a moment I thought him playful. I thought his mood had shifted by some personal release, and he wished me to turn or dive as one with him. Wrapping my arms and legs around, I squeezed tenaciously, determined not to express fear, attempting with that fierce gesture to express a willingness to die with him if that was what he required. In spite of my resolve, when I could no longer breathe and he showed no sign of reversing our position, I panicked. Releasing my right arm from his back, I pulled it under the surface. Thrusting my fingers between his legs to gently seize him, I exerted no pressure, merely asserted a claim to my life and his love. He reversed our positions. Shuddering, I sucked at the air, filling my lungs. I remembered the bath. Was it he, then?

Reaching shore, he scooped me into his arms like a piece of flotsam, and crashed through the rolling surf. He held me so tightly that my chest and thighs burned. I tried to lower myself, but he would not release me. I laughed nervously, but was silenced by the rage I saw in his eyes. Wrapping my arms around his neck, I rested my head on his broad, tight shoulder and struggled to keep from weeping. He was causing me physical pain; I could not comprehend anything beyond that. I tried to deny it: he doesn't understand. Yet, when I shifted my position, attempting to wriggle free, he clamped his hands, squeezing me practically senseless. I shouted, stupefied, then begged him not to hurt me anymore. I was crying, trembling with terror. Jones. I thought of poor Jones as we stalked toward the shore.

"Donough," I whimpered, "Donough, I'm afraid."

He threw me down to the wet sand. When I tried to rise, he kicked me and straddled me, emanating fury and muttering brutal, vicious oaths. Pressing his fists to his eyes, he wailed and howled dementedly. I knew he wished me dead. I crawled blindly, vanquished by horror. Like an osprey swooping on its prey, he lunged; his body ground my stomach and chest into the cutting sand. I pleaded with him not to kill me. He cuffed me on the left side of my head. The earth tilted. Waves, cold as death's tongue licked around us as he savagely forced my legs apart, lacerating my thighs and knees on the sharp pebbles and shells. I punched at him. He pounded my head into the wet sand. I screamed, outraged by the pain, damning him, while he tore his way to plunging, growling spasm, releasing a hot wrath beyond my ken, beyond all relation to my self. Pulling himself free, he stumbled away.

I lay unmoving until he was gone. Then slowly I rolled over. The summer stillness and the cloudless, star-bright sky were as they were; yet, everything was different. I was alive. Choking with tears and mucus, I stood and walked back into the sea. I was alive. I never wanted to die. It would happen soon enough; it needed no assistance from me or anyone else. I would die for no one, not even for myself in the name of love.

I swam until I had no strength; then I drifted with the current. The salt water scalded my wounds but it cleansed and embraced me, covering me and my shame. What had I done wrong? Why had I not fought harder? I was no longer a tiny child; why had I behaved as one? And I kept responding with a question: How could he hurt me? Exhausted, I made for land. I walked. I wandered up the beach with no known destination. Oblivious of reason, I could not comprehend why he would hurt me if he loved me. In deep melancholia, I strayed among the dunes. I have no idea how I reached Nanny Welles.

"There is too much I don't understand, Nanny."

"In time you will see," she soothed, tucking me into a bed.

"When?" I begged, convinced I would never see.

"When you are ready, child."

"Tell me!"

"I cannot."

"How do you know I will see?"

"We all do . . . eventually. And, occasionally, before it's too late."

"I don't understand love."

"We never question love until it brings us pain."

"Shouldn't I ask questions?"

"In matters of the heart, only those with answers, child."

"He hurt me!"

"I know. He told me. He told me everything. Did you do nothing to him? Did you not hurt him?"

"No! I would never hurt him. And if I did, I never meant it. He should know that. He should never have hurt me. *Why* did he hurt me?"

"You're right. He should never have hurt you. He never means to hurt anyone. He was afraid . . ." She trailed off, and bid me sleep.

Sleep? Who can sleep? I thought before sleeping.

The afternoon was warm and hazy. A churning, sandy sea brought up its secrets and deposited them along the shore. A block of cloud covered the sun, turning the sky milky white. As I walked in the surf back to Gaywyck, wearing a caftan Nanny Welles had given me, I thought of Donough Gaylord and knew some immense change had occurred within me. His act of violence had transformed me as radically as the storm had altered Gaywyck's terrain. I felt detached, *whole*.

We never question love until it brings us pain.

I walked slowly, in no hurry.

He did it from his pain. He can't accept our love. He didn't mean to hurt me. He's afraid of love.

And what about me? I recalled his body weighing me down, and the various terrors. My body tensed. I stopped walking and looked out to the horizon.

Only fools and madmen and late-nineteenth-century romantics die for love. Equating love with death and pain: it will not do! It's easier to die for love than live with it or without it. "*Men have died and worms have eaten them, but not for love.*"

On the shore, in the far distance, a male figure paced at the foot of the jetty. I am certain a faculty develops in human beings enabling us to recognize our loved ones no matter the distance, no matter the crowd. Donough Gaylord waited for me. Nanny must have sent him a message. I walked up over the dune and sat in the upper branches of a toppled tree. I wondered if we could save the tree by pressing it back into the earth. Could the roots be returned to their original canals, restored like a great tooth to its socket? It wouldn't be the same, but mightn't it healthily live on?

He's ashamed of our love. He wanted to kill it.

And what about me?

Scrambling from the maze of the dying tree, trying to avoid making metaphors, I walked farther from the water into the meadow. From the beginning, *he* had fought against loving, like a perverse alchemist turning gold to lead. I sighed with grief. I could not fathom it. Of his hurting me, it had been impossible to conceive. Yet, it had been done. He had done it! I could do nothing about it now; I could only make certain it never happened again. I would leave Gaywyck.

Distracted by a bee climbing a Jacob's ladder, I sat to get a closer look. I knew its instincts had led it to that purple flower as surely as mine had led me to Donough Gaylord. When we collided in the hammock, he and I, it was right and it was good. I knew in the circle of our loving that my life was unfolding according to its own correct sequence of discoveries. To be held by him was, for me, sublime comfort. It was my truth. In that embrace, I had welcomed my eternity, and everything else had dissolved, become inconsequential, incidental, one with my need for him. I had wanted him, and I had needed him to eradicate me.

And what about me?

I no longer wanted to die in any way. I wanted no part of a love that required such grand sacrifice. And he wanted no part of a love like ours. My love could not change him, could not make it right and good for him. "Love cannot *do* anything," the sage says; it exists, like the stars and the earth and the sea. It exists to be experienced and enjoyed. I did not want his pain, yet he seemed unable to love me unless I accepted it. Contrary to his own instructions, he wanted me to love him because of and in spite of it. I would leave Gaywyck.

Certain he was grieving for what he had done, I rose and walked to the jetty.

And what about me?

I love him. I don't want to leave him. There must be an explanation for what he did and why he did it. How will I know unless I ask him? I can't read his mind. I'll talk with him. I love him. Perhaps . . . I must trust myself to do what's right. I must trust him. I'm no longer a child. I can take care of myself. I've changed. I've learned. Can't he change? Can't he learn? I love him. I know he loves me. There must be a chance if we love one another. I love him. I love him. We can change. We *can*!

He stood with his back to me, watching the sea, waiting. He wore a collarless white linen shirt and gray trousers rolled up over his slim, bare ankles. Quietly I cleared the wood. He turned, sensing my approach. I remembered the first time I had seen him. Like then, his beauty dazzled. He smiled and moved toward me. The clouds parted, covering us with warm, golden sunlight. I stopped, stunned by what I saw and knew instantly to be true.

He took me in his arms. I hung against him, unable to speak. How had I ever mistaken the other for him?

"Cormack will never hurt you again," he whispered.

Suddenly I grasped what Nanny Welles had meant by *seeing*. Having seen myself, I was finally able to see others. The blind could see. And, it had not been too late.

Twenty

Hᴀɴᴅ ɪɴ ʜᴀɴᴅ, ᴡᴇ ᴡᴀʟᴋᴇᴅ ᴀʟᴏɴɢ ᴛʜᴇ shore. We did not speak. I glanced at his profile and marveled:

One face, one voice, one habit and two persons,
A natural perspective, that is and is not!

The differences were legion, however. Cormack's beauty was coarser and worn: where Donough's face, unmarked, unlined, shone like a child's silken flesh, Cormack's was creased around the eyes and mouth. His hair was shaggy, his body not as supple. That I had ever confused the two seemed inconceivable. Yet, I had done it.

I accepted without reservation the silence between us. I reckoned it natural for Donough to be confused and withdrawn, distant from everyone. Why had Cormack caused such suffering by disappearing? And who was buried in his grave? As with his mother, did his tombstone mark an assemblage of stones? And why the masquerade? I felt compassion for Donough's turmoil. I wanted to help him. When I reached for his hand, he kept it back from me.

As we walked, there was a palpable sense of intimacy shattered. The spiraling tension between us forced me to speak. I tried to share what I had just discovered within myself. After stumbling over a few short declarative sentences, I fell back into the silent void. To reveal was to justify, to explain was to defend.

"It isn't necessary," he managed weakly, clearing his throat. "I understand."

"Understand what?" I exclaimed, struck by the dissimilarity in their voices. "Did you *know* Cormack was alive?"

"No!" he whispered in the tone of a defeated child.

I was confounded by his brooding, hurt expression. He mumbled some broken phrases, one related to Cormack's mystical power over people. Taking his meaning, I saw my way free.

"Donough," I interrupted, taking his hand. "I mistook him for you."

Releasing my hand, he stopped and stared at me with incredulity. I struggled to stay calm and rational.

"What do you mean?" he stammered almost comically.

"Each and every time I was with *him*, I was certain I was with *you*! What else could I have thought?"

He studied my face. In his wide eyes I could read the greatest ferment. What had he been thinking? Had he been waiting at the jetty to forgive me? To give *me* another chance?

"It happened, Donough, because I needed him to be you. I needed you so. I refused to see he wasn't you! He *had* to be you! Who on God's earth *could* he have been? You told me Cormack was dead. He only came to me when you were in residence here. He answered to your name. He used your words. He wore your wristwatch. *He* stole my wristwatch!"

I laughed maniacally. He stared at me in frantic disbelief. I was desperate.

"Donough!" I shouted. "Donough, I thought *you* were loving me, Donough! And he encouraged me to think so. I wanted to be cherished, and he cherished me, or seemed to, masquerading as you. How could you think . . . ?

I moved away from him. He grabbed me. He turned me to face him. I could only repeat, choking on rationalizations and excuses, my throat constricted by rising sobs presaging embarrassing tears.

"I thought he was you. . . . I wanted you to . . . cherish me, Donough!"

He pulled me close. I pushed away. I turned and ran. He shouted my name. "Robbie! Robbie! Robbie!"

Throwing the caftan off, I angled my path and splashed into the low tide. The clear green water closed around me. Held aloft, distanced from my anger, I felt serenity descend. On the shore, Donough Gaylord crouched with his head buried in his arms. He looked up imploringly. His lips moved. I heard him without hearing, whispering: "Robbie, Robbie, Robbie! Robbie!"

The notion that I would knowingly seek Cormack was unforgivable; it implied not only a disgraceful collusion on my part but a monstrous betrayal of *him*. I could have

GAYWYCK 337

punched him, my beloved Donough Gaylord. I remembered my frightened father accusing me of my mother's descent into madness. He had been afraid, not of me or for her, but for himself: his weakness—*his* weakness. Donough had believed me guilty of the sins for which he flailed himself. He had not seen me in the hammock with Cormack, he had seen himself. Just as I had not seen him. Just as *I* had unjustly accused him of an act of brutality contrary to his nature.

I had been as wrong as he. I could not escape it. I, who had fancied myself Florimund on first approaching Gaywyck, had been the one asleep.

I lay poised on the crest of a wave. He was standing on the shore watching. I tumbled with the breaking, frothy curve. When I surfaced, he was swimming toward me, his clothing spread like a banner on the sand. Trembling, I waited for him to reach me. He stopped a yard away. We trod water, only our heads visible, as each of us waited for the other.

"Forgive me, Donough," I pleaded.

"Forgive me, Robbie," he responded, our words overlapping.

"Love is deaf, dumb, *and* blind!"

A wave swelled and thrust me into his arms. We laughed together. I kissed him, at first tenderly, apologizing one last time, before kissing him as I had wanted to from the moment I saw him. He frowned and looked surprised; then responded with such ardor that we were nearly taken by the current. I led him to the far, seaward end of the jetty, to the flat promontory exposed by the low tide. We did not speak until love had been answered. In each other's arms, we repudiated suffering, accepting the pleasures of loving. No longer a neophyte, I knew my desires. We met as equals in the most exciting of combats. We achieved manly estate.

My laughter surprised him, but triggered a similar response.

"You are magic," he sighed.

"You seem relieved," I teased, stroking him, probing all the while.

He fell silent. Stretching his full length, he reclined on his back. I washed him with seawater. The thick black hair on his body formed curls similar to the small waves lapping at the base of the rocks. I put my head on his chest, resting beside him. He touched my face. I continued stroking him. He rose magnificently; I did as well.

"I am relieved," he answered solemnly. "For the past thirteen years, I've been impotent."

One hot August night, he and Cormack spied on their father's "meeting" with Steven, and began to mimic their games—at first playfully, but then with frenzied urgency. Cormack took their father's role; Donough, Steven's. Mesmerized by the scene, the impressionable Donough had totally transposed himself into the protégé's position and experienced the forbidden passion of the father he adored. At the moment of that volcanic orgasm, he fainted, awakening with his priapic capacity blasted. He had been to several doctors abroad, had been hypnotized by Dr. Charcot in Paris, and had shared in Dr. Freud's work on hysteria; but until the recent night his robe opened in my room, he allowed himself little hope.

Sharing memories of that August night had aroused him. He blushed, but I stroked him more lovingly and kissed him and took his love and knew what worship is. How could we deny ever again the feelings we brought to one another?

"We must forgive the past, Donough," I whispered. "We did the best we knew how."

Our laughter the third time broke spontaneously and at the same moment. Splashing into the water, I swam, calling him to follow. Over my shoulder I watched him stand and stretch in the full-blazing day, proudly bearing the mark of our love. We swam together, splashing and playing like boys, then sprawled on the beach to dry. A congregation of piping plovers scurried along the surf's edge while we spoke.

"I wish I were braver," he said. "I wish I were stronger."

"You are brave. You are strong. I love you entirely."

"Cormack was always the courageous one."

"Nonsense! Cormack is just quicker."

He laughed loudly, frightening the birds. "Robbie, I used to believe loving hateful."

"Do you still think it so?"

"No! *Not* loving is!"

After a deep silence he added, "Does Cormack love you?"

"Yes."

"Then I pity him. He is more afraid of love than I."

He dropped into a reverie. He was stupefied by Cormack's being alive. He could not speak coherently. I changed the subject, dismissing the twin from our conversation. I would manage Cormack Gaylord. Arrogantly I regrouped my strengths, believing I held all the cards in matters of the heart. By my denying his existence, I believed I had provoked his wrath. I would never do *that* again. He loved me. I could manage Cormack Gaylord.

"How did you get here to save me from Keyes?"

Another tale unfolded.

Two days before, while I had sat secreted in the cottage examining the contents of Jones's suitcase, Brian had decided to go for a walk. He dressed warmly against the rain in his mackintosh and his tweed cap and set out for the beach; but the force of the slanting wet prompted him to seek cover in the birch grove, where he perambulated for a time, eventually detouring to the waterfall to view the flowering water lilies before returning to the house for tea.

By the time Cormack realized he had mistaken Brian for me, the duplicitous game was ended. Brian recognized him immediately and fled. He ran to Donough's study, but downed wires rendered the telegraph useless. Without a word to anyone, he ran to the gatehouse, and taking a motored tricycle, caught the market train for New York City.

I, in the meantime, having finished minding everyone else's business, returned to my rooms, was assaulted in my bath and drugged after dinner by Keyes.

Brian burst into Donough's study at 15 Gramercy Park. He could do little but gasp and sputter and cry out in bewildered rage. The shock at the sight of him was minor compared to the effect of the message. After several hasty telephone calls, Donough and Brian sped by motorcar to the ferry, and then across the East River, and then on to the waiting, steaming, single-coach train, making no stops but one, to arrive at Gaywyck in breathless time to save my life!

"Who would believe it!" I concluded, having snatched the narrative from him at the point where he and Brian boarded the express train. "It's better than a novel!"

"Yes, it is! Unfortunately, it didn't happen that way."

He and Brian had arrived at Gaywyck in breathless time, but I was collapsed on the jetty and Keyes was already in flight up the beach to the house.

"Keyes must have seen you coming to my rescue! *No!*
I heard your shout! I remember hearing you yell my name
to frighten him away!"

"I never shouted."

"You did! Or did I dream it?"

"Or was it Cormack?"

"*Oh!* Of course! Well . . . it doesn't matter. It's all
over! Isn't it nearly time for tea?"

We sat around the table with Denvers, who seemed in
a black mood. We ate in silence, due, I assumed, to Keyes's
death. The tutor's body was laid out in his rooms waiting
for the coroner to collect it.

"Whatever possessed Keyes?" I asked with my usual
style and tact.

"The urge to kill, my dear, what else? It happens to the
best of us. We usually aren't brave enough to have a go is
all."

"Brave enough?" I sputtered, nearly spooning my soup
into my ear.

"I'm told," Donough interrupted, "Keyes hasn't been
himself since Jones died."

"Who *do* you suppose he's been?" Denvers wondered,
a sharp edge to his voice making the words sound barbed.

"An unknown woman in a Rossetti portrait?" I offered
foolishly.

"Nonsense!" he retorted. "He dressed that way to lure
you to the rocks. The old fool! A siren to the last!"

He was the only one to laugh.

"Why was Keyes drugging me and dressing as the portrait long before Jones died? Why was he so afraid I
would steal Donough away?"

"We'll never know." Denvers shrugged. "Cormack's
being alive must come as a shock to you, Donough. Or
are you going to tell us that in your heart of twin hearts
you've known all along?"

"No. I thought him dead," he stammered, flushing dark.

We lapsed into a murky silence. Donough's distress was
unbearable to me. I was appalled by Denvers. I wanted to
ask if he knew Cormack was alive, but I was afraid to
mention the name in Donough's presence for fear of a
violent response. I suggested to Donough that we saunter
in the shrubbery. We were barely out of the tutor's hearing when I expressed my dismay. Donough heartily con-
curred. The night of his hasty return, after the doctor

administered to me, he had attempted a conversation with Denvers but had found him impossibly obfuscatory.

"What did you do?"

"I went to Nanny."

The old nurse had been straightforward with him. She advised him not to leave me unguarded.

"*He* has always wanted what you want and taken what you've marked as yours."

"How long have you known him alive?"

"Always."

"The doctor saw him dead! Who is that buried in his grave?"

"Steven."

"But Steven wasn't with Father that night."

"I say he was, Donnie! It was a fearful thing, a suicide pact, and we lost our heads and *he* ran wild: he ran away, so we covered his tracks as best we could, lest they think—"

"You lied?"

"Yes, we lied. God forgive us."

"*We?*"

"Yes, we. Denvers had a part in it as well. It was he who found Cormack with the bodies. They took their own lives, God forgive them."

Donough had not been able to confront Denvers. He had avoided him, prowling the grounds when not at my side, dreading the inevitable meeting with his twin. Although no link between Keyes's attempt on my life and Cormack's presence could be uncovered, he took the inexplicable reappearance as a fatal omen.

"Why hasn't Cormack come to see you?" I asked, as the waves capped over the promontory where we hid after leaving the shrubbery.

"I don't know!" he flashed fiercely. "He's not a creature of our species. I thought I had freed myself of him. He will never release me alive!"

His agitation frightened me. He was breathing heavily, and words were brought out with the greatest effort. When I placed my hand on his chest, I could feel his heart pounding. I was afraid to ask why Denvers had not told him Cormack was alive. Had Cormack, in fact, murdered his father and Steven, then coerced Denvers into keeping the secret?

"How could he *dare* approach Brian?" Donough de-

manded of me. "He should have known Brian would recognize him!"

"He thought Brian me. I don't understand why he revealed himself without the cover of your presence here."

I stood to dive into the water. I was so overcome with
nausea that I had to sit, and I found it necessary to accept
Donough's offer to carry me back to the house. He helped
me into my trousers, pulled on his own, and lifted me with
a soft grunt. I made a feeble joke about no longer being
a little boy. He agreed I'd matured since our meeting.
I noticed the round redness of his nipple, and took a violent spin in a suffocating vortex before losing consciousness. I surfaced in my room with Dr. Anders staring down
at me squeezing my wrist. I smiled at him as if we were
meeting in a country lane.

"Shock," he pronounced dramatically. "Has he been out
of bed since I saw him yesterday?"

I did not remember seeing him yesterday.

"Yes," Donough answered meekly.

"He's done everything he oughtn't . . . several times!"
Denvers said, hugely amused.

"Has he had a fall?"

A vase of immense, perfect peonies placed on my bed
table took my attention. I love the peony.

"A fall?" Donough echoed.

"Yes, a fall! I don't remember this welt on the left side
of his head, nor this bruise, nor these scratches on his
body."

"I fell," I said, smiling, pulling my wrist from his grip.

"This is not a joking matter, young man! I will not be
responsible if you don't remain in bed. You've had a nasty
time of it!"

He lectured me. He need not have. I felt wretched. I
had no intentions of budging.

"Peonies are my favorite flower," I said aloud.

"What?" he demanded.

"I want to sleep," I said petulantly.

He gave instructions to Brian about my diet, and stern
orders to Donough and Denvers about my rising only for
emergencies. He actually slammed the door behind him!
I sat up. The three jumped as though a shot had been
fired.

"What are you doing?" Donough demanded.

"Don't worry! I'm not going anywhere! I feel as if I've been thrown by a wild horse."

"You have been, dear!" Denvers quipped.

"Where's Cael?" I whined, defeated.

Brian opened the sitting-room door. Cael sped to my side, squeaking in annoyance at being locked out. I took great comfort in his nudging me with his cold nose, demanding a proper welcome. Then exhaustion again overtook me. I suspired, sliding into a supine position. The doctor was correct; it was not a laughing matter, nor one for Denvers's acerbic tone, which I tried unsuccessfully to avoid by closing my eyes.

"Tell me, dear boy, before you doze, how long have you been meeting with Cormack thinking him Donough?"

Brian gasped. Suddenly he understood why Cormack had approached him. I smiled at him dumbly. He did not smile in return. Then I turned my attention to Donough, who seemed as startled as I.

"Nanny Welles told *me*," Denvers announced, filling the silence, and delighting in our perturbation.

"How did *she* know?" Donough asked.

"Dear boy! Nanny knows *everything!*"

"She's known all along?" I asked, feeling the fool.

"No . . . I wouldn't surmise *that*. Only our Cormack's known *all along*. Seeing what a sweet adventure he was having, I don't wonder at his reluctance to spread the news."

"Why didn't she tell me you didn't know?" Donough directed to me.

"Did you ask her, dear boy? No? Well, she probably assumed you trusted Robbie's puppy-dog faithful heart. Who would believe our Bob was no longer white?"

"You knew Cormack was alive?" Brian asked Denvers.

"Yes. But he had gone to sea for his own protection."

Brian demanded an explanation. Donough offered one, growing so distressed that Denvers crossed to his side and said in a tender, affectionate voice, "Try to be calm. You aren't a child any longer. He can't hurt you. He never would harm a hair on your head."

"He wants me dead!"

"Nonsense!"

"He wants Robbie. *And he wants me dead!* I know that's why he's returned. He wants to destroy us."

"You need sleep, dear boy. You could also use a double brandy."

Denvers seized control of the room. He organized my "honor guard." I made a feeble protest, but each man had suffered from Cormack's violent temper; not one could be dissuaded. They planned a "duty" of four hours to lessen the chances of a careless snooze. Brian attempted to theorize that he, too, had been drugged, but Denvers ignored him and requested the first watch. "Donough and Brian are exhausted. *I* am not. They will sleep; I will sit here, alert, while Robert sleeps. Donough will relieve me for a late supper, and Brian will relieve him at one. Simple?"

Nothing here at Gaywyck is ever simple, I thought as I nodded. Are we to maintain this charade forever? When I am well, am I to join you all with my own four-hour shift?

They all nodded in turn, grunting, agreeing it was a fine plan. The drawbridge was up and the castle dressed for war! Yet surely they knew underneath the bravado that if Cormack Gaylord wanted entry, not even Karl von Clausewitz on his brightest day could prevent him. Donough looked distraught.

Finally Denvers commanded them, "Leave! Leave! Let the dote sleep!"

"We need our rest, too," Brian insisted as he moved toward the door.

Denvers ushered them out in his grandest manner: " '*So get thee gone, good night.*' " Then, turning to me, he asked: " '*Mine eyes do itch. Does that bode weeping?*' "

" '*'Tis neither here nor there,*' " I answered correctly, receiving a smile of approval.

He busied himself about the room: adjusting the windows, drawing the drapes, banking the fire, straightening my bedclothes, fluffing my pillows. As he moved from task to task, he sustained a monologue, absorbing my monosyllabic responses into its flow.

"Poor dear, sweet Keyes. Yes, it's true; he'd not been himself (or anyone else), but *not* since our Jones got himself drubbed. No! Long, long before that: since Gaylord's passing. And who has? Who has had the heart to be? There was a *man*! Jones was . . . something else. I know how you despised him. Perfection he was not, but he was *all* we had. Say what you will, we have always encouraged others to feel what they feel even if 'bitter as coloquintida.' That may be the cause of all this unraveling. Jones, dear Jones . . ."

Jones, dear Jones indeed! I thought. *He* certainly put money in *his* purse!

". . . Perhaps, just perhaps . . . Oh, what *is* the use? Will you want one more blanket? Yes? I'll use this one here. Will that do? Fine! Do try to sleep."

I closed my eyes. He sat. The rhythms of his speech changed.

" 'There are many events in the womb of time which will be delivered.' The bedlam must be planted for starters."

"That word again," I noted, arranging my body under the covers, longing for Cael's comforting presence. He had followed Donough.

". . . He'll not rest without a grand send-off, without spiffy obsequies. Beethoven's *Missa Solemnis* would be fitting and proper, I think. But it's going to be difficult. Suicide fires everyone's canons. Do you think we should tell a fib and say . . . ? You're quite right to be so adamant. What *was* I thinking? We've had a surfeit of fibs surrounding deaths and burials in this family. But would one more . . . ? Yes. Yes! Of course, of course! I was but jesting. I wonder where *he's* been all these years. Does he still . . . ? No! I won't embarrass either of us. How dreadful of me to even . . . Zounds, Denvers! Hold your peace! But one *does* remember! Maybe later? Mary Rose, the mother of this all, reminded me the other morn that I am growing older. She wished me a golden age, but I most seriously doubt it . . ."

He knows *everything*, I thought, turning to eye him carefully.

". . . She thought you her sister, and you thought Cormack Donough, and Cormack thought Brian you, and I thought Cormack's deeds Keyes's and Keyes thought himself Beethoven—all the elements of a jolly farce, not a tearful pavane along the edge of the river Styx. Oh my, oh my! Go to sleep, Robbie. Pleasant dreams to you. . . ."

When did he think Cormack's deeds Keyes's, I wondered.

I pretended a restful state I did not own. I was uneasy but not endangered. If he had violent longings toward me, I knew he would not personally execute them: he could not abide contaminating himself. I remembered a conversation when he spoke of his admiration for Iago.

"Yes! Yes!" he had exclaimed as he sat in the library teaching me whist. "We know the 'Spartan dog' is but the dark side of the noble black's too alabaster soul, but in the course of human events he manages his work commendably well. To some, he is a 'hellish villain'; to me, he is no worse than the 'great of heart.' He's certainly a good deal smarter. It's all in the playing."

I replied it depended on how he defined "smart."

"Semantics!" he bellowed, scattering the cards just as I was securing the odd trick.

Now I squinted, watching him settle into the chair by my bed. I could see the loquacious mood was gone; his mouth hung slightly open and he stared blankly ahead, unblinking. I wanted to ask why Mary Rose would take me for her sister, and what power Denvers had over Keyes, but it would have been senseless. His black expression clearly stated:

> Demand me nothing. What you know, you know.
> From this time forth I never will speak word.

I dozed. I woke to find the wind strengthened; the rustling trees sounded like applause at the opera. Denvers had never moved. He looked small, shrunken, like a leaf withered where it had been blown. I remembered the first night we met. *You will change everything*, he had said. What had he meant? I now repeated: *Love cannot do things*. From the first, Gaywyck's secrets had divided us. Looking at his aged, worn face, I felt regret. I slumbered suddenly.

I was pleased when Donough arrived. His sweet presence stirred me. There were things I wanted to ask, things I wanted to tell, and things I wanted to do. Thinking me asleep, he whispered some words to Denvers. The tutor stood, and both withdrew. For an instant, I feared his not returning. Fragments of a dream recurred, bearing forgotten discordancies. Where would I have gone had I left Gaywyck? What would I have done with the rest of my life? Isn't life what we cause to happen? But don't things happen without us? Yes . . . yes. . . .

He came in quietly, shutting the door carefully behind him. He walked to the windows and thrust them open, filling the room with the fragrance of wisteria. The scented, discourteous breeze billowed the curtains, lifted the collar of his white silk shirt, and ruffled his hair. He stood in profile, lost in reverie. I loved him past telling.

"*'Mais ne suffit-il pas que tu sois/ l'apparence/ Pour réjouir un coeur qui/ fuit la vérité?'* " he said softly.

I wanted to call, but I needed to watch—to fasten the moment firmly in the eternal present. When he turned, our eyes met. Slowly I raised my arms. He eagerly crossed to me, looking calmer and relaxed. The shadow of Cormack was momentarily gone.

"I love you," I said.

"I love you, too, my shining boy."

A knock on the door forced us apart. Ambrose wheeled in the dinner; he began to serve, but Donough dismissed him. It was lovely being alone with no one hovering about; it was the first time we had ever been thus. I reveled in the privacy. He served the food and sat by my side on the bed. I wanted to watch him eat. Eating is an act of hope and an act of faith. He laughed and kissed me, delighted at my perception, confessing a similar one.

"We are fragile creatures," I elaborated, "easily punctured and poisoned, fit *only* for loving."

He was wonderfully serene. Some sprays of honeysuckle had been thoughtfully and beautifully arranged on the dinner tray; he reached for one and fondled the delicate buds.

I remembered a flower in a letter to my mother carelessly lost and mysteriously recovered. Ghosts? Poachers? How long had Cormack Gaylord been wandering the grounds of Gaywyck?

"What are you thinking about so intensely, Robert?"

"Letters. . . . I found one written by a house guest, an actress named Margie."

"Where?"

"In a book of Poe."

"I think I liked her! She was a superb Orsino, if I recall her correctly. What else have you found?"

"Jones planned to blackmail you, I know for certain now. He said Keyes told him Cormack killed your father."

"The man was mad!"

I told him about the hidden suitcase and the stolen

treasures, but mostly I told him about the love letters from Keyes, the threatening note, and my conviction that the music teacher had murdered his pupil in a jealous frenzy.

"Was there nothing else in the suitcase, Robbie?"

"I hoped to find my watch, but that was before—"

"I mean belonging to me."

I knew what he meant. Studying the peonies, I envied them their mutability. He left my side.

"Did you look through everything? At the dinner table, Jones mentioned photographs. . . ."

Nodding slightly, unable to lie to him, I said weakly, "I glanced."

With a shock, I knew the photo was of me and Cormack in my bed. Donough had not lied. When did all this begin? Why had Denvers never told Keyes that Cormack was alive and end the grief?

Donough sat in the chair on the opposite side of the room and turned his face away. I feared he would become frigid and withdrawn. I spoke the only words I could. "I love you. Please, I love you."

"I know. I don't know why the photographs should humiliate me after what I've told you. I don't know why I never destroyed them."

"It isn't important any longer, Donough. You were a child."

"We were *never* children! How can there be such a thing as childhood in a world without innocence, a world twisted and gone rancid with mendacity!"

Springing to his feet, he bounded to the windows. "I can't breathe in here! Cover yourself if you're cold!"

I did so, and waited for him to continue. When he spoke, the harsh tone in his voice frightened me.

"I should never have allowed you to live here. I should have forbidden it, but I thought the horrors over, finished. I thought *them* dead. I hid the Rossetti and thought that would take care of everything."

"I love you," I whispered. "Please, I love you."

"You *love* me?" he shouted, turning to face me. "He nearly killed you, and you love me?"

"What has *he* to do with you?"

"It's always been the same. I allowed it to happen."

"It happened. It had nothing to do with *you*. Cormack did it, and I did it! Denvers is right. You're not a child anymore. He can't hurt you, Donough. There is nothing he can do to hurt you."

"Except take you from me."

It was out. He had said it. He slumped into the chair and wept. I went to him and knelt with my arms around his knees. He stroked my head. I held his fingers, kissing them. I loved him, but how does one teach another to trust? No! It was more than that. He had shared too many secrets not to know trust.

"Why do you say that?"

"Why not? You can't honestly tell me that I'm . . ."

"That you're *what*, Donough?"

". . . that I'm as *good* as he is."

I did not understand. I told him so. He studied my face, then laughed without humor. "As potent? As *exciting*?" he spat out, closing his eyes.

"Donough, it's you I want again and again. I love *you*."

He snorted.

"Don't be jealous of him, Donough. Don't! It's I who should be jealous."

"*You*?"

"You still love him."

He lurched away from me and stood in front of the fireplace. Had I trespassed fatally?

"Donough! I want you to love him. If you don't love him and forgive him, we may never have a life of our own. He'll always be between us."

"Like he was between my father and Steven?"

"I don't know your father and Steven. You tell me."

"He was my father's catamite. He often lay with Steven and Papa."

"Did you ever?"

"No!"

"Why not?"

He remained silent.

"Donough, why not?"

"They didn't want me."

He was crying again. I placed my arms around him and rested my head on his shoulder.

"They didn't want me," he sobbed, distraught.

C IS NOW WITH PAPA AND S OFTEN.
I HEARD PAPA TELL S IT WAS TO
MAKE C MANAGEABLE.

"Didn't you believe what your father said?"

"No! Steven accepted whatever Papa wanted until the end, when they fought. I've always believed they fought over Cormack. I wanted . . ."

"I know what you wanted. I'm sure they wanted you as much as Cormack, but couldn't find such a plausible excuse."

He turned. He asked me to hold him close. The tears had never stopped, but now they built into a torrent. I led him to the bed, and we lay together. I wrapped myself around him while he cried for every wrong that had ever been committed against him. At first, I tried to comfort. Then I began to weep from the joy of his deliverance. When his tears subsided, I kissed him. Effortlessly I commanded him. Surrendering, he commanded me. I was taken with a loving force and propelled further than I had ever gone. I took him as he had taken me. Ecstasy was the reward: benediction beyond bounds.

"I love you" were the only words spoken, whispered, shouted.

This is for all time, my Donough Gaylord.

As though reading my mind, he pressed his hand over my heart.

We slept, limbs entangled. I dreamed I was at the pond feeding Tristan and Isolde. Cael sat on my shoulder, perched like an owl. Suddenly he stretched his right paw and pointed to Denvers riding on a broomstick over our heads. I fled along the shore, following the strains of Schumann's *Traumeri*, knowing they would lead me to Donough Gaylord.

Cormack called me. I awoke and instinctively reached for Donough. He was not there. The bedclothes still held his warmth. Again, Cormack called my name. This time I caught in the plaintive tone the whine of a beaten cur. I stood and reached for my robe, noticing that Donough had taken only his trousers. Where could he have gone in such haste? Then Cormack called again. I hurried to answer him.

When I stepped out into the warm night, I could hear voices raised in the vicinity. I also smelled smoke. At the foot of the portico steps, Cormack waited. He wore his dark cape, and his hair was wet from the sea. In the light from the gibbous moon, his beauty revealed was startlingly unlike Donough's: rough-hewn, it seemed unfinished, the

way Michelangelo's uncompleted figures are captives of
the stone but no less powerful, present, defined.

"Forgive me," he demanded gruffly. "Forgive me,
dammit! I'm leaving tonight. You'll never see me again."

I nodded.

"Walk with me, Robert."

"No!"

"I give you my word: I won't hurt you. Please! Walk
with me a short distance."

"There's a fire. We must help."

"It's only a ruse. Denvers set it to give us time. Walk
with me! I'll explain everything."

Shaking my head, I backed away. Climbing the steps,
he nimbly thrust his fingers between my legs to gently
seize me, exerting no pressure, merely asserting a claim as
I once did.

"Where do you want to go?"

"To the dolmen. Hurry, we haven't much time."

He seemed much larger than Donough. Side by side, we
walked in silence down the avenue of lindens; barefoot,
he strode with a feral grace not unlike his brother's. I
allowed him to take my hand. The skin on his palm was
rough.

"Why did you show yourself when Donough wasn't
here?" I asked directly, coldly, determined to hold my
distance—arrogant and too certain of untested strengths.

"I wanted to warn you," Cormack replied. "Keyes was
going to kill you, and I wanted to warn you."

We stepped down the broken stones and entered the
dell. He yanked me toward him and kissed me hard on
the mouth. I pulled myself free; he gripped my wrist and
smiled a teasing half-grin. I was anxious, but not frightened. I was strong and able to defend myself.

"I've given my word I won't hurt you, lad. You needn't
be so standoffish." He laughed, mocking my stern counte-
nance.

"How did you know about Keyes?"

"Denvers told me. He said I wasn't needed anymore."

"What do you mean?"

He moved tightly against me. I did not move away,
though he no longer held me.

"I would never hurt you, lad. I was angry. I wanted to
tear you out of my soul. I love you, Robert. Say you
believe me."

I did. The blood rushed to my heart. I was frightened.
"Yes, Cormack. I believe you."

"I couldn't leave without seeing you. I knew you forgave me. Now you must say you love me."

"But I don't love you, Cormack."

"That isn't true, lad."

He insisted I loved him. He kissed my hair and rubbed his head against mine. Suddenly I felt nervous and less certain of my position.

"It *is* true, Cormack! How could I love you? I barely know you."

He laughed, kissing my cheek, darting his tongue in small, hot circles. His beard scraped against my chin and made me sigh.

"Yet what you know of me best, you love. Can you lessen what we've shared by refusing to use its rightful name?"

I looked into his eyes. When he smiled again, my own closed in confusion and undeniable pleasure. He opened his hands to me. I clasped them.

"Say it, lad."

"Yes . . . I love you, Cormack. I do love you."

"I had to hear you say it. Let me hold you."

It could not mean I loved Donough poorly, or less well. But, yes, I did love this man. I tried to understand, to qualify the love I felt for him, to distinguish it from the all-pervasive love I felt for his brother. There was no denying it: the need I had for Cormack Gaylord was a kind of loving. I loved the menacing free spirit I had imagined him to be, what everyone had told me he was.

He embraced me. I responded to the sweep of his gestures as he stripped off my robe and pressed his hard, damp body against mine. His heady smell mingled with the tart smell of the sea. He kissed my lips. I behaved like a tumescent schoolboy never before handled by a passionate man: I blushed, I stammered, then I cleaved to him, begging for every pleasure at once. I wanted him to swallow me whole. He understood perfectly. He fondled, he caressed, he brushed aside whatever scruples blocked my way until I begged for him.

"Come away with me, lad. We'll take the world, you and I, together—always. Come with me lad, come . . . come. . . ."

There was no laughing. At the center of me there was a savage longing not quelled. There was *tristesse*. I faced a void, an unfilled space. Created by Donough, he alone had access; it echoed with his name.

I clung to Cormack, full of anger and remorse for wishing what I knew could only bring grief. I wanted to leave with him. I intended to be by his side. I wanted his love without danger of pain, without the danger of death. I, alone, would be immune to its ineluctable perils. A panic seized me.

"Oh, God! Cormack! Why are you here?"

"I'm here to 'save' Donough." He laughed, confident of his powers, trying to calm me with more kisses and caresses. "I was to dispose of you for Denvers."

He often visited Nanny Welles and Mary Rose, arriving and leaving unseen in the night. The previous October, he had found a note from Denvers. Donough, it said—proud, naive, *simple* Donough—needed to be saved from a scheming cousin, a venal, evil whore of a beauty who planned to control the Gaylord fortune and who threatened Denvers's long-range plans to return Cormack to his brother's side.

"I was to help him drive you mad, and save our precious Donough from himself.

"Mad? Drive me *mad*?"

Having inherited weakness in the head, a slight nudge was to send me over the edge. My hysterical reaction to Mary Rose's image was encouraging; my collapse over Whitman, more so. Even in my heavily drugged condition the third night at Gaywyck, my response to Cormack as Donough was perfection, and Denvers had taken a photograph for later use to further blur the demarcation between fantasy and reality.

"When he put on all the lamps to take the photograph, lad, I saw he was lying. You were none of the things he said. I was your first. I knew I was your first. I loved your sweetness and the trusting way you opened yourself to me. I was too rough. But I was more careful the second time. Wasn't I? *Wasn't I?*"

Cormack concealed his feelings from Denvers. He said the plan would take more time. After finding the letter to my mother, proof of my innocence, he lied to Denvers: pretending to leave on a voyage, he lived in the attic of the cottage, plotting to have and to love me as his father had and loved Steven. Until he devised a way, he would masquerade as Donough. He spied on me. He stole my watch, read my journal, eavesdropped on conversations to foster conviction. He gave me orchids and watched over me while I slept. Now hopelessly entangled in his own pound net and satisfied in the deception, he fell more and more in love with me. The death of Jones complicated matters. Denvers demanded quick revenge.

"Poor Denvers!" Cormack sighed. "First he was convinced Donough did it; then he turned on me. I assured him it was Keyes, his cat's paw, Keyes. After Keyes killed you on the jetty, Denvers was planning to poison him and claim it a suicide."

"Did you meet Jones?"

"He didn't recognize me either! The guttersnipe played blackmail games. I rolled him over and he squealed like a stuck pig. He died happy."

What had begun as a roughing-up to teach poor Jones a lesson ended in murder.

"I didn't intend to kill him, Robert."

"Did you *intend* to kill your father?" I blurted angrily.

"My father and Steven were already dead," he answered softly, wincing as I recoiled from his touch. "They'd swallowed cyanide rather than live apart. They died for their love. I would do the same for you."

I did not want anyone to do the same for me. The voices beyond the trees still shouted, but seemed like distant thunder.

He had gone to comfort his father over the loss of Steven, the beloved Steven. The two men had been fighting continually. Steven wanted to live openly with Gaylord, to avow their love publicly, but Gaylord was unwilling. Steven fled, then returned the next week in the middle of the night. They died together.

"I soaked them in oil from the lamps and made a funeral pyre. I knew what was required of me."

"Why did you run away?"

"Denvers said no one would believe me. There was no note. He said he would work things out with Nanny. He loved me. He wanted me safe. He loved my father, and he lost my father. Now he doesn't want to lose Donough, too. He's helping us to get away."

"He's done all this in the name of *love*?"

"I'd do all this and more for you."

We heard the sounds of a fire engine, and the towns-people arriving by horseback and wagon.

"I want to go back, Cormack."

I was wrong, I thought. He will kill me, too, in the name of love.

"That's no longer possible, lad. We're bound together now. You've made your choice. You're coming with me."

"I can't go. I love Donough."

"You must come. You belong to me."

"I *won't* go! People don't *belong* to other people."

He pinched my waist with angry fingers. The muscles in his arms knotted, swelling with impatience. I recognized a sense of helplessness in the face of his darkening tem-per. He forced me to share his cape as we struggled down the path that connected the sunken garden to the beach.

"It's what you want, lad," he said sternly. "Once we're away from here, it will be clear again, as it was a few moments ago. I'll make certain of that, Robbie."

This is madness, I thought, meekly complying. Does he expect us to *walk* where we're going, dressed in this one cape?

When we reached the beach, I broke from him, intend-ing to view the fire. We both knew I could not escape by running; he did not give chase. I stopped. Out on the waves, the steam yacht waited to bear us away. I turned to face him. He glared at me, snarling at my evident surprise, aware I had underestimated him. I spun and ran to the jetty. I would be seen; people would save me. I leaped up the rocks to the top. In seconds he stood beside me, his arm around my waist. Together we gazed on the conflagration consuming the room occupied by Keyes's corpse. The fire engine pumped water. People carried buckets and carted the treasures from the house.

I saw figures running down the beach toward us. Cael led Donough and Brian. I turned to look at Cormack. He was signaling the steam yacht, which had begun to ap-proach the jetty. He pulled me to the end of the stone pier.

"Cormack, I won't go with you."

"Then we'll die together, lad. It can't be any other way now."

I shoved him, knocking the cape from his shoulders. I expected him to drop, deflated by my full force. Instead, he cuffed me brutally. Enraged, he called me "Fool!" I stepped backward. He grabbed a fistful of my hair and

clutched my throat with his left hand, instantly squeezing
me breathless. The searing pain paralyzed me. The fury in
his eyes was murderous. My legs buckled. My nose started
to bleed. I gagged on my screams.

Cael clawed his foot. Cormack eased his hold enough
for me to suck in air while he raised his leg to kick the
animal into the sea. Cael! My Cael!

Cormack brought me to my knees. He dragged me
close and pressed my face up into his groin, bending me
backward to snap my spine. With my last strength I bit
him. Howling, he released my throat to shake me loose.
Clenching my jaws against his blows, I bit harder. Blood
spurted down my neck.

Donough shouted his name.

A gunshot! He flew back, releasing me completely. My
neck and throat felt scalded; the side of my head, numb.
I was shaking uncontrollably and the blood I feared flow-
ing down my thighs was my urine. Brian murmured loving words. He held a smoking pistol. I wanted to hide, to
cover my face and hide myself from shame and self-
loathing.

Donough knelt by Cormack's side, cradling his head in
his lap. I crawled toward them and stopped halfway. Cormack raised his hand for me to come near. I knelt at his
other side. A bullet had torn open his chest; blood spilled
from the wound.

"Dote," he whispered to his brother, "dear dote! He
did not want to go. I tried to take him with me, but he
did not want to go from you."

"Cormack!" Donough sobbed. "Stay with me!"

"I think I'm dying, dote. This isn't what I planned."
He laughed. "I wanted to come back, but Denvers said it
could not be. Said I would be hanged. I nearly died without you. I used to sneak into your room and watch you
sleep. You never knew. I was looking after you like I said
I always would."

He took my hand and gave it to his brother.

"I nearly got away with him." He grinned. "I love you,
dote."

Donough kissed him on the cheek. Cormack lifted his
arm and threw it around his brother's neck.

"There's not a one like you in the world, Donnie. I
know. I looked. Go with your lad. He loves you. He loves
you. He loves you the way only I . . ."

"Cormack!"

"My Donnie. I've come home."

"*Cormack!*"

"He's dead," Brian whispered.

I covered him with the cape.

Donough raised me to my feet. Unbuttoning his shirt, he stripped it from his back and wrapped me in it. He carried me down to the beach, where Cael sat cleaning his drenched body.

"There's Denvers!" Brian shouted clearly.

I glanced past the gun he held, toward Gaywyck. At first I thought the heart of the great house was ablaze, but it was the moon glinting on the surface of the window. The fire was nearly contained, reduced to streams of writhing smoke. To my dazed and swollen eyes, the sight of Denvers wrapped in flames plunging through the oval window amidst shattering glass and splintering light could have been a magic lantern image of Lucifer's fall from grace.

"Cormack didn't kill your father," I said, forcing the words from my searing throat. "They—"

"I know, Robbie. Keyes poisoned them."

"Keyes?"

"He didn't want them to leave Gaywyck. My father was planning to live abroad with Steven."

"But—"

"No more, dear boy, no more! Later we'll talk."

I could not bear it. All those years Cormack had thought them classic, tragic lovers embracing death. He was willing to give his life—had given his life—for what he believed was *their* truth. I could not bear the lie.

I looked at the oval hole where no sunrise would shine that morning.

No more Polyphemus.

". . . only complex, earthly loving." I sobbed, hearing the cock crow.

Twenty-one

ALTHOUGH DENVERS HAD REMOVED THE treasures from Keyes's rooms, and the Botticelli from the music room, and most of the valuable books from the adjoining library wall, the smoke damage to Gaywyck was extensive. He had soaked Keyes's body with oil from the lamps and set it ablaze, then called Donough to lead the fight against the spreading conflagration. As soon as the village fire brigade arrived and the fire was under control, the two returned to my rooms. I, of course, was gone. Denvers then revealed the "truth" about Cormack and me. Displaying the photograph he said Jones had taken, he claimed Cormack and I set the blaze to gain time for flight. "Now it will be the way it was meant to be—just the two of us."

Donough banished the demented old crone. "He told me he did everything for *me*! Had Keyes kill my father to spare *me* the shame! Brought you and Cormack together to show me what a whore you were . . . *are*! I wanted to strangle him! He *knew* you would not go with Cormack. He knew Cormack would kill you then kill himself. He planned to have his revenge on you both for the death of Jones."

"Poor Denvers!" I whispered hoarsely. "He must have hated himself beyond bearing. Why else would he fall in love with men he could never have? He was too long with the Jesuits."

Donough laughed and kissed me. He had not laughed for days. It was good to see him doing something besides sighing and staring at my heavily bandaged face and neck. (Dr. Anders was very liberal with the gauze. I think he was trying to tie me down.)

Denvers had lied about the Jesuits. He claimed his disenchantment with their intellectual standards forced his departure from the order; but, in fact, it was they who cast him out, finding his obsession with the sufferings of Christ unhealthy. They needed a Latin scholar; Denvers

was eager for the glories of martyrdom. He had come to
Gaywyck and remained for one reason only: Mr. Gaylord. During their brief interview, Gaylord enticed and
tantalized him. Overly proud of his virility, the twins'
parent saw the attraction and tormented the shy, repressed
man, charming him into a cruel submission, treating him
like a precocious schoolboy who might, one day, have his
way. It also worked with Everard Keyes. Gaylord thrived
on their fanatical love, knowing it united them to one
purpose: keeping the twins in line. He also knew their
attachment was bereft of reason, but he never expected it
to be the death of *him.* "He failed to remember that wasps
feed off their hosts," I whispered. "And many a cobra has
misread his mongoose."

I became distressed. I had beseeched Donough to tell
me, then found I was not yet ready to hear. He resumed
reading *Pride and Prejudice* aloud for an hour before
administering my medication and sternly ordering me to
nap. He excused himself and returned to his study, where
he sat by the hour perusing the journals of Julian Denvers
and Cormack Gaylord Sr., found in Denvers's rooms.

"Everything was calculated. Keyes did his bidding. They
kept tabs on their progress by reading your journals."
Donough spoke as though giving a weather report.

"What power did Denvers have over Keyes? Keyes
thought Cormack was dead, yes?"

"Uh-huh," he answered, having at some point adopted
my speech mannerism. "To keep his accomplice quiet,
Denvers told him Cormack died instead of Steven. The
deed sent Keyes into paroxysms of guilt that deranged
his mind. Had there been an autopsy after the fire, Denvers
planned to blame the deaths on Cormack, whose flight was
witnessed by the respectable Nanny Welles."

"Of course," I croaked, raising my hand to ask for a
respite.

Cormack Gaylord Jr. had seriously damaged me. I must
not make light of it. He broke my nose and blackened my
left eye. What with various contusions and damaged muscles in my neck and throat, swallowing and speech were
made painful for over two months. There were great welts
on my neck, a mean purple bruise under my left ear where
his thumb had lodged, and my cheek was swollen to the
shape of a healthy cantaloupe. It was a miracle he hadn't
fractured my jaw or knocked out my eye or uprooted a

dozen teeth; but in the immediate aftermath of our confrontation, I found it difficult to be grateful for anything, once I was over the relief of being alive.

Swathed in bandages, I cried a great deal. It exasperated Donough, who—ever patient—insisted on changing the wet gauze every time. I blamed myself for everything that had happened. There were a million ifs.

"If you hadn't gone willingly," Donough comforted, "he would have dragged you."

"You don't understand."

"Yes . . . I understand. It happened. It's over."

I began to cry. The doctor became worried. My state of mind, he warned, was detrimental to the healing process. I would never recover if I did not eat and shake the depression that gripped me as tightly as Cormack's fist. On the fourth morning, Donough handed me a letter from Father Howard. My mother was recovering. Donough decided to bring her to Gaywyck.

"We're cousins," he revealed, grinning.

He had just been informed of our connection by Father Howard, who was party to the deepest Gaylord secret, and who had clandestinely acted as intermediary between Mr. Gaylord and the family of Whyte.

Mary Rose Reagen's twin, Rose Mary Reagen, disappeared from Boston Common one hot July afternoon in 1851 while their nurse, Clotilda Honeywell, dallied with the butcher's son on the far side of a great elm. Why only one child was snatched from the double carriage added to the controversy that made good copy in the newspapers. A huge reward was offered, and every Gypsy expelled from the city. (There was a large convocation of Gypsies in Boston and its environs that year; it was generally assumed that the child was abducted to beg or to dance for pennies or to climb through windows and rob the homes of respectable people.)

The child was never found. Thirty-two years later, at the opening of the Metropolitan Opera House, Mary Rose Reagen Gaylord was introduced by her confidant, Father Collins, to his friend from seminary days, Father Howard, who happened to be in New York City on parish business and who was a guest of James, Cardinal Gibbons, in the diocesan box. Stunned by her physical likeness to his own parishioner's wife, my mother, he mentioned the coincidence to Father Collins, who mentioned it to Gaylord.

The very next day, Steven was dispatched to investigate. Rose Mary Reagen was discovered living happily as Prudence Whyte in a small, comfortable town in upstate New York, a town practically owned by Gaylord crude-oil investments.

They debated how best to manage the reunion, when a moratorium was declared on the subject as Mary Rose became less and less well. Gaylord decided not to make us aware of the relationship, being loath to instigate fears of inherited mental weakness.

Father Collins was requested to invite Father Howard to New York for a holiday. A meeting was arranged with Mr. Gaylord. The Whytes were to be assisted in every possible way, but were never to know. Under the aegis of Gaylord, my father quickly progressed from assistant schoolmaster to principal of the new school built by a private donation. The only other direct interception was the conscription of Miss Grimmond to supply my voracious reader's appetite with books and literary journals. The shy recluse was asked by Father Howard to help ease my difficult adolescence, and she, dear friend, had been willing to do whatever was required.

One of Gaylord's last acts was to set up a trust fund for me. Whatever career I chose was to be facilitated; there were to be no obstacles money could remove. If I had not won a scholarship to Harvard, a "sponsor" was to come forward and eventually be credited with leaving me an annuity in his will upon my graduation. My mother's sudden collapse and my refusal to go the expected route complicated matters for Father Howard, who was appointed, upon the death of Gaylord, executor of my trust. He wrote to Father Collins, who hastily applied to Donough Gaylord for advice, assuming him cognizant of my history. Wary of stressing familial allegiance lest there be none, he stuck to my history.

Donough offered the position of librarian without asking questions, touched that "young Robert Whyte's mother's gone mad." He had been totally unaware he was under obligation to an unknown cousin languishing in the foothills of the Allegheny Mountains. He was recently returned from a month in Ireland and was distracted by the mounds of work. He had been relieved the business with Father Collins was so amicably dispatched in under ten minutes.

"The most important ten minutes of my life," he added, kissing my hand.

"How large is my trust fund?" I asked, patting his head.

"Very large. My father was absurdly generous."

"Does it still exist?"

"What *do* you take me for?" he shouted in mock amazement.

"So! I'm no longer a poor relation dependent on charity?"

"Correct!"

"Couldn't be more attractive!"

"What are you going to do with your newfound wealth?"

"Paint this room."

We had moved into the cottage because the necessary repairs begun on the main house made it impossible for me to rest, and Dr. Anders had insisted I sleep days on end or, as usual, he would not be held accountable. He suggested my removal to a hospital, but I refused to leave Donough. I had become so agitated that he relented on certain conditions: 1) sleep, days on end; 2) Brian was to nurse me and provide a special diet; 3) a throat specialist was to see me immediately; 4) Donough Gaylord was to remain at Gaywyck.

Margaret Davis was entreated to augment the staff. She arrived immediately with her three children, insisting it was no inconvenience. Assuming the responsibilities of housekeeper, she assured Donough she would manage quite well with Brian's able assistance. They managed brilliantly. In two days the entire cottage was cleaned. As when Donough had lived there, the second-floor parlor with the great wych elm outside its windows was my bedroom until the first night, when I pronounced it *ours*. I did not want separate bedrooms. I wanted him by my side. I did not want a cot brought in for him; I wanted us in one bed.

"What do *you* want, Donough? Is it too soon?"

"No."

"We can have separate rooms if you wish."

"No! Why?"

"The world's disapprobation?"

"Life is a breath . . . too short to worry about the world's disapprobation!"

Mrs. Davis decided it would be best if she lived in the

main house for the time being. Mary Rose had been settled into my old quarters, and there was such a tremendous amount of work to be done that the housekeeper preferred to be close to the disorder. I had no complaints about being far from the children.

"You don't mean it!" Donough insisted.

"*Yes*. I do! I dislike children because they frighten me: they're so *complicated* and noisy and demanding . . . too demanding—all that attention! I've always disliked children; children and dogs!"

"Robbie!"

"It's true! Dogs are just like children: they're stupid and noisy and demand attention and shit all over the floor. Cats say: 'It would be in your best interest to love me.' Dogs say: 'Love me! Love me! Love me!' "

"Well, now that we've settled *that*!"

"Do you mind terribly?" I croaked, hugging Cael.

"Obviously not about children, but I rather like dogs."

Very soon after this conversation, I happened to glance out the window during my breakfast. A small boy of about five years, shadowed by a tiny black terrier, stalked Tristan and Isolde. The boy carried a bow and arrow, taut, ready for action. I could not shout; my voice was barely producing normal tones; Brian had returned to the main house; Joshua was fishing; Donough was at the farm; the downstairs maid was downstairs; and my swans were about to be slaughtered.

Luckily, Donough insisted I wear a heavy nightshirt during the day; otherwise, naked, I could have done serious damage to myself as I clambered down the wych elm. Rushing across the lawn through the flowering wild thyme, I waved my arms, to the delight of the boy, who lowered the arrow and saved himself from being throttled or directly drowned.

"I'm hunting!" he announced proudly.

The puppy licked my bare feet. I lifted it. It had a beautiful face with large brown eyes and short, erect ears; there were flecks of gold in its curly black fur. I put the puppy down. Cael hissed and howled. I lifted the puppy until Cael collected himself.

"People don't hunt swans," I said, trying to look stern behind my mask of bandages, and trying to be heard over Cael's disgraceful ruckus. The child had huge eyes and fortunately resembled his mother.

"Why?" he asked.

"Because swans are our friends."

At the sight of me, Tristan and Isolde were leading their family over to see if I had some food. They traveled slowly, wary of Cael's temper. The child was delighted to see them approach.

"What *do* people hunt?"

"In the house: rats, bats, mosquitoes, flies, wasps, little boys, and dogs."

He laughed. I was charmed. His teeth were good.

"And outside?"

"Only what they need to eat."

"Can y'eat swans?"

"No. Swans are tough, like cats."

He nodded thoughtfully. I wondered if there was anything else I should specifically designate as "tough." "One must hunt rats only with people who know their prey's tricks or one can get hurt. Where did you get that bow and arrow?"

"I found it. See?"

"Uh-huh. Did anyone say you could use it?"

He shook his head.

"May I have it? Please?"

"Are ya gonna tell my ma? She'll paste me!"

"No. Why should I? We all make mistakes."

He handed me the bow and arrow.

"What's your name?" I asked.

"Robert."

"So is mine!"

"I knew two kids in the city called Bobby."

"Uh-huh. Well, I've never had a friend named Robert before."

"What's prayer's tricks?"

"Excuse me?" I asked, on my best example-setting behavior.

"You *said* ya hadda know a prayer's tricks to hunt."

"Prayer's tricks?" I muttered dumbly, growing uncomfortable.

"Yeah, ya said—"

"Oh! You mean a *prey's* tricks! P-r-e-y, prey. That means an animal you hunt. To *pray*"—I clasped my hands and glanced at the clouds—"is p-r-a-y. They're homonyms: they sound alike but have different meanings. There are lots of words like that."

"Oh, yeah?"

"Yeah! 'Buy' and 'bye.' " I mimed the different meanings and spelled the different words for the kid, who seemed enthralled. " 'Time' and 'thyme.' "

"Children and dogs," Donough suggested over my shoulder.

"Oh! Mr. Gaylord! I assume you know Robert Davis?"

"Yes, we've met. Your mother has been looking for you, young man," he said to Robert, who turned and scurried away.

"Wait!" I called, straining my throat.

"Robert!" Donough shouted for me.

The boy stopped and nervously glanced over his shoulder. I ran to him and relinquished the sleeping puppy.

"You forgot this," I said, smiling. "Come and visit me sometime. I live in the cottage."

"I know where *you* live," he said. "And I know what happened to ya, too."

"Oh?"

"Ya got throwed by a horse."

"Yes," I said sweetly, making a mental note to tell Brian I was not amused.

"Goin' hunting?" Donough queried on our way back to our room.

"Uh-huh! The kid nearly killed Tristan. Look at Cael shredding the lilac bush; he's furious with me!"

"I think you've made a friend."

"Isn't it odd his name should be Robert?"

"No. Now, if it were Hans or Vincenzo . . ."

Robert became a frequent visitor to our home. Of the three Davis children, I discovered an affinity with this middle one, who was charming and intelligent and soon loved to read. (It was *I* who encouraged his interest in medicine. He grew up to become a fine neurosurgeon; his child Roberta, my goddaughter, seems to be following in her father's footsteps. But I digress. I have just skipped decades.)

I considered reading more of Denvers's journal after luncheon.

"Robert, please don't," Donough insisted.

"Oh-oh! You're angry with me."

"I'm not angry with you," said Donough finally.

"Why aren't you?"

"My anger has passed."

I was silenced. Because tears were imminent and the bandages fresh, I grasped his hand and asked him to tell me about the people who had raised my mother.

He had written to Father Howard asking for information about my Quaker grandparents. My mother, Father Howard responded, declared her "parents" dead when they informed her she was a foundling; she had accused them of unspeakable treachery for not having told her from the beginning. She married my father to be free of them.

My mother came to live at Gaywyck. She and her sister became companions. Unlike Mary Rose, who was quite mad quite often, my mother suffered from depressions that debilitated but never disoriented her; she found her sister's company remarkably beneficial. They became mistresses of the main house, entertaining the two prelates, my grandparents, my Aunt Emily, Sister Theresa (recently made mother superior of her convent), and Miss Grimmond, who, keeping her promise to Donough, came for a week and stayed six months.

I brooded about Denvers and composed journal entries to fathom what seemed to be idiocy and bravado but filled me with pity and terror. Mary Rose gave me the clue when she said Gaylord's rejection had unhinged him. Closeted with his passion, he festered. Everyone was made to suffer for his self-dread and loathing, which the alchemy of egotism converted into anger. He was not what he seemed. He knew his value, yet Cormack received Gaylord's love and I received Donough's. He wanted us both removed. He railed against his fate. Everything was beyond his control but the lives of others. Trying to destroy Gaywyck after his last attempt to dupe Donough failed, he was devoured by teeth of flames. With the journals, we discovered his severed fingers lovingly mummified in a Fabergé cigar case studded with amethysts the color of his grief, the color of his rage.

The first weekend during my recovery, I was gratified by the sudden appearance of Goodbody and Mortimer. Goodbody brought me a huge Whitman's Sampler box of chocolates ("I know how fond you are of the man!") and a gigantic bouquet of peonies. I was grateful to them for being there, for I had not been able to discuss Cormack's death rationally with Donough, and I was certain he was grieving horribly but had not wished to burden me; he

consistently dismissed my queries with a casual response.
I thought his friends might console him where I could not.
And there was another reason, a more personal one. The
moment Goodbody and I were alone, I opened discussion.

"Have you always been faithful to Mortimer?"

"Good Lord! What a question, Robbie!"

"You know about me and Cormack?"

"Yes. Donough told us. I hope you don't mind. He
hadn't intended to, but it was impossible not to relate—"

"No, I don't mind. I'm glad, in fact. I don't ever want
to have any secrets from you, Goodbody."

"You must call me Timothy, Robbie."

"Yes . . . I will. Thank you. Chocolate?"

"No. They're for you. Donough said you weren't eating.
I thought they might fatten you up."

"I love chocolate."

"Good. Now! Your question. I don't see why you're
upset; you thought you were with Donough. At least
that's—"

"Until the last time, the night of the fire. I knew he was
Cormack then."

"I see."

"I loved him."

"Yes . . . I see. . . ."

There was a long pause. I felt on the verge of distress
again and distracted myself by locating caramels with the
help of the chart on the lid of the box. This question had
been tormenting me. Before I discussed it with Donough,
I wanted to have some thoughts, besides guilty ones, on
the subject.

"Timothy, I've tried to think of it in terms of wanting
Donough and needing Cormack, but I need Donough and
I wanted Cormack, too."

"Yes? Those nice differentiations aren't much help at
times like this. They're fine for dallying but not for understanding motivation, which is usually too complicated for
such simple fare. You know it isn't a question of guilt or
innocence?"

"No, I don't. I feel terribly guilty."

"Why?"

"If I love him, why should I want someone else?"

"You think love focuses sexual attraction?"

"I think it *should*!"

Then I understood. It was my unwillingness to accept

the boundaries of love. I was confused by the slightest change of direction on the *carte de tendre*.

I explained this to Timothy, adding, "I'll have to think on it. Love *can* do things. If we love ourselves, we can use it to change ourselves."

"Yes . . . but it doesn't just *happen*. Once you realize you want a monogamous relationship, it then acquires force and meaning of its own. Nothing should bind us together but love. *Now* we can discuss wanting and needing. I know many men who stay together because they have houses and carriages and mutual investment funds. I love Eugene. Yes, I've been *faithful* as you call it, but only because I want to be. It isn't always easy, trust me! There are many attractive men in this world, but I love Eugene. He is the best for me, and sharing my body is connected to everything else. There aren't many monogamous love relationships of our kind, Robbie, but then, there aren't many in marriage, either, and fewer by choice."

"It's what I want."

"Yes? It's what Donough wants, too."

"What if you should meet someone who is better for you?"

"God knows! If that happens, I'll confront it then. Life is full of 'what-ifs.' "

"Chance and change?"

"Exactly! Something else to be afraid of instead of just living our lives."

That night, in Donough's arms, I felt as if a great weight had been hoisted off my heart. I did not feel guilty anymore. I felt *wiser*. And, I felt wonderful.

"I'm relieved to feel the tension gone," he said.

"Mm," I sighed, snuggling closer.

"You were pleased to see Goodbody and Mortimer?"

"Oh, yes! Did you get a chance to talk with Mortimer?"

"What about?"

"I thought you might be able to talk with him about Cormack. You don't have to tell me about your feelings if you don't want. I understand."

"No. No, you don't, my dearest boy. I've told you how I feel."

"You haven't, Donough. You've said nothing but 'I'm all right.' "

"I am."

"How do you *feel?*"

"All right!" He laughed, squeezing me tightly.

All right was not distraught or untangled or any of the things he had been the first time Cormack "died." *All right* was calm, saddened, accepting. He was not ill. He was not hallucinating, and the world was not two-dimensional or colorless: a black-and-white photograph in motion. Having a replica of oneself, a different being yet in many ways the same, was conducive to infantile oneness. They were everything to themselves. They trespassed on each other's souls as they had shared and divided the same ovum. It had taken him three years of psychic laboring to experience life as a separate being. With the help of doctors in Paris and Vienna, he had gradually seen himself as one whole person, and not as a reflection of another; when Cormack "died," Donough's self-image expired.

"Last week, I wasn't afraid of Cormack," he whispered, "I was afraid of what I would allow him to do with me. I needn't have worried. I'm all right, my dearest boy. That *is* how I feel. I grieve that we will never meet as men, but I have forgiven myself and mourned for us both."

The next morning brought a glorious summer day. A cloudless lilac-scented sky and a spectacularly clear sea were reported by Donough at breakfast. It was agreed I was strong enough to picnic at the cove. I was not to swim ("Wade?" "Perhaps!"), but I could sit and walk (slowly), and toss a football (indolently). Just as I was finishing my last cup of tea, Brian and Joshua and Lonnie brought in my Cézanne. The Crevelli already hung in our room; I wanted the Cézanne on the wall opposite the bed, not in the sitting room, where it had originally been settled. It was easily accomplished. When the three had gone, I asked Donough what his first impression of me had been.

"Your eyes totally disarmed me," he whispered, stretching out on the bed by my side. "Then I thought you were trying to impress me with your enthusiasm for my pictures."

"You took me for a sycophant!"

" 'An overeager beauty,' I thought. Can you forgive me, my dearest boy?"

"I remember your scent: you smelled like autumn flowers. You are lovely, Donough Gaylord. Take off your clothes."

He blushed and looked shocked. I could read amusement in his eyes, even though he had not yet adjusted to my new boldness. The shy recluse was no more. Would he miss him? He looked away, then returned my stare to see if I were serious. We had done a great deal of laughing that morning before breakfast, and we hadn't much time before the picnic. He grinned a wide and foolish grin. I was so full of love for him—so serene about the way we were, the way we thought, the way we felt—that I burst into laughter.

"I love you so much. It just washed over me like a great wave."

He took me in his arms. I cried with fine gusto. When I pulled back from his shoulder to take the napkin from my breakfast tray, I saw he was weeping. "I love you," he said. "I love you."

We probably would have spent a teary, laughing morning if Mortimer had not called from the garden bemoaning the loss of the day's best moments. I dressed quickly and we joined our friends under the raintree. Donough had not exaggerated the splendor of the morning. Except for my brief excursion to rescue Tristan and Isolde, I had not been out of bed for a week.

Goodbody was in high spirits. He sang a bawdy ditty about a judge and a jury, then pounced on the peonies blooming by the pond, and with a courtly bow presented me with one.

"Donnie says these are your favorite flowers. How lovely of them to be in bloom for you now! They are my favorite, too, and I'm always anxious to make converts. I wish someone would develop a strain with a longer blooming season. They aren't with us long enough, and *please*, no metaphysics!"

I was reminded of Denvers and Keyes and felt saddened and diminished by the loss of them. Goodbody and Mortimer had accompanied Donough to a service for the two tutors in the village the previous afternoon. Donough must have felt a similar loneliness, because he put his arm around my shoulders and hugged me to him.

"You've grown more!" he whispered. "You're nearly as tall as I."

I nodded, pleased. I was soon to become a man of equal measure.

"Nature," laughed Goodbody, "is so *natural*."

"Very profound, Goodbody!"

"It *is*, you know, Mortimer. At the club the other day while awaiting you, I overheard two asinine gents discussing Wilde's 'illness.' They said there are unnatural goin's-on in nature. They are incorrect, *a priori* and *a posteriori*."

"Indeed they are, Goodbody. I beg your pardon."

Reaching the sand at that instant, I broke free to test the temperature of the sea. Fortunately it felt cold and uninviting; I had prepared an argument for why I should be allowed a short swim.

Down by the jetty, Brian and Mrs. Davis played a game of catch with her two sons while Robert struggled to raise a box kite, and Nanny Welles sat on the rocks knitting. The nurse had resumed residence in the main house; her former third-floor quarters were operating as nursery for the three boys, on an outing that morning to allow the newly painted dado to dry.

"They look like a marvelously healthy, happy family," Mortimer observed.

One year later, practically to the day, Brian and Margaret Davis were married. Their courtship is one of the finest, most enduring memories of our first year together; their evident happiness was a variation on our own and carried love from the cottage into the main house and over the three hundred acres of Gaywyck. Donough gave the bride away; I was the best man. When they left for a honeymoon in Ireland, I complained that *I* had never seen Ireland. One month later, Donough and I left for a year abroad, with more adventures and happiness than I could relate in one hundred volumes. Their first child they named Donough Robert.

On the beach that glowing morning, we joined in their games. Robert and I lifted the papered frame into the wind. Aloft, it provoked applause and seemed to shudder with our excitement.

"I wanna fly!"

"So do I!"

"Why can't I fly?"

"No wings."

"Why not?"

"We have a thumb that wiggles instead, a tensile digit. If we had wings, we couldn't fly this kite. Ya gotta make do, kid!"

When we parted from them to continue our walk, I

told Donough how much I enjoyed their company. He smiled as if presented with a gift.

"Ever since our conversation about children and dogs, I feared I had made a dreadful error inviting Mrs. Davis and the boys to live here. Now I'm certain things will work out."

"Children *and* dogs?" Mortimer asked, frowning. "What kind of American are you? I'd hate to handle your case in court."

Those halcyon days, full of fruit blossoms and sunshine, knew but two dark hours: the one I spent with the journals of Julian Denvers; the other asking questions of Donough because I could not bear to read more.

"Just tell me quickly how he knew your father was leaving."

"Steven told him."

The last night, Denvers heard Steven arriving and went to meet him. Gaylord had sent him a letter agreeing to go abroad. Steven showed Denvers the letter, thinking the tutor would be pleased for them, having no idea Denvers had offered himself as slave to Gaylord that very afternoon and been laughed out of the room. Keyes poisoned the brandy they used for a farewell toast.

I went under the covers, wanting to go under the bed, and would have stayed there if Donough had not insisted we walk and ride the horses. I was pitched into another foul depression and gripped by fear. The devious workings of the human mind terrified me; my tendency toward depression was a manifestation I could not understand. Depression covered my other feelings like a mask the face. Would the mask endure? Had I inherited the Reagen legacy? Was I destined to crumble slowly into madness?

While we walked, he offered comfort, but his tenderness tormented me. How much of his love was a response to this weakness within me? Was it love he felt, or pity? Perhaps my mother had been right. Had he recognized in me a displaced feminine soul?

I could not speak to him. I could not verbalize any of it. He guided me to the oakstand and told me we would not return to the house until I explained myself.

"Why do you love me?" I asked, hoping it would lead me to the rest.

"I love you because . . . because you are the man you are."

As usual, his choice of words was perfect.

"Could I ever be a wife to you?" I forced myself to utter, compressing a dozen queries and turning plum-colored from the effort.

"God, no! We are both men. We cannot be otherwise with one another or we will be untrue to ourselves. We will share our lives. I have seen men who wish to be women and wives to other men; it isn't possible."

"What will I be?"

"You will be Robert, my comrade in perfect manhood."

"And if I go mad?"

"And if *I* go mad? I have already entered death's dominion once."

"Aren't you afraid?"

"Madness is fearful, yes! There are many doctors now who offer theories contradicting heredity. I take my hope there and trust in my strengths."

"I'll save you from . . ."

"You'll save me from what?"

". . . from hearing promises I cannot possibly keep."

"Dearest boy, you *are* a promise kept."

On the way back to our room, we met Goodbody and Mortimer riding along the shore. They offered to dismount and join us, but we excused ourselves and wished them good exercise.

"I'm tired and I'm thirsty," I complained to Mortimer unbidden.

He reached into his vest pocket and offered me the flask I had given him for Christmas.

"No, thank you. Too early for me."

"It's Saratoga mineral water," he said, chuckling at my surprise.

I drank a toast to us, thanked him, and took my leave.

"No more toasting Jefferson Davis?" I asked Donough.

There had been little drinking on this visit, none of the requisite Manhattans or brandies or wines before, during, and after each lavish meal. I had been too self-absorbed to take it as anything but a gesture to *my* uninterest in alcohol.

"Mortimer has stopped drinking."

"Completely?"

"Yes. He's had a difficult time of it these past six months."

"I didn't know."

"He's doing well. He's fine now."

My ignorance saddened me.

"I want to know everything about everyone." I sighed.

"No, you don't! It would make life unbearable. It's hard enough remaining ambulatory knowing about oneself."

We laughed and hurried back to our room. We had grown closer to one another, had found it easier to share more of our private realities. We spoke frequently of Cormack to exorcise his ghost. He was buried near the dolmen. We would sit by him and talk of love, our shadows one.

I returned with Donough to Gramercy Park in the autumn. He had his work. It was unreasonable for me to expect him to retire to Gaywyck. He was deeply involved with the Gaylord enterprises; they intrigued and gratified him. He was not interested in becoming a country gentleman; he was an urban creature. The cultural pleasures of Gotham were the axis of his life. I wanted to share in all of it.

At first I lacked an aptitude for finance. Leisure was most appealing. Then I learned. Reader, you might never infer from this memoir that I am abundant in the rare and precious commodity known as common sense. Undeniably, I possess the ability to look at two items and see them both; to store them and find them again; to combine them and make two; to connect them and perpetrate a synthesis.

In time, I became his efficient deputy, dividing the responsibilities. It was my idea to eliminate the less lucrative peripheral business interests rather than embrace Taylorism. I convinced Donough to found the Gaylord Foundation as a means of distributing the yearly profits more efficiently. The foundation has become our primary interest.

On our second New Year's Eve together, 1901, we joined Goodbody and Mortimer at the opera. It was a performance of *Tristan und Isolde*. Again, I was profoundly moved. We parted from our friends in front of the opera house and walked up the snow-decked streets, through the throngs of other happy couples, to our bridge in Central Park. That evening Donough informed me he had begun the business of adoption. He wanted my name to be Robert Whyte Gaylord. In the eyes of the law, we would share one another. Privilege and duty would deftly conjoin.

Snow began to fall as we stood on the bridge spanning the frozen pond. The full moon blessed us as we leaned together, dizzy from the weight of our love.

"I'll gladly be your friend, Donough Gaylord, till death us do part."

"Not beyond that, Robert Whyte? Not to the edge of doom?"

"Like an ever-fixed mark."

"Not admit impediments?"

"Never! *Never!*"

Bells began to ring all over the town. It was midnight. We kissed and discovered each of us laughing.

This is for all our time, Donough Gaylord.

Yes . . . yes . . . I say yes. . . .

For all our time, time out of mind. . . .

Epilogue

DONOUGH GAYLORD DIED AT MIDNIGHT.
He looked up at me, surprised.
Bells tolled, the sea continued, our love endures.